ALL HAIL THE KING

and QUEEN

R SULLINS

THE NIGHTMARE DUET

R SULLINS

www.rsullins.com

rsullinsauthor@gmail.com

Published by: NEA Ink, LLC
The Nightmare Duet cover by: RJ Creatives
The Nightmare King cover by: Dark Fox Cover Designs
The Queen of Nightmares cover by: RJ Creatives

FOREWORD

I will never do justice to this story, I already know that, and it wasn't my goal. My only goal was to create something entertaining, something you can get lost in and take your mind off the reality of the world we live in.

Jack is one of my favorite characters. He is so nuanced, with so many layers to him. He feels the weight of the responsibility which he readily accepts, but he also feels the pull toward something... *more.*

I hope I managed to do this incredible character justice as I created a world for him in which he ruled a slightly different Halloween town.

Welcome to Pumpkin Patch, Utah.

TRIGGER WARNINGS

Trigger warnings...
- Violence
- Attempted (s)assault
- Adult situations for 18+
- Language
- Murder
- Hand necklaces
- Harm to animals
- Lots of blood

THE NIGHTMARE KING

THE
NIGHTMARE
KING
THE NIGHTMARE DUET
R SULLINS

For all the fanfic writers. Keep going...

There are people out there who love what you do.

My body trembled from the pain and cold as I whimpered. I tried to look deeper into the dark and damp room but could barely see beyond the table I was strapped to. I had no idea how long I'd been trapped in the room, and I didn't even know where I was. I only knew that I had been taken after work.

"Someone, please help me..." My plea was barely over a whisper, and my throat was raw from all the screaming I had done for so long over the last however many days I had been trapped. I heard a noise and immediately clamped my teeth tight, but I couldn't stop the whimper that escaped at the thought of the man coming back.

I listened intently for any sound of his footsteps coming from overhead. That was the only way I knew I was probably underground because of the sound of footsteps coming from above whenever the man appeared. This time, the room was silent other than my ragged breathing and the echo of my blood slowly dripping down to soak into the concrete flooring.

I closed my eyes, and as I lay there trembling uncontrollably in jerks, I was tempted to beg every deity I had ever heard of for death. For an ending to this ongoing torture.

. . .

I BOLTED UPRIGHT in the chair, my heart beating out of control, my hair stuck to my forehead and neck. I slammed my heels down on the carpet with a distressed cry. Resting my face in my hands, I took several deep breaths of stale air and concentrated on the feeling of the clothes on my body, the movement of the air being stirred by the lazy fan.

I was safe and alive. I hadn't been a prisoner in that basement for over six months. Most of my injuries had healed, even if I was left with intense scarring all over my entire body. Only the worst of the cuts that had become infected during my time with the doctor had taken much longer to heal. And out of those, only a few spots still needed daily antibiotic cream and bandages.

I opened my eyes and took in the room. I was in a waiting room off the long hallway of the courthouse. I breathed in deep through my nose as my mind fought to accept that I was safe and not still chained to a makeshift operating table. I was safe, and I was sitting all alone while I waited for the next step in the process of the eventual conviction of Dr. Stein.

Dr. Stein was a well-respected doctor to Hollywood's richest and most famous. Those with hoards of cash would consult with him and pay hefty sums for a little nip, a little tuck. If you wanted a perfect nose, Dr. Stein would give you what you wanted. If you wished to have Angelina Jolie lips, that was exactly what you would get. Never too much, never too little. He was considered a magician with a scalpel, and his hands were pure magic. Except with me.

I had been his receptionist not long before my nightmare began. I had gone to Hollywood, just like so many others before me, and many more that would follow. So many others would go there, searching for their big break into the movie industry. I was a small-town girl from Kentucky with big dreams. In the few months I had been in Los Angeles, I had only managed to snag a role in a commercial. It was almost clichéd, really. I had made my start on the slow climb to the big screen by taking a part in a toothpaste commercial.

In order to pay my rent for a small apartment I shared with three other girls, I managed to land a receptionist position at the respected doctor's clinic. I had been ecstatic. The pay was fantastic and allowed me to continue my quest for a real acting role. I had no idea that I had caught the attention of a monster.

I listened to the foot traffic outside the door, waiting for someone from the District Attorney's office to let me know if Dr. Stein was going to await his trial behind bars or if he was going to get the house arrest that they had assured me was the most likely scenario. Sitting in the witness box to testify at the bond hearing had been one of the hardest things I had ever done. Facing the man who had systematically tortured me for months was almost as cruel as the actual torture had been. But what made it so much worse was having to sit there to be ogled by spectators.

My scars were horrific. Why the man with the magic hands had decided to experiment on me was unexplainable. But he had. From my head to my feet, I had long scars that he had carefully sutured to maintain as much scarring as possible. For a man who could create miracles with his scalpel, he was equally capable of creating nightmares.

That's all he had left behind. Long gone was the beauty that had driven me to become an actress. My pale peaches and cream skin now had a network of thin pink lines over it, the dots from the sutures clearly visible. He hadn't even been kind enough to ensure that the cuts healed as invisibly as he did with his clients. I was his patchwork doll. It was the name he had called me from the moment I woke up in the basement of his Malibu mansion.

Footsteps sounded from outside the door, and instead of fading, they came closer. I sat up straighter and did my best to brush the drying sweat from my face, pushing my dark red hair back from where it had stuck during my little unexpected nap. I looked up expectantly as the doorknob turned, and the Assistant DA walked in carrying her briefcase. One look at the grimace on her face told me I wouldn't like whatever she had to say.

She stepped into the small room and closed the door softly

behind her, taking an extra long second before she finally turned around to face me with an apologetic look on her face. I shook my head, dread already filling my stomach.

"I'm sorry, Sally."

"No." I gripped the handles of the chair until my knuckles turned white and my fingers began to ache. All I could concentrate on, though, was the words that were coming out of her mouth.

"As a well respected Doctor with no priors of any kind, the judge felt that he wasn't a flight risk." There was anger in her voice, and it was clearly written on her face that she didn't agree with the ruling for the doctor's bond. "He is released on his own recognizance with a bond of one million dollars."

"No house arrest?" My voice was small, weak, and disbelieving.

"No, I'm sorry, Sally."

I squeezed my eyes shut. She could repeat how sorry she was over and over, but it still wasn't going to keep me safe. "He swore that he would get me back," I whispered. "He said I was his. He promised me so many times that I would always be his and that if I ever got away from him, he would get me back. And he would make me pay."

She sat down in the chair next to me and laid her hand over my arm. I immediately flinched from the contact. She quickly withdrew her hand and clenched it into a fist, setting it into her lap. "The judge doesn't think that Dr. Stein is a threat to you since he has been arrested. You have been issued an order of protection, but that's it." Her voice trailed off as I swung my head around to face her, incredulity marking my features.

"An order of protection? A piece of paper to stop him from doing what he promised?" I waved a hand, indicating all of me. "This meant nothing to the judge? Was he paid off?"

The tightness around the ADA's mouth gave me all the answers I needed. I nodded and turned to stare back at the wall. Out of the corner of my eye, I saw her hover her hand in the air as if she wanted to comfort me again, but she knew already from our many meetings that I didn't like being touched. Not anymore.

"I—shit," she let out a long sigh before dropping her hand. "If you need anything, don't hesitate to call me, okay?"

"When is the trial set to begin?" It was the only thing I needed to hear at the moment. How long did I have to disappear?

She stood and picked up her briefcase that she had set on the floor by her feet. "Six months."

I closed my eyes and breathed, taking air in and out of my lungs slowly, methodically. Too long. It was too long. If the judge had been somehow paid off to keep Dr. Stein out of jail without an ankle monitor, what were the chances of him actually being found guilty and sentenced to prison?

I listened to her walk out of the room and, once again, softly close the door. As a tear tracked down my cheek and stopped its descent to fill in along the line that was scarred into my flesh from the corner of my mouth to nearly my ear, I let out one broken sob.

TWO

I sat up when my alarm went off, jarring me out of yet another nightmare. I ran my hands over my face, then gripped my long, thick braid, giving it a harsh tug. I finally reached over to the old alarm clock, which sat on the nightstand of the motel room, ignoring the pounding and yelled curses coming from the wall against the headboard.

It had been about two weeks since the bond hearing. The first thing I did when I left the courthouse was head to the apartment I had once shared with the other girls. When I had disappeared, they reported it to the police, but they'd had no choice but to rent out my room to someone else when so much time had passed without any sign of my return.

Luckily, they hadn't gotten rid of my things. Not that I'd had much to begin with. Just two small suitcases with everything I had brought with me to California. One of the girls had stuffed them into her cramped closet and was more than happy to return them to me once I'd shown up at the door fresh from the hospital.

Even though someone new had taken over my room, they had let me crash on the couch in the living room. I had learned quickly to protect myself by ignoring their whispers and stares of pity. I knew I would have to get used to it. This was my life now. I didn't really have a choice. I also couldn't go anywhere else. I'd saved up a decent amount of cash from my well paying receptionist job, but in L.A., it would hardly get me by in a hotel for a week. Not like the cheap motel I had found when I arrived in Utah.

Going home to Kentucky was one of the last choices I would ever make. My family had too many mouths to feed, and they had been glad to see me go when I had jumped on the bus to Hollywood. We hadn't parted on bad terms, necessarily, but it was clear that I wasn't to return when I failed. And they had promised I would as they waved me out the door. So, no, I couldn't go back home.

Instead of crawling back to my parents, I had closed my eyes and circled my finger over the map, buying a bus ticket to the town where my finger had landed. I quickly found it was a small town filled with pumpkins, bikers, and hardly anything else.

Pumpkin Patch, Utah. It was kind of ridiculous, honestly. The town was some sort of Halloween mecca, a tourist stop on the way to wherever their real vacation was. It was only summer, but there were shops all up and down Main Street that were dedicated to the celebration of Halloween. And pumpkins.

Pumpkin bread, pumpkin spiced lattes, pumpkin soap, pumpkin figurines. Though I would outwardly scoff if anyone asked, I would never actually admit out loud that the town had charmed me at first sight. I had climbed down from the bus, ignoring the whispers and stares from the passengers who had been pointing and talking to their companions about me, and began walking. I pulled my cumbersome suitcases behind me over the surprisingly well-tended sidewalk until I saw a sign for the Pumpkin Patch Motel.

Within two days, I had found a bar willing to hire me even though I was only nineteen. It then took me another two hours to figure out that it was a biker bar and that they didn't give a shit about laws. It didn't matter. I was away from California, away from the monster that had imprisoned me, and was staying in a motel that let me pay by the week. With my pay, tips, and the money I had saved before my Nightmare began, I was doing just fine.

I swung my legs over the side of the creaking mattress and stood up, past the instinct to grimace at the sensation of the old, stained synthetic carpet under my bare feet. All I cared about was that I was safe. I walked into the bathroom, flipped on the light, and turned on the shower as the bulb flickered a few times before staying steady. The water was never going to get steaming hot, but it was warm enough to soothe my aching muscles. No one had warned me how tiring being a bar waitress could be.

Once I stepped out, tucking the thin towel around my breasts, I opened the drawer that held my waitressing attire. They were just tiny spandex shorts that luckily covered more than they originally appeared, though not much more, and a cropped tank top that stopped just above my belly button. They were both black, and the top had the bar's name across the boobs.

When I had first seen the bar, I had thought it was just a regular bar in a small town, similar to the ones dotted around Kentucky, but it didn't take more than one shift to realize that the aptly named Devil's Bar was owned by the local club, The Devil's Nightmares. It was surprisingly well run, for which I was grateful, but after working there for two weeks, it was apparent there were things wrong with it, too.

I used the ancient hair dryer that came with the motel room, just grateful that the rundown place even supplied one. After my long hair was finally dry enough, I started on my makeup. I didn't wear much; I never really gained a talent for it, usually sticking with lipgloss and mascara. However, since the whole ordeal of being used as some sort of experiment or whatever the doctor had considered it, I'd begun using foundation to cover the pink lines. I couldn't do anything about the raised scars, but at least they didn't stand out as vividly as they did with a fresh face.

I left my hair down as a shield against stares. Even though I knew it did little to hide my body, it was still comforting. With nothing left to do to prepare for my shift, I slipped on my jeans and a hoodie to hide the skimpy outfit. There was no way I was going to walk through town wearing next to nothing.

The bar was fairly quiet when I arrived, with only a few regulars sitting at the bar and a couple of the servers being friendly with the few men who were sitting at the tables. It was a cozy atmosphere most of the time. The bar was all wood inside. There were wooden beams across the ceiling, and the floor was made of planks that had been worn smooth from years of hundreds of feet walking across it every single night.

The bar itself was about eight feet long, with the register in the middle. There was room for two bartenders, but in the two weeks I had been there, only one guy was ever behind the bar. I didn't know for sure, but I figured he was the owner. At the very least, he was the manager. He had been the one to hire me on the spot, letting his eyes drift down my body first. He had stared for a long time at my face, and I had become so self-conscious that I was getting ready to mumble, never mind about the job, when he had grunted. He'd offered me the job and warned me that the guys would be handsy, but if anyone gave me any kind of shit, to let him know immediately.

I was surprised to realize that they didn't have any bouncers that worked for the bar. When I had mentioned it, he just grinned, pulled a shotgun out from under the bar, and thunked it down on the wooden surface.

"This is my bouncer," he'd said with a tap of his forefinger to the barrel. "Besides, this place is the Nightmare's. If someone wants to get out of hand, they have more problems than getting bounced." The look on his face was kind of terrifying, and even though I hadn't seen anything yet to indicate that the Devil's Nightmares were even remotely scary, I just nodded and scampered away to take more drink orders.

But that night, when I arrived for my seven to midnight shift, everyone seemed on edge. It was as if there was a current of electricity humming through the bar, almost like a storm was brewing and everyone was waiting for the show to start.

I passed the long wooden bar, nodding at Mac, the older, tall, skinny bartender with shaggy brown hair, and headed down the long hallway. There were several rooms down the hallway with restrooms, storage, and a changing room in the far back where the girls kept their belongings while on shift. I didn't carry a purse or even an I.D. on me. I hated leaving anything in the hotel with the flimsy lock, but I hated even more to leave anything valuable in the open cubbies. I pulled the jeans down my legs, folded them up, and lay them in the cubby I had started to think of as mine. After unzipping and taking the hoodie off, I put it with my pants, ready to get the night over with.

I decided to ignore the weird atmosphere and just do my job. I hoped more people would arrive since a busy night meant not only were the tips better, but the whole night would go by faster. On my days off from work, I didn't know what to do with myself. I wasn't used to being sedentary. Growing up, I had been responsible for a lot around the tiny house I shared with my parents and four siblings. Most of my responsibilities included taking care of the kids, but I also had plenty of other chores that kept me busy. It was the one thing my parents had been so upset about when I told them I was moving away. They were losing their free babysitter and house cleaner.

I walked up to the bar and reached for a round serving tray. "Hey, Mac." I ducked my head, allowing the darkness of the dim bar and my hair to conceal most of my features. "Is there any place in particular you want me tonight?"

The open space was large, with several round tables with enough seating for four spaced out over the floor, along with a back area filled with four pool tables. Instead of there being tables around the billiard section, there were several bar stools lining the wall. It usually stayed pretty busy back there, and I had been assigned the section several times already.

Working the main floor was usually divided amongst two girls. I had noticed that no one sat at the table in the front corner. It was a cozy spot, which sat shrouded in darkness with little of the ambient lighting reaching that far into the corner. To me, it seemed like it would be a great spot to sit in and have a drink. Not that I could legally drink yet. But I couldn't help but wonder why that table always remained empty despite the crowd of people.

There was also a kitchen that served easy, mostly fried foods like french fries and onion rings. They also had nachos, which seemed to be the most popular food item on the meager menu. When it was a busy night, sometimes Mac would assign one of the girls to do nothing but run food out to tables. I had done that once, and it had sucked. Not because it was hard but because there were no tips involved. The servers were supposed to share tips, but they were stingy with them. Or maybe it was just me they didn't want to pay.

Mac gave me an uneasy look I hadn't seen on his face before. "Uh, why don't you stay around the bar tonight? I could use some help pulling beer. You can also take the tables closest while you're back here if the other girls get too busy."

I looked at the nearly empty bar and back at Mac. I wouldn't get many tips that night if I only had a couple of tables, but he was the boss and I wasn't going to argue. As it stood, there weren't even any people sitting near the bar other than a couple of guys on stools at the other end who were flirting with the other servers.

I shrugged a shoulder and set the tray back down. "Sure, Mac."

His weird look hadn't left his weathered face, and he was fidgeting with the bar rag he was holding. The way he was acting started to make me nervous, and I stiffened with apprehension, wondering if he was planning on firing me. Maybe they didn't need so many waitresses, and as the most recent hire, I was the one most likely to be let go. I knew it wasn't because of my performance. I was damn good at my job, mostly because I actually did it. Unlike most of the others, I didn't spend the whole night trying to flirt with one of the bikers. I couldn't even understand why the girls would. They were mostly old men who were overweight and looked like they could barely hold a motorcycle up anymore.

"Listen, new girl—"

Whatever Mac had been about to say in his nervous agitation was cut off when Meg, a cute little brunette, came running in through the front door. Her uniform barely covered her assets, the shirt showing a whole lot of underboob from the hack job she had given it. Her eyes were excited, and I had never seen her look so animated. Usually, all I got from her were sneers and a cold shoulder.

"They're here!"

As one, everyone stood up straighter, and the old bikers that hung around the bar night after night held up their beer bottles and yelled as if their favorite football team had just made the winning touchdown. It was then that I finally realized only bikers were in the bar that night. Not a single other person without a patch or server uniform was in sight.

Startled, I turned back to Mac to ask him what was going on when I heard it.

Dozens of motorcycle engines.

THREE

SALLY

That weird feeling that had been buzzing through the bar's atmosphere started to get stronger and was no longer possible to ignore. I started feeling it myself as I watched everyone in the bar straighten their shoulders, fix their hair and makeup, and share nervous glances. I had no idea what would be coming through the doors, but based on everyone's reactions, I wasn't sure I would like it. In fact, I was itching to run out the back door.

I turned back to Mac with wide eyes on the verge of panic to see him staring at me. He gave me a shrug and a chin lift as if to say, "Good luck, new girl. You're on your own now." I had to fight back a glare, pissed that he was throwing me to the wolves with no warning. I didn't even know what was happening or what I would be facing in the next few minutes. He could at least have given me some kind of heads-up that something would be happening tonight.

I debated with myself for a few long minutes as, one by one, motorcycle engines shut off, the thunderous sound of all those engines dying away into the night. I watched as Daisy, a gorgeous girl with bright pink hair who hated me on sight, continued to primp, plumping up her breasts and arranging her top, making sure the sparse fabric barely covered her nipples at all. She tugged on her shorts, and I couldn't hold back a wince as she gave herself a wedgie. Sure, it made her legs look even longer but was the uncomfortable sensation of having fabric flossing your asshole really worth it?

Suddenly, the front door flew open, and I knew I had wasted precious time I could have been using to escape. As I watched, men began pouring through the door like bugs swarming through a crack in the foundation. Cheers went up from everyone inside the bar, and the bikers entering pounded their fists on the tables as they passed.

Some of them went toward the pool tables in the back. Some found tables to sit at. Several crowded in around the bar, forcing me to step back until I was hiding in the back corner by the hallway. It was a good position to watch from. I was able to stare at the sight of at least thirty men openly. All were dressed similarly in jeans and black leather vests. There were subtle differences; some were wearing leather pants while others wore black jeans, but all of them had the same large patch on the back of their vests. The embroidered skeleton with a large full moon in the background was sinister look-ing, but I couldn't deny that it was pretty fantastic artwork. Whoever had come up with the design was very talented.

A giggle from the opposite side of the bar caught my attention, and I wasn't surprised to see that Daisy was being felt up by a biker. The man had bright green hair and a broad smile on his face, showing lots of teeth as he shoved his hand up her top, clearly palming her naked breasts.

With flaming cheeks, because I had not wanted to see that display, ever, I turned my head only to see a tall, slender man with a devilish grin bending one of the other servers over a table and palming her crotch through the thin shorts that made up our uniforms She certainly didn't seem to mind the attention as she let out a loud squeal of delight, encouraging the biker to do more than I was prepared to see.

Suddenly, a lot more girlish squeals came from the front, and I watched as every single server I had worked with at one point or another over the last couple of weeks came through the doorway. There were a few other women, too, I hadn't seen before. The newcomers weren't wearing a uniform like the rest of us who had come to work that night. Instead, they were dressed in outfits that were even skimpier, if that were possible. One wore a short blue sequin dress that barely covered her ass and started at the top of her areolas. Another was wearing jeans and a tank top, but the top was basically see-through, and her denim shorts had so many cuts and tears in the fabric that it revealed more than it covered. It looked like the group was ready to party.

I glanced over toward Mac for answers. I was confused, anxious, and even a little angry that I hadn't been warned. Based on how quickly the girls had arrived, everyone but me knew that the motorcycle club would be returning home, but no one had thought to tell the new girl. That could be what was Mac's problem earlier. Perhaps he was going to tell me what to expect, but too little, too late. He was frantically grabbing beers by the handfuls from the cooler behind him, so, with a sigh, I dipped under the hatch where I was standing to pitch in.

He gave me a tight smile as I leaned in to help, grabbed four bottles at once, and handed them over. He hesitated slightly but knew he couldn't turn down the help while we were so busy. Together, we were able to get a beer in everyone's hands before anyone could get too upset. As soon as the beers had been handed out, Mac immediately started pouring glasses of whisky. Instead of beginning tabs and checking who the drinks were going to the way it usually went on a regular night, hands just snatched up the glasses as quickly as he could pour them.

"Start filling up glasses with draft beer, will ya, new girl?" he shouted over the raucous laughter and yelling coming from the crowd. Someone had turned up the hard rock that was coming from the speakers in the corners of the ceiling, making it even harder to hear. The whole place was chaotic, and my nerves were making me jittery.

I could do nothing but nod, all at once glad to be behind the bar instead of having to thread my way through the crowd to serve drinks. In the brief glances I'd managed to take between grabbing bottles of beer, it didn't look like any of the girls were actually serving drinks. I turned away quickly after one particular look around. I was positive that I had seen Stephanie, one of the nicer girls I had worked with a few times already, being pounded from behind as she was held down by the back of her head against the green felt of one of the pool tables.

If I had to place a bet on it, I was certain that every single one of the other girls was probably getting railed, too, or was well on her way to it.

Glass after frosty glass, I pulled beer straight from the tap, trying to remember what I had seen Mac do when he had filled my orders. I was sure I was filling the glasses up with too much foam, but I couldn't help it. I tried angling the glass more, but it didn't seem to be helping. I tried filling it a bit slower, but that took too long, and I didn't think the foam was any smaller than before with that method, either. In the end, I just said fuck it and filled the mugs as quickly as I could without making too much of a mess and ensuring at least half the glass was beer instead of foam.

"Too much head!"

I ignored the yell, knowing that I was screwing it up. But I was doing my best with no prior training and filled the next glass before thunking it down on the wooden bar top and sliding it away. I twisted to the side to pull another mug from the cooler, noting how low the stock was getting.

"Hey, bitch! Did you fucking hear me?"

The name calling caught my attention. I looked up with startled eyes to see some guy standing in front of me with an angry snarl on his face. When I felt the coldness of beer begin to pour over my fingers, I jumped and looked down to see the glass I was currently filling was overflowing.

"Damn it!" I looked around, unsure what to do, but I realized that the glass had less foam in it than all the others I had already filled. With triumph at my victory, I smiled wide, set the glass down on the bar top, and pushed it toward the man who had been yelling at me, sure that a fresh glass of beer would help calm him down.

Unfortunately, instead of making him happy to get a free mug of ice-cold beer, he just looked even angrier. I looked down in confusion. Yes, the glass was covered in spilled beer, but who the fuck cared about that? It was free beer! The foam was actually nearly absent. I would have thought he would be happy with it.

As I contemplated the mug of beer, I let out a small shriek of surprise as my arm was yanked hard, causing the beer to topple over. The liquid quickly spread across the surface of the bar. Only the small lip on both sides stopped it from pouring onto the floor. Instead, my small crop top was working on soaking it up since the man had yanked me off my feet and seemed determined to pull me right across the top of the bar.

"What the hell do you think you are doing?" My screech was loud enough to hear over the thumping music, but the man didn't seem to give a shit. He completely ignored my outrage, the look of anger on his ugly face becoming twisted by some sort of desire that I had no intention of delving into. I was way past done dealing with the asshole. My arm hurt where he was grabbing me, and my ribs were aching from being dragged over the hard surface.

I slapped my free hand at the man before clenching it into a fist and swinging as hard as I could. Which, admittedly, was actually not very hard at all with the awkward angle I was in. When I heard his condescending laughter, my face grew heated, and anger quickly began to override the fright that had started growing.

"Let me go, asshole! Let me go! Mac!" I screamed for Mac, but he was down at the opposite end of the bar, surrounded by other big guys wearing leather vests. If the motorcycle club was okay with a woman being abused this way, they could all rot in hell. I certainly wasn't going to spend any more time working in a place that would allow it. Mac had told me that if I was ever being harassed, I should just get his attention. A lot of good that was doing me now.

I looked around wildly, but it seemed like most of the guys had their backs turned, all holding their drinks and having a grand time. I caught the eye of the one with the dark hair who'd had a devil's grin. That same grin was on his face as he watched me struggle. He was no longer with the girl from earlier. Instead, he was leaning against the wall by the front door, his legs crossed. He held up a bottle of beer in response to the pleading in my eyes and lifted it to his lips.

I shut my eyes and screamed as my hip made it over the counter. It would be an effortless yank from there to have me onto the other side and entirely at the man's non-existent mercy. I opened my eyes one more time, hoping to get Mac or anyone else's attention as my free hand slapped around, trying to find purchase on anything that would allow me to slow his progress. Instead of seeing the devil's grin again, I saw the devil himself. Or someone the devil would shit his pants over seeing in a dark alley.

Striding toward the bar was a man unlike any I had ever seen. I wasn't even sure what I was seeing, to be honest. His dark eyes pinned on my arm where the guy gripped hard enough that I was sure I would have distinct finger bruises.

He was tall; that was obvious by how he towered over everyone he passed. His shoulders were broad, and his thighs were thick enough to fill out his jeans to the point the seams were working overtime. He was wearing the same leather vest everyone else was wearing, but his seemed to be covered in patches, whereas most of the other biker's had very few. I suddenly realized that the guy I was being manhandled by had none at all. I knew nothing about motor-cycle club hierarchy, but that had to be significant.

But the thing that caught my attention and held me spellbound despite the terrifying situation I was in were the tattoos. From his neck down, going below his black T-shirt, then reappearing down both arms, was solid black tattoo ink. Except for the stark white. He was tattooed to look like a walking skeleton. Why was that so fascinating? And why did I want to see if that ink covered him in places that weren't covered with clothing? I continued to struggle, though I couldn't take my eyes off the tattooed biker.

The man finally stopped yanking me, but instead of letting me go, he took my legs and swung them around so that my body was facing him. The fear instantly came back. I was a fucking virgin, and there was no way in hell that I had fended off all the immature cowboys back in Kentucky, and then the wannabe movie stars in California, just to end up being raped in a bar in front of at least forty people.

I opened my mouth to scream louder than I ever had before when the man froze. I looked at his face to see his eyes glued to my stomach, and I knew what he was seeing. What a strange fucking world to be saved by the scars that had ruined my life.

"What the fuck is this?" He laughed and pushed my top up, and my hands immediately covered my breasts to stop him from revealing my boobs to the room. He traced his rough fingers over my skin, not even trying to be gentle about it.

I slapped his hand away. "Don't touch me!"

"I can touch you if I want, whore. That's my right as a Devil's Nightmare." He looked down at my body, his face twisted in disgust. "I don't know why your cut-up ass is here, but pussy is pussy. So shut the fuck up and take my dick."

He had one hand pressing hard against my sternum, the pressure beginning to make my chest ache, and the other hand went to his belt buckle. My chest was heaving as my breaths came in heavy pants while I tried not to completely lose my shit while panic began to take over. I bucked my hips and fought as hard as I could, twisting my body back and forth as much as possible when the pressure was suddenly removed from my chest. The man let out his own scream, causing my eyes to widen with surprise.

In confusion, I looked down at the hand that had been holding me down to see it pinned, covered in blood, a wicked-looking blade sticking out of the top of it. With relief pouring through me, I let my eyes slowly trail up from the blood that was mixing with the beer pooling next to my hip until my eyes met deep, black, bottomless pools.

I lay there panting, trying to catch my breath and stared at the man as he stared back at me. Both of us ignored the asshole who was screaming like a little girl and holding his arm, tears and snot running down his face. As if trapped in a spell, my gaze was locked with the man who was covered in black ink and amazingly lifelike tattoos of bones.

A chuckle sounded from next to us. Reluctantly, I forced myself to drag my eyes away from the hypnotic ones that didn't seem to want to let me go. I blinked in disbelief as the man with the devil's grin smiled.

"The Devil's Nightmares don't force women." It was all he said before turning and disappearing into the crowd. I had thought he was just going to watch from the door as I was assaulted, but instead, he had left to get help. I turned back to thank the skeleton man, but when I glanced around to where he had been standing just a moment before, he was gone.

FOUR

SALLY

After shoving myself away from the still screaming asshole, I rolled away, but not before I used his body as leverage. I may or may not have managed to kick him in the nuts a few times. I also might have shoved my foot into his arm, which was still pinned to the bar when he tried to grab me as I moved away. The pervert predator should have thought twice about laying his hands on me again.

I quickly shoved my way through the hulking bodies of bikers until I could rush to the dressing room, practically running to get away. I dropped onto one of the hard plastic chairs and put my head in my hands as I took several deep breaths, filling my lungs to capacity before letting them back out again slowly. It didn't stop the trembling in my hands, but my racing heartbeat started to decrease gradually.

One of the girls I had enjoyed working with popped her head into the room to stare at me with wide eyes.

"Are you okay?"

I looked up and dropped my hands on my legs. "Uh, hey, Kara."

She stepped in, taking a look around before dropping to her

haunches next to me. "Are you okay?" she asked again, reaching out and taking one of my trembling hands. I stared down at where she was touching me and fought back the instinct to yank my hand away. She was being nice to me, and I desperately needed to feel like someone cared.

"What the hell was that, Kara? What's going on tonight?"

She gave me a gentle squeeze and then let go of my hand, standing back up. She walked over to the large mirror on the wall by the door. "To answer your second question, The Devil's Nightmares have returned from a rally they have been at for the last two weeks," she waved a hand as she used the other to tidy up the eyeliner at the corner of her eyes. "Somewhere. I'm not sure." She turned back to me, looking over my body, and I glanced down to see the beer that had soaked into the black shirt. I groaned because I only had one uniform and hated the thought of smelling like booze for the rest of the night. Not that I wanted to go back out there at all.

"To answer your first question, that guy that grabbed you—" I snorted because I could handle being grabbed. That was almost to be expected when working at a bar full of bikers and the other kinds of men drawn to such a place. She grimaced but continued. "He was a prospect for the club. Maybe he didn't know the rules or was too drunk to care, but you don't lay a hand on the girls if they don't want you to. He will probably get kicked out of the club after this." She shrugged. "Good riddance. Nobody wants a guy like that around."

I didn't know if I should be relieved or worried. If the prospect got kicked out, then he might try to come after me in retaliation. I shivered at the thought. Staying in Pumpkin Patch might not be the right thing to do after all. I thought of my other choices and couldn't come up with anything good. I could try the same as before; I could just close my eyes and randomly pick another place to go, but what if it ended up being worse? Home to Kentucky was still out of the question. That would forever remain my very last option.

"I wouldn't worry too much about him coming after you again," she said softly, watching me through the mirror. "He would be given a warning that would mean his life if he tries to hurt you."

"They would kill him over me?" I wasn't shocked that they'd kill someone; it was a one percent club, and I doubted they ran it like Sunday School, but I was a nobody to them.

She shrugged a shoulder, then fished a tube of lipstick from the side of her bra, expertly sliding it onto her already cherry-red lips. "Not necessarily over you. More because of the disrespect he showed by breaking the rules. Technically, you aren't club property. But you do work for the club, so that gives you protection. But, just saying, even if you were just a girl in the bar having fun and got assaulted, the reaction would have been the same."

She turned to face me while tucking her lipstick away again inside her bra. "The Nightmares are a lot of things, most of them bad. But there is one thing they would never do, and that is force women or hurt children. They don't traffick, and they don't rape. It's a hard line they won't cross as long as Bones is the president. Even before then, it was something that most frowned on. I guess even those living in the deepest shade of gray won't cross into certain black areas."

I nodded absently, part of me very relieved to hear the news that they didn't treat women that way. It didn't mean they were good to their women. Some may cheat on or even beat their women, making them utter assholes. But part of me was stuck on what she had said about the president.

Bones.

It didn't take any explanations. If I hadn't been freaking the hell out when I first laid eyes on him, I probably would have been able to see it immediately. It was the way he held himself. There was an aura he gave off that was commanding, almost regal. He was more like a king than a president. The Skeleton King. *The Nightmare King*.

"Here, you can wear this. You are a bit smaller than me, but this should work well enough so you don't have to wear that one all night." She held a clean top out to me while gesturing to my beer-soaked one.

I grimaced again and stood up from the chair, glad to see that my legs weren't so shaky anymore and my knees were holding me up. I gingerly lifted the top over my head, careful not to drag it over my face, knowing that even though I couldn't see it through the black fabric, there was blood on the shirt, too. I dropped it onto the table and pulled the clean one on. It was baggy, much baggier than the other one, but it covered well. It was nice of her to say I was smaller than her instead of just calling my boobs small. She was well endowed and super curvy. She looked like a goddess with her long honey-blonde hair shining under the lights. But her sweet personality was what made her truly beautiful.

I looked up at her with gratitude. "Thank you. I appreciate it."

She waved away my thanks but smiled. "Are you ready to head back out there?"

I took a deep breath but nodded. Kara took my hand and pulled me along, not giving me a chance to second guess myself. When we entered the main room, it was as if nothing had happened. The bikers were all still partying, drinking their bottomless drinks, chatting with their buddies as if they hadn't seen them in decades, even though they had apparently been partying for the last two weeks together.

The man who had been pinned to the bar was gone, the blood wiped away. I saw the knife still lying on the counter, and my hands itched to grab it, to keep it. For some reason, I felt like it would protect me. Because it was his.

I slipped behind the counter and returned to filling mugs of beer. It was a relief that no one was making a big deal from the experience. A few curious looks were thrown my way, but no one said anything other than to call me sugar or babe while thanking me for the beer I slid across the bar top to them.

Mac had glanced my way several times with an apologetic look that I ignored. It wasn't his fault. I didn't think he had even noticed what was happening. It had been so quick, and Mac had been busy since the first biker had stepped through the doors. He barely had a chance to wipe the sweat from his brow as he poured glass after glass of whiskey and tequila shots.

I settled into an easy routine of filling glasses and sliding them down the smooth wood to whoever's hand was sitting there waiting. Whenever I had a chance to breathe, I would take a quick glance around the bar, just searching for the president. It wasn't until hours later when I noticed it was close to two a.m., that I saw him sitting at the corner table by the front door. The same table I had always thought was the best one in the place. Now I understood why no one had ever sat at it. It was his throne.

It was too dark, and there were too many people in the way, but I could have sworn he was staring at me. I shook my head as I poured an almost perfect mug of beer with only a little too much foam. I was being ridiculous. He was a fascinating man, so, of course, I was thinking about him. That quiet, commanding aura demanded respect without having to utter a word. The strong build. The tattoos. What he wasn't was watching me, a nobody, covered in so many scars that not even my mother would be able to look at me without wincing.

Now that he was seated at his table, I noticed that many of the bikers gravitated toward him. They carried their beers and whiskeys as they stood nearby, close enough to talk without actually entering his domain. The only ones that seemed to get close and even sit at the same table were the green-haired one with the cocky attitude and the dark-haired one with the sinister smile. There was another who dropped down into a chair next to him with light hair that almost looked blue but was difficult to tell in the dark. It seemed like they were his inner circle, even though it looked like they irritated him at times.

It took a while before I caught on to what some of the bikers were saying. Once I heard it, I made sure to keep my ears cocked to listen. They were complimenting him. As I strained to listen, I began to hear nearly all the bikers expressing how great he was. There was talk of how he had defeated various other men. I didn't understand what they were going on about, but I was more than intrigued. The president, though, looked like he wished they would all shut up and go away.

I noticed he wasn't drinking much. Daisy had come over to snatch a beer I had just filled and carried it over to him, her hips swaying like a pendulum and looking like she was ready to hop onto a stripper pole to put on the show of a lifetime. I had held my breath as she carried the glass over to him. Daisy stood there with her hip cocked to one side, clearly offering more than a beverage, but I didn't think he even glanced her way. The green-haired guy just laughed loudly and snapped his fingers in her face until she set the glass down on the table hard enough to slosh some of the beer over the side.

She flounced away, her hair bright pink flying behind her. She had a look of rage on her face, and when she caught me looking at her, she bared her teeth at me as if she were snarling like a wild animal. I had no doubt that she would have clawed my eyes out if she hadn't been sidetracked just then by some biker who wrapped his arm around her waist and tugged her into his hard body. He was attractive and muscular, and she must have thought so, too because she pulled his head down and took his lips in a kiss that wasn't suitable for the public.

I poured another beer and slid it to the next biker, giving him a small smile at his thanks. When I glanced back towards Daisy, I saw their kiss breaking off and Daisy turning to me with a triumphant grin on her face. I just shook my head. I had no idea why she would feel like she won anything. I wasn't after anyone at the bar. I had no desire to get involved with anyone. I lifted my head to glance back at the corner table and shuddered.

When the last of the bikers were finally stumbling out the door, and the place was empty of everyone except Mac, me, and a couple of younger guys that had vests on without the patch, I slumped against the wooden top of the bar.

"You did real good, new girl."

I sighed and looked up at Mac through my hair. I had no idea when he was going to stop calling me new girl, but whatever. "Is it like this all the time?" I started to brush the hair back from my face but looked at my sticky fingers and grimaced.

"Nah. This was a party only because the Nightmares had come home after being gone so long. After tonight, everyone pays for their drinks, so there won't be so many hanging around. Nothing draws the club in like a party and free booze."

I nodded tiredly, thankful it wouldn't go the same way every night. I hadn't earned many tips. Only a few of the guys had slid a few dollars to me. Most just thanked me or even just grunted before walking off with their fresh mugs. At least I was getting a salary for the work I had done.

We cleaned up quickly, and with the help of the young prospects, we had all the empty glasses picked up and the tables wiped down. One of them placed the chairs on the tables so the floor could get the mopping it seriously needed.

"Why don't you mop, and I'll get the glasses through the washer?" I nodded gratefully at Mac. I always ended up soaking wet when I tried to wash up. The spray was so strong and took a lot of strength to squeeze. I could imagine how badly my hand would be aching by the time I was finished. I'd much rather push the mop around. Truthfully, I had the better end of the deal since I was sure the back was pretty full, and he'd be at it long after I was done.

"Should have made those prospects stay longer," he grumbled to himself as he walked away, heading into the kitchen.

I entered the mop closet, pulled the rolling mop bucket over to the sink. I used the cut-off hose attached to the spigot to fill it with steaming water before dumping a dose of cleaning solution into it. I pulled the bucket with me and started at the pool table end of the bar and slowly, methodically, made my way from one end to the other.

When I was finally done, my arms felt like limp noodles, and my back was protesting, but I was proud of the job I had completed. I was sure my arms were getting stronger, and I would earn myself defined muscles before long. I started to push the bucket back toward the mop room and stopped short, making dirty, soapy water slosh over the side.

I stared up at the man leaning against the end of the bar, watching me with his deep, black eyes. I swallowed hard, jerking my gaze away and squatting down with the bar towel I had tucked into the side of my shorts. I started nervously wiping up the spill, hoping he wouldn't see the way he made me tremble.

I heard his footsteps before I saw his huge black biker boots stop inches from my hands. I paused, fighting the urge to look up at him, to see what expression he might have on his face, and terrified that I wouldn't see any at all. I couldn't read the man, and somehow, that scared me more than anything.

The bucket started to roll away from me, and I jerked my head up to see his back, the large sinister reaper staring back at me from the vest he was wearing, Devil's Nightmares, printed above, and Pumpkin Patch, Utah, below. It took me several seconds of staring with my mouth hanging open before jumping up, dripping rag in hand, and following him. By the time I turned the corner, he was already pouring the dirty water down the drain.

He didn't even look at me. He just turned around and walked down the hallway until I heard a door close with a thud. I looked down at the mop before dropping the wet rag in the basket for dirty linens. With just a shake of my head, I turned on the water so I could rinse the mop and bucket. And men complained that they couldn't understand women.

FIVE

THE NIGHTMARE KING

I sat on my Harley, watching Barrel run his fingers through his thick green hair, trying to tame the wildness from the wind. Of course, that was about all he did as he strutted like a fucking peacock through the door being held open by one of the prospects. I couldn't help the shiver of revulsion that slithered up my back at knowing he was about to rut the first pussy he came to.

"One day, Prez, you're going to find a pussy that doesn't turn your stomach!" The quiet laughter from my Vice President, Lock, had me turning my dead stare his way. He just held up his hands as he backed away, that stupid fucking creepy smile pasted to his face. He, too, turned around and walked through the doors.

Nearly all of my men had shoved their way in through the doors of the bar that the Nightmares owned, ready to start celebrating their triumphant return to their home turf. As if they hadn't just spent the last two weeks fighting, fucking, and drinking. There were some days I couldn't understand the needs that seemed to ride them.

I sat on my bike, smoking a cigarette, debating starting up my engine, and heading to the house I owned on the club compound. I wasn't in the fucking mood for all the noise and press of bodies. The music was already turned up loud enough that I could still make out the song playing even through the now closed doors. And I was sure my dog, Zero, was anxious to see me.

After a while of sitting in the near black night by myself, I was done. The club could go on without my presence for the night. I was just done already. Just as I reached for the key hanging from the ignition, the door opened, gaining my attention. Lock stood just inside the door and gestured with his head, a clear indication that I was needed. If he was calling on me to handle shit, it was because the President of the club was needed.

I let out a frustrated sigh that nobody but me would hear. Once I got to the door, I grunted at Lock. "This better be fucking important." I fingered the blade at my side, long and wickedly sharp. Lock glanced down at it, then back up to meet my eyes without flinching. There was a reason why he was my VP.

He gave me his stupid grin. "I think you're going to want to handle this one yourself, Bones."

Most people thought I had earned my road name due to the tattoo that covered me from my neck down to my toes, but they'd be wrong. I had an affinity for blades. And my favorite thing to do with them was to slice flesh down to the bone.

I stepped over the threshold, holding in my wince at the thumping music. I started to ask Lock what the fuck the problem was since all I saw was the usual bullshit that came with a Nightmare's party. There was drinking and fucking everywhere I looked, until I saw it. Until I saw *her*.

The waitress Mac had told me he hired the day we left for the rally was on her back on the bar. Her dark red hair was spread over the wood, looking like spilled blood. Something moved through my veins at the sight. My back went straight, and my muscles tightened.

Heat curled through me, urging me to go to the goddess, to spread her legs and feast in a way I never had before. I'd never felt my heart pounding so hard for any reason, and I clenched my jaw, willing myself to get back in control. I would never allow myself to be weakened by a woman. Then I saw the man over her, and the heat in my veins turned molten.

I had never in my life been jealous over anything before. Unquestionably, never over a woman. To feel the darkness crawling up my spine, telling me to cut off the dick that was inside of what was mine, had me ready to turn around and walk the fuck out. I didn't want a woman. I didn't need a cunt to get off on; I had my hand for that. It was the only way to ensure no one could get close to me.

I took a step back, not caring that I was essentially running away. I started to turn around, but then her eyes met mine, and my feet started moving of their own accord. As I took in more of the woman, the fire in my veins turned instantly into ice-cold fury. She wasn't being fucked. She was trying to fight off a fucking prospect that wasn't taking no for a motherfucking answer. My blade was in my hand before I had taken two steps. The tears that filled her eyes as she struggled made me want to gut every motherfucker in the room.

As I grew nearer, I took in the rest of her. Her face was as pale as her stomach, but there was something more. Thin pink lines became more visible in the dim lighting with each step I made that took me closer. She was covered in what looked like knife marks. Her soft looking belly, exposed by the ridiculous outfits that came with being a server at the Devil's Bar, was crisscrossed with more healed knife wounds than I could easily count. Looking down at her legs, I realized there were just as many. I felt a raw hunger to peel off her clothes so I could trace every line.

I was usually cold as ice, ready to extract a pound of flesh with nothing more than a cold detachment. I had never felt the need to bathe in anyone's blood before, but the prospect holding her down with a hand to the center of her chest had me aching to cut it off and then feed it to him. A red haze had steadily filled my vision as I moved forward.

I reached out, seeing the stark white of the bones covering my hand against the pitch black, reminding me that I was a monster.

One that could do whatever the fuck he wanted. I had the prospect's hand pinned to the bar within my next steady breath.

As he screamed like a bitch I met the eyes of the girl. I watched as the bright blue irises cleared of fear. She stared back into my cold, dead black eyes without flinching or cowering away. I studied her, wondering why she would be the only one in my life who could hold my stare without flinching.

Lock said something, causing her to turn her head to look at him, breaking whatever fucking spell she'd had me under. I watched as her eyes went soft, and a look of gratitude swept over her features. It had me taking several steps back and then turning away. I looked toward the door, back to where my bike waited, the keys still in the ignition, but turned to head toward the back of the bar instead.

I kicked the door to my office open and headed straight for my desk. As I sat there, I wondered why the fuck I wasn't just leaving the way I had planned. The way I wanted to. I didn't want to be in the bar. But the girl...

I shook my head and pulled open the bottom drawer, pulling out a bottle of whiskey. Before I could raise it to my lips, I saw blood-red hair going past my door. She was likely going to change out of the wet shirt she was wearing. I hadn't missed how she had been soaked in beer while lying there. My hand tightened on the bottle. The fucker was going to pay for what he had done. He had broken one of the only rules I had laid out when I took over the club. No forcing women. Ever.

A minute later, one of the other waitresses hurried past my door. She glanced inside as she passed, flinching when she saw me sitting there but tried to cover it with a small, forced smile. Fuck her, too. I was grateful, though. Because I knew she was one of the good ones. She would help the other girl without being a bitch about it.

It was several minutes later before they both reappeared together, the tall blonde girl pulling the redhead along with her. The girl looked shaken up but not traumatized. Good. If she were going to hang around a biker bar, she would need to have some steel in her spine. I grunted as I took a shot of whiskey.

It took a long time of sitting in the darkness with only my bottle of whiskey as company, before I finally couldn't take it any longer.

For the rest of the night, I sat in my reserved seat, ignoring everyone that wanted to talk, growling at Shock when the crazy motherfucker tried to tell me stories I already knew about the trip we had just taken. The only thing I was interested in was watching.

Her blood-red hair flowed down her back as she worked behind the bar. Every smile she gave to one of my men had anger flowing through me, only her glances my way, telling me she was as aware of my presence as I was hers, calming me, and keeping me from cutting the eyes out of every single one of my men.

I watched as she hid herself while in plain view. She used her long hair as a shield, as if she could hide her essence from my eyes. I wanted to stalk over there and demand that she show me her scars. The scars that didn't take away from her beauty, only enhanced it.

I sat there and wondered how she got them. They weren't self-inflicted. Someone had done that to her. Someone had touched her flawless flesh and carved himself into her. I wanted to carve myself into the man who had done it until he no longer existed. Until he was nothing but a pile of bones and blood. I would hand her his heart since mine was black coal in my chest.

But I wouldn't. Because I would not go to her. She was as untouchable as I was. My filthy hands had no place on her. But neither did anyone else's. That was a promise I made to myself as I sat there in my dark corner, alone while surrounded by others.

SIX

SALLY

"Hey, new girl!" I stopped in my tracks on my way back to the bar. I looked around and noticed several of the guys who had been drinking were standing up. Most of them were chugging down the last of whatever was in their glass as if they would never get another drink again. I hurried over to the bar.

"What's up?"

"Look, we normally wouldn't do this, but a couple of the girls are sick tonight. They wouldn't want to miss tonight if they could avoid it, so it must be pretty bad. I heard a stomach bug was going around town."

I was used to his rambling, but right now, I just wanted him to get to the point. "Mac, what is it?"

"We need you to work the fight tonight." He stood there expecting something from me, but I wasn't sure what. Unfortunately, I had nothing to give him. He sighed heavily as if he had just realized how hopeless I was. "The club hosts a huge fight night at a warehouse down the road once a month. It's a big deal around here, and it brings in a fuckton of cash. The girls that work the fights make a fuckton, too. As I said, they wouldn't miss it if they had a choice. So we need you to step up tonight." He gave me a narrowed-eyed stare, sizing me up. "You think you can do that, new girl?"

I had already been working at the bar for close to a month, and I hardly considered myself a new girl, though I was definitely an outsider compared to the rest. But serving drinks at a fight club? It sounded dangerous, and it was on the tip of my tongue to say hell no when a snicker came from behind me.

"You're joking? Right?" Daisy plopped her tray down on the scarred surface of the bar with a loud clatter. "This... thing working the fight night? She'll scare the crowd."

"Now, Daisy..." Mac started, but I was already stepping forward.

"I'll do it." I lifted my chin and stared him in the eye, challenging him to agree with the stupid bitch that had taken every chance she had to belittle me and tried to make me feel like shit over my appearance. I ignored her snort of derision as he gave me a curt nod, a glint of approval in his eyes.

"Good, good. I need you to go into the back room where the extra clothes are for the girls. Find the ones that are different from what you wear here. Can't miss 'em." He turned to give Daisy a glare. "Get moving, or I'll tell them to leave you behind."

I didn't wait around for any more of her shit and left my tray sitting there. Mac would put it away behind the bar. I assumed the place would stay pretty slow for the rest of the night if the exodus of bodies was any indication.

I found the clothes in stacks where he said they would be. He was right; they were different from what we usually wore. While our uniform at the bar was a black crop tank top with black shorts, these clothes were white. It wasn't a typical crop top, more like a bralette, though there was a built-in bra so my breasts wouldn't hang out of the bottom. The white boyshorts looked like they were made of leather, but as I examined them, I realized they were the same stretchy spandex material as the black shorts.

It only took me a few minutes to swap out my clothes, and I was pleasantly surprised at how comfortable they were. Honestly, they would have been great workout clothes if the top was a little more supportive. As it was, the top molded to my body, coming to a stop just a couple of inches below my breasts. The shorts only rose as high as my hip bones, leaving a large expanse of flesh visible.

I looked in the mirror and realized for the first time since I had been taken that I had lost a significant amount of weight, but more than that, I had gained muscle. Since leaving high school, I had put on those dreaded "freshman fifteen", probably plus a few. Before now, I would have had a bit of a muffin top and would have been able to pinch a good amount of flesh from my belly. Even while I was in captivity, I hadn't lost much weight since the doctor had made sure to keep me fed and healthy for his "experiments". Now, though, I was slim, as slim as I used to be when I swam daily for the high school team. What I didn't like about the outfit was the god-awful camel toe that made me feel self-conscious.

I plucked the stretchy fabric at my crotch and wiggled my hips, hoping to make the material slide down a little more, giving me enough room to cover my vagina better.

"There's nothing you can do about it." I turned to look at Kara as she strolled into the dressing room, wearing the same thing I was. "We've all grown to get used to it." She reached down to adjust the seam between her legs. "Though I do hate the fucking wedgies."

She walked over to me and circled me while humming. "You look good. Great actually. You can almost see a hint of a six-pack in your abs." She scrunched her nose. "I wish I had the motivation to do crunches, but I'd rather eat a bowl of cereal."

"I think you look great, too," I offered. She really did. Her curves were amazing, and she carried them well.

She grinned at me, making me almost want to smile back. "Thanks. So, I was told to make sure you had a tattoo before we left. There will be a lot of guys from other clubs at the fight, and it will let them all know that you are off-limits. No one is allowed to force a woman while at the fight night; the Devil's Nightmares would chop off their dicks if they tried. But it's important to have their MC logo visible, just in case. They tend to get handsy. But if you get scared, just look for any one of the Nightmares, and he is obligated to put a stop to it. Okay?"

It all sounded great to me, but I was still stuck on the word tattoo. "You are going to tattoo me? Here? Now?"

She giggled and walked over to a small plastic box on a nearby shelf. "Not exactly, but yeah." She took the lid off the box and reached in, withdrawing something.

"Is that a temporary tattoo?" Honestly, it was pretty clever. I was all for having something that would help protect me from a bunch of drunk, lawless assholes. She waved it in the air as she grabbed a paper towel and a bottle of water.

"Isn't it great? It will only last a few days but should work like a charm tonight. Just make sure you don't rub it too much and don't get alcohol on it." She folded up the paper towel and waved me over. "I need your wrist." I held it out to her, and she turned my hand until I was in a position that she approved of. In less than a minute, she was lifting the drenched, folded up paper towel and slowly sliding the back of the tattoo off. The image left behind was identical to the one I had seen pretty much everywhere in the bar and all over each member's vest.

Kara held up her own wrist next to mine. "It obviously isn't real, but no one will notice, and that's all that matters." She chucked the trash in the bin by the door and tugged at her crotch one more time, muttering about wedgies before giving me another huge grin. "Oh! One last thing. You should pull your hair back. It gets super hot in the warehouse with all those bodies packed in there. There isn't any air conditioning. If you leave your hair down, it will be stuck to your arms and drive you crazy. Trust me." She gave me a wink and turned around, walking through the door. "Be outside in five minutes, or you'll be left behind!" With that parting comment, she was gone down the hall, her curvy hips swaying in a sensual way I could never hope to emulate.

I turned back to look at myself in the mirror and cringed. I had been using my long red hair as a shield since I was rescued. I considered leaving it down, but Kara was right; sweaty skin and long hair didn't mix well. With a sigh, I reached up and began to braid my hair into a French braid, starting at the top of my head. I was adept at it, my fingers flying through the process I had become used to almost daily for years. I always French braided my hair before putting on my swim cap to keep it from becoming a tangled mess.

Once I was at the end of my hair, I held it together with one hand and looked around for anything that I could use to tie it back, but there was nothing. You'd think with so many women around, there would be at least one stray hairband, but nope. I decided to try my luck with asking for help. One of the girls could have an extra around her wrist and wouldn't mind sharing.

I walked down the hall and passed an open door, grunts coming from inside it, catching my attention and making me look despite my better judgment. I had one glance before my head was spinning back to face forward. I never wanted to see that shit ever again. Barrel, the green-haired club enforcer, was pounding into a bent over Daisy, taking her hard. I shivered in repulsion and quickened my steps until I approached the next door.

I knew it was the President's office. I rarely saw him sitting, brooding in the dark, at his table in the bar. But he showed up to dump my mop bucket every night before leaving me standing there watching, never saying a word. My curiosity and, yes, my yearning to see him had me slowing down as I passed, doing my best to ignore the grunts that were getting louder. Why couldn't they shut the door? Freaks.

I spotted a rubber band sitting right on top of the desk next to a few pieces of paper and what was probably Bone's cell phone. I paused. I didn't really want to use an actual rubber band on my hair, that shit pulled and wasn't good for the strands, but I needed something. And there was something right there, just a few feet away. I glanced up and down the hallway, not seeing anyone. If I darted in and grabbed the rubber band quickly, no one would know. It wasn't like I was going to be stealing secrets or anything. It wasn't a big deal. Right?

Yeah, it was a shit idea, but I was going to do it anyway. With determined steps, I crossed the threshold and walked over to the desk, snatching up the rubber band. I let out a startled cry when I suddenly felt myself being pushed back before I could even comprehend what was happening. My feet were shuffling against the floor until my back hit the wall. A large, calloused hand wrapped around my throat and squeezed. My gasp came out as a squeak when I looked up to see bottomless black eyes glaring down at me with murderous intent.

"Tell me, little girl, do you want to die?" His gravelly, monotone voice had goosebumps popping up on my arms and the fine hairs on my body standing on end. I was looking into the face of a killer, someone I knew was far more dangerous than the man I had been rescued from.

I tried to speak, to explain myself, but his fist just tightened further. I couldn't take a breath, and my brain flew into panic mode. I dropped the end of the braid and grabbed onto his wrist with both hands, frantically trying to pry him away from my throat as my vision grew hazy around the edges.

He tilted his head to the side and watched me as I struggled for a breath that wasn't coming. "Only someone with a death wish would come into my office and take from me."

I shook my head as well as I was able while being held in his unbreakable grasp. I held up the rubberband that I was still clutching and jabbed it in the general direction of his face as my world grew darker and darker. He let up fractionally as he focused on what I was trying to show him. Just that much was enough to allow the smallest amount of air into my lungs. I sucked in as hard as I could, but it still wasn't enough.

"What the fuck is this? You were stealing a rubberband?" All I could do was nod as he loosened another fraction. "Why?" he demanded and shook me by the hold he had on my neck, my head lolling backward as I closed my eyes. "I could have killed you. Over a fucking rubber band." It almost sounded like he was speaking to himself rather than me. His gravelly voice lost the monotone edge, turning angry at the thought of killing me over something so minor.

Suddenly, the pressure was gone; only his hand remained, collaring me without stealing my breath. I sucked in huge lungfuls of air as tears rolled down my cheeks, across my scars, only to slide against his flesh where it met mine.

"Needed...for...hair." I gasped and choked, only his hold on my neck and my hold on his wrist keeping me upright instead of a heap of flesh and bones on the wooden floor.

"You needed the rubberband for your hair?" His monotone was back the same as when this had started, with no infliction to indicate if he was shocked, angry, confused, or amused.

"S-sorry. I'm s-so sorry." I wanted to beg for my life, but what reason did I have? My life was as useless as a used tissue. I probably should have been more afraid at that moment, but I honestly thought that the only reason I was scared at all while he was choking me was because of pure natural human response. Now that I was no longer in the clutches of death, I almost didn't care what he did with me.

His hand left my neck, and I dropped the hand that had been holding his wrist down to my side. I let my head fall forward. I didn't know what his next move would be, but I knew that it would have the potential to change my life for the worse forever.

When his hand reached behind me, I forced my body to relax my tense muscles. I kept my eyes closed when I felt him moving his hands, just focusing on clearing my thoughts, trying to slip into a meditative state so I could shake off the residual terror I felt at having my life squeezed from me.

When I heard his deep intake of air, I let my eyes open to see my braid dangling from his hand. I lifted my chin and followed the red plait to his heavily inked fingers. He had the ends of my hair pinched between those fingers, fanning out the strands, the rubberband securely tightened around the hair. And he was taking in my shampoo scent with his eyes closed as if he were enjoying it.

I stared, dumbfounded, as his eyes opened and focused on mine.

"Next time you need something, you come straight to me. Understand?" I started to nod until his hand returned to my throat, making me stiffen in anticipation of being choked again. But instead of tightening, I felt a feather-light caress of his fingers where I was sure to have a bruise by morning. "Good girl."

He stepped back, and before I could blink, he was gone from the room, and I was left standing there, confused and running my fingertips where he had just caressed me.

SEVEN

SALLY

As I sat in the back row of the van, I thought back to the conversation I'd had with Linda, the Assistant District Attorney. The Doctor was seen going about his day as if nothing in the world bothered him. He'd had his license pulled and would never work in medicine again. Apparently, he had taken up horticulture since the bond hearing.

The trial was still slated to start in January, and I would be expected to be there to testify. I had assured her I had every intention of returning. I had a driving need to see him behind bars for the rest of his miserable life. Linda had also told me that there was a quiet investigation going on behind the scenes regarding the judge and whether or not he was taking bribes. It was slow going, though. These people were good at what they did, but finding a money trail was challenging when there were so many ways to hide one.

I fingered the end of my braid, fanning it out the way Bones had. I brushed it over my lips and closed my eyes as I thought back to the way his tattooed fingers had brushed softly over my throat. It was almost as if he were apologizing, but at the same time, I got the impression that he had liked seeing his fingers there, collaring my throat, holding my life in his hands.

I shivered. A part of me had liked it, too. It was actually scary how much I liked it now that I was looking back and not terrified that he was actually going to squeeze the life out of me.

The van turned down a road, making my body sway with the momentum. I opened my eyes to peer out into the darkness. There didn't seem to be anything for miles around. After a couple more minutes, though, I caught a glimpse of lights in the distance.

I knew I wasn't fully prepared for what the night would bring, but at least it was a change from the norm. I glanced down at my wrist and traced a finger lightly over the temporary tattoo there. It was easy to tell up close that it was fake, but since it was to help keep unwanted attention away, I hoped that it would do the job. I didn't know what would happen once we arrived, but I assumed it would be similar to waitressing at the bar. In other words, a lot of drunk, horny bikers that would be showing off for their friends, acting like idiots, and trying their luck with all the girls.

My standoffish attitude had helped the regulars at the bar see early on that I wasn't interested in having a good time with them. Over the last month, they had all learned to keep their hands off me. I was sure the display that first night back hadn't hurt either. Not with the way Bones had come to my rescue.

I rarely saw him outside of the shadows, where he tended to lurk. The white of the bones tattooed on his skin were almost eerie with the way they were all that could be seen in the darkness. As if there really was a skeleton watching me.

There was a yearning I felt in my belly whenever I looked up to see his black eyes fixed on me. I wanted to lean forward as if it would bring us closer together. Feeling his touch for the first time had ignited something inside of me I wasn't ready to name.

The van rolled to a jerky stop, and I gasped at the sight of the parking lot that was already filled nearly to capacity with what looked like hundreds of bikes. The other girls had been talking quietly amongst themselves as I sat alone in the back but grew louder in their excitement while doing a final clothing and makeup check. There would be a few more of us, but some of the girls had chosen to ride with the guys on the back of their motorcycles. Looking at the number of motorcycles in the lot, I hoped the other clubs had also brought plenty of help.

Kara turned to me, an assessing gaze eyeing me. "You good?"

I merely nodded as they started to climb out. I waited for the van to clear so I could stand up, hunched over, and make my way to the door. As I stepped down gingerly where Kara waited for me, she hooked her elbow with mine and began to lead me to the wide-open double doors that were the entrance to the rather huge metal warehouse building.

"It's going to be wild inside. I hope you're ready. Remember, there are rules. No guys are allowed to force you to do anything you don't want to do. The tattoo is there to declare that you belong to the Nightmares, but even without it, they aren't supposed to give you a hard time. Unfortunately, the clubs that will be here tonight aren't as strict as ours. That means, sometimes, it takes more than one no."

She looked down at me with serious eyes. I was hesitant to hear whatever else she had to say, but I got the feeling that it was necessary. "There is a club in the neighboring county that has always been a little... darker than most. They are the Boogeymen. They have been the Nightmares' top rivals forever, and whenever there is a major dispute, they are almost always the cause. They would take over the whole region if it were up to them. Bones, along with the other presidents, have kept them in check, stopping drugs from flooding our streets and preventing trafficking. Each club has its own territories that no other club can invade without a war breaking out. That means there are things that they do that the Nightmares can't stop—unless it spills over across county lines. This warehouse is called The Four Corners and is on the edge of Nightmare territory, right where the other counties meet. It is considered neutral territory, so even if the Boogeymen want to break them, they have to follow the rules if they don't want three other clubs to go to war with them."

She pulled me to a stop just outside the doors as the other girls passed through, tossing hair over their shoulders and swaying their hips, ready to get to work. "Just stay away from them, okay? If they realize you aren't actually Nightmare property, they might try to press their luck. Look for a Nightmare and get his attention, okay?" She stared me down until I nodded my agreement. "If they manage to get you outside and away from witnesses, you could disappear, and the Nightmares would have a difficult time convincing them to give you back."

My breath started coming in short pants as I tried not to panic at what she said. "Why would they bring me here if I was in danger?" I didn't like the way my heart rate had sped up, and I could feel cold sweat trickling down my back.

"I'm not trying to scare you, Sally. But you need to know how important it is for you to stay away from them, okay?"

I hesitated before nodding. I took a look over my shoulder, but I knew I wouldn't find a way back to town. All I could do was follow her instructions and hope that the night went smoothly. Mac had said the club needed my help, but I couldn't help but feel a small flare of anger that they had been okay with putting me in this position.

Kara turned back to the doors and tugged me along with her. "I promise everything will be okay. The fights are actually really fun to work. The tips are amazing."

"Fights?" It wasn't until we were several feet through the doors and into the lit interior that I saw the large ring in the middle of the floor. It looked just like a boxing ring seen on the television, except the dingy white floor was stained in many places. There were no chairs around the ring, just picnic benches spread evenly throughout the building, except for a large, bare space around the center to allow spectators to stand and watch up close.

I saw bars set along each wall, similar to the one at the Devil's

Bar. There were already bikers standing behind them serving drinks to the crowd that had grown even larger since we'd entered. As I stood there, taking everything in with a bit of awe, more motorcycle engines could be heard coming up the long road.

"The guys fight here?"

Kara giggled. "It's really hot, you'll see. Every guy wants to be the one to win, but there's only been one undefeated reigning champion for a few years now."

"Who is it?" I thought of the bikers with the Devil's Nightmares. Lock was cold and sinister. He was muscular but slender, and I didn't think he'd be big enough to beat some of the guys I saw walking around the warehouse. He was too wiry. Even if he were fast, a few good hits and he'd be out. There was really only one Nightmare I could think of that was big and strong, but there was no way...

"Bones, the President of the Devil's Nightmares, of course!" She tossed me a wink before dragging me across the room to the far right side of the warehouse. I recognized the two guys manning the bar as a couple of the prospects who sometimes helped out at work. I hadn't really talked to either one of them, but they were always polite to me.

Kara leaned her head closer and lowered her voice. "When the guys are done with their fights, they are always fired up from all that adrenaline, you know?"

I blinked at her, not getting what she seemed to be hinting at. She giggled again and gave me a playful push. "You really are an innocent little thing, aren't you?" I blushed but refused to take the bait. She huffed in exasperation and pulled me closer, talking right into my ear. "They are always looking for a fuck after a fight. Fucking a biker when he's high on adrenaline?" She waved a hand in front of her face. "Fucking hot."

I held up my hands and shook my head emphatically. "Not interested."

"That's damn a shame for you, because it's the best sex I've ever had."

A thought hit me, and my face got even hotter. I was sure my cheeks matched my hair, even through the thick makeup I was wearing to cover my scars. "Does Bones..." I couldn't finish the thought. I had never seen him even look at another woman while he'd been around. He was always lurking in the dark after the bar closed, only coming out of his office to dump the stupid mop water for me, just to disappear again. But he was always alone.

Kara was already shaking her head without me needing to continue. "No, never. He always grabs a whiskey and heads to his table." She indicated an empty table near the bar with a tilt of her head. "But, between you and me, that boy needs to get laid." She looked around quickly as if to see if anyone was within hearing distance and might have heard her talking shit about the president. "Just, maybe don't mention to anyone I said that?"

I burst into giggles, surprising myself, before clamping a hand over my mouth to stifle them. I couldn't remember the last time I had laughed at anything. But seeing Kara look around, full of worry that someone would have overheard that their president needed to get laid? It made me feel lighter, almost relieved. Hell, I was lying to myself because the feeling of tingles in my belly was definitely relief to know that he hadn't been sleeping with any of the club girls.

Together, we walked up to the bar and grabbed a tray each, ready to get the night started. The room was already getting full. Nearly all the bikers I recognized had filled in the section of the warehouse that seemed to be designated as the Nightmares. Some were wandering around the other clubs, shaking hands or just talking. It was good to see that they seemed to get along well without a lot of animosity. I had been a little afraid that there would be a lot of fistfights and rivalry, but it was as if they were colleagues of a sort. Similar to rival businesses that had respect for each other.

I began the night like any other, walking from table to table, taking drink orders and cash, pocketing tips that appeared to be a little more generous than they usually were. The guys were all respectful, barely talking more than to give me their orders and to thank me.

I people-watched as I did my job. Everyone seemed to be really enjoying themselves. I saw Daisy leaning over to run her red fingernails up the arm of a biker I had never seen before, who gave her a salacious grin at her blatant flirting. Kara was doing her own bit of flirting, but she passed it around to everyone, more like she was just highly enjoying herself as she served the bikers. There were a few other girls from the club whom I worked with frequently, and a couple that I knew were club girls who didn't work at the bar but often hung around. I was curious to know if they worked in other businesses I'd heard the club owned or if they just spent time as a club girl when they could. I hadn't noticed any of the guys in serious relationships. I couldn't help but wonder if they kept their wives or girlfriends at home. Surely, at least a few had to be in a relationship.

A loud ringing had my head whipping around to face the center while I was heading back to the bar to fill another drink order. Everyone else grew quiet as they waited for the bald man in the center of the ring holding a microphone to speak. It was when he welcomed everyone back to the fight night and a deafening cheer went up from the huge crowd, that my eyes caught on the tall, imposing man walking my way.

EIGHT

SALLY

Bones walked straight up to me, invading my space. I swallowed hard as his intense eyes bore into mine. His hand went up to my throat, the same way he had done in his office, but this time, he didn't push me into the wall. His eyes weren't filled with rage. His face was as impassive as always, not giving a single emotion away. But deep inside his black eyes, I saw what looked like concern. And a hunger that he seemed to be winning a battle against.

His thumb swept over my pulse as it fluttered wildly in my neck before his hand tightened with just enough pressure to make me stiffen without causing me to panic.

"Stay on this side of the warehouse." His words were stiff and gruff, an order given and expected to be obeyed. Since I had no desire to wander into a group of unknown horny bikers, I nodded. Or I tried to. His hand tightened more. "Say the words, little girl."

"I will stay on this side of the warehouse." My voice was quiet, barely above a whisper, as I met his stare with wide eyes, but he must have heard me because his fingers flexed then loosened, lightly resting on my skin as his thumb once again swept over my racing pulse. His eyes left mine, wandering over my face as he seemed to search for something. His attention to what I knew was my scars had me swallowing hard and shamefully lowering my eyes to his chest. I heard a rumble that almost sounded like a growl coming from him, causing my eyes to fly back up to meet his again. After another long moment, he grunted and stepped back before turning away from me and striding over to the table Kara had indicated was reserved for him.

I quickly turned back to the bar, ignoring the probing eyes of the bikers and the girls around me. I gave the prospect my order and waited as I stared at the bar. I had always struggled with having the attention of others. I had no clue why I thought I could be an actress, but with the damage that had been done to me, I couldn't stand the stares of others anymore.

Behind me, the bald guy was making announcements that I was barely paying any attention to as I waited patiently for the drinks I would need to return to the table with. But when I heard Bone's name being called out and another deafening cheer, I couldn't resist glancing over my shoulder toward his table.

Bones had a mug of beer gripped in his hand while Daisy stood just to the side of him, trying to gain his attention. But like every other time I had looked toward him in the last month, his eyes were locked on me. I gave him a small smile with just the barest tilt of my lips, but his blank expression never wavered. I let my smile drop and turned back to the bar when the prospect grunted out my name.

I thanked him, quickly loaded my tray, then headed back over to the table with their order. Through their laughter and playful shoves, I managed to get everyone settled with their fresh beers and pocketed the money they gave me. I was sure that they had massively overpaid, but each of them waved me off when I offered them their change.

As I approached the next table, the first two fighters were called to the ring. The night continued just like that, with roars of excitement and even some jeers from the crowd as each round of fighters entered the ring, bare-chested and full of testosterone. Most of the fights lasted several minutes as the guys pounded each other's faces until they were bloody. A few times, the fights ended up on the floor of the ring as the men grappled for dominance until someone finally surrendered or was knocked out. The club the defeated biker belonged to always dragged the unconscious man away, and I couldn't help but worry. There didn't seem to be any medical personnel in the warehouse to help if anyone got seriously injured.

Often, after a biker won his fight, a girl stood waiting for him at the edge of the ring. One girl had climbed inside and thrown herself into his arms as he had been roaring to the crowd in victory. I had thought they were going to start fucking right there for everyone to watch until the bald guy laughed and pushed them toward the ropes, ignoring the snarling man as he tore his mouth from the girl and pulled his hand from inside her skirt.

I patted my heated cheeks at the display and couldn't help but let my eyes wander back to Bones. His face was just as stoic as always, but there was no denying the heat in his eyes as he stared back at me. I was beginning to realize that, though the Devil's Nightmares president was outwardly impassive and unemotional, there were hints of what he was feeling in the depths of his black eyes if you looked close enough. I was beginning to think he just never let anyone that close. The only reason I could see anything at all was because his eyes were always on me.

I had a tray full of empty glasses when his name was called to a roar of excitement from the entire crowd. My breath caught in my throat, and my full tray nearly toppled over as my body jerked convulsively at the sound of his name. Excitement swept through me, and right on its heels was a healthy dose of fear. I had seen how brutal the fights were. There was a reason why the mat of the ring was stained. There were already fresh splatters of blood covering the surface that I knew wouldn't wash out whether they attempted to clean it or not.

My eyes flew to Bones, and I watched as he squared back his

broad shoulders and stood up slowly from the bench he'd been sitting on. His eyes met mine, and he raised a head to gesture to me, crooking one finger in a come here motion. Without stopping to think, I left my tray where it was on the edge of the table and walked to him as if in a trance.

He methodically took his vest off and folded it carefully. When I reached his side, he held out his vest, which I took in my arms without thinking. I pulled it close to my chest, knowing it was a significant move on his part. My mind was too overwhelmed to give it too much thought, but I knew it was essential to keep it safe. Then he reached behind the back of his neck with one hand and, gripping the collar of his black T-shirt, he pulled, taking it off in one swift motion.

I barely noticed when he dropped the shirt onto the top of his vest in my arms. My eyes were taking in every inch of his chest. The same ink covering his arms and neck covered every inch of his torso. I knew then there was no doubt that the ink would be everywhere else on his body. He looked like a walking skeleton, but under that black and white was the body of a god.

When I was finally able to tear my eyes away from the muscles that formed the deep V disappearing under the edges of his black jeans, I saw the barest glint of humor in his eyes. With unspoken words between us, I promised to keep his vest safe. He grunted, then turned away, stalking over to the ring. In one smooth move, he slid under the bottom rope, quickly jumping back to his feet. Then I watched with my tummy clenching as he cracked his neck from side to side.

"Wow, girl, the sexual tension between you two is enough to get every girl in this building pregnant." Kara's words, coming from next to me, had me yanking my gaze away from the sight of Bones' dominating presence in the ring. I glanced over to see her waving a hand around her face, pretending to cool off.

"It's not like that," I muttered, pretending her words weren't lighting up my insides and having bubbles fizz in my gut.

She nudged my shoulder with hers, a smirk covering her face as she smoothed her hand over her slick blonde hair. "I think you're in denial. But, girl, if you have a single shred of smarts in that brain of yours, you'll take that cock for a ride. You do realize that he's never been seen with a woman, right?"

I jerked my eyes back to the ring to see another man sliding into the ring from the other side. He was huge, one of the largest men I had ever seen. Bones was tall, six-foot-five, if I had to guess, based on how my neck had to crane back to look up at him as he towered over me, but the other guy had at least a few inches on him. I hadn't thought about who he would have to fight, but seeing the man who was as big as a tank flexing his arms and pounding his fist into his other hand dramatically had worry slamming into me. I looked over to Bones, who seemed completely unfazed by the guy's muscled bulk, shaved head, and the spider tattooed on his face. I thought about what Kara said. "Maybe he doesn't like women?"

She snorted as she played with a strand of her hair, curling it around her finger before smoothing it back out over her ample chest. "No men, either. The man is like a robot when it comes to fun of any kind."

"I should hold those." The obnoxious voice came out of nowhere, and hands suddenly reached out to snatch away the leather vest and T-shirt from my arms.

I jerked back, holding the items tightly to my chest. I glared at Daisy. "No. He gave them to me. If he wanted you to hold them, he would have called you over instead." She would have to pry them out of my cold, dead fingers. I didn't know why it mattered to me so much, but, well... here we were.

"You're not even a Nightmare girl."

She spat the words at me with a sneer, much louder than they needed to be. My mouth dropped open in a shocked gasp, and I quickly glanced around nervously. I knew Daisy didn't like me, but spreading that kind of information could put me in massive danger. The Devil's Nightmares knew I was an outsider but respected me anyway; other clubs wouldn't have that same compunction. I didn't like that there seemed to be quite a few unfamiliar eyes on us.

"You need to shut the fuck up and back off before I tell Bones the kind of shit you're trying to pull, bitch." Kara took a menacing step into Daisy's space. I had always thought of Kara as sweet and kind. I certainly hadn't thought that she would have the side of her that I was seeing now. Somehow, she had morphed into protective mode over me, and I had to swallow back the grateful lump that developed in my throat. Not even my parents would have tried to stand up for me, instead letting me fight my own battles with the excuse of it making me stronger or some such bullshit. Maybe they were right, but it also taught me that I couldn't rely on them for anything.

"You better watch your step," Daisy leaned in and hissed at Kara. "You are going to regret speaking to me that way."

"Yeah, I don't think so," Kara scoffed, then I felt her hand wrap around my elbow just before she dragged me away from Daisy and closer to the ring. "Ignore her, okay?" She was so pissed off that her words came out in a snarl.

I swallowed hard, my gaze meeting Bone's from inside the ring while he stood there ignoring his opponent, who was prancing around the ring showboating for the crowd. Instead, he seemed to be paying close attention to what I was doing. My eyes darted from the other fighter to the referee, to the crowd, and back to the black eyes that made me nervous. I watched as they narrowed almost imperceptibly, then left mine to land behind me.

My curiosity got the better of me, so I turned to look over my shoulder. Daisy was glaring daggers at my back while standing cozied up to a guy I had never seen before. The guy was looking at me with too much curiosity, making me immediately want to back further away. It was a look I had seen before. There were many times the doctor would stare at me like that when he was filled with morbid interest, right before he would satisfy his curiosity by doing something that hurt.

I was battling back the panic trying to crawl up my throat, when first Daisy, then the biker, seemed to realize they were being watched. Their eyes widened, and before I could make sense of the sudden change, the man turned, walking away quickly with Daisy rushing to follow after him. I wondered if Bones had done something to warn them somehow, but when I turned back to face the ring, he was facing his opponent with his usual dead stare, somehow even more intimidating than usual.

The sound of a bell rang out, immediately starting a flurry of activity inside the ring. Everyone on the outside stood on their feet and cheered for their favorite to win. Bones did a lot of ducking and dodging, seemingly playing some cat-and-mouse game with the giant man. For every third or so swing he avoided from his opponent, Bones would send a sharp jab somewhere into the man's body.

There was blood dripping down the large barrel chest of Bone's opponent from a cut above his eyebrow, and a large bruise was already forming on the side of his ribs. He had yet to make full contact with Bones, though he had grazed his chin at one point when my small squeal of worry had his gaze jerking to me. Though he still managed to pull his head back, he hadn't avoided the fist completely as it ran across his jaw. From that moment on, I clamped a hand over my mouth and bit my lip to hold back any sounds that could distract him.

For being such a tall, muscular man, he was quick on his feet and almost seemed to have a sixth sense for his opponent's moves. Bones avoided blows as if it were a choreographed dance. It wasn't until the other man was panting heavily, his swings becoming sloppy and sluggish, that things changed. And then the crowd truly went wild.

The sounds in the large warehouse were deafening, but nobody seemed to care as every man and woman went wild as they watched Bones suddenly begin to beat the living shit out of the other fighter. The huge man swayed on his feet with every punch, his head jerking back with each impact. I truly didn't understand how he was even still on his feet.

Bones didn't even look winded. Just a thin layer of sweat covered his exposed back, making the stark white of the bones that created the effect of a ribcage gleam under the fluorescent lighting. The rippling movements of his muscles were easy to see, and see I did.

I stared, fascinated, as he decimated the much larger man, my breath shallow and my heart beating like a runaway train. If anyone needed a drink refill, they were out of luck unless they found someone else to serve them. After a particularly vicious uppercut, the biker was knocked backward several steps. He began pinwheeling his arms, trying to maintain his wavering balance, and I became aware of a prickling sensation going down my spine. The feeling of being watched made me regretfully pull my eyes away from the Nightmare President. I darted my eyes around as I subconsciously rubbed the back of my neck, trying to soothe the tension the feeling of being watched caused.

My gaze scanned the crowd, looking for anyone who had their eyes on me. Daisy was still cozied up to her biker, but neither seemed to be paying me any attention. Instead, they were practically fucking in the middle of the crowd. His hand was clearly inside her stretchy shorts and moving at a rapid pace as she panted against his mouth. I looked away in disgust, a full body shiver running over me and had me shaking out my arm, not holding the clothes, trying to get rid of the icky feeling. I had already seen Daisy getting railed way more times than I ever cared to. I didn't care how often she got it on. I mean, good for her, I guess. But I *really* wished the girl would at least try to keep it behind closed doors.

I continued my scanning of the warehouse, but it wasn't easy to see anything through all the people standing and yelling toward the ring. No one seemed to be looking at me openly, but the sensation wasn't going away. A loud thump and deafening cheers had me forgetting about anything except for Bones as I spun around to see Bones turning away from the big man who was sprawled on his back, arms splayed out. I couldn't see his face, but it was pretty obvious he was knocked out by the stillness in his body. I might have been concerned if it weren't for the steady rising of his chest. Instead, I was panting as if I had been the one in the ring. I hadn't thought I was the kind of girl to get turned on by senseless violence, but watching the man I had a deep fascination with dominate in such a vicious, undoubtedly primal way sent all kinds of delicious shivers through my body.

As I stood staring, clutching the clothing tightly to my chest, the Devil's Nightmares president slowly turned until he faced me, his face an expressionless mask. He took slow, measured steps to the side of the ring, ignoring the yelling and congratulations from the guys who had jumped into the ring to celebrate his victory. He lifted a leg to step over the top rope, barely pushing it down to do so. His other leg came next until he was balanced on the edge of the platform. Then Bones hopped down to the warehouse floor, all without moving his dark gaze from mine. Several men and women rushed up to him, but he ignored all their congratulatory yells and back pats as he strode toward me.

I took a long, deep breath before letting it out in a shaky exhale. My whole body felt tingly, from my scalp down to my shaky knees. Before I could convince my body to step forward and meet him halfway, Bones was in front of me. Without saying a word, I started to extend my arms, offering his shirt and leather cut back to him, but before I could move my arms more than an inch, he snapped out his hand. In less than a heartbeat, his large palm wrapped around the back of my neck the same way he had wrapped it around the front of my throat earlier.

With a squeeze of warning and pressure to direct me, Bones pushed me forward. My feet began to move, obeying the unspoken order to walk. The crowd parted around us as he propelled me through the warehouse floor. I did my best to ignore the whispers and stares coming from the people all around us, but felt my cheeks heat at the blatant glares from some of the women, including Daisy.

With the way Bones towered over me without saying a word, I had no way to judge his intent. I didn't know if he was angry or pumped up with adrenaline from the fight. The other fighters had immediately celebrated with whichever girl they had grabbed, huge grins of victory on their faces as they took their pleasure. Bones was impossible to read.

We walked past the bar on our side of the warehouse, and I saw the sign indicating the restrooms, assuming that was where we were headed, but more pressure on the back of my neck had me making a sharp right turn. I didn't have to look around for more than a second to realize exactly where I was being directed. A heavy metal door was propped open, leading to the darkness outside.

We stepped through the doorway, and I immediately spotted a few tables situated in the packed dirt. One dim yellow bulb highlighted the outdoor seating area with just enough light so a person wouldn't have to stumble their way through, but it did little to actually light up the space.

A few people were outside sharing a joint while others were smoking cigarettes. One woman was on her knees in the dirt, her head bobbing enthusiastically, while the biker held her hair in a makeshift ponytail, directing her movements. The president stood there, silent and imposing, surveying the small group of people silently. They each looked up, likely sensing the menacing presence of someone even more dangerous than they were. They began elbowing the others that were a bit more oblivious.

As if an order had been shouted, though not a word was said, they stumbled to their feet quickly from where they had been lounging at the wooden tables. Cigarettes were tossed onto the dirt without a second thought, and they all shuffled toward the door. The girl who had been on her knees was pulled up roughly, the guy thankfully using a hand under her arm instead of just yanking her by her hair.

As she stumbled past, wiping the corners of her mouth, she looked Bones up and down, her pupils blown and her steps unsteady. She was probably high on something, but it didn't stop her from dragging her feet as she gaped at Bones before coming to a stop in front of him to smile suggestively. A sharp tug on her arm had her following behind the man she had been blowing, but not without a significant amount of reluctance, as she seemed to have trouble taking her gaze off him.

Once everyone was inside, the door swung shut with a loud clang, making me jump. The hand at the back of my neck tightened again, then pressed me forward, intending for me to head toward one of the tables. I didn't know why, exactly, he had brought me outside, away from everyone else, but I wasn't naive enough to not have a guess. The biggest problem was, I didn't know what I would do about it.

As a virgin, I wasn't keen on having my first time on a dirty table outside a huge biker warehouse with a hundred or more people just on the other side of the metal wall. On the other hand, I couldn't deny the pull the president had on me. Ever since the first night I had seen him, I'd been having fantasies of what it would be like to be the sole focus of the mostly silent man. I'd never been in the presence of so much dominance. He was the kind of man who didn't have to force others to obey him. He led because he was born to do it. If this were a different century and a different place, he would have been a general if not a king. I couldn't imagine him bowing to another soul.

More pressure on the back of my neck had me bending my knees to lower myself. I glanced at the ground, thinking of the woman on her knees. I didn't want to, but I also didn't want to say no. I would do it because he demanded it, even if I knew he wouldn't actually force me. Somehow, I knew he had honor. He could have forced any woman to bend over for him whenever he wanted, but he never did. He wouldn't. He didn't allow women to be used against their will by his men, and he led by example.

As I began to lower to the ground, he stopped me with a firm squeeze of his hand. I glanced up, startled, not understanding why he stopped me. My head pressed into the back of his hand where he held me firmly, a question in my eyes. He looked behind me, so I craned around to see what he was indicating, only to see one of the wooden picnic benches behind me. With my face hot from embarrassment, I stepped back and gingerly lowered myself until I was sitting primly, my hands still holding his clothes in my lap, and waited to see what was next. I could ask him, but it felt like breaking the silence was wrong.

Finally, his hand left me. Immediately, I missed the comforting weight. I felt bereft, almost sad, that he had let me go. Having him there felt like he had claimed me in some meaningful way. Losing it felt like losing something important I'd never fully had.

I lowered my eyes to the shirt in my lap and blinked several times, trying to understand the confusing thoughts racing through my head. I was a spinning wheel of emotions all of a sudden without him there to guide me. His hand came into view, and I watched as he grabbed his clothes and lifted them from my lap. I resisted the urge to yank them back to my chest, not wanting to lose those, too.

A finger lifted my chin after Bones dropped his shirt and leather vest onto the table next to my shoulder. I allowed him to raise my head, tilting it back until I could see into his black eyes. My breath caught, not expecting what I saw. No longer was his expression cold and emotionless. Inside the depths of his eyes, those fathomless pools of darkness held a raw and fierce hunger. If I weren't already sitting, my knees would have given out on me.

Without a word, he lifted his other hand and reached for his belt. His hold on my chin loosened enough to allow me to watch him unbuckle the silver clasp with deft movements. My tongue darted out to wet my lips as his fingers lowered to the button to his jeans, popping it open. With his fingers grasping the tab to his zipper tightly, he paused. I glanced up breathlessly from his hold on the zipper and met his gaze again.

As I stared into his eyes, I saw the vulnerability. There was a question there he wasn't asking out loud, and he was expecting rejection. He was asking me to perform this intimate act with him. I could see he wanted it badly, but he was giving me the choice. I paused for no more than a second as a multitude of thoughts ran through my mind, not the least of which was— if I refused, would he let me walk away? Would he ask another woman instead? Would it be Daisy? Or even Kara? I began to question myself whether or not I really wanted to do this with him, but I knew the answer before I could even fully form the question.

I looked back down to where he held his zipper tightly, seeing the thick outline of the cock held tightly back by the denim, and wet my lips again. Yes, I wanted to give this man pleasure. I wanted to be the only woman to do so. It felt imperative to prove to him that I was all he would ever need. I was terrified, too. I knew that if I took this step, I would be ruined in the best way. Even without us actually having sex, the intimacy would cement a fragile bond that had been growing between us since the night he saved me. But, if broken, it would break me in two.

Decision made, and with a deep exhale, I reached toward his jeans, silently telling him that I was willing. Bones suddenly grabbed my hands and yanked them to my sides. I gasped, but before I could protest or question why, he pressed my hands firmly against the wooden bench. I jerked my head up to see his jaw clenched tightly. With his eyes narrowed, there was a warning in his gaze that didn't entirely extinguish the desperate need burning there. I understood the gesture for what it was— a warning not to touch.

I curled my fingers around the edge of the bench and nodded once. His hands relaxed, hesitated, then left mine where I had them clenched tightly to the wood. One went back to his zipper. The other went behind my head to grab hold of the thick braid there. With a firm grip on my hair that held my head immovable, he finally lowered his zipper.

TEN

SALLY

Once he had the zipper halfway down, the lack of pressure allowed his cock to push forward, causing the zipper to slide down the rest of the way on its own. His cock was hidden behind black boxer briefs that did little to hold back the thick length of him and nothing to conceal the sheer size. The head of his cock was easily outlined through the cloth, and I followed the line of what could only be a vein running along the side of his cock. Even in the dim lighting, there was no mistaking that the man was huge.

I swallowed thickly, wondering what having him stretching my mouth out would be like. I still wanted to try it, but there was now a heavy dose of apprehension mixed in with the anticipation. With both dread and desire, I watched anxiously as he hooked his thumb into the waistband of his briefs and pulled. He had to pull up and over to release the head of his dick before pulling down, finally revealing exactly what his boxer briefs had been struggling to hold back.

Just the head of his cock was enough to make me lean back involuntarily as if to get away. Thick and round, it was shiny with the precum he had been leaking. He didn't let me get far, the hold on my braid keeping me in place as he continued yanking down his boxer briefs until he was fully exposed.

I was what some would call innocent. I had grown up in a house full of younger siblings, and my time spent at home was mainly as the caretaker to the whole brood. I had to share my bedroom, so there was never any privacy, and I had no opportunity to date since my parents needed me at home to take care of the children. I could never touch myself to explore the needs that came with puberty. I didn't have the opportunity to explore with boys. I didn't watch porn. Only after I had moved away did I begin to explore the world of sex.

Being young and frightened in the big, new city I had moved to, I hadn't been ready to date yet. I had planned to dive in as soon as I felt more comfortable, eager to get it over with. But that ended once I had been kidnapped and held by an insane doctor. So any experience I'd had regarding sex was from watching porn on my phone and touching myself quietly so my roommates wouldn't hear me through the paper-thin walls of our shared apartment.

Now, I was finally seeing a real man's cock for the first time, and I was overwhelmed, excited, and greedy. Because I was finally, *finally*, getting the chance to live.

He didn't even have to guide me. I immediately leaned forward and swiped my tongue over the head of his dick, lapping at the glistening wetness there. I closed my eyes and took in the experience, cataloging every sensation. His skin was hot against my tongue. The flesh was soft but firm. The taste was slightly salty, a little bitter, but not at all unpleasant. I wanted more. I *needed* to experience more.

With a muffled groan, I opened wide and engulfed the head in my mouth, remembering the videos I had watched of the porn stars doing this very thing. I had to open even wider than expected, the stretch on the corners of my mouth pulling uncomfortably where the doctor had sliced me open, only to stitch me back together again. I was fully healed, but the skin there was thinner than it had been before the incisions, and it caused a sudden jolt of panic to rush through me. Worried that the skin in the corners of my mouth would tear, I pulled back with tears in my eyes and looked up at Bones, ready to apologize for my fear of hurting myself. As soon as I saw his face, though, I froze.

Even a moment ago, when his desire was plain to see, the features of his face still held onto that mask of indifference. But now, he was anything but indifferent.

Bones squeezed his eyes shut, and his lips pressed into a thin line as he clenched his jaw. His cheeks were red, and at first glance, it looked like he was in pain, but I realized it was intense pleasure he was feeling. Just that short time of having him in my mouth had brought him so much pleasure that Bones had let his mask drop.

His eyes opened as I stared at him with my mouth open in wonder, lips still wet from my saliva. He looked into my eyes and, without saying a word, pleaded with me. It was then that I knew I wouldn't stop. I would never stop. I had done that to him, only me. And I wanted to do it to him again and again until all he thought of when he looked at me was the pleasure I gave him.

Without further hesitation, I dropped my head back down. Now that I knew what to expect, I was careful, taking it slow, allowing my mouth to stretch around his girth. I took him down as far as I could go, testing myself and pushing myself to my limits. When he hit the back of my throat, I swallowed convulsively, trying to stave off the gag that threatened me. When I swallowed, squeezing the head of his cock with my throat muscles, he groaned low and deep. Hearing the sound of his pleasure felt like the greatest victory of my life.

Needing to breathe, I slowly pulled back up, letting the flat of my tongue glide over that long, thick vein I had seen through the black cloth of his boxer briefs. I felt it pulse against my tongue, so I pressed harder and felt his whole body jerk as he let out another deep, guttural groan.

I wanted to see him, to watch his face as I took him inside my mouth, but our positions didn't allow me to do anything except bend forward. It felt like I was missing out on the best part of the experience, but at least I got to listen to the sounds he was making. I slid back to the tip, swirling my tongue around the head, and was thrilled when I tasted a new release of his precum.

I took a deep breath to prepare myself, then quickly lowered my mouth over his cock, swallowing it as far as possible. I knew I had gone too far, too fast, when I couldn't hold back the gag. Tears immediately filled my eyes, and I tried swallowing several times to regain control. My fingers flexed at my thighs, needing to grab onto him so badly, but I knew I couldn't without ruining everything.

I swallowed and gagged, pressing my tongue hard against the shaft in my mouth, but refused to give up. I was nothing if not determined. I had always been stubborn with a need to prove myself. While fighting my instinct to pull off, I shallowly bobbed my head up and down, refusing to give up. I felt him grow thicker, the added stretch nearly overwhelming, and widened my eyes. I knew I couldn't take anymore. My lips were stretched to their limits, and the fear of tearing came rushing back. But before I could react, Bone's hand on my braid tightened, pressing my head down as his hips pushed forward for the first time.

I was on the verge of struggling for freedom when the first spurt hit the back of my tongue. Within seconds, several more spurts of come shot out, triggering my instinct to swallow before I choked. I didn't even have a chance to taste what he was giving me. All I could do was make sure I could breathe, knowing the best way to do that was to swallow.

Through the buzzing in my ears, I heard a shout followed by another deep groan. Once his cock had stopped pulsing, it softened enough that I no longer felt in danger of tearing, allowing me to finally relax. He left his cock sitting there on my tongue for several breaths before eventually withdrawing slowly. I licked my lips once he was gone from my mouth, my tongue grazing the head of his cock and making him jerk from the contact.

I sat back, panting, and looked up at Bones with a small smile playing on my swollen lips. His chest was heaving with his breaths, rising and falling rapidly, the stark white bones of his tattoo appearing to be flexing. The muscles of his abdomen glistened with more sweat than had been there after his fight. It was mesmerizing, but what took my breath away was the look on his face that he wasn't trying to hide.

The look of wonder as he stared down at me had me squeezing my thighs tightly together as I dug my fingernails into the wooden bench. That, right there, was why I had wanted to do this to a man who had barely spoken to me in a month. He stared down at me with lust, approval, and a hint of surprise. I had a strong feeling that I had just given him his first blow job and felt insanely proud of myself for being able to give him that experience even though I hadn't known what to do above the very basics.

He stepped back, taking slow, deep breaths, calming himself quickly. I watched as the remaining pleasure I had given him melted away and wanted to cry when that familiar mask of indifference stole over his features once again. As the smile fell from my face, he turned to his shirt and leather vest. He quickly pulled the shirt over his head and shrugged into the vest. His shirt had fallen over his open pants that were pulled down below his hipbones, hiding the cock that had only partially softened.

I frowned as I watched him use both hands to tug his jeans back into place and tuck his hard dick away. He swiftly had the fly of his jeans zipped, buttoned, and his belt refastened before I could even consider offering a protest or beg him to let me do all that again. The last thing he did was run both hands through the thick black hair on his head while letting out another long breath. Once he had finished righting himself, he was again the president of the Devil's Night-mares, and I was back to being the girl who worked for him.

I dropped my gaze to my lap, blinking rapidly, hoping like hell I could hold back any tears of sadness or frustration that threatened to escape. I didn't want him to see me as weak or desperate, even if that was exactly how I felt at that moment. I should have expected this ending. Bones had never pretended to be anything other than the man who was gazing down at me with his dead-eyed stare and emotionless expression. I had given what he wanted willingly, almost desperately, so I had no one to blame but myself.

He took another step back and then just stood there, waiting. With an internal sigh, I stood up and brushed off the back of my spandex shorts, only just then remembering that I was wearing white. I hoped they weren't stained or ruined from sitting on the dirty bench. It wasn't until I bumped the tip of my finger against my leg that I felt a slight jolt of pain.

"Ow," I muttered, brought my finger close to my face to look at it in the dim light, and hissed under my breath. I hadn't felt the splinter as it happened, obviously too engrossed in what I had been doing at the time, but it had started to throb the moment the pain had registered in my brain.

My eyes were downcast while I studied the small splinter in my finger. When heavy boots entered my vision, I refused to look up. I wasn't willing to let Bones see how badly his rejection had hurt me. He reached for my hand, grasping it firmly in his tattooed fingers as he held it up to the yellow outdoor light. I darted a glance at his face, expecting that blank mask still in place, but was stunned when what I saw instead were concerned eyes that looked pained.

"I'm sorry," he said in a low voice, barely audible but clearly full of remorse.

"It's fine," I shrugged one shoulder, fighting the urge to yank my hand away. "It's just a splinter. I'll take care of it once I get back to the motel tonight." I bit my tongue on the impulse to tell him that he could carry on his night without the concern he was showing. Maybe a part of me was holding a grudge, that stubbornness I had rearing its head. After his reaction, I was feeling used and cheap, unlike the way I had when I'd brought him so much pleasure.

He jerked his gaze to mine, his jaw clenched tight, his eyes narrowing. Without another word, just one last look at the tiny piece of wood under my skin, he dropped my hand and stepped back again. He raised his arm, gesturing at me to walk ahead of him, so I did. I passed him with my chin up, refusing to show weakness. I could have sworn I heard him inhale deeply as I walked past his tall body. When I approached the door, I reached out to open it, but he got there before me, twisting the knob and jerking it open with a hard yank. I expected him to enter first and paused for it. But he stood back, gesturing again for me to enter first. The man managed to shock me on every level.

ELEVEN

SALLY

The rest of the night went by in a blur as the hours passed swiftly. Several more fights went on as the bikers got drunker and more rowdy by the hour. By the time people began to filter out, my feet and back ached more than they ever had in my life. But every time I glanced down at my chest, I knew I would do it all over again in a heartbeat. My bra top was stuffed full of folded bills with denominations ranging from ones to twenties. It was bulky and uncomfortable, but I knew what that kind of cash could mean for my continued survival. I had four and a half months remaining until the trial would begin. This one night of having my boobs stuffed awkwardly with scratchy money meant even if I had to pack up and leave suddenly; I would be okay.

When the other girls and I finally stood by the van, ready to pile in, I was practically dead on my feet. For once, I couldn't wait to get back to my stinky motel room with the stale air and questionable stains. I was leaning against the dusty side of the vehicle with my eyes closed, waiting while everyone else climbed in when the fine hair on the back of my neck raised. I snapped my eyes open and subconsciously rubbed at the goosebumps that covered my arms while I glanced around nervously.

During the day, there was nothing but fields full of corn and pumpkins as far as the eye could see. In the dark, there was nothing but blackness. It had warning bells exploding in my head, the creep factor just dialing it up to ten. I looked back toward the bikes that were still parked, hoping to see Bones, knowing he would protect me even after the way he had distanced himself when our intimate moment was over. Unfortunately, only a few guys were left in the parking lot, smoking and talking shit to each other. The rest of the bikers were long gone. I had no choice but to shrug off the feeling and hope my nervous mind was just imagining things.

It was finally my turn to climb in, and I couldn't move fast enough, settling into the seat directly behind the front passenger. Kara was already laying her head back against the headrest, her breath evening out quickly. I wished I could sleep as easily as she seemed to be able to, but my mind was just too chaotic to shut down. The driver had the radio turned on low, a rock song I couldn't quite make out playing softly in the background as the girls around me tried to sleep. Instead of resting with them, I stared out into the darkness, my eyes itchy and dry.

The miles passed quickly. When the driver pulled up to the bar, everyone stumbled through the mostly empty bar to grab their belongings before heading straight back out to their cars with mumbled goodnights and tired waves.

Kara gave my shoulder a quick squeeze as she passed me.

"I'll see you later." She yawned, her mouth gaping open wide, then shook her head, blinking at me. "You did good tonight, hun."

I gave her a small smile as I pulled my pants on over my skimpy outfit. "Thanks. See you." With a final wave, she was gone, and I was left standing by myself in the back room, gathering my things.

My footsteps echoed as I briskly walked down the hall and into the main room. I let out a startled yelp when movement came from a table by the door. I puffed out a breath while grasping my chest, waiting for the panic to recede. "Holy shit, Mac!" I hadn't noticed the bartender sitting there when we had first arrived.

"Sorry to startle you, new girl. Are you the last one?" Mac stood up and stretched, then moved to the door while blinking red eyes.

"Umm, yes." I still had my hand pressed to my chest, willing my racing heart to calm.

"Are you okay?" He tilted his head as I stood there, gathering my scattered courage. I still needed to walk to the hotel, but after the slight scare he had just given me, added to the eerie feeling I'd had of being watched back at the warehouse, I dreaded making the trek home. Not that the dingy hotel room was home, but it was all I had for the next few months.

I gave a jerky nod and blew out a breath. I gave Mac a tight smile. "I'm good. You had just scared me. I wasn't expecting anyone to be sitting in the dark."

He shrugged while hiding another yawn behind the back of his hand. "Sorry," he apologized again. "I had to come back to wait for you all to come get your things so I could lock up."

I blew out a breath and nodded, my movements a little less jerky. "I understand. I'll see you later this evening."

"Okay, new girl. Get home safe." He closed the door behind me before I could give in and beg him to walk me to the motel. I hefted my bag higher on my shoulder and began to put one foot in front of the other while trying to convince myself that there was no reason to be scared. The town of Pumpkin Patch may seem spooky with all the Halloween decorations at times, but it really was just a quirky, fun tourist spot on the map. I had yet to see anything to be truly frightened of in the time I'd been staying there. I was betting that having a notorious biker club calling it home actually helped keep the crime level low.

As I walked, I started to relax as I breathed in the cool night air. It was only a couple of hours later than I usually headed home, and the only difference I noticed on the walk was that it was quieter than usual. By the time I had reached the motel room I'd been calling mine for the last couple of months, I had calmed enough to start feeling the lethargy pulling at me. As much as I desperately wanted to shower the night away, I could barely keep my eyes open. I ended up shrugging off all my clothes, not caring as wads of cash fell to the floor. I dropped face-first onto the hard mattress and hugged the extra pillow to my chest. Within seconds, I was out.

The sound of a motorcycle engine pulled me from an exhausted, dreamless sleep. I blinked blearily at the red lights of the small clock on the nightstand to see I had only been out for an hour. Once the sound of the engine faded, I fell right back into sleep.

It was only another half hour later when another motorcycle rumbled past the motel, jerking me awake again. It wasn't a common occurrence at that time in the morning. I sleepily wondered if it was some of the guys just getting back from the warehouse. I huffed out an irritated sigh and turned over onto my other side.

A few hours later, my phone ringing had me reaching out to aimlessly slap my hand around in the general location where it usually sat until I made contact with the cool surface. With a bleary squint at the screen, I swiped my finger across it and muttered out a raspy "hello," then cleared my throat and tried again.

"Hello?"

"Sally, it's ADA Ramirez. I know it's early, but I wanted to give you a quick heads up."

That had me sitting up, clutching the bedcovers tightly to my naked chest. Usually, receiving calls from the ADA was comforting. She would let me know that things with the case were progressing smoothly while reassuring me that all was still well. Hearing the tone of her voice over the phone this time was the complete opposite.

"Oh god. Did Dr. Stein disappear? Is he coming after me?" Even I could hear the panic rising as I spoke.

There was a tired sigh coming across the line. "No, he's still here. But there's been a small development in the case," She paused, but before I could begin firing more questions at her, she pressed on.

"Another girl stepped forward. She—fuck! I'm sorry, Sally. Damn, I hate to even say this to you. This other girl has the same sort of scars you do. She gave an official statement that she was a willing... victim. She claims that Dr. Stein and she had a relationship and an agreement. She let him..." her words trailed off hesitantly for a moment before she continued, barely disguising her disbelief. My breathing grew more labored with every word she spoke. "...work on her and in exchange for a great sum of money. They were also lovers."

It sounded as if she was taking a drink of something, and I could just picture her gulping down a large cup of coffee. Then, the heavy thunk of a mug being set harshly down on a wooden desk could be heard clearly, all but confirming my suspicions. I rubbed my forehead. I was too tired to focus properly, and the distress from this new development was making my mind want to escape from reality. "Sally, I don't have to tell you how damaging this type of statement could be for your case. It paints a picture that you agreed to whatever he did to you and then changed your mind later. The defense attorney will run with that narrative to get the jury on the doctor's side."

"But it's not true," I whispered as I stared blankly at the strange pattern of the thin carpet covering the motel floor.

She sighed again. "I know, Sally. I know. We will keep looking into this, okay? I needed to let you know. We will do everything we can to fight the accusations so we can find you justice. Okay?"

I swallowed through the lump in my throat while nodding into the emptiness of the room. "Okay." My voice was barely more than a whisper, but ADA Ramirez heard me well enough.

"Okay, sweetie. You take care, alright? Let me know if you need anything, and I will contact you again soon."

I nodded silently again and waited until the beep sounded in my ear, letting me know that the call had disconnected. I brought my phone down to my lap to see the words CALL ENDED on the screen before it suddenly went blank. With numb fingers, I lay the phone back on the table and then sat in bed for several minutes, just staring at the wall without seeing it. With tears sliding down my cheeks, I lay on my side and hugged the extra pillow to my chest. I blinked while staring at the slight crack in the curtains.

It was morning, and the sun was trying to slip into the room, but all I could see were the white painted cinderblock walls of the basement I had been trapped in for months. I let out a shuddering breath, not allowing myself to fall into the hysterical cries my mind desperately needed to. Crying wouldn't change anything. All I could do was keep moving forward.

The numbness I had felt since the phone call stayed with me all through my shift at the bar. I spent the night moving on autopilot, ignoring the snide looks and remarks that Daisy threw my way. I barely registered the comments about being unable to please the president and, frankly, didn't give a shit what she had to say. I knew I had pleased him; there was no denying that. It was when the whole thing was over that he had grown cold and distant again. But I couldn't find my way out of the numbness to argue.

I had just finished mopping the floor and was rolling the bucket back over to the closet when I bumped into a table, sloshing dirty water on the floor. I gave a mental shrug, deciding I would wipe up the mess with a towel once I was done dumping and rinsing the bucket. I managed to prevent any more mishaps inside the mop closet and returned to the main room with a towel in hand before dropping to my knees with a defeated sigh.

As I wiped up the last of the dirty water from the floor, the air changed, and I felt him. I looked up to see him there, standing near the hallway, the low lights making the white of the bones stand out sharply on his arms. It was the Devil's Nightmare president. He was silent as usual, but I could feel his stare as if he were shouting at me. His steps came slow and steady toward me. Even though he was light on his feet, his heavy boots sounded like gunshots in the quiet room. When he stopped in front of me, I swallowed hard and craned my head back from my kneeling position on the wooden floor.

His hand went to his belt, already slipping the leather through the metal. I wanted to shout at him, to deny what he wanted. I urged my head to shake, my mouth to protest. Instead, I waited with bated breath. I could tell myself I didn't want this, didn't want to be used by him again, but it would have been a dirty lie. Though I felt a sliver of shame for it, I wanted it. I wanted to see his face change the way it had the night before and know that it was me that caused his mask to break into pieces.

He held his throbbing erection in his hand, not moving toward me. He was waiting for me to make the decision the same way he had the night before. I found myself leaning forward, my lips opening eagerly, carefully keeping my hands in my lap. Unlike the night before, I was in a position that allowed me to watch every change to his features as he sank into the bliss. I was already addicted to the thrill of breaking his carefully constructed façade, but being able to watch it crumble thrilled me. I controlled his plea-sure. It was me that he needed.

When he growled out his release and backed away, breathing hard, his chest heaving, I licked at my swollen lips. He turned and walked away from me, heading toward the hall and out of sight, again not saying a word, but this time, I didn't mind.

He had made me feel something other than numb for the first time since I woke up that morning. It was power, and I smiled.

TWELVE

THE NIGHTMARE KING

I stood in the shadows, watching to make sure the girl made it safely into her motel room, the same as I had done every night for the last few weeks. As soon as the door closed and the light turned on, I turned to leave, walking down the sidewalk back to the bar where my bike was waiting for me.

Everything was changing, and I wasn't sure how to feel about it, and that pissed me the fuck off. I needed to be in control of all that was around me. This little girl with her blood-red hair and the scars that she failed to hide was taking control from me. I never permitted another human being to see me vulnerable, not since I was too young to be the one in control. But somehow, I allowed this one person to.

I sat on my bike, starting the engine, trying to forget about the girl. Instead, the memories cascaded through every thought. Taking her mouth on the floor of the bar was a compulsion I couldn't walk away from. That alone pissed me off. I couldn't control myself when it came to her. Watching her face while she swallowed me, witnessing her stare into my soul, her blue eyes seeing what was impossible to hide, made me want to rage in anger. I should kill her and be done with it. But the mere thought of harming her made my blood run cold.

I would stay away from now on. It was a promise I already knew I would be breaking the moment I saw her again. There was a pull to her I couldn't fucking explain and couldn't stop. A part of me didn't want to. Because for the first time in twenty years, I wanted to be close to another living being that wasn't my dog.

As I rode past the clubhouse and turned onto the short road my cabin sat on, I could already hear Zero's happy barking. A white blur in the night ran straight toward my bike and began running alongside my tires, always careful not to get too close but not scared in the least of the engine's roar as I pulled into the drive. As soon as I turned off the engine, Zero began prancing around, waiting for me to climb off the motorcycle.

I reached into my vest pocket and produced the dog treat I always kept there and held it up. His rear immediately hit the dirt, his tail wagging excitedly, but his eyes glued to the dog bone. I tossed it in the air, and even though it was dark outside, Zero had no trouble catching it and chopping it down in just a couple of bites. He let out a happy woof and instantly began his prancing again, telling me without words that he was happy to see me.

I got off my bike, bending over to pet the white mutt. I had no idea what breed he was and didn't give a shit. I had found him in one of the many pumpkin patches that lined the back roads of the town. He had been a white smudge in the distance that had caught my eye, and something compelled me to stop. I had walked out through the pumpkins that day, stepping over vines and half-ripe gourds until I got to him. He'd been huddled under one of the larger pumpkins, barely bigger than my hand. Without a second thought, I picked him up and tucked him inside my vest.

"Come on, boy, let's get to bed."

He gave an approving bark and raced to the door, disappearing through the dog door before immediately reappearing, barking, then disappearing through the flap again. For a brief moment, I wondered if he would like Sally.

As I walked through the doorway, my cell phone rang. I considered ignoring it, but there were very few people who had my number and even fewer who would dare disturb me this late at night.

After glancing at the screen, I growled. "This better be fucking good, Lock."

"One of these days, you're going to answer with a different greeting than that. I just know it."

My silence made him sigh, and the forced cheerfulness dropped from his tone.

"I've received reports from some of the spies around town that a Boogeyman has been seen driving through town more than once. Before you ask, no one got a good look at the guy's face, but they were able to make out the patch on the back of the cut."

I cursed under my breath. There were clear rules when it came to club territory. If one of my guys had been spotted in Boogeyman territory, they would have either shot him on sight and dropped his head on my doorstep, or kept him prisoner just for the joy of torturing him.

"Double patrols. Church in the morning." I hit the end call button and tossed the phone on my bed. Shrugging out of my cut, I pulled my T-shirt off. The cut went to the chair in the corner, and the shirt went into the pile of dirty clothes on the floor.

Zero hopped on the bed, going straight to his chew toy as I walked into the bathroom, where I stripped off my jeans and then headed into the shower. I didn't want to wash the feel of Sally's mouth off my cock, but I needed to clean the day off me. As I lifted my face to the steaming water, I wrapped my hand around my hardened cock, which had begun to stiffen as soon as the girl's face hit my mind. The memory of her big blue eyes staring up at me with her mouth full of my dick had one of those guttural groans rising from my chest.

I was an expert at stroking my cock; it was all I'd felt since I was old enough to know that pleasure existed in that way. But her mouth was something entirely different. My hand no longer did what it used to, and when I came, shooting my come onto the shower floor, it was with a disappointed sigh. I should never have given in to the desperation that filled me last night. The adrenaline high from the fight and seeing the fucking going on around the building had put ideas in my head that had never been there before. Now I knew what it felt to have a woman's mouth on me, to feel her tongue glide against my shaft.

Now, I couldn't shake the need to know what else I had been missing out on. I wanted to feel her cunt wrapped around me, squeezing me. I needed to fill her up and watch my seed ooze out, just so I could press it back inside with my fingers.

The thoughts running unbidden through my mind had my cock swelling as if I hadn't just come down the drain. With a snarl and a curse, I slammed off the water and stepped out of the shower without bothering to dry off. I dropped to the floor and began doing pushups until my arms began to shake, and the muscle fatigue had me gritting my teeth. By the time I slapped off the light switch and climbed into bed, I was dry. But my dick was still hard.

"Why the fuck is a Boogeyman in my territory?"

It was the only question I needed an answer to as I looked around the large wooden table at the clubhouse. Church was in session. All of my club members were present except for the prospects, of which we were down to two since I had kicked the other one out of town after cutting off his hand as a punishment for touching what wasn't his.

The members glance at each other nervously, a few of them fidgeting in their seats like pussies at my growled question. Shock leaned back in his chair, flipping a coin over his knuckles and between his fingers.

"All that we have been able to find out so far is he drove back and forth a couple of times down Main Street before taking off back out of town."

I looked at him as my mind raced with different possibilities. "Main Street? Nowhere else?"

"Sorry, Prez. Just Main Street." He tilted his head. "There's a rumor that the prospect you kicked out last month went to the Boogeymen after leaving here."

I ran my hand over my face in frustration while suppressing the string of curses running through my mind. "Get someone to do some recon on that. I also want to see his background check." I glanced around the table, taking in everyone's expressions. "Who vouched for him to prospect?"

One of the newer patches, Repo, a street name given due to his day job, flushed and started fiddling with his hands like a naughty school kid. "Uhh, that was me, Prez. I met him at the bar and got to know him. He seemed like a cool dude. When he said he was inter-ested in joining, I guess I thought he'd be a good fit." He shifted in his seat as I stared him down. "Sorry," came his mumbled excuse for an apology for fucking up.

Barrel strode back into the room from where he'd run off to grab the background check and slid the folder in front of me before retaking his seat with a fucking smirk tossed the kid's way as he pulled out his knife and started cleaning under his fingernails with it. I ignored everyone as I slammed the folder open to see the picture of the dumbfuck staring up at me.

To be honest, I never got a good look at him the night I cut his hand off. As president, I didn't concern myself with the matters of the prospects. I had men that were responsible for that. It looked like I might have several guys that dropped the fucking ball in this situation.

His folder read like most of the others. His age, twenty-five, his address, some low-rent apartment on the edge of town, no family listed. I glanced up and eyed every man in the room before settling my glare on Shock.

"You're my Sergeant at Arms, isn't that right?"

His chin ticked up a notch as he grunted out his affirmative.

"You run the background checks and ensure the prospects and girls that want to officially join the club are legit." It was a statement, not a question, because, yeah, it was his fucking job. "You didn't see anything wrong with this?" I held up the sheet that had virtually no information on it.

"I ran the check. Nothing else came up. I figured the guy was an orphan or some shit. Everything else checked out fine." His eyes narrowed before he relaxed, his body almost melting into the seat as he looked over at Repo, who looked like he was about to shit himself. "I'll make sure that in the future, we have everything, even if I have to dig his granny up from her grave to verify. That's on me, Prez."

He was pissed at being called out for this fuck up, but it was his mistake.

"Looks like I will have to tighten shit up around here. I'm going to have to follow around behind your asses to make sure you're doing your jobs right." I glared at Repo. "And you are on probation. Congratulations, you get to prospect with a cut on."

He swallowed hard but nodded, knowing that I could have just taken his patch and said fuck it. But he wasn't the only one that had fucked up. If I took his, I'd have to take Shock's, too. As much as he pissed me off at the moment, he was one of my best men, and his title in the club reflected that. He'd been with me since the beginning, him, Lock and Barrel. No one said a thing as my words settled in the room as hard and heavy as the gavel by my side.

"This guy was a plant by the Boogeymen. We let him waltz right into this club. There's no telling what kind of information he might have managed to steal. Our only saving grace is that he was only here for a few weeks, and prospects aren't allowed around sensitive information."

"Pres, do we know for sure that he was a mole?" Barrel fluffed up his green hair and yawned like he was fucking bored. "I mean, maybe he is just a pussy that decided to hop to another club when he was kicked out. What's better than to go straight to our rivals when he's licking his wounds."

I raised an eyebrow. "And the Boogeyman just let him in with arms wide open?"

"Sure, it seems suspect, but," he shrugged, "punk ass bitches do shit like that all the time."

It was Shock that spoke up at Barrel's words. "I will dig so deep into his background that I'll know what time his momma takes a shit every day. This fuck up won't happen again."

I stared back at him, and he met my heavy stare without flinching. "I know it won't, Shock." The barely concealed threat hung in the air as the rest of the Devil's Nightmares held their collective breaths.

THIRTEEN

SALLY

I had the night off from the bar, and not knowing what to do with myself, I spent the last couple of hours at the local library. Considering how small the town was, it was a lot larger than I had expected.

I browsed through all the usual sections I went for, pulling out books of my favorite go-to authors. Then, my fingers trailed across a title that had me pausing. Slipping the book out of the tight space, I flipped it over to look at the cover. My face heated, and I glanced around to see if anyone was paying attention, not that they would know where my mind went as I held the motorcycle club romance.

The man on the cover stared back at me as he straddled his bike, his leather cut open over a naked chest. He was hot in that cover model sort of way. But I couldn't help but superimpose his image with a different one. One that was tall, handsome in a scary way, and literally covered in tattoos. I flipped the book over to read the blurb on the back, knowing that I was going to be reading it no matter what the story was about.

After a quick scan of the blurb, I tucked the book between two of the others I had already grabbed and made my way to the checkout desk, unable to slow my steps in my haste to get back to the motel room and start reading. There was no question about which book I would be diving into first.

I set the small stack of books on the counter and gave a small smile from behind my hair at the elderly woman who had helped me get set up with a library card. I kept my head down, using my hair as the shield it had become in the last few months.

"Found some good books, dear?" She quickly started scanning the books, and I couldn't help the relieved sigh that left me when I noticed she only gave each book a cursory glance. I wasn't ashamed of my chosen reading material, but it felt like there was a neon sign over my head letting everyone know that I was a hussy crushing on the local motorcycle club president.

It didn't seem like the town was overly fearful of the club. In fact, I had gotten the impression that they appreciated the club's presence in town. There was a noticeable lack of petty crime that I was sure was attributed to the club keeping the riff-raff out. While working at the bar, it had become evident that they didn't like anyone who came into their territory and caused problems.

"Thank you," I murmured as I scooped up the books and placed the receipt she handed me in the top book to use as a bookmark. It was a helpful reminder when they were due back. After sliding them into my bag, I kept my head down and exited the library, hoping that preventing eye contact would deter others from attempting to speak to me.

My stomach growled, making me realize exactly how much time I had spent browsing the shelves. I spotted the deli I had eaten at a few other times, noticing it was still open. It would be a quick, filling dinner, plus they had premade sandwiches, which meant more avoidance. The bell jingled merrily when I pushed open the door that had hand-painted jack-o'lanterns on the glass door. The decor in the town was typical of Halloween, family-friendly, and fun. Honestly, I wondered if they ever got tired of the same theme year-round. But then again, there were several towns around the country that were dedicated to Christmas, so why not Halloween?

After perusing the available premade sandwiches in the refrigerator and grabbing a bottle of water, I walked my purchases up to the counter, where a bored looking teenager was playing with her phone. Without even looking up once, she gave me my total, and I was out of the door before my anxiety even had a chance to spike.

I tucked the bag with the sandwich under my arm and looked up to the sky, breathing in the fresh evening air. It was something I had missed while living in Los Angeles. In Kentucky, we had more open spaces. You could see the stars and breathe unpolluted air. In L.A., there was a layer of brown smog covering the city. While I lived there, I considered that it was a trade-off, something I had to live with in order to chase my dreams. Somehow, I let myself forget. Being here in Utah, I realized it was just one more thing that hadn't been worth it. It wasn't that I had just given up on my dream of being an actress, but I had definitely second-guessed what I really wanted in life.

I filled my lungs with the clean air and let it out slowly as I contemplated my future. I had no destination; I couldn't see the outcome anymore, and I let the wave of melancholy sweep over me. I sighed while cracking open the bottle of water and continued on my way back to the motel that I could see up ahead. I raised the cold water to my mouth and then cried out as the bottle fell from my hands.

At first, I didn't know what had happened. I was in a weird state of confusion as I looked down at the ground, the amount of water inside the bottle getting smaller, the puddle of water growing larger, engulfing the bag with the sandwich in it that I hadn't even realized had fallen as well. It wasn't until my back was thrown against a wall, my head hitting hard enough to see stars, that my brain started to comprehend what was happening. I had let my guard down, taking in the beautiful night, in doing so, I had left myself open to an attack I hadn't seen coming.

Tears immediately filled my eyes as all I could think was, "No. No. No. Not again." I didn't realize how badly I was shaking until I lifted my hands to grasp the one that was wrapped around my throat in a cruel grip. My mind screamed that this was nothing like the way Bones would grab my throat. His hands were firm and unyielding, but they didn't hurt. It was comforting. This was something entirely different.

I pried my eyes open and blinked, trying to clear my vision, seeing my trembling hands wrapped around a normal, flesh-colored arm devoid of black tattoos. Looking up, I finally saw who was cutting off my air.

The snarling, irate face was familiar, but in my panic, I couldn't place where I had seen him. I tried to speak, but all I could get out were garbled sounds that didn't make any sense, even to my own ears.

"I'm going to make you pay for what you did to me, bitch." The words were spoken against my face, spittle flying to cover my cheek as he leaned in. A shudder of revulsion ran through me as I felt him lick my face from my chin to my forehead.

"I don't even care that your scars make you look like a freak. First, I'm going to fuck you up a little bit, add to those ugly scars you can't hide. Then, when you're nice and compliant, I'm going to fuck you in every fucking hole on your body." He punched me hard in my stomach, my ribs protesting as a woosh of air made it through my constricted throat. I heard him laugh, even though the sound seemed pained. "Fuck, that hurt. Something else you're going to be paying for, cunt."

I was yanked forward for a heartbeat before my body was slammed back against the wall. The man let go of my neck, letting me fall to the ground, whimpering and coughing through the pain of my bruised throat and the punch to the gut. I rolled over, attempting to get away from the man that I still couldn't place in my frantic thoughts. My face hit something soft, so I started blinking, hoping to clear my vision of the blackness from having my head so violently bashed against the wall.

I realized that it was my bag that was against my cheek. It must have fallen when I was tossed against the wall the first time. All I could think of was the knife I had hidden in the side pocket. The same knife that had been left behind on the bar the night Bones saved me from being raped by the prospect. My eyes widened at the realization that finally hit me.

Even though he had been above me and I was struggling against him, I hadn't paid much attention as I had been panicking and fighting. Now that the memory had surfaced of that night, I realized who was doing this and why. I reached for the side pocket, ready to protect myself, but it was too late.

With a scream of frustration and pain tearing out of me, I was viciously yanked back by my foot. I felt the skin of my hands and stomach from my shirt sliding up, tearing as I was dragged over the rough ground. A hard kick to my gut had my whole body rising into the air for the briefest of seconds before hitting the ground again, landing on my other side. The cruel laughter from the prospect was followed by a taunt.

"What's wrong, bitch? No one here to save you this time?" I heard what could only be a belt buckle jingle. I moaned, trying to use my hands to crawl away from the nightmare, but I felt too weak to hold my body up. "I'm going to enjoy every second of this."

Another kick sent me to my back, and through my watery eyes filled with tears, I had a hazy view of my attacker. He was holding something up. "By the time I'm done with you, you are going to be missing so many body parts they won't be able to put you back together again."

I blinked rapidly to clear my vision. His words and the way he spoke them had me trying to search for the reason. And then I realized why I couldn't figure out what he was holding up. He wasn't holding anything up except for his hand. What was left of it, anyway. There was a dirty bandage wrapped around what was too small to be much more than a stump, the end seeping blood. I thought of the way he had wheezed in pain when he punched me and realized the blood was from him hitting me. Good. I hoped he was suffering.

I shook my head, the movement making me dizzy, but I couldn't let my eyes close. I had the overwhelming need to keep the man in my vision, the same way you would watch a wild animal, readying for the moment it pounced. "I didn't know that had been done to you." I wheezed out. Not that I cared. I only wished that I had been able to watch. Had I known that night would lead to this moment, I would have asked Bones to just take his life. Because I knew the damage to the man could have been done by no one other than the Devil's Nightmares president.

He barked out a bitter laugh. "It doesn't fucking matter, now, does it, bitch? This happened because of you, and now you're going to be the one to pay." He slid his zipper down, and I swallowed hard, willing myself not to vomit as he reached inside his boxers with his good hand.

"You don't have to do this!" I pleaded as he took a step towards me. "I didn't do anything!" My words fell on deaf ears. He continued to struggle to get his pants down far enough to pull out his dick, looking equal parts frustrated and smug.

"Cry all you want, cunt. I want to see your tears."

It occurred to me at that moment that I hadn't screamed. I couldn't when his hand was gripping my throat, but since I had been lying on the ground, all I had done was whimper and cry. We weren't in a large city where most people would walk by, ignoring the crime around them, not wanting to be involved. It was getting darker by the moment, but there would be someone around who would hear and come running.

With as much effort as I could put into it, I rolled myself toward my bag that was just a couple of feet away. As I rolled, I let out the loudest scream I could muster through my raw throat. It wasn't nearly as loud as I wished it could have been, as it should have been.

But it had to be loud enough. That's all I needed— was for it to be enough.

As I reached into the pocket of my bag, I heard him curse and grab onto my ankle again. I kicked as hard as I could while letting out another smaller scream. I felt the cool handle of the knife, and just as I wrapped my hand around it, getting a steady grip, I heard what sounded like a pack of wolves snarling viciously.

I rolled onto my back, brandishing the knife, ready to cut the dick off the prospect the second he tried to do anything else to me, only to realize there was no pack of wolves. There was only one dog. It was smaller than I would have expected for the display of violence. I blinked as a spray of blood hit my face from the throat that had been ripped open. Then I blinked again, shifting my gaze from the sight of the dog and bloody man to the one that stood over me.

My head moved, allowing me to take in who I already knew was there. "Bones," I breathed out before my whole body went numb and my vision went dark.

FOURTEEN

I lay on the bed in my motel room, the usual scent of aged carpeting and rust from the bathroom sink filling my senses. I dreaded waking up fully, knowing that there was something I didn't want to remember. It wasn't until the sounds in the room came flowing into my consciousness that my eyes flew open wide, and a whimper left my throat.

At my sound of distress, the movement in the room paused briefly before starting again. I heard a drawer close before another opened and tried to piece together what was happening. Someone was in the room with me. They had to have brought me back from the alley, but who?

I squeezed my eyes shut as I thought hard about what had happened before I lost consciousness in the alley. There were snarls; a white dog had appeared out of nowhere, ripping into my attacker's throat.

"Bones," I whispered out the one name that brought equal parts terror and relief to me. The bed jostled underneath me at my raspy voice, making my eyes fly back open. What was supposed to be a white snout covered in what was likely my attacker's blood pressed in close, sniffing my cheek. I was about to jump away screaming when that mouth opened, only to have a long pink tongue take a wet lap up my cheek. I only had a second to process that the beast wasn't about to maul me before I grimaced at the slimy trail it had left on my face and the nasty smell of coppery blood on its breath.

"Ugh." I didn't dare put my hands on the dog to push it away. Instead, I turned my head to look over at the small dresser where I had heard movement. There, I spotted Bones pulling my clothes out of the drawers and stuffing them into one of my suitcases haphazardly. "Is your murder dog going to eat me next?"

I winced with pain as I pulled my arm up to cover my mouth and nose, afraid that if I moved too quickly, the dog that looked like it was smiling at me would change its mind and attack. My forearm did a decent job of keeping the warm, fetid breath out of my nose. As I looked back at the dog again, my stomach twisted, threatening to revolt at the sight of the matted blood on its face.

Bones grunted at my question, then snapped out a command. The dog immediately jumped off the bed, going to its master's side. I watched as it sat there obediently, staring up with adoring love. I couldn't believe how small he was. Barely reaching Bone's knees, he wasn't big at all, though his protective behavior and the way he had shown no hesitation in attacking, you'd think he was a massive beast. It was kind of endearing, though I still didn't want to take any chances on having him turn that protectiveness on me.

"He won't hurt you." His tone was as gruff and final as every other time I had heard him speak, which, admittedly, wasn't much. Bones was a man of few words. He hardly paused in his packing as he opened the next drawer, pulling out the few pairs of pants I owned. If he'd already cleared the other drawers, then that was the last of my clothes to be packed.

"Ummm," I cleared my throat and tried again. "What are you doing?" I lowered my hand to my throat and rubbed at the pain there, wincing from the injury that had been inflicted when the man had choked me.

Bones frowned at my movements, his stoic, handsome face showing his displeasure at my pain. It sent warm tingles flowing through me. Thinking that he cared enough to save me, to be angry about me being injured, did things to my weak little heart that it shouldn't. I had yet to properly shield my heart from him. I loved what we had done together, even though I knew I shouldn't, knowing that a man like him would never want a girl like me. Why would the president of a motorcycle club want to keep a scarred, petrified mess like me? If he wanted a woman, there were plenty around, ready to drop to her knees for him at a snap of his fingers—beautiful, undamaged women.

I carefully leveraged myself up, using a hand to hold me steady as the other went to my ribs, grinding my teeth to keep from crying out at the pain.

"Stop moving," he gritted out, dropping the suitcase he'd zipped up to the floor before moving to the end of the bed where I had been lying. He reached for me, to do what I had no idea. Force me to lay back down? Help me sit up? But a knock on the door to my motel room had us both freezing and our heads whipping to the door.

The dog let out a menacing growl and stalked over to the door while baring those sharp canines, ready to tear through anyone who tried to gain entry.

"Zero, sit." I blinked at the command as I watched the blood-stained dog, Zero, drop to his haunches and wag his tail once before resuming his terror inducing snarling.

Bones stalked over to the door, and as I watched, he pulled a wickedly sharp blade from a holster on his side. He glanced through the peephole, then reached for the security latch, pulling it back before wrenching the door open. I didn't know what to expect, but seeing a handsome man wearing jeans and a black T-shirt wasn't it. He had salt and pepper hair, tattoos covering most of his arms, and carried a small black medical bag.

Bones stepped back with a grunt, allowing the man entry while Zero stood up, his tail wagging wildly. He didn't jump on the man, but he did push his snout into the man's hand. He petted the dog for only half a second before pulling back with a grimace, turning a glare toward Bones. He held out his now bloody hand.

"What the actual fuck, Bones? That's just nasty." He turned his glare to Zero while holding his hand out in front of him. "There better be some soap in that bathroom. And a fucking good explanation for why I'm here in this dump."

He took a few steps, heading straight for the bathroom, before stopping in his tracks when his eyes caught on me, still half sprawled across the faded bed cover, as I stared up at him with wide eyes. He gaped at me for a long minute, his eyes raking over my body, not in desire but in a clinical way, as if he were mentally accessing my injuries. He turned his head back to Bones but shook it without saying a word and continued heading into the bathroom.

I watched as he stalked past me, staring after his back, then turned back to look at the MC president. He stood there next to the door still, with his tattooed arms crossed over his broad chest. He was glaring at me. All I could do was raise an eyebrow in question. I had no idea what I had done to make him mad this time other than to cause him the aggravation of having to be here at all.

In no time, the man, a doctor, I presumed, considering the bag he was carrying in his freshly washed hand, stepped back into the room and straight to the end of the bed where I was lying.

"So, what happened?" He didn't look over at Bones; his question was directed straight at me. I swallowed, wincing slightly at the pain there, and began speaking, the words coming out raspy through my raw throat. As I told him what had happened, his face softened, then grew hard in turn. Before I had finished my explanation, he was already moving, setting his bag down and reaching for my shirt.

I heard a growl and froze, looking over at Zero, but he was sitting quietly, watching every move the doctor made. I looked up at Bones to realize he was the one making the sound of a pissed-off wolf.

"Relax, man. I've got to check her injuries. That involves being able to see them." He raised an eyebrow in Bones' direction but carried on what he'd been doing without waiting for an answer. Bones moved over, away from the door and closer to the bed. I watched as he grabbed the chair from the corner of the room, pulled it closer, then sat sprawled on it. All without taking his eyes off me.

The doctor chuckled as he revealed my bruised ribs, probing with gentle fingers that still hurt like a bitch. "Never thought I'd see the day."

I tore my eyes away from Bones' gaze, which had been holding me captive, and looked up at the doctor, wondering what he was talking about.

"Shut the fuck up unless you want me to feed your tongue to Zero." At Bones' growled words, Zero thumped his tail on the floor. I scrunched up my nose at the disgusting visual. After what I'd seen the dog do, I had a feeling he wouldn't be opposed to eating a man's tongue.

"Ewww," I muttered, causing the man to chuckle again.

"I get it, man. But that's fine. If you want to pretend it isn't happening, that's on you." He turned to meet Bones' gaze. "But don't kid yourself. And don't wait too long, or you might watch it slip from your fingers before you even have a good grip." He turned back and winked at me before resuming his thorough exam.

Bones seemed to choose to ignore the cryptic words, and before long, I had been bandaged from my scraped up knees and palms to the wrap around my ribs that made breathing a little bit easier. He stepped back when he was done examining my throat and snapped off the gloves he'd been wearing. He stuffed them and the rest of the discarded trash back into his bag.

"That's about all I can do. You probably should have an antibiotic shot to ward off any germs you picked up from the alley, but I don't have one in my bag with me. I'll come by the compound in the morning to check on you and bring one then. Overall, I'd say you're lucky. Your ribs aren't broken, but bruised ribs can hurt like a bitch and will take four to six weeks to fully heal. Your throat is damaged, but nothing permanent. I suggest soft foods for a few days to allow the swelling to go down." He snapped his bag closed and turned to Bones. "You don't expect to take her on your bike, do you? I can drive her if you want."

I watched as Bones' eyes narrowed dangerously, the black irises seeming to glow with dark flames. Again, the doctor chuckled. "Yeah, I get it. But you don't want your girl to be in any more pain than she needs to, right?"

My mouth dropped open at his words. "I'm not his girl," I spluttered, stumbling over the words. I didn't want him to get the wrong idea and have Bones angry at me for this man that I still couldn't tell was a friend of his or not misunderstanding the situation. "He just... saved me," I trailed off as both men stared at me. One with amusement and a raised eyebrow and the other with a dangerous glare that had me snapping my mouth shut and swallowing hard.

Bones stood abruptly, walking over to my suitcases and wheeling them to the door. "You can drive her," he grunted before wrenching the door open and stalking out into the night. I thought that was all he was going to say, but he paused, Zero on his heels, wagging his white, furry tail. "But don't touch." Then he turned on his heel and strode over to a black SUV, opened the back, and deposited my every earthly possession inside.

"Hey!" I protested, my voice croaking painfully as I raised it in panic. "What are you doing with my things? I need those!"

"I think, beautiful," the doctor winked as he took my arm gently, helping me to stand unsteadily, "that you won't be staying here anymore." He looked around the room with disgust, wrinkling his nose. "It's not safe, and you need to have someone watch over you while you heal."

"But," I began, thinking over what he said. "Where am I going?"

"Somewhere safe, I promise. Where the Boogeymen can't get you."

I swallowed as a wave of terror washed over me. "You aren't talking about the mythical boogeyman that likes to hide under the bed, are you?"

He led me to the door and out into the dark parking lot, swinging the door closed behind us. "Some monsters are worse than the ones in our nightmares, Red." He looked over to where Bones was sitting astride his huge all black motorcycle with his arms crossed over his chest, shooting daggers with his dark eyes. "And, sometimes, it takes a monster to keep you safe."

I ducked my head to avoid the dark glare sent my way. I caught myself rubbing the center of my chest as the thoughts of Bones hating me sent jolts of pain through my system. Once we made it to the SUV, the doctor held the door open for me, but I couldn't climb up without my ribs screaming in agony. In the end, he had to boost me up. The positioning was awkward, and one hand ended up on my ass. I jolted at the feel of his hand there and gave out a muffled squeal.

Suddenly, the hands that had been holding me up abruptly disappeared, and for a split second, I was in a freefall. My heart lurched just as my entire body tensed up painfully, preparing for a fall to the hard pavement. Only, it never happened. Instead, strong arms wrapped around my body and held me tight to a broad chest. I didn't have to look down to see that the arms were covered in solid black ink except for the places that showed shadowed bones.

"Breathe with me. You're okay." The rough voice whispered directly into my ear, making me shiver. But I did as instructed, feeling the chest behind me rising and falling slowly. As my frightened breathing slowed to a bearable pace, I dropped my head back on his shoulder. After a couple of minutes, when I was calm and ready to move again, Bones maneuvered me into the seat with more gentleness and care than I would have thought he was capable of.

He smoothed back the tangled hair that was still in my face and ran his eyes over my body, ensuring I was okay. "I'm sorry. I shouldn't have done that." His jaw was clenched tight as he spoke, almost gritting out the words. But I could see the remorse he was feeling just beneath the surface. "I just... didn't like seeing his hands on you."

I nodded with acceptance, unsure how to respond to this new side of Bones. I hadn't expected him to be so possessive. Or maybe he was jealous. He had fucked my mouth—twice, after all. Perhaps he was the type of guy that didn't like to share. I had no idea what was going on, but I couldn't deny the little thrill of excitement.

He stepped back with his fists clenched tightly at his sides, and I had the distinct feeling that he didn't want to leave me alone with the other man. But then, without another word or glance in my direction, he slammed the door shut and stalked back to his bike. I watched as he let out a shrill whistle, calling Zero to him. In a swift, graceful movement, he swung his leg over the motorcycle and started it with a ground shaking roar. In the next second, he was gone, nothing but taillights disappearing down the street and the blur of a white dog running behind him.

FIFTEEN

SALLY

"I'm sorry I, uh, touched you there."

The doctor's voice pulled me from my musings, causing me to turn my head to look at him in the dim light of the vehicle. "What?" My thoughts were so jumbled at the moment I had a hard time figuring out what he was talking about. He glanced over with a sheepish look on his handsome face.

"I didn't mean to grab your ass. I was trying to help you in and didn't know where else to touch you that wouldn't hurt with the position you were in."

My face heated at the sudden memory. Maybe if I hadn't acted like a frightened virgin, Bones wouldn't have shoved him out of the way. But then again, I couldn't feel sorry for the gentle way he'd held me as he helped me calm down. "It's okay. Really. Don't worry about it."

There was silence for a minute as we drove down the darkened streets as we left town behind. The silence was broken again a moment later by his deep baritone. "He's actually a really good guy under all that darkness he carries around."

I didn't have to wonder, that time, what, or who, he was talking about. When I stayed silent, he continued.

"He's had a rough life. I probably shouldn't be telling you this, but I think there are some things you should probably know when you deal with him."

I interrupted with a question that had been bothering me since the motel room. "What's your name?"

He chuckled, glancing over at me again before turning back to the road. The motorcycle was long gone, with no traces of the lights in the dark. "Everyone just calls me Doc. It's been my name so long that it became permanent."

I just nodded. "Are you in the Devil's Nightmares, too?"

"Ehh, no. I am what you would consider an ally, I suppose. Instead of joining, I stayed on track with my work. My residency kept me too busy to prospect. Now, I just stay available to the club when they need me."

"And Bones is okay with that? He trusts you?" I had to question. It seemed they would have a hard time trusting an outsider around their club. I had already felt that during my time as a waitress. The other girls who had been around longer and who were considered club girls got more attention and often took off with one of the patched members of the club. I'd also heard of club parties. Ones that were private and weren't held in a public setting like the bar. I had never been invited to one of those, whether to waitress for them or to party. Not that I actually wanted to. But curiosity was a dangerous thing.

"As much as any brother could, I suppose."

I swiveled my head to stare at his profile. "Do you mean club brother?"

"Nah, Red. I mean blood brother. Or half-blood anyway." He shrugged, but I could see his white teeth in the dash lights as he grinned. "That's what I wanted to talk to you about, actually."

He had my full attention. If I could turn sideways in my seat and rest my back against the door to really take in the story, I totally would. Instead, I had to keep my head turned so I wouldn't miss a thing. "Like what?" I may have sounded overly eager, but I didn't care as long as my curiosity about Bones was fed.

He cleared his throat and shifted in his seat as he thought about where to start. Or maybe whether he should start at all. If he changed his mind about spilling the story about Bones' past, I might scream.

"So, as I said, we are half brothers. My dad had an affair with his mom. Kind of." He side-eyed me, judging my reaction to his next words. "His mom was the town whore. From what I've heard, she was beautiful, a real knockout. And she used it to her advantage. She was paid well for her services."

"What happened to her?"

His tone turned solemn. "When Bones was twelve, she was killed in a fit of jealousy. She was with a guy, doing her thing, and one that had become obsessed with her shot the guy and then strangled her with his bare hands."

"That's awful," I breathed out. My heart ached for a young Bones. He was at such an impressionable age. I could understand why he was so quiet and angry all the time.

"It gets worse," Doc warned. "Bones walked in on them just after."

"Oh no!" I gasped in shock.

"It was our dad." The words were like a bomb in the vehicle. I could do nothing but gape in horror. "When he realized what had happened, Bones grabbed a knife from the kitchen block and slit our dad's throat."

I tried to swallow back my tears, but some fell anyway. "You don't hate him for that?"

"How could I? My dad was a piece of shit that ruined more lives than you could imagine. He'd cheated on my mom for years until he broke her spirit. He wouldn't let her leave, so she left the only way she knew how."

He didn't have to spell it out for me; I could figure it out. How horrible for both boys.

"So, when he called me to tell me what he'd done, I left work and headed straight to the trailer where he and his mom lived. Together, we cleaned up the mess and got rid of the body. When the police came around asking questions about his disappearance, I told them that he had probably run off after he killed the other two." He shrugged as if it were nothing, and my heart continued to break for the guys.

"After that day, Bones changed. I took him in as his guardian, but I was gone a lot. Being a young doctor takes up a lot of time. He was always a quiet guy, but he became filled with rage. He got into trouble, doing stupid shit. It wasn't until he'd made one of the guys in the MC furious for vandalizing his bike that things got better."

"What? That doesn't make sense!"

He chuckled again as he turned down a dirt road, driving slowly to avoid any potholes. I could see lights up ahead and figured we had finally arrived at the motorcycle compound.

"Instead of stringing his ass up like he deserved, they took him in. Taught him what it meant to be in a brotherhood and gave him an outlet for all that anger. It turned out the president was actually his estranged uncle. From there, it's, as they say, history."

I stared at the lights as they grew bigger, trying to process everything he'd told me. It was a shitty story, one that Bones had lived through. Doc was right, though. It did help me understand him a little better. Though, I still didn't know what I was supposed to do with the information.

When Doc drove past the large building with a row of motorcycles in front of it, I turned back to him. "Uh, what now? I thought I was staying there?"

He shook his head and pointed ahead. In the distance, not too far away, I could make out a single light. "You're staying there. I don't think my brother would be able to handle seeing you around so many men."

I shook my head. "I think you have the wrong impression here. Bones doesn't see me that way. I'm just another waitress to him."

As he pulled to a stop, he turned to look at me fully. "Are you sure about that?"

"Uh, yeah. Pretty sure," I insisted.

"How many other women have you seen him look at?"

I looked out the window as I thought, but there wasn't much to think about. "None."

"Does he look at you?"

All the time. Just about any time I glanced in his direction, he would be watching me.

"By your silence, I'm going to take that as a yes."

I looked back at him just as the front door to the cabin-type house opened. Bones stood in the doorway, blocking out most of the light with his arms crossed over his chest. I couldn't see his expression with the light behind him, but I was certain there was another scowl sitting there.

"But that's only when he's around. When he's not—"

"He's busy working. Trust me, Red. He has never looked at another woman."

With that, he opened his door. When he moved to the front of the SUV, Bones was already there, having grown impatient. Doc said a few words, then slapped Bones on the shoulder before moving to the back of the vehicle to retrieve my suitcases. Bones was the one to walk to my side of the car. He opened my door just as I unbuckled my seatbelt. With only a grunt in greeting, he slid his hands under me, one under my legs and the other behind my back. He lifted me effortlessly, turning toward the house and leaving the car door for his brother to close.

Neither one of us said a word as he carried me through the open doorway and into the small house. I didn't get more than a short glimpse of a modestly furnished living room with just a couple of comfortable looking black leather recliners and a dog bed in the corner by a fireplace. After that quick non-tour, we entered a hallway with only a couple of doors on either side before entering the first door on the right. I thought he was just going to dump me on the bed. Instead, he carefully lowered me onto the mattress, propped against a small mound of pillows leaning against the headboard.

Looking around the room, I realized it was even more sparse than the motel room I had just left. I could only surmise that he never had overnight guests and was actually surprised that he even had a spare bedroom furnished.

"One of the club girls insisted that I keep a spare room available a few years ago when I built the place." He rubbed the back of his neck as he looked around the room as if seeing it for the first time. "I can bring in a TV or a chair. Just let me know." After his statement, he dropped his hand and glared at me, the moment of awkwardness over. "Don't leave this room without help. I don't want you hurting yourself more by trying to do things on your own."

"How can I get help when you have to do... presidential things?" I waved my hand towards the door. "I won't be able to hold my pee while you're gone. What if I get hungry? What if there's an emergency?" I didn't want to be waited on hand and foot, but I didn't know what his plan was if he kept me locked away in bed all day. I was sure he was a busy man, and he obviously lived alone with only his dog for company. At least, I assumed he lived alone.

"If I'm not around, I'll have one of the club girls sit with you."

I grimaced at the thought. Not that I was opposed to it being a club girl, really, but I wasn't sure about someone being forced to babysit me. "You use club girls a lot," I muttered while looking down at my fingers playing with the hem of my shirt. I realized I hadn't cleaned up yet from the attack as I stared down at myself. I was still covered in grime and dried blood.

"Do you think I can, uh, take a shower?"

We both turned to look out the open doorway and across the hall to another door, which I figured was likely the bathroom. My cheeks started flaming at the implications of what taking a shower would entail. Even if he left me alone to shower, he would still need to help me get undressed. I watched as every muscle on his body tensed up before he slowly turned back to face me, a hungry look in his eyes that couldn't be mistaken.

After giving me a look that had me tightening my thighs together, Bones turned on his heels without saying a single word. I watched him push open the bathroom door and flip on the light, though I couldn't see inside with the way the doorways were situated. I heard the water turn on and some rustling going on. As I listened to the sounds of the motorcycle club president preparing to help me shower, my body heat began to rise to uncomfortable levels. All I could do while trying to regulate my breathing was fantasize about how involved he would be.

I watched him leave the bathroom without looking in my direction and stomp in his heavy boots back down the short hallway to the living room. The anticipation of what was to come next was killing me. I could hear the water running in the bathroom, and steam was starting to billow out into the hall. He didn't leave me waiting for long.

Bones walked back into my room carrying a suitcase. With only a quick, heated glance up and down my body, he tossed the suitcase on the bed and flipped it open. I watched as he dug through the clothes he had half-haphazardly thrown inside an hour ago. I bit my lip as I eyed him, wanting to tell him to stop, knowing he was sorting through my underwear, but he'd already seen the plain cotton panties and bras. I only had a couple of nice, lacey bras. They were ones I'd snatched up on clearance when I had gone to a sale at one of the lingerie stores near where I used to work.

Finally, he held up one of my only cute nightgowns. Even that one was just cotton with flowers on it. But the material was soft and one of my favorites. I noticed he didn't grab a change of panties before he turned to me. He tossed the nightgown in my lap, and before I could do more than put a hand on the material, he bent down and scooped me back into his arms. I would never say it out loud, but I was getting really comfortable being carried by his strong arms. I certainly wouldn't have any problems being toted around by him for the rest of my life.

It honestly took all my self-control not to snuggle in and lay my head against his strong shoulder. Bones may appear to be a murderous asshole with no conscience, but there was much more under the surface. All of his glares and growls never stopped him from trying to help me, and he never hesitated to save me from the guy who wanted to do more than just hurt me.

We stepped into the bathroom, the heavy steam immediately coating my body in slick moisture. I glanced over to the open shower curtain, surprised to see a plastic lawn chair in the tub. I jerked my gaze back to Bones.

"When did you bring a chair in here?" How did I miss that?

He sat me carefully on the counter and grunted before ducking his head, trying to look busy as he turned back to the water, testing the warmth. "It was already in here."

I paused in my next question, knowing if I pushed too hard, he might clam up on me completely, but my curiosity finally won out. "Why?"

He huffed out an annoyed breath, turned back to me, and gripped the hem of my shirt before I could react to his abrupt movements. "I sit in it when I wash my dog." We both froze as he yanked my shirt over my head, me with gritted teeth against the quick, sharp pain and him with wide, apologetic eyes. He reached out to smooth back the hair that had fallen wildly around my face. "I'm sorry, I shouldn't have..."

"It's fine." I blew out a slow breath as I tried to get past that initial shock of pain. "You didn't mean to, I know." I closed my eyes and drew in another breath through my nose.

A finger under my chin had my eyes flying open and forgetting all about my breathing exercises. "If I could kill him all over again, I would."

It felt deeper, more intense than a declaration of love. Coming from this man who was obviously emotionally repressed, it might as well be. As I debated on the best way to respond, he had obviously gotten over the moment of weakness because the next thing I knew, he was unbuttoning my pants and shimmying them over my hips and ass with little help from me. I didn't even have time to brace myself or to lift my hips up, and the pants were already down to my thighs. It wasn't until he was on his knees in front of me that I remembered which bra and panties I was wearing.

My eyes squeezed shut in mortification. Every woman had them, the panties they saved for their period, so they didn't ruin even more panties. I just happened to be wearing mine on the day the man I was hopelessly falling in love with was undressing me. Bones, the hottest motorcycle president on the planet, was kneeling face to face with my vagina, and I was wearing stained panties. Fuck. My. Life.

I let out a strangled sound and then took in a deep inhale of breath before daring to crack one eye open. I had to dip my chin to see, but as soon as I could, I felt a wave of heat wash over me. Bones was still in front of me, both of his hands on the waistband of my jeans. As I watched, his eyes closed, and he dropped his forehead to one of my knees. I didn't dare make a sound, didn't even take a chance on breathing too hard. I just stared, fascinated, as this incredible man lost his shit over my pussy.

Suddenly, he pulled the jeans down and off my feet, taking my slip-on shoes with them. Then he twisted his head and nipped the inside of my thigh. Before I could do more than yelp in surprise, I was back in his arms as he stepped over to the shower. He set me down in the plastic chair, and I blinked up at him as the water immediately soaked me. He shoved the shower wand in my hand and then stepped back.

"I can't remove your shit," he gestured up and down my body. "If you need me, call out." He paused at the doorway without looking back to where I was sitting with my mouth agape as I held loosely to the shower handle with my hand.

"Don't need me," his growly words made me shiver as I looked down at myself. I was still wearing my plain white cotton bra and stained period panties. The white gauze was still wrapped tightly around my ribs, and I also had bandages on my scraped knees and hands.

I looked at the small shelf next to me to see the body wash and 2-in-1 shampoo. I grimaced as I thought of what not using conditioner would mean for my hair, then sighed. I didn't know why I thought Bones was actually going to bathe me. He hadn't even fully undressed me.

"What the fuck?" I mumbled the words under my breath. "How am I supposed to wash myself without getting all these bandages wet?"

"It doesn't matter. We can replace them when you're done."

My head whipped around to the door. If I had to guess, I'd say he was sitting on the floor with his back to the door. He may have left me alone to bathe, but he hadn't abandoned me completely. His words were muffled but clearly understandable. A slow smile made its way across my face. He was scared. Why that should make me feel so powerful, I wasn't really sure, but it did.

"What about my bra and panties?" I asked without raising my voice. I had a feeling he was listening intensely to everything coming from this room.

"Leave them on." The words were a clear order.

"But won't it be easier to take them off before I get them all..." I let the words trail off before finishing. "Wet?"

There was a small thump against the door, and I could just picture him banging his head against the door in frustration. "You don't want to play with me, little girl." What was it about that deep, growly voice that got me so worked up? As much as I wanted to try out this new found vixen inside of me that wanted to see how far my teasing could go, there was a stronger, louder part of me that was screaming not to tempt the beast.

I sighed, letting the cowardice win. It wasn't that I was afraid Bones would hurt me, far from it, actually. I had somehow found myself trusting him more than anyone else in this world. But I hated to admit it, even to myself, that I was still that scared victim who had been trapped for months in a cold basement. Bones wasn't the monster in my story. The monster was a well-respected physician who played nice with society. It's strange how that works.

I sighed and began to wash my hair with one hand, the other wrapped tightly around my bandaged ribs. No matter how slowly I moved, my ribs screamed out in agony. I couldn't bring myself to do more than brush a hand over my skinned knees, barely rinsing away the dried blood that had settled onto my skin. By the time I had rinsed away the last of the suds from my body, I was sagging in exhaustion and pain.

I couldn't reach the holder for the shower wand, and the towel was too far away to grab, so I ended up sagging back on the plastic chair in defeat, sniffling back tears as I felt sorry for myself.

"What the fuck are you doing?"

The enraged question had me jolting in shock. I dropped the shower handle to grab hold of the curtain, as I almost sent myself crashing to the floor when I jumped. My gasp of pain from the sudden movement had Bones snarling profanities. He ignored the water shooting full blast at him from the shower wand as it spun wildly on the floor of the bathtub. Instead of caring that he was getting soaked, he swiped the towel from the top of the curtain rod where he'd left it.

In swift movements, he had me wrapped in the towel, and the water turned off as he scooped me up again. I couldn't enjoy the feel of his strong arms holding me again, unfortunately. I was too busy attempting to hold back my sniffles and moans of pain.

"You stupid girl. Why the fuck didn't you call me to help you?" He stomped across the hall to my new bedroom, depositing me gently on the end of the bed. He went back into the bathroom for another towel and returned before I could do more than wipe my nose on a corner of the soaked towel I was draped in. "You don't ever sit there and suffer when I can help you. Do you understand me?"

His glare told me he expected an acknowledgment, so I just nodded glumly, feeling sorry for myself more than I cared to admit. Without a word, he whipped the wet towel off of me, sending it flying, landing with a wet plop in the bathroom across the way. My wet bra was next, making me gasp and rush to move my arm from around my ribs to my breasts. Bones didn't even pause as he took the fresh towel and began to dry me off, starting with my legs and working his way up to my hair.

When he rubbed much of the dripping water out of the soaked strands, he went back down, shoving my arm out of the way to dry me there, too. Before I could do more than squeak in protest at the feel of his cloth covered hands rubbing over my nipples, he began to unwrap the soaked bandage.

"Lift your arms out to your sides," he commanded me in a stern tone that I pictured him using on his motorcycle club members. With a face flaming as red as my hair, I did what he commanded. I couldn't tell if he was taking in the view of my puckered nipples as he knelt beside me on the floor. I could lie and say that it was from the cold, but that would be a damn lie. The man had just been rubbing my breasts. No matter how much pain I was in, I couldn't deny that it was enough to make me want more. Maybe later, when I wasn't shivering and my ribs were healed, though.

He stood up, taking the wet bandage with him. I immediately brought my arms back around to conceal my nakedness and blinked up at him as he pointed a finger in my face. "Don't. Move." I jerked a nod up and down, wishing I could use my hair as a shield, too.

He was as quick as always, returning to the room with a long strip of cloth that looked like it had once been a bed sheet. "Up," he commanded again in his rough tone. With a sigh, I lifted my arms back out to my sides. He knelt back down in front of me, right between my legs. I watched his face, trying to see if he was looking at my stained panties or taking glances at my puckered nipples, but he never took his eyes off the new bandage. He wrapped it tight around my torso quickly and efficiently. By the time he was done, I felt a million times better, the support helping me feel like I wasn't about to fall to pieces.

I glanced down to survey his handiwork. "It looks like you've done this before," I said, impressed.

He grunted and sat back on his heels. "Once or twice." His tone suggested he was bored with the situation, but as I glanced down at him, I couldn't miss the hard outline of his cock pressing firmly against his leg. More than a little thrill went through me at knowing I actually did affect him after all.

He stood up again, not even bothering to conceal his erection. Once again, he strode out of the room, only to return mere seconds later. He held up my nightgown and frowned. It had been attacked by the water after I had dropped the shower wand, along with the rest of the bathroom. I grimaced, glancing over to my suitcase, still open a couple of feet away from me on the bed. Instead of reaching for a dry nightshirt, he stalked out of the room again.

I stared after him, dumbfounded. I had no idea what he was going to do next. I shook my head and reached over toward the suit-case with one hand extended, trying not to use my core muscles to lean over. With a grimace, I had to stop. My clothes were just a smidgen too far out of reach. As I sat there contemplating my next move, he strode back in, holding a black T-shirt.

In deft moves, he had the shirt over my head, guiding my arms through as if I were a doll. I blinked up at him as he pulled my wet hair out of the neck hole. I glanced down at myself to confirm that he had, indeed, dressed me in one of his shirts instead of just using one of my own. I ran a hand over the fabric, feeling how soft the material was from being well-worn. It had to be one of his favorite shirts. I wanted to ask so many questions about his actions from the entire night, starting with why he had shown up in that alley when I needed help the most, but I knew I wouldn't get any answers from him.

He surprised me further when he pulled out my brush and sat on the bed behind me. He slowly ran the brush through my hair, carefully detangling every strand. By the time he was done, my eyes could barely stay open, and I had yawned more times than I could remember. The last thing I knew, he was lifting me carefully and placing me between the warm, dry sheets. I didn't even have the energy to blush when he slid my wet panties down my legs so I wouldn't get the sheets wet.

I wished he would hold me in his arms. I couldn't remember my parents offering me comfort when I'd been hurt or ill. Bones had shown more concern for me and had taken care of me more than I could remember receiving during my entire childhood. It made me feel warm inside, causing my infatuation with him to grow stronger. If only he would lie next to me, whisper that everything would be alright. I squeezed my eyes shut and turned to my side carefully, mindful of my injuries, and wished for sleep to take me quickly.

I could have sworn I felt him place a kiss on my forehead as I was falling asleep, but I was too far gone to know for sure. But my heart warmed at the thought.

SEVENTEEN

THE NIGHTMARE KING

The woman was driving me insane.

I tried to stay away, to spend most of my time in the President's office at the club, but she kept drawing me back. I knew I could trust the club girls I had assigned to watch over her, but over the last four weeks, more and more every day, I wanted it to be me who took care of her needs. If she was hungry, I wanted to be the one to feed her. When she needed to bathe, I wanted to be there to help her. Well, I still did that. No one else was allowed to see the woman naked but me.

She had somehow burrowed under my skin. In the beginning, I thought it was just attraction that had me going back night after night, watching her from the shadows until I couldn't hold back anymore. The two times I had all but forced her to suck my cock, I thought it was just because no one else had ever done it before. I knew even then that I was a fucking liar. I could tell myself all I wanted that it was just the experience of having it done, that any woman would do, but it was her. Only her.

Now that I had spent the last few weeks with her under my roof, watching her cuddle with my dog, brushing out her blood-red hair every night...

She was driving me insane.

And now I was sitting here in church hearing that the motherfuckin' Boogeymen were looking for her. Like fuck they were going to get anywhere near my woman. I slammed my fist down on top of the wooden table, making the gavel clatter next to me.

"I want their fuckin' heads. Whoever broke into her motel room, whoever is asking questions. I want them strung up in the shed. It's fuckin' bullshit that this has been going on for weeks, and no one has seen anyone lurking in town."

Barrel sat back in his chair with a long sigh. "Prez, we all like the girl. But this is a lot of manpower when we should be planning the next weapon run."

I slowly turned my head, showing him exactly what I thought about his opinion. Like the intelligent man he tried to pretend he wasn't, he quickly held up both hands in surrender. I glared around the table with a dare. "Anyone else have anything to say about the matter? Am I taking up too many mother fuckin' resources trying to hunt down our enemies that have been successfully infiltrating our territory? They are making us look like fuckin' morons holding our dicks while they run circles around us." I stood from my chair slowly and leaned over the table, bracing my tattooed knuckles on the polished wood. At the silence in the room, I nodded. "This has gone on too long already. I'm hearing more shit about drugs being passed around at the high school, and last week our warehouse, which no one is even supposed to fuckin' know about, got raided. Double the patrols. Triple 'em. Find these fuckers!"

I stood back up straight. Grabbing the gavel, I slammed it down on the table. "Church dismissed!"

I strode out of the room, my anger at the entire situation making a red haze fall over my vision. Pumpkin Patch was a fuckin' ridiculous town, but it was my town. I'd be damned if these lowlife assholes were going to run drugs through it and destroy everything I had worked so hard for. The cops were worthless hicks, too drunk on their coffee and donuts to protect it the way it needed to be protected. That was where the Devil's Nightmares came in. The mayor couldn't do jack-shit to keep the Boogeymen from infiltrating the high school with drugs. But I could. I was the motherfuckin' Pumpkin King, and Pumpkin Patch belonged to me.

A commotion from the front of the building drew my attention just as I was about to head out the backdoor. I was eager to head back to my house to check on the woman that made my brain itch, but I detoured to the common room to see what the fuck was going on. Just knowing that whatever was going on was probably bullshit had my anger ratcheting up another degree.

"What the fuck is going on in here?" I demanded as I entered the large room we used for parties and general gatherings. There were several club girls huddled together, raising a ruckus, shouting and upset. I glanced at a couple that looked like they were crying, dismissing them instead for someone who had half a brain who could explain without giving me a migraine.

The girls parted, revealing a blonde huddled in on herself, crying almost violently. At my voice, she looked up with relief. I stumbled back a step as she ran over, throwing her arms around me, soaking my T-shirt with her tears, and getting her makeup all over me. I was going to have to throw the goddamn shirt away.

"Bones! Thank god. I need you!" She burst into a fresh wave of tears and buried her head in my neck. I grimaced at the feel of the wetness but more so at feeling any woman's arms around me but Sally's. It was like fighting with an octopus, trying to get her off me.

I held her back by her upper arms as she blinked up at me with a hurt look on her face. She looked like I'd kicked her fucking dog. It wasn't until I had her set away from me that I recognized the club girl. Out of all the girls I allowed to hang around the club so my members wouldn't mutiny on me, she was the one I couldn't stand the most. She was pushy and bitchy, lording it over everyone that she was the fuckin' queen bee of the club girls. I had no clue where she had come up with that idea, but I usually ignored the drama, choosing to stay far away from it. I never wanted one of the women. Just the idea of having one of them touch me sent a wave of revulsion through me.

This one, though, she'd been trying to get herself a title of old lady since the moment she strolled through the doors. When she wasn't attached to Barrel's cock, she was trying to climb mine. It didn't matter how many times I told her to fuck off; she didn't want to take no for an answer. I was guessing her dreams of old lady would only be satisfied with being the head bitch. Too bad for her, only one woman had ever come close, and I wasn't ready to admit it yet, even to myself.

Her face was a mess, with makeup smeared all over her, so it took a second to notice the black eye and split lip. I frowned. "What happened to you?"

Her lips curved up at my words, seemingly pleased that she finally got a piece of my attention. She tried to push her way back up against my chest, but I held her away from me with a firm hold on her shoulders. Her pleased smile quickly turned into a scowl. Before I could blink, she burst into tears again. I shook my head. The woman was mercurial as fuck.

"What the fuck?" Barrel walked up next to me, staring at the chick he'd been banging off and on for the better part of two years. "What happened to Daisy?"

At his words, the girl, apparently named Daisy, tore away from my hold and flung herself into his arms. Relieved I was no longer the one dealing with her, I stepped back, crossed my arms over my chest, and waited for an explanation.

"Barrel! Some guy beat me up! He tried to r-rape me!" It was hard to understand her through her increasingly annoying sobbing, but her following words had ice running down my spine. "The g-guy said that it w-was a message. They want the redhead delivered to them, or they would hurt someone else."

As I stood there with my mask in place, not letting anyone see the icy fury raging through my blood, I saw her peek at me from under her lashes. She was looking for something. A reaction, maybe, but she definitely wanted something. Her words were going to get something, alright, but it wasn't what she was hoping for.

"How did you get away?" My cold tone had everyone turning from her to look at me.

She leaned back from Barrel to look up at me, seemingly confused. "What d-do you mean?"

I waved a hand in her direction, indicating her body. "You have a black eye and a split lip. You say he tried to rape you. How did you get away?"

"Prez," someone hissed at me, but I ignored them. I was smelling bullshit, and we weren't anywhere near a farm.

"No, I want to hear this. We need to know what happened. In detail." I looked around the gathered crowd of patched members and club girls before returning my gaze to Daisy, who was back to scowling at me. "Your clothes aren't torn or dirty. I don't see any bruises anywhere else. What. Happened?"

All I could picture in my mind was a replay of the night I had been staking out Sally's motel room as I usually did when she wasn't at work. Hearing her frantic cries of pain coming from the nearby alley scared me more than I had ever been in my life. I could still see her lying there in the filthy alley, bruised and bloody, her clothing torn, and the fucker preparing to violate her in the worst way a woman could be. If Daisy had been attacked, why wasn't she a mess, and why was she even standing here at all?

"How did you get away from your attacker, Daisy?" My voice had sunk into the menacing tone I usually used when I was in the middle of torturing a man for information. I watched her swallow hard and then look around at the gathered faces, looking for someone to help her out. "Look at me!" I barked, making her jump. "Tell me, now."

"I d-don't know! He jumped out of nowhere and started punching me. He said they want the scarred bitch, and they would leave the rest of us alone." She pouted and crossed her arms over her chest. "I think we should hand her over. She's not even one of us. Why should the rest of us be threatened and hurt when we could just give her to them? Who fucking cares?" She jutted her chin out defiantly, and it took all my willpower not to hit a woman for the first time in my life.

I turned to look at Barrel, but he was already stepping away from her, shaking his head in disgust. Daisy turned to look where I was and immediately dropped her arms, her eyes tearing up again as she reached for him. It was his turn to cross his arms as he glared at her.

"Barrel…"

"No," he spit out at her. "Fuck no. What the fuck Daze? You're working with the Boogeymen?"

Her mouth dropped open in shock before swallowing several times. Her eyes ran back and forth over the faces that had gone from understanding to pissed at her words. What she didn't seem to understand was that everyone liked Sally. Since she had started working at the bar months ago, she had been nothing but sweet to everyone. There wasn't a single person other than Daisy who disliked the girl.

"No! I swear it! I would never!" She wrapped her arms around her middle, and the tears that came to her eyes, I was sure, were finally real. "I swear, I'm not lying. I don't like the girl; we all know that, and I shouldn't have said what I did. But I swear, I'm not lying. I wouldn't work with the Boogeymen." She looked up at me with pleading eyes. "Please, believe me, President?"

I still had my doubts, but she seemed sincere. And for once in her fuckin' life, she was acting respectful. I shook my head and turned to leave. "Clean her up, get the full story. And watch her. If I find out she's lying, I won't send her back to the enemy; I'll feed her to Zero piece by piece." After barking out my orders to no one in particular, I strode from the room, needing to escape the clubhouse and all the bullshit.

As soon as I got to my bike parked out the back door, I hopped on and revved the engine, not waiting around for anyone who might have something to say. I had no patience for traitors, and it didn't matter if they had a cock or a cunt. I would make them bleed on the end of my knife. I wasn't called Bones because of my tattoos. It had been too long since I'd flayed a man open with my blade.

The corner of my mouth tipped up in an expression I had forgotten I was capable of making as I turned up the long drive to my secluded cabin away from the club. Sally still had my favorite knife. I knew she kept it under her pillow every night, and since she had started spending more time in the living room, she slid it under the couch, within easy reach during the day. It obviously made her feel safer with it near. As long as I was alive, I would make sure she kept it on her at all times when I wasn't around.

EIGHTEEN

SALLY

I waved at Emily from the doorway as she walked out to her car before closing and locking the bolt securely. It had been four weeks since the attack, and though I was grateful for all the help and the company over those weeks, I was starting to get cabin fever.

I twisted my torso back and forth, then bent over from side to side. The pain was mostly gone, with only a twinge every now and then if I moved too quickly. It was time to leave. I had been relying on the club president's charity long enough.

His attitude towards me seemed to have thawed over the last couple of weeks. I figured being in close proximity with someone had a way of doing that. I could only be glad that he had; the alternative could have been a nightmare. If he had ended up getting pissed about me taking up so much of his space instead, I probably would have found a way out long ago, even if I had to crawl.

He had surprised me. He didn't seem to mind me being in his small home, which really went against the nature he projected. But he never went as far as he had the first night he brought me to his cabin. He didn't try to undress me, and when I needed my ribs rewrapped, he allowed me to hold my shirt up out of the way, keeping myself covered. I still caught the erection he couldn't hide, but I figured that was simply a reaction to being so close to a woman's body.

Other than the nightly routine he had started of brushing my hair, he rarely touched me. He seemed fascinated by my hair, though, spending long moments running the brush through the strands, careful not to pull any. As much as he liked doing it, he was also unaffected, while I had come to crave the time we spent together, even if it was in silence. It hurt that I yearned for so much more from him while he only tolerated my presence. That was why I needed to go now that I was pretty much healed.

I walked into the bedroom I'd been occupying and looked around. The second day I was here, I watched from the bed as Bones emptied my suitcases, putting away my meager belongings in the dresser. Then he turned to leave me alone without a word.

I stepped to the end of the bed and knelt down on the floor to look where I remembered he had slid the empty cases once he was done. Seeing a black handle, I grabbed it, tugging it out into the open. When I stood back up and lifted it onto the bed, I waited to see if it would cause any pain to my ribs, then breathed a sigh of relief when nothing hurt.

I was just finishing up, placing the last piece of clothing neatly into the first suitcase, when his voice boomed from the doorway. I jumped, letting out a startled scream.

"What the fuck are you doing?"

I spun around, my hand over my racing heart, to see the man himself stalking toward me with a murderous expression.

"I asked you a question, little girl. What. The. Fuck. Are. You. Doing?" He didn't give me a chance to answer before he grabbed my suitcase, dumping all the carefully folded garments into a pile on the bed. Then he took the newly emptied case and flung it toward the hallway. I watched as it landed with a bang against the wall. I turned back to him, my mouth open in shock.

"Why did you do that?" I flung up my arms in exasperation and tried to step around him to retrieve the case, but he stopped me with a hand on the center of my chest.

"I'm not going to ask you again," he snarled down into my face, pissing me the hell off. I pushed against his chest, but it was like trying to shove a wall. All it did was make me stumble back a step. It was my turn to glare up into his stupidly handsome face.

"There's no reason for me to stay here anymore. I'm all better now!" I lifted my chin defiantly. "It was kind of you to let me stay here to heal, but it's time for me to go."

For some reason, I couldn't understand, my words only seemed to enrage him further. At one time, I may have been scared of that look. He was a mean motherfucker, someone I knew could, and had, killed without mercy, but after spending so much time, limited though it was, with him, I had come to realize that he would never hurt me. He was always careful with me, as if I were made out of glass. His glares could be considered lethal, but they were nothing but bluster when it came to me. I still didn't understand why he was so angry at seeing me pack. I would have thought he'd want me gone from his home.

"You aren't going anywhere," he said in a tone so final I nearly dropped my mouth open in shock again.

"Why not?" I demanded with my hands firmly on my hips. "I don't need you anymore!"

He froze, his glare turning frosty cold, sending shivers up my spine. I wasn't sure what to make of his change in demeanor at my words, but it was too late to try to take them back.

"You are better now?" His tone went quiet, almost calm, instead of the fierce anger he had displayed only seconds before. "You're healed and aren't in pain anymore?"

Confused, I shrugged. "No, I'm not in any more pain. I can move around just fine. Which you could see by how I had managed to pack the suitcase you just dumped all over the place."

"Good." His hand shot up before I could even think to react. I gasped at the restriction around my throat and felt his fingers flex when I swallowed.

"Bones?" I froze at the sudden move, then brought my hands up to hold onto his forearm. He wasn't hurting me; his grip was more firm than tight, allowing me the freedom to breathe normally. "What are you doing?"

"Something I've waited too goddamn long for."

Then he was jerking me toward him. His mouth landed on mine in a brutal kiss, our teeth clashing. His tongue invaded my mouth as soon as I opened it reflexively to gasp. Several seconds passed while my brain tried to catch up to what was happening. As soon As I realized that this man was actually kissing me, my eyes drifted closed. With a throaty moan, I surrendered to him.

At my capitulation, his movements slowed. He didn't gentle his kiss, but he was no longer harshly taking me. His tongue slowed, swiping over mine in a rough caress that had my belly doing somersaults. With his hand still firmly around my throat, he pushed me until the back of my knees hit the bed. When I landed on my butt, he followed me, still pushing until my back was flat on the mattress. I felt the bed dip as he crawled on top of me, his knees caging in my legs as if to keep me prisoner. Little did he know, escape was the last thing I wanted to do.

His mouth tore away from mine, causing me to open my eyes and blink up at him in confusion. His face was his usual blank mask, but his eyes were blazing with an intensity that filled my body with molten heat. There was so much that he could barely keep hidden in his gaze. Passion, lust, desire, hunger, and other emotions I was too overwhelmed to try and figure out at the moment. His dark eyes ran over my face. Whatever he saw there had him letting out a deep, throaty sound. For one second, his hand tightened almost too tight, but it was there and gone before I could even try to gasp for air.

He removed his hand from my neck, and I almost cried for him to return it. I was afraid he would get off me, to leave me a mess of wanting more from him, but he wasn't rejecting me the way I feared.

Instead, he reached with both hands to the front of my dress. In a firm grip, he yanked, tearing the material down the center, jerking my body with the rough movement.

I couldn't breathe as I watched him look over my body with a primal hunger I had only dreamed I would one day see coming from him. It was as if he were more beast than man at the moment. As if my threat of leaving had finally unlocked something, and the man was no longer in control.

"You aren't going anywhere." His words were as cold and emotionless as they had been when I told him I was well enough to leave. "You're never going anywhere."

I swallowed, hearing the threat in his tone. It was a demand so final I had a sudden fear of what he would do when I would have to. It wasn't that I would want to; I never wanted to leave. But eventually, I would need to go back to California. I had never told him why I had come to Pumpkin Patch in the first place. He had no idea that there was a trial date looming in the very near future. He didn't give me a chance to respond before he dipped his head to my breasts that were still encased in my one lacey bra.

I gasped and arched my back, pressing more firmly into him when he bit down on my nipple hard enough to send a shock wave of pain through me, just shy of being more than I could handle. I didn't know why it would make me want to beg for more. I didn't know why moisture had flooded into my panties. By all accounts, I should be frightened of being held immobile while having pain inflicted on me, but instead, I longed to see what else he would do to my body.

I felt movement and opened my eyes that I had closed when he'd bit me to see him reaching for something behind his back. The snick of metal sliding against metal had my eyes going wide. Instantly, a wave of terror washed over me so violently that I could do nothing but freeze in shock. My eyes followed the path of the blade as it lowered to my flesh and slid under the band of my bra. With one flick of his wrist, my bra was sliced open. I wished I could feel relief that the blade hadn't been meant for my skin, but I was firmly trapped in a nightmare from the past.

His black gaze took in the flesh he revealed, slowly running up my chest and back to my face before making the slow trail back down again. Then he paused, darting back up to my face, taking in the expression of terror as I stayed trapped in my memories. From a corner of my mind, I watched as he looked from my body and the scars that covered me, then to the knife he was still holding in his hand. His expression morphed into one of horror, and then he quickly tossed the knife away.

I flinched as it hit the wall. It was several long seconds or minutes—I had no way of knowing for sure—before my mind allowed any sound other than the whooshing of my own heartbeat to penetrate.

It's gone.

Baby, I'm so sorry.

I didn't know.

It's gone, I promise.

Come back to me.

As soon as the pleading words broke through, I let out a sob and threw my arms around him, holding tight. I knew I was shaking like a leaf, and I was probably scaring him, but I couldn't stop. When he tried to pull back to look at me, I held on tighter with my face buried in his neck, clinging to him with all my might.

"Baby," it was the softest tone I had ever heard come from him, his chest rumbling against mine. The rich, deepness of the timbre filled me with a sense of safety and security I never thought to feel again. "Tell me."

I knew what he wanted, but I couldn't give him my story. Not yet. Not right now. I shook my head. "Not now," I whispered, unable to control the tremble in my voice.

I felt him stroking my hair with those big, tattooed fingers and wanted to cry at how right it felt to be held and caressed by this King of Nightmares.

"What do you need from me?"

I finally pulled back so I could look him in the eye, letting him see my sincerity and desperation. "I need you to make me forget."

He studied me for a long second, and I was afraid he was going to insist that we stop. But then he let out a tortured groan. He swooped down, retaking my lips as I sighed with relief into his mouth. The kiss was no less explosive than the first time, but there was suddenly tenderness, too. When he pulled away from my lips, it was to trail kisses over one cheek and then across to the other. Then I felt his lips sliding up the side of my face, continuing to my forehead. It wasn't until I felt his lips glide across my neck and down the center of my chest that I began to cry silent tears. He was kissing every jagged scar. Every ugly memory was being replaced by the tenderness of his lips.

When his lips found a nipple and latched on to it, sucking it deep into his mouth, I arched and cried out. "Bones!"

He stopped abruptly, pulling back with a glare. "When I'm with you, you call me Jack. I'm Jack to you. Do you understand?"

I realized, with a wrench in my heart, that he was giving me a precious gift. *Him.* He was giving me the real him. Not the MC President. He was giving me *Jack*, the man. I lifted a trembling hand and caressed it over the dark stubble on his jaw.

"Jack," I whispered.

NINETEEN

THE NIGHTMARE KING

The sound of my name coming from her sweet lips was enough to make me lose any control I had been clinging to. I felt the thread I'd been barely holding onto snap, and I could no longer hold myself back. For the last couple of months, I had been lying to myself in an effort to not do what I was about to. I wasn't a gentle man. Never had been. I was a fucking beast that was only kept in check by my iron will. But now that she said my name, something I hadn't heard since the day my mother was murdered, I was done.

I needed to know what had happened to her. I had a burning need to know who the motherfucker was that had taken a blade to my girl, turning her into what resembled a patchwork doll, but she had asked me to make her forget. She had no idea what she was asking for.

With a carnal groan, my vicious need for this woman took over every rational thought. I was going to give her sweet and gentle as well as a man like me could, but she had unleashed the beast instead.

I lowered my head back to her breasts and bit down on the swell, hard enough to leave a mark without breaking the skin, then sucked. I would brand her in more ways than one before the night was through. I couldn't remove her scars, but I would give her something else to look at when she looked in the mirror with those eyes of hers that were always filled with sorrow.

Her cries of pain mixed with pleasure made me so hard it was causing my cock to ache and throb. I needed to get my jeans off before they left a permanent outline of my zipper etched onto it. As I made my way down her belly, licking and nipping at every scar on my way to her cunt, I reached down to pop the button on my jeans. The pressure of my hard cock trying to escape the confines pushed free without me even having to lower the zipper. The only thing holding me back from plunging into her body was the cotton of my black boxers.

As soon as I made my way to the small patch of dark red hair at the top of her pussy I stopped to stare for a long moment. I had never been up close to a cunt before but knew after this I was going to need to put my face in hers every fucking day. I shoved her legs wide to make room for my shoulders but also to get a good view of the treasure she kept hidden there.

She was pink everywhere, while wetness coated her pussy lips and was smeared onto her thighs. Her scent filled my senses, making me feral for her taste. I needed my mouth on her more than I needed my next breath. As I shoved my face into her cunt, sinking my tongue in as far as I could reach, her flavor made come leak from the head of my cock. It was nearly more than I could take.

I reached down with one hand while using the other to hold her thigh open. I squeezed my cock as hard as I could, the pain making me wince, but it helped to stop the come that was threatening to explode from me. I wasn't ashamed that she already had me on the verge of coming within seconds of finally getting a taste of her, but I didn't want to waste my seed in my pants. I had always heard that once a guy came, he was done for a while. That was unacceptable to me. I refused to come anywhere but deep inside her cunt while she screamed my name in pleasure.

I dragged my tongue from her entrance and through her lips until I reached her clit. It didn't take a fucking rocket scientist to figure out where a woman's clit was. It was right fucking there, swollen and needy, just waiting for me to wrap my lips around it. I sucked, then swiped my tongue repeatedly over the hard nub while listening to her cries and moans. It wasn't until I put some pressure on it with my teeth and rapidly stroked my tongue back and forth that she nearly bucked me off her. With a satisfied hum, I let go of my cock and placed my hand on her pelvis, pushing her firmly back onto the bed.

I never let up my assault on her clit, knowing that what I was doing was exactly what she needed the most. I was tempted to stick a finger inside her, to feel that warmth and softness I knew was waiting for me, but a depraved part of me wanted my cock to be the first thing that entered her. I may have stuck my tongue in her, but it could only reach so far. My cock was going to be what breached her and stretched her wide open.

Her legs were trembling, and her hand was gripping tightly to the hair on my head as she moaned while calling out my name over and over. I couldn't bring myself to give a single fuck. She could rip every hair out by the root if she needed to as long as she came all over my face.

I felt her entire body stiffen, her thighs clamping so tight I could barely keep them held open. I glanced up her body to look at her face from my position between her legs and almost blew my load again at the gorgeous sight of her breasts heaving and her eyes squeezed shut.

I growled into her pussy. I wanted to order her to come, but I didn't dare stop what I was doing. I had found what worked to bring her pleasure, and I wasn't quitting until she came. Then finally, with her screams ringing in my ears, she broke, her orgasm making her clit throb in time with my thrashing tongue. I let up on the pressure but didn't stop until her whole body collapsed, going slack against the mattress. With a satisfied grunt, I let go of my hold on her. I slid up her body while shoving my pants and boxers down over my ass.

Without warning, I lined my cock up with her entrance, knowing that what I was about to do would hurt her. I notched the fat head of my cock there, pressing in just enough to make sure I wouldn't slip back out. Then, I wrapped my hand around her throat and waited for a beat. As soon as her eyes flew open at the feeling of my fingers squeezing to get her attention, I held her gaze with mine.

"Jack," she whispered hesitantly. "I've never done this before." Her face was red with her embarrassment. I flexed my fingers around her neck at her words. Suspecting it and knowing were two different things, and it brought the fierce possessiveness I'd been fighting for so long to come raging inside me.

"Neither have I." She stared up at me with eyes wide at my words.

With a hard thrust of my hips, I shoved my huge cock into her tight as fuck hole. I had to fight to keep my eyes open on hers, not wanting to miss a single reaction. Her cunt squeezed me like a vice, making me wince, and I fought hard to control my instinct to pound my lust into her. I watched as her eyes widened dramatically and then watered. A single tear slid from the corner of her eye, and I couldn't hold back from leaning down to lick the teardrop away, savoring it on my tongue.

"Your pain tastes almost as delicious as your cunt. I love knowing that I am where no man has ever been before."

She whimpered as I pulled back an inch, testing her reaction. As soon as I entered her, she froze from the shock and pain of the intrusion. It felt amazing, but I didn't want to hurt her any more than I already had. That wasn't the kind of pain that I wanted to give her.

I tightened my fingers around her throat until she gasped for the small amount of breath I allowed her. At the same time, her cunt spasmed around my length.

"This cunt is mine."

I loosened my grip again and watched as she took in a full breath. "It's yours, Jack." Her whispered words broke something in me, breaking me apart and rebuilding me again into another man. With her admission, she sealed her fate. She agreed she was mine, and now she would have to live with the consequences.

The King had found his Queen.

SALLY

With a savage snarl, he withdrew until I could feel that he left only the head of his dick inside me. I held my breath, knowing that he was about to wreck me in the best way possible. I knew going into it what I would get from this man. He was ruthless and brutal, and I didn't know what it said about me that having his hand around my throat, fully controlling my very breath, turned me on beyond my wildest dreams.

I stared directly into his eyes, trying to convey to him that I was all in. I was willing to submit, knowing that submitting didn't take away my power but gave me more. He stared back at me with a look full of gratitude and something else I knew I might never hear come from his lips. But that was okay because I knew beyond a shadow of a doubt that he had fully committed himself to me.

He slammed his hips forward again, and the shock of every nerve ending inside me lit up like fireworks, making me cry out in pleasure. Without pausing, he set a relentless pace, keeping me from sliding up the bed with his hand collaring my throat and a rough grip on my hip. His fingers were digging into my flesh, and I knew he was probably going to be leaving bruises by the time we were done, but that was another part of what I accepted from him. His mark was something that I would wear with pride and never try to hide. I wished his bruises could cover every scar he had kissed earlier, doing his best to show me that he didn't see me as less than because of them.

Both my cries and his grunts grew louder as he fucked me relentlessly. The headboard was banging loudly against the wall with every thrust and was probably ruining the wall, but I didn't think he would care, now or ever.

I tightened my fingertips on his shoulders, digging my nails deeply into him, causing me to have a moment of regret that we weren't skin to skin. He must have had the same thought because, in the next instant, he was kneeling over me while making sure to stay lodged deep inside of my pussy and tore the shirt over his head. It was the second time I had seen his chest, but it was the first time I had the opportunity to slowly rake my eyes over every dip and valley. I slid my hands from his shoulders to run my fingertips over his broad chest. He felt glorious under my hands, but I could feel what he had hidden under the ink that was covering every inch of his flesh. He ignored my furrowed brows, narrowing his eyes to growl a command.

"Put your nails back on me. I want my Queen to mark her King."

A sob caught in my throat at his words, overwhelmed by the intensity of emotion they brought, as he resumed his brutal pace. I did what he ordered, wrapping my arms around his shoulders and grabbing onto him with both hands. When he felt the bite of my nails digging into the flesh on his back, he hissed in pleasure.

I felt my legs stiffen almost painfully as another orgasm began to crest inside of me, and knew I wouldn't be able to hold on much longer. I briefly considered the fact that he was fucking me without a condom and that I wasn't on any birth control. It wasn't a good time in my life to even consider having a baby. But he wasn't slowing down. Even as I opened my mouth to warn him, a sinister smile curved his lips.

"I'm going to come deep inside your little cunt. You know that, don't you, my Queen?"

"Jack!" My cry wasn't one of panic, and his smile widened,

making me realize he had felt the way my pussy spasmed around his cock at his words.

It was all I needed to send me over the edge, that wicked smile and the words that all but bound us together permanently. I wanted to be owned by this man. I wanted to be the queen he had called me. I flung my head back on the pillow with a scream. My orgasm had him throwing back his own head with a shouted curse. He stilled his hips, pressing deep as he ground our pelvises together. I felt his cock jerking inside of me, and the warmth of his come filled me until it started leaking out from where we were joined.

He held still for long moments, his head hanging down, and his hands braced next to my head to keep him from collapsing on top of me. I sighed through my panting, my heart giving a flutter that he was trying not to crush me with his weight. He dragged heavy breaths into his lungs, and his skin was coated in a light sheen of sweat as if he had just run ten miles. Once the aftershocks of our orgasms subsided and our heart rates returned to something closer to normal, he slowly withdrew. I already hated separation.

He had taken me roughly, and I could see he thought it was too hard by the expression on his face. I didn't want him to have a single regret, so I lightly ran my fingertips over his jaw until he looked at me, his expression going soft for a brief moment. I was grateful I now had the right to touch him freely.

He sat back on his heels and spread my thighs wide enough to get a look at my pussy. I knew he had intended to check for damage, and I couldn't help but blush profusely. But as he stared, mesmerized at the sight of his come trickling out of me, I saw his cock thickening from where it had just been lying spent against his thigh. The sight was so erotic, seeing the lust sweep over him, that I wanted him to fuck me all over again.

Instead of giving in to what we obviously both wanted, he leaned forward, inhaling the new scent of both of us mixed together. He took his tattooed finger and slowly pushed his come back inside me. Once he was satisfied that he was back where he belonged, he began to lick me clean. He seemed to be chasing the flavor of both of us combined. It wasn't something I had ever considered before when I dreamed of him taking me, didn't know it would be so fucking hot.

"Come on." He pulled back once he was satisfied he'd cleaned me, stood up from the bed, and held his hand out to me. I took it without question, making him tip his lips up again. I had never seen him smile before tonight and vowed I would do my best to make sure I saw that expression on his face every day from now on. Everything was already changing, and I had never been happier.

He led me out of the room I had been staying in, down the short hall, and through his bedroom straight to the bathroom. He stopped at the toilet, pushing me down gently on one shoulder. I laughed while turning red from embarrassment.

"What are you doing, Jack?"

"I read that women need to go pee after they have sex to avoid getting a UTI." He turned away, walking over to the shower, which was much larger and nicer than the one in the hallway. His whole bathroom was better, done with gray walls and black tile. It was one of the only rooms that he seemed to have actually put money and time into in the whole house. Who knew that Jack would have a taste for luxury bathroom decor?

After he turned on the water to get hot, he turned back to me, but I had peed as quickly as I could, not ready for him to witness me doing something so intimate, which, when I thought about it, was kind of funny, given where his mouth just was. He watched as I stood up after flushing the toilet. He grinned wickedly as he watched a blush cover me from my hairline to the breasts I was trying to hide with one arm.

He held out his hand again. "Come shower." His voice was low and husky, making me think about the other things I had imagined him doing to me inside a shower. I squeezed my legs together at the filthy thoughts.

"Let's get you cleaned up so I can dirty you again."

TWENTY

As much as I had been going crazy inside the cabin, I hadn't really wanted to find myself spending my days at the clubhouse.

It honestly wasn't that bad. I got to sit in the office with Jack, curled up on the leather sofa while reading a book. I had ample opportunity to stare at him under my lashes, watching him glare at the laptop that seemed too small for his large hands. He also had a ton of paperwork. I wouldn't have expected a motorcycle club to have so many records to keep. But he had explained to me that the club, and he in particular, owned several businesses in town, which included the bar. I had known about the bar, of course. What I didn't realize was that he seemed to own more than half of the other businesses in Pumpkin Patch as well.

He had been rather open about things since we had spent our first night together just a few days ago. I learned that he was a silent partner in most of the businesses, financially backing them while letting the part owners run things as they saw fit. As long as they ran a good company, didn't try to embezzle money from it, and treated the other residents of the town right, he was content to allow them to make most of the decisions. But from what I understood, he was a very rich man.

"I invested in the first business when I was eighteen. On my birthday, the town lawyer revealed a trust I hadn't known was being held for me. Apparently, my mother had been setting aside money for my future for years." I watched as he stared vacantly off into the distance as if sinking into memories of his mother. It made me think of the scars I had felt on his chest, the ones I ran my fingers over every night as he fucked me in the bed that he now considered ours. I wasn't sure what they were from. A part of me wanted to hate the woman if she were responsible, if she had placed them there herself, or if she hadn't stopped someone else from doing it.

"I had no idea she had been saving money instead of using it to buy things we needed." He blinked and looked back at me. "The first business I gave money to was the deli."

"The deli?" I tilted my head, looking at him curiously. "Why the deli?"

He looked away from me and back to his laptop. I thought that was the end of the conversation and reluctantly picked up the book I had been reading and opened it again. My eyes darted back up as he spoke gruffly without glancing back at me.

"Because they fed me when I was younger."

After the silence stretched on without further explanation, I opened my mouth to ask questions, then shut it again with a click of my teeth when he suddenly slammed the lid of his laptop shut.

"Storytime is over. Come here." He pushed his chair back, making room for me in front of him on his desk. I wanted to protest, wanting to learn more about him as a boy and about why he would need to go to the deli for food, but his expression warned me not to ask. Plus, his eyes heated as they swept over me. I was still too entranced by him and under the spell he wove on my body every time he got his hands on me to deny what he was offering.

I closed the book, setting it next to me, not caring about losing my place, and stood. His eyes turned wicked as he watched me walk to him. I was wearing a pair of shorts that were practically indecent. They were something I would never have considered wearing outside of the bar during shifts. But Jack had been showing me with his actions how much he loved every inch of me. If I tried to cover my scars, he would get angry, telling me to be proud of what I had overcome instead of being ashamed of it. We still hadn't had the discussion yet about where I had gotten my scars. Just like we hadn't broached the subject about where he had gotten the ones covering his chest. Sometimes, I wanted to ask him if my scars were such a badge of honor, why did he go to such lengths to hide his?

As soon as I was within reach, he shot out a hand and gripped a hip tightly, yanking me into him hard. His hand went straight to my throat, making me moan with the desire already beginning to course through me. He had that effect on me. A single look, a single touch, a hand collaring my throat. He made me feel desired and worshiped. Owned. It was what I had always dreamt of as a young teenager while lying on my top bunk in the bedroom I shared with my three sisters. A man who would care for me and would take me away from the life I had. I hated what I had gone through. But I couldn't hate that it led me here to him.

"Jack," I whispered right before he brought our mouths together in a searing kiss. After that first night, he seemed to get better at literally everything he did with his mouth, hands, and cock. I hadn't known it could get better than that first time, but with time and practice, he had begun to play my body like it was his own personal instrument. I should have known he would be great at sex. He was the best at literally everything he did.

His hand stayed around my throat as the other skated down my body, over my breasts, down my flat stomach, and started inching under my shorts. He popped the button and slowly began to slide the zipper down, his fingers sweeping back and forth over the flesh he revealed inch by inch.

Just as he pulled the zipper as low as it could go and shoved his hand inside the minuscule panties he had bought along with the shorts I was wearing, the door to the office flew open.

"Hey, Prez, there's an emergency. Oh shit." Shock stood a couple of feet inside the office with a stupid grin on his face. "Hey, Sally. Sorry for, uh, barging in. Not used to the Prez, uh, having anyone in his office." The man didn't attempt to back out of the room or even pretend that he wasn't enjoying the rare opportunity of seeing his President with a woman.

I turned my head back to look at Jack. I had whipped my head around at the unexpected disturbance, but Jack hadn't looked away from my face. The dark look of lust was still clinging there, along with a heavy dose of annoyance. I expected him to pull his hand out of my panties at the disruption. Instead, he slipped his hand in even further until his middle finger found my opening. Then, with his eyes still on mine, he sank that finger deep inside me while his thumb brushed over my clit in one, then two circles.

He slowly withdrew his hand before standing up in front of me, the hard outline of his cock unashamedly on full display. I itched to reach out to grab it, to protest him leaving after barely touching me, but I swallowed back the words.

"I want you to stay in this room and wait for me to get back. Understand?"

I tore my eyes away from his hard dick and blinked up at him. I watched with glazed over eyes as he stuck the digit that was glistening with my moisture in his mouth and slowly sucked. A chuckle coming from behind me made my cheeks heat but also knocked me out of my lust induced stupor. "Yes, Jack."

He stepped into me and traced one of the scars that stretched from the corner of my mouth. "Good girl." And then he was gone, both he and Shock leaving with a quiet snick of the door. I sighed and glanced down at my open shorts. I'd heard of sexual frustration, but this was bullshit.

I hopped off the desk and straightened my clothes, fixing my zipper and refastening the button. I walked over to the couch and dropped down with a groan. I eyed my book but had no desire to pick it up. Instead, I grabbed the throw blanket off the back of the couch and laid down, using the throw pillow that had shown up along with the blanket a couple of days ago. I'd never taken Jack to be such a considerate man, but he always seemed to be attuned with my needs, often anticipating them before even I did. He was always bringing me a bottle of water or something to snack on. Then there were the clothes that appeared a few days ago.

With those thoughts swirling through my head, I lay there staring at the big wooden desk that Jack occupied most of the day. I must have drifted off to sleep at some point because a knock at the door had me jerking awake and looking around in dazed confusion. The sky was darker outside the window, telling me it had been at least a few hours since Jack left to take care of business.

A second knock sounded from the door. "Sally?" It was Kara. I hadn't seen her since just before my attack. I sat up quickly, then stumbled to my feet while trying to finger-comb my hair into place. I twisted the knob and pulled the door open to see Kara raising her hand to knock again.

"Hey, Kara," I said softly, unsure about how I should act around her now that my situation had changed so drastically.

She looked me up and down slowly. "Wow, you look great. You're practically glowing. And here, I'd heard that you had been attacked and nearly died! I wanted to come see you, but the Prez was only allowing a few people around. He took you to his house, huh? That's crazy!"

I tucked a strand of hair behind my ear, not knowing what to say to everything. "Yeah, he saved me, then took me to his house to recover."

She studied me again, her eyes lingering on the faint, barely noticeable fingertip marks on my neck. In Jack's defense, my skin bruised entirely too easily, not that I was ashamed of the way he branded me with his fingers. Looking at them made me feel warm and tingly inside. I wondered what she'd think of the much more distinguishable marks on my hips.

After a long silence that I was beginning to hate, she finally spoke again, a grin spreading over her face. "So, you and the boss, huh?"

Before I could come up with an answer, a voice yelled from down the hallway. "Kara! Come on! Get your ass moving. They are barely able to keep up at the bar. Get Sally, and let's go." The voice was only vaguely familiar. In my mind, I could picture one of the guys who worked the night shift at the bar, but I couldn't place which one.

Kara's smile dropped into an apologetic look. "Yeah, so that's why I'm here. We are slammed at the bar tonight and need help from anyone who can pitch in." With another quick glance at my throat, she asked me if I was well enough to work.

"I'm not supposed to leave." I grimaced and glanced back at the couch. "Jack told me to stay put until he got back."

She grinned. "Jack, huh? I didn't even know that was his name." She sighed as her grin dropped. "Well, shit. Are you sure? We could really use you." Loud stomping footsteps came down the hall, and we both looked over to see the guy, Craig or Carl, I couldn't remember, coming our way with an angry scowl.

"I told you to come on." He turned a dark look my way. "You're still on the payroll, are you not?"

I gave a reluctant nod. I hadn't known any different. Jack hadn't said anything about me not working for him anymore.

"Then let's fucking go." He turned on his heel as if his word were final.

"Wait!" I called out. I didn't want to disobey Jack. It wasn't as if I obeyed his whims mindlessly, but I also didn't want to go against him either. I was also not comfortable leaving the safety of his protection, and leaving the clubhouse or his house without him seemed dangerous. "Jack, uh, Bones, told me to stay until he got back." I finished weakly when he'd turned around to give me a death glare.

"You work for the Devil's. If you think the President wouldn't want all his bitches to earn their keep, you are more delusional than you look." He scoffed, then turned his back and walked out of sight.

Kara looked at me apologetically. "It's okay, Sally. I'm sure we'll be fine without you."

I chewed on my lip for a minute, but the guilt of leaving the rest of the crew to a bar full of rowdy patrons won over my need to stay put. "No, it's okay. I'll come."

She hesitated. "Are you sure?"

I gave a decisive nod. "Yeah, I'm sure." I closed the door firmly behind me as I stepped out into the hallway. "I don't have my uniform here, though."

"I'm sure we can find an extra for you somewhere in Mac's supply room."

We hurried down the hall together, neither one of us wanting to face the wrath of Craig. Or Carl. Whatever his name was.

TWENTY-ONE

SALLY

I was dressed in borrowed clothes, a tray in my hand filled with mugs of overflowing beer, and my back was killing me. I had forgotten how rough waitressing could be on a body, especially since I was wearing the sandals I'd dressed in that morning to go to the clubhouse.

I delivered the drinks to the table full of drunk and obnoxious men, dodging hands while ignoring their rude comments about my scars. As if I had never heard them before. I rolled my eyes. Most of the guys that came into the bar stayed on the side of respectful, knowing they were in a business owned by Devil's Nightmares. But sometimes, when they got a little too intoxicated, they let caution go and let whatever asshole thing that came to their tiny little minds free. The first few times, I had been embarrassed and hurt. I'd had to let it go quickly if I was going to be able to do my job. I was sensitive about my scars and tried to cover them as best as I could, but Jack had done a lot to help me accept them.

I walked around checking on my other tables, taking new orders, and gathering empties to return to the bar. There was no clock visible inside the building, so I had no idea how long I had been working. I couldn't help but worry my lip as I thought of Jack returning to find me gone. I wondered if I should have left a note for him so he wouldn't worry. I didn't know if anyone would tell him where I had gone. And then there was the worry about whether or not he was going to be angry at me for ignoring his order to stay put.

I set my tray down on the end of the bar and stretched out my back as discreetly as possible. My feet were tired from running around the bar all evening, but the soreness between my legs made me shiver every time I felt it. The memories from last night rolled through me, heating up my core and making me shift my legs, trying to dissipate the ghost sensation of Jack's face there.

I was waiting patiently for the Mac to get to me when a loudly whispered conversation finally penetrated my lust-filled memories.

"Look at her," The snickered words of Daisy were purposely loud enough for me to hear; I was sure of it. I looked around to see who else might be within earshot, but no one else was close enough to hear over the sound of music and boisterous laughter coming from a nearby table. "She's so pathetic."

I really thought those kinds of conversations between mean girls had ended in high school, but apparently, Daisy and her sidekick never grew up. I kept my back to them, pretending I couldn't hear their cruel words.

"She thinks she has half a chance with Bones. We all know he's going to get tired of looking at her fucked up face soon." Daisy had been playing this same broken record ever since I arrived with Kara.

"Hey, do you think her cunt is cut up too?" The question came from the friend, pissing me off and making my face turn red that they were having fun at my expense. Their giggles had me grinding my teeth.

"Ewww. I think I lost respect for Bones if he's willing to stick his cock in Frankenstein over there." Daisy's words had my back snapping straight and my muscles going rigid. How dare she?

"Frankenstein's Monster, you stupid twit." My words were gritted out through my clenched teeth, but even though my back was to the girls, I knew they still heard me. If I had to guess, I'd say her goal was to bait me into reacting and was just waiting for me to lose my shit. I was playing into her hands and couldn't find myself to care.

"Excuse me, whore?" Daisy's insults weren't very creative, but the venom in which she spewed them could curdle milk.

I slowly turned just my head so there would be no mistaking my words and eyed her nasty smirk. She was standing with one hip cocked out, her hand resting on it like she was a diva. "I said, his name is Frankenstein's Monster. Frankenstein was the doctor that created him, you uncultured swine. Maybe spread the pages of a book every now and then and give your legs a break for once."

The outraged gasps had me grinning wickedly despite myself. I turned back to stare at the side of Mac's head, trying to use my non-existent mind powers to make him hurry up.

The unexpected sharp pain on my scalp from having a fistful of my hair yanked had a gasp bursting from me. I hadn't thought she was stupid enough to actually lay hands on me in front of Jack's men, but I guess I underestimated her lack of intelligence.

I still had a hold of my tray when she swung me around and slapped me hard enough to have my head turn from the impact. It took a second for the hit to register through my shock, and then I felt a sting on my cheek and knew she had scraped me with her claws. I hoped she washed those fingernails. At least I'd had a tetanus shot recently.

Without thinking it through and relying solely on instinct, I jabbed the edge of my tray into her stomach as hard as I could. When she bent over with an oof full of pain, I brought the tray to my side and swung it like a baseball bat into the side of her head.

I watched in a strange kind of detachment as she fell to the floor, gasping for breath and clutching her stomach. Her self-cropped bar shirt had slid up, revealing her fake tits and pierced nipples. I didn't know why my eyes were drawn there, but I couldn't stop focusing on the flash of silver in the darkness of the bar.

When someone grabbed my chin, jerking it up roughly to meet their gaze, I realized I was breathing heavily. Jack's eyes bore into mine, looking murderous. I met his gaze without flinching. When I heard the metallic snick of his favorite switchblade opening, our eyes held steady. When he brought that blade to my cheek, I leaned into the metal, letting the flat edge of the cold steel soothe some of the sting from the scratch. The first night we had been together, I'd had a panic attack when he'd brought out his blade, and all I'd done was see it move toward my skin. I couldn't explain why now nothing this man did frightened me. Well, that wasn't entirely true. He was a scary motherfucker, and danger radiated from him. But I knew beyond all doubt he would never harm me. He'd gained my explicit trust with every look, with every thoughtful gesture. Every time he laid his hands on my body and held me close to his side at night to sleep, he had cemented my trust in him.

If there was one thing in this world I was absolutely certain of, it was that Jack would never hurt me. Now Daisy, on the other hand—she had probably sealed her fate by drawing my blood. His eyes roamed over my face as a mixture of concern, relief, and anger waged a fierce battle. He gave me the tiniest hint of a grin that I was sure nobody else would have been able to detect. There was also pride as he slowly slid the blade over my stinging cheek.

He turned away from me then and stood over the crying Daisy. She was still lying on the floor with tears making her heavy eye makeup melt down her cheeks as she clutched her abdomen. I winced as I thought of the pain she was likely in. I felt terrible that I'd hurt her. I wasn't a violent person and hadn't been in a real fight before.

She was wailing like a wounded animal, garnering the attention of everyone within earshot. When she noticed who was standing there, she dialed that shit up another notch, and I couldn't stop my eye roll if my life depended on it. My sympathy for her didn't last long. She would have done what I had to her and worse if I hadn't fought back. That girl hated my guts and would do anything to see me cry.

"Bones! Do you see what that bitch did to me?" She held her stomach and cupped her cheek as she got to her knees in front of Jack. Then, she had the audacity to reach out and try to touch his thigh. I was about to rip her hand away when Jack's hand shot out and grabbed a fistful of pink hair on the back of her head.

"What did you call my woman?" His voice was deep and gravelly, making a shiver run down my spine while, at the same time, a wave of lust rolled through me. He looked murderous as he glared down at her, yet somehow, it revved my engine.

Then Daisy's eyes went from pained and pleading to menacing in a second, and my breath froze in my lungs at her swift change of demeanor. All pretenses dropped as she showed her utter contempt. My blood ran cold as she made it clear to Jack how much she hated him. "Your woman? I pretended to have more respect for you than that. But if sticking your cock in the sliced-up whore is what gets you hard, then you're even more vile than I thought." She spat out her words with so much hatred and venom I was surprised she had been able to conceal it as well as she had.

I turned, darting my gaze around the bar to see who was watching, hoping to see one of Jack's trusted men nearby. The bar was too full of the town's people. I was afraid if he gave into his instincts right then, someone would see and report it. The people of Pumpkin Patch might appreciate the Devil's Nightmares for what they did for the town, but I didn't think they'd be quite so forgiving about witnessing casual murder while tossing back a few beers. When I caught sight of Shock pushing his way through the crowd, I relaxed a fraction. That was until I turned back around to see Jack bring his blade to Daisy's cheek.

I inhaled sharply as the blade made contact. Jack didn't press it in but held it there with the promise of death in his eyes. Daisy just stared up at him with hateful defiance; her chin jutted forward in a taunt.

Jack spoke quietly, the deadly menace evident in his gravelly voice. "Who do you work for?"

Daisy's eyes flickered with panicked terror before quickly concealing it with more hatred. "Go to hell where you belong— below the Devil's feet as his little lap dog. You're nothing but Nightmare scum." Her tone was full of scorn and contempt as she refused to give in to Jack's threat of violence, but I knew I hadn't imagined that quick flash of fear.

Jack canted his head to the side as he studied her closely. "Did you think that the name 'Devil's Nightmares' meant I worked for the Devil? No, sweetheart, I bring nightmares to the Devil himself. Didn't you know? I am the mother fucking Nightmare King."

My nerves were shot as I watched. I wasn't one to chew my fingernails, but there I stood, gnawing on my thumbnail with my eyes bouncing back and forth between my man and the woman, who was obviously a mole. As he pressed the blade ever so slightly into her cheek, a tiny bead of blood welled up on the surface of her skin, right where she had made me bleed. She whimpered, breathing hard through her nose at the pain, but clamped her lips closed tight. I looked over my shoulder with alarm, needing to check if anyone had seen what he'd done, but nearly sagged in relief against the bar when I saw the wall of club members surrounding us. There wasn't a single outsider close enough to see or hear. Whatever Jack did would be risky, being that we were in public, but at least he was shielded by his club. Even the girl who had been with Daisy was gone, likely having run off the second Jack showed up. My heart finally started to slow its frantic racing once I realized Jack had backup and that his club members would keep him safe from backlash.

"One more time, Daisy. Who. Do. You. Fucking. Work. For?"

"Go fuck yourself, Nightmare King," she sneered.

I covered my eyes, peeking through my parted fingers, expecting him to slice her throat right then and there, but instead, Jack just smiled wickedly, making Daisy swallow hard. Though fear was fairly wafting off her in waves, the hatred she carried for Jack was palpable. I wondered in awe how she had been able to hide it for so long. Those were some acting skills I would have killed for a year ago. I winced at my internal thoughts. Bad idiom to be using at the moment. Jack let her go and backed up a few steps. She wavered on her knees at the sudden release of her hair but straightened her spine before she could tumble over. Without taking his eyes off her, he called out quietly.

"Take her to the shed."

One of the bikers who had been helping to block any view of the bar patrons quickly stepped forward and snatched Daisy up by her elbow, hauling her to her feet. Daisy allowed him to lead her away without a single word of protest. With her jaw set in defiance, she glared at Jack and then moved her loathing on me. Her look was so full of venom that I shivered.

Jack's hand broke our eye contact by gripping my chin and lifting it gently. He studied my face, eyes carefully blank when stopping on my bloody wound again before grunting. "I am sending Barrel to take you home. You're to stay there. This time, you don't leave for any reason." I nodded my head while my gut churned and biting on my bottom lip. I had fucked up by ignoring what he had told me to do. I wasn't scared, but I didn't like the thought of him angry at me, either. "We'll talk when I get home." I nodded again.

"Let's go." Barrel walked past me, so I turned to follow him, giving Jack one last, long look, hoping he would be able to see how sorry I was. It was my fault that all this had happened. But, then again, if I hadn't, they might not have found out that Daisy was some kind of mole or plant. At the very least, she was a traitor. I sighed in defeat, my shoulders slumping.

Following Barrel outside the bar, we came to his bike, and I hesitated for just a beat. Jack was the only person I had ever ridden with. It almost seemed too intimate an act to be pressed up against anyone other than him. Barrel stopped next to his motorcycle and looked back at me, then down to the bike. He cursed under his breath.

"Fuck. Prez would have my nuts if I put you on the back of my bike." He looked around until his eyes landed on the van that had taken all of us girls to the fight night at the warehouse. It felt like years ago, since so much had happened since then. "Come on, we'll take the van. That way, I can keep my balls intact. I'm kind of fond of them."

I couldn't help the small laugh that bubbled out of me. I hadn't had much interaction with Jack's men other than taking orders and the occasional hello, so I hadn't realized that Barrel was actually kind of funny and charming. By the time he had pulled up to the cabin, my cheeks were aching from laughing and smiling so hard. I finally understood why so many of the girls seemed to fall all over themselves to get his attention. Once you got it, he gave it all to you. I could imagine that, for a lot of girls, having his undivided attention was a heady thing.

"Thanks, Barrel," I said, wiping a stray tear from the corner of my eye. "I appreciate the ride."

"No problem. Do you have a key?"

I grimaced, thinking about how I left my things behind at the bar in the back changing room. "I forgot it. But I know where the spare is." Thank goodness there was a hidden key for times like this.

"Good. I'll wait here until you get inside." He jerked his chin in that way I noticed the bikers tended to do as I just smiled and climbed out of the van. It took me a couple of minutes to locate the correct rock, but finally found the spare key. After waving off Barrel from inside the house, I closed and locked the door, making sure to set the alarm so I didn't piss Jack off any more than I already had.

With a heavy sigh, I walked down the quiet hallway and into the primary bedroom before peeling off the skin-tight bartending clothes. Unable to stand the smell of alcohol and stale beer any longer, I took a quick shower. After blow-drying my hair until it was no longer damp, I crawled into bed and stared at Jack's pillow. I finally reached over and grabbed it, hugging it to me.

TWENTY-TWO

THE NIGHTMARE KING

I slammed the door open so hard it banged off the wall as customers scattered out of my way. With my fists clenched tightly at my sides and my teeth grinding together, my gaze went straight to Barrel's bike. Seeing that it was still sitting there, I relaxed fractionally, realizing that he had been smart enough not to take home my woman on the back of his motorcycle. Even though I had ordered him to, I would have had to hurt him if she had wrapped those arms around him.

"Ready, Prez?"

I grunted in response to Shock's question, heading over to my bike and climbing on. Side by side, we rode out of the parking lot, kicking up gravel as we headed toward the club compound where the shed was located.

The shed was more like an oversized garage with a drain in the middle, an industrial-sized walk-in freezer, and a furnace in the back. It was likely the cleanest place on the entire compound with the amount of bleach that we used to wipe away any traces of blood. Just to be certain, if any questions were raised as to what the building was used for, it doubled as a deer processing room. Which was also why we had an industrial-sized walk-in freezer full of deer meat. It came in handy whenever we held club cookouts. Win-fuck-ing-win.

Shock and I came to the outside of the shed and stopped next to the bikes that were already parked there.

"Looks like Lock brought friends," Shock raised his hands to cup around his cigarette as he lit it and squinted at me through the haze of smoke. "How do you want to play this? We've never had a female guest before. It kind of goes against our creed."

"What goes against our creed is spies, liars, and traitors. That woman in there has been working for someone and has shared who knows how much information with them for over a year." I shook my head. "Fuck, I don't even know how long she's been here. Longer?" It didn't matter. Even if it had only been a day, I couldn't allow what she'd done to stand. If word got out that someone had sent a spy to our club and I let them walk away, I'd look weak. It would open the door for someone to try to take our territory or challenge me for my position.

Besides, the woman had hurt my Queen. I should have kicked her out weeks ago after I'd seen her catty attitude towards Sally one too many fucking times.

I strode to the door and punched in the code. After waiting for the light to turn from red to green and the door to beep, I yanked on the handle, striding into the large open space. Usually, when we had interrogations, we stripped the man of his dignity first. By making him hang from the hook in the middle of the room completely naked, he was left feeling vulnerable. It tended to lower their defenses, scared the piss out of them, sometimes literally, and got them talking faster. Dealing with a woman was going to cause unique challenges.

I wasn't surprised to see Lock standing with his arms crossed in front of a pissed off Daisy, looking uncertain about how he should proceed. All of my men knew my stance on women. They were to be respected, not treated like disposable blowup dolls for their pleasure. And above all, they were always to only be used with consent. So, knowing that I wouldn't want to strip a woman naked in order to make her vulnerable during interrogation left him floundering about how to proceed.

I stalked to the table where tools had already been laid out. They were all clean, scrubbed, and soaked after the last time they had been used. I glanced around until I spotted a rope lying coiled in the corner of the room after someone killed a deer. Pulling out my knife, I went over to the rope, sliced a length off the long coil, and brought it over to the woman with her wrists bound, standing over the drain in the middle of the floor with a glare on her face and a gag in her mouth.

"She wouldn't stop running her mouth about how we would all regret laying hands on her 'when her brother finds out'." I grunted at Lock's use of air quotes. I could imagine how much the woman had likely ranted. That was fine. She'd be telling me what I wanted to know soon enough.

I tied a loop and a knot around each end of the rope and hooked one end to the hook. The other end went around her wrists after a slight struggle before Shock held them still. She was a fighter. I had to give her credit. Her muffled curses were easy enough to make out through the gag, so I didn't bother removing it yet.

Once I had her hands secured with the rope, I jerked her arms above her head and pulled the rope tight at the knot, shortening the distance between her wrists and the hook until she stood on her toes. It would be uncomfortable. Her shoulders would be screaming in agony soon, and fear would be setting in quickly. It wouldn't take long for her to realize that she was truly stuck with no way to escape. I hoped it was all the tactics I would need to use to make her talk. If it wasn't, well, I would just have to do what I had to do.

"This can be easy, or it can be difficult. I'm not going to lie. I hope you make it difficult." I made sure she could see the dead-eyed stare I gave the world, letting them know that there was nothing they could do that would affect me. It made anyone who saw it swallow in fear. You couldn't intimidate a man who felt nothing.

I yanked the gag out of her mouth and tossed the damp material to the floor. "You stupid mother fucker!" I crossed my arms over my chest and tilted my head as she screamed at me. Regardless of how it might appear to my men, I didn't want to be here. I had more important places to be, and dealing with this woman was just keeping me from getting to my Queen. I knew Sally was upset and had sensed how angry I was. I didn't like leaving our business unfinished, and I needed her to understand that she couldn't disobey me, not when she was jeopardizing her safety. But I would do whatever was required to discover the information this woman was hiding before I went home to deal with my little Queen.

As the screaming continued for several more minutes, I simply stood with my arms crossed and stared her down until she finally stopped. With her chest heaving and her breasts threatening to escape the short shirt she was wearing, Daisy began to tremble. Whether it was from the discomfort of having her arms wrenched up painfully or the reality of her situation finally settling in, I didn't care.

"Who is your brother?" It was a simple question I didn't expect an answer to... yet. But she would talk. They all did.

"Fuck you, Bones. You are nothing. The Boogeymen are going to take everything from you, starting with your freak of a woman. I hope they split her apart as they take turns destroying her cut-up cunt."

My eyes narrowing was the only outward sign I gave that I was a heartbeat away from slitting her throat. "So," I said as calmly as I could while walking back over to the table of sharp, as well as not-so-sharp, implements. I perused the options available as distaste filled my gut for what I would have to do next. "Your brother is a Boogeyman." I finally selected a pair of pliers and walked back over toward her, holding up the pliers, allowing her to clearly see what I was holding. "What have you told him about the Nightmares?"

She licked her lips as she danced on her toes, letting her weight settle on one foot before switching to the other. She eyed the pliers nervously. "Look, just let me go and he won't kill you or your bitch."

I chuckled darkly. "That wasn't what I asked you." I placed one knee on the ground in front of her and studied her toes. If she were a man, I would have just started cutting body parts off. Seeing a woman helpless and being abused brought back too many dark memories that I found difficult to push back.

I placed the pliers against one of her big toes and clamped down on the red-painted nail with the pliers, squeezing hard with a firm hold. I paused, looking up at her, disgust and self-hatred roiling in my gut. "Who is your brother?"

Her lip trembled as a tear escaped from one eye. But she narrowed those hostile eyes at me, and I knew what she would say before she opened her mouth. Her screams rang out as I pulled, removing the first painted toenail from her foot. I shifted the pliers to the next toe and asked the same question.

It took three more attempts, creating a small pile of red-painted nails, before she broke, spilling her secrets. Curses rang out in the room as all of my men straightened their backs and looked like they were already mentally preparing to go to war.

"Why would Oogie send his sister into the Nightmare's lair?" I asked her as I stood back up to loom over her. She was shaking so hard that the chain the hook was attached to rattled as she sobbed into her arm.

Oogie was the president of the Boogeymen. He was a big, mean motherfucker, and the stories about the shit he had done to both men and women were enough to have my blood turn to ice in my veins. If he got ahold of my woman, he wouldn't hesitate to hurt her precisely how Daisy had described earlier. He wouldn't stop at a few toenails. No, Sally would never be the same. If she survived at all, death would be a kindness. I would never let that happen. Every Boogeyman would be a pile of ash and bone before even one of them laid a single goddamn finger on her.

"H-he hoped I could lure you into bed. I w-was supposed to slit your th-throat. But you never even l-looked at me twice."

I shook my head in disgust. "It would never have been that easy. He had to have known that. He threw you to the devil, not expecting you to come back."

"No! You're wrong!" She screamed, spit, and snot running down her chin. Thick rivulets of black-tinted tears ran down her red cheeks.

I sighed at her denial of the truth. "What secrets have you told Oogie about us? About me?"

"Nothing, I swear! I was never able to get close enough to learn anything important."

I believed her. I glanced over at Barrel, who was standing frozen in the corner with his arms crossed over his chest. His green hair was sticking up in every direction like he'd been repeatedly running his hands through it. He met my stare with hard, cold eyes and slowly shook his head. No, he wouldn't have given any of our secrets away.

I was about to do something that went against my instincts. At the same time, I couldn't let Daisy return to the Boogeymen. I pulled the knife from my back pocket and pressed the latch. The sound of the metal sliding against metal rang out loudly in the room. Her eyes went to the blade as I lifted it, and her body shook as she sobbed quietly. Regret and terror clouded her eyes until she squeezed them shut.

I raised the blade higher, and with one swift swipe of the knife, the girl fell to the floor. We all stood there in silence as she continued to cry pitifully until she opened her eyes and stared up at me in confusion.

I crouched next to her and danced the blade close to her face. "I'm giving you a gift, Daisy. Something I've never given to another soul that's ever been brought into my shed. A chance."

"Wh-what?" Her whispered word was hoarse and disbelieving as her eyes darted from my face and back to the blade repeatedly.

"I'm letting you live." I closed the blade and slid it back into my pocket, standing up to my full height as I stared down at her. All the possibilities of my actions played through my head as I questioned my sanity. "I'm going to give you money, and you are going to get on the next bus out of town. You're going to ride that bus far, far away from here. You will forget you ever knew this life, this town, and these people. You don't have a brother. You were never here." I stared hard at her, letting her see her death in my eyes. "If I ever see you again, you won't get the chance to take another breath."

I stepped back, giving her room to scramble to her knees. She winced as her foot scraped against the floor, but what I saw in her eyes told me all I needed to know. She was going to take the out I was giving her. She also knew I wasn't the only one who would slit her throat if she ever returned. Her own brother would do it before I ever had a chance to.

TWENTY-THREE

SALLY

The shift in the air woke me seconds before the mattress moved with the weight of another body. Before my brain could fully come awake, I was being caged in. Jack's large body loomed over me, with his arms on either side of me and his legs trapping mine.

"Jack," I whispered, relaxing my cheek back into the pillow. I wanted to know what had happened while, at the same time, I didn't. I hated Daisy. Hated the way she treated me, hated the way she had betrayed the Devil's Nightmares, but I didn't want to hear that Jack murdered her.

"You were a bad girl," His deep, gravelly voice rasped into my ear as he ran his nose down to the back of my neck and nipped me there. "You disobeyed me when I distinctly told you to stay in my office."

I whimpered, pushing my rear up against his front. I could feel the naked, hard length of him brushing against my thigh where my nightshirt had ridden up in my sleep. He ran a hand down the center of my back, pausing at my ass. He palmed the cheek there, and I pressed into it, telling him I wanted more without saying the words.

I would be ready to beg him in another minute of his continued teasing.

"I'm sorry," I moaned. "They said they needed the help."

His hand disappeared a second before heat exploded on my ass. I gasped as he smoothed his palm over me, rubbing away the sting he'd caused. "You obey no one but me. You follow no one's instructions but mine." He shifted until he was lower on the bed, his arms next to my hips. In another quick movement, my thighs were jerked open.

"Bad girls get punished."

I whimpered again, wondering if he was going to spank me some more, wondering if I wanted him to. I had never been spanked before. My parents were shitty at parenting their kids, but they had never laid a hand on any of us. I had a feeling that even if they had, this would be far different than anything I might have experienced as a kid.

The nightshirt was yanked up my body and over my head before I knew that he was going to do it. My hair went flying in every direction, obscuring my vision in the dim lighting of the room. The shirt trapped my arms and hands, and all I could do was feel as his big, calloused hands roved over my scarred back and down to the globes of my ass. Jack yanked my hips up roughly until I was on my chest and knees, with my face turned to the side on the pillow. My every breath caused strands of hair to blow out as it covered my face. My arms stretched out above me kept me from being able to reach back or pull the hair from my face.

"This is what's going to happen, little Queen," his voice rasped from above me while his hands continued to roam as if he couldn't get enough of the feel of my skin. "I'm going to spank this delicious little ass. Then, I'm going to fuck you. You will take it like the good girl I know you can be." He lifted a hand, and even though I expected it, I still couldn't help the startled cry as his palm connected with the flesh of my bottom.

I stiffened my muscles, readying for the next blow, but instead, he soothed the sting again. The combination of harsh and soft kept me on edge, never knowing what to expect. Each time he spanked me, the heat grew, not just in my ass but in my belly, then spreading to the rest of me. By the time he had spanked me a dozen times, moving the blows to different parts of my bottom, never striking the same spot twice, I was a panting, quivering, crying mess. I was crying because of the pain, but I was also crying because of the sexual frustration I hadn't known I'd feel. I wanted him inside of me with a desperation that was new to me.

Jack shifted behind me, and I knew he was lining himself up with my core. I felt him swipe the head of his cock over my entrance and heard him hiss.

"You're soaked, little Queen. Did you enjoy me spanking your magnificent ass?"

I whimpered, shifting my knees, wishing I could see him. He sounded different and had a gruffness to his tone that he generally didn't have when we were alone. Whatever he had done with Daisy had affected him. He needed me, needed this. I could help him work through the demons that were eating away at him.

"Fuck me, Jack. Make me pay for being a bad girl."

He growled low in his throat, and suddenly, I was filled with a hard thrust that had my knees sliding out from under me. With a curse, he wrapped an arm under my hips, lifting me back up, and held me there, keeping me in place for his brutal thrusts. Every stroke lit me on fire inside, targeted every nerve ending, and sent shockwaves of pleasure zinging through me. I choked on my cries of pleasure, hair sticking to my cheeks wet with tears.

"More, Jack!" I screamed, needing more. Needing everything.

He hammered into me harder than he ever had before, and I loved every second of it. I soon found myself teetering on the edge of the most immense orgasm I had ever experienced. The sheer magnitude of it scared me. I was afraid of who I would be when it was over. I didn't know what would be left of the person I was.

A hand swept up my hair, gathering it in a fist, finally allowing me to take in a full breath of air. My head was tilted back, pulled by the solid grip on my hair. My cries got louder, and my legs began to tremble with my impending release.

"Do. Not. Come." Jack's words were a command as he increased his pace further. I was on the desperate edge of a knife's blade, needing to fall but not wanting to disappoint him. I squeezed my inner muscles desperately, trying to hold myself back. He hissed harshly between his teeth as my walls fluttered and clenched tightly. "Fuck!" He bellowed loudly. Then, his other hand let go of the bruising grip he had on my hip. A hard slap to my ass made me scream in agonized pleasure.

"Fuck! Fucking come. Come all over my cock. Soak me! Come now!" He roared. With his permission finally granted, I sobbed and squeezed my eyes shut as wave after wave of fierce satisfaction swept through me. Goose bumps covered every inch of me as I fell head first into the orgasm he'd wrung viciously from me.

I vaguely heard his curses and yells as he thrust once, twice, then stilled deep inside me, spilling his warmth and filling me up. I lay there, my face half in the pillow as I struggled for breath. My whole body shook with aftershocks. His body blanketed mine, pressing me firmly into the mattress, and I welcomed his weight and warmth.

Too soon, he rolled to my side. I whimpered as his weight left me, his cock withdrawing left me feeling empty.

"Are you okay?" He ran his fingers through my tangled hair, smoothing it away from my face. I didn't bother looking at him. I was still trying to get a hold of my emotions. Somehow, he had wrung me out until I felt almost hollow inside. It was a good feeling, even as it left me feeling bereft. "Little Queen, look at me. Please?"

It was the plea that finally had me cracking my eyelids open, blearily looking up at his concerned face. "I'm okay," I croaked, my throat feeling dry and raspy. I must have screamed more than I thought.

He swept my face clear of all the hair and gently pulled the shirt from around my arms, tossing it to the ground beside the bed. He gathered me in his arms, turning me until I was cradled in his warmth. I sighed and snuggled my cheek against his smooth chest.

He rumbled out a low chuckle, running his thumb over my cheek. I blinked up at him, finally able to see him clearly, and smiled.

"There she is." His deep voice in that adoring tone had another shiver running over me.

"I love you, Jack." My words were soft, mumbled in a sex-drunken slur, but they were unmistakable in the quiet room. His entire body froze for a solid second before he pulled me closer to him and nuzzled into my hair.

"I don't know what love is," he rasped out against my head. "But what I feel for you has taken over every part of me. I've never wanted another woman before you. I never thought I could touch a woman and feel what I do for you. If I lost you, my world would stop spinning. Life would cease to have any meaning."

I lifted my hand and ran it over the stubble along his jaw, tears blurring my vision. "That's love, Jack."

He sighed and kissed my head, then rested his cheek against me. "Then, my little Queen, you better hope that nothing ever happens to you."

When he remained silent after those ominous words, I pulled back and looked at him in his black eyes. There was a depth there I hadn't seen in anyone else. They were so deep that a person could drown in them, swallowed up by the darkness in the bottomless pits. "What would you do?" It was spoken softly, letting him know I was scared of the answer, of the truth. I didn't want to be responsible for this man's sanity, but at the same time, I couldn't live without him, either. So, didn't that make me just as desperately insane as he was?

"There would be nothing left once I was done."

I swallowed hard as we stared into each other's eyes, seeing the truths we each held. I couldn't promise him what he needed. There was no way to guarantee that I would never be hurt or taken from him. Life was a bitch, and good people died every single day from illness or accidents. Young children and innocent babies died. People who had never hurt another living soul became ill. I couldn't promise that would never happen to me.

"I'll do whatever I can to stay safe." It was all I could promise him. It was the only truth I could give. But it was the truth. I would make sure I kept my oath for as long as I could. Because I loved him enough to never want to cause him pain.

"I was kept as a prisoner for months," I began, knowing that it was time to tell him everything. He was committing himself to me, and if I was going to give every part of myself to him, I needed to give it all, including the ugliness. His whole body went rigid as he waited for me to elaborate. "It was my first real job. I left home, looking for more than I could have in our small town. If I had stayed, I knew I would be stuck there forever. I would have a million babies, just like my mom. I would have married the first man that asked. And I would have been miserable for the rest of my life."

I shuddered, looking away from his probing eyes. I knew my story was already all over the place, jumping from one thing to another as my brain tried to form a coherent thought. "I took all the money I was given as graduation gifts from family, packed a suitcase, and got on a bus bound for Hollywood. Becoming a star wasn't as easy as I thought it would be." I sighed. I ran a fingertip over the tattoos covering his chest, tracing the white bones that made up the ribcage of the skeleton he wore on the outside of his body.

"I found a job as a clerk at a plastic surgeon's office. I was so happy to have been able to find a job like that. Most people that went to Los Angeles looking to become a movie star ended up working in dead-end jobs as waitresses, or worse, found themselves on sketchy casting couches that ended up being nothing but porn studios." I shuddered at the revolting thought. "Instead, I found myself strapped to a surgeon's table in what could have been an operating room. But it was really just a basement. At least it was clean."

I continued on, knowing that if I didn't finish my story, I would lose the nerve to do so. I could also sense that Jack wouldn't be able to hold onto his rising anger much longer. "He was well respected, the plastic surgeon to the wealthiest clients in Beverly Hills and Hollywood. Apparently, though, he had a dark side that no one knew about. He was considered the best. Always left his clients completely satisfied with his perfect technique, never leaving the trace of a scar behind."

I felt him shift his hand, and he lightly ran a calloused finger over a scar on my shoulder, then moved his finger along my skin until he was tracing one of the long scars over my cheeks. I held back a flinch at the touch there. "While he was delivering perfect results to the wealthy clients, he was operating on me, leaving me with the worst scars imaginable."

His fingertip left the scar, and his whole hand cupped my cheek, tipping my head back until I was looking back into his dark eyes. "You're the most beautiful woman I have ever seen. These scars," he said, his eyes roaming over my face, taking in the lines that closely resembled stitches on a patchwork doll, "they tell me how strong you are. You are a survivor. Not everyone survives their scars. Not everyone comes out with their soul intact."

TWENTY-FOUR

SALLY

I ran a finger past one of the tattooed ribs and over one of the scars hidden beneath the black ink that covered his chest.

"What scars do you hide, Jack?" I whispered.

He sighed deeply, and I thought he was going to refuse to answer. It made me sad because, though he wanted my past, he didn't want to share his. But then he lowered his head and kissed my lips sweetly with his before placing his forehead on mine and closing his eyes.

"My mom was a complicated woman. She had demons that I couldn't understand. She turned to drugs, alcohol, and sex well before I was born. After she had me, nothing changed. She continued the same lifestyle; she just had another mouth to feed. I learned at a young age to stay away when she was... entertaining.

"I was around six years old when the first man came into my room after my mom passed out." It was my turn to stiffen as burning hot rage began to fill me. I blinked back the tears that filled my eyes, knowing he didn't want or need my pity. It was hard, though, not to pity a defenseless little boy. "The man liked to use his knife. He was a regular of my mom's, so he was around a lot." His eyes grew vacant as he stared out into the dark room.

"When my mom realized what was happening, she kicked him out, but not until he had beaten her bloody, virtually left for dead. It was the first time I had threatened a man. I used his own knife on him, slicing him to the bone on his arm. He never returned. It was a couple more years until the next man came along, attempting the same thing. I still wasn't big enough to fight back. A locked door never stopped those men."

I closed my eyes as desperate grief filled every part of me.

"Eventually, though, I was bigger, stronger than whoever came after me. I stopped any man who tried to get rough with my mom. We had a couple of good years. As good as they could be with her still drinking and doing drugs nearly every night. Whoring was all she knew. All of that changed when my father murdered her." He looked at me then, focusing those eyes back on me, letting me see the rage, the helplessness, and the pain. "And then I slit his throat."

My voice was a choked whisper. "Good."

He held me tight and pulled the blankets up over us. "Sleep now, little Queen."

I nodded, though I wasn't sure how I'd ever be able to rest well ever again with the picture of a young little Jack being abused by monsters, turning him into the man he'd one day have to become to survive.

THE NEXT TIME I woke up, it was by stretching my arm out, reaching across the bed, and feeling nothing but cold sheets. I cracked one eye open to verify that I was indeed alone. A sound from the end of the bed caught my attention. I turned my head on the pillow, swiping back my tangled hair, internally groaning at the feel of the mess on my head. It was going to take a lot of conditioner to get the strands smooth again.

Zero sat up, wagging his tail at me. I smiled at him as he padded across the covers to my side before huffing and curling up next to me. "He left you to guard me, didn't he?" I ran my hand over his soft white coat, thinking back to the first time I had seen him. I wasn't sure what Jack had used to get all that blood out of his fur, but whatever he'd done had Zero looking shiny and pristine.

We lay together for a while as my mind went over all we had discussed late last night. Some of what we'd done was a blur of passion and excitement. I felt my face heat at the memory of his hand spanking me. I wiggled a little bit to check, and, yes, I still felt the sting there as my skin brushed against the sheet. I had a feeling it would last most of the day. I couldn't bring myself to mind, not when it had been such an erotic experience. I didn't think I'd want to be spanked often, but every now and then? I could get behind that.

Did I really tell him I loved him while half out of my head, drunk on orgasm afterglow? I wondered if he thought I was just saying it as a heat of the moment thing. But he also gave me his own confession. One I would hold close to my heart forever. He hadn't exactly told me he loved me. But the words that he said might as well have been written by one of the greatest romantic minds of the past.

I gave Zero one last pat and scratched behind his ears, then scooted out of the bed, padding over to the bathroom with a grimace on my face. Jack usually cleaned me up after we had sex. He had a habit of making me go pee afterward, too, wanting to ensure I wouldn't end up with a UTI. It was adorable, though I'd never tell him that. I think it amazed and shocked everyone around us that he was so different with me. Though they saw him soften towards me in public, even then, they didn't see how he would smile at me and how gentle those hands that had likely killed many men could be when he touched me. I liked that I had a part of him that nobody else would ever have. Except for maybe our children one day.

The thought of children with Jack had a wistful smile growing on my face. As I reached for the handle in the shower, I froze. A wave of cold dread, then shocked delight, washed over me as I stood there half in the shower, half out, my hand hovering in the air.

"Little Queen?"

Jack's gravelly voice knocked me out of my dazed state, and I stared up at him with wide eyes. My reflection caught the corner of my eye, and I turned to see the mirror. I was a mess. My hair was tangled around my shoulders from where he had gripped it roughly in the night and had been caught in my nightshirt after he pulled it over my head. But it was my face that had my attention. I was paler than usual, my widened eyes full of shock, making the blue stand out brightly. There was fright, easy to read, but there was also a hint of hope.

"Sally?" Jack gripped my chin gently and raised my face to meet his concerned gaze. "What's wrong? Are you hurt?"

I opened my mouth to speak, but nothing came out. I closed it again, swallowed, then cleared my throat. "I, uh," I darted my eyes to the side. I had no idea how he would take the news. We had never spoken of the possibility, though the fact that we hadn't used protection in the past couple of weeks since we'd started sleeping together was as much on him as it was on me. Maybe it was too soon? Perhaps I was just late because of all the changes in my life lately. I cleared my throat again and moved my eyes back to look at his beautiful face. "Jack..."

I didn't know what to say. I could be wrong. I was only a couple days late, though I was never late. Not even when I'd been held captive in that horrid basement. My mind flew through the possibilities of what I should do, what I should say. Then Jack held up a bag, and my eyes became mesmerized by what was clearly visible through the plastic.

I darted my gaze back to his to see him smiling. "I thought you could use this."

With trembling fingers, I reached for the bag, but he pulled it away before I could touch it. "You bought a pregnancy test?" I whispered as I watched him step to the counter and set the bag down. He reached inside and plucked the box out, quickly ripping the top open and withdrawing a test wrapped in white. Without hesitating, he had the wrapper open and the test held in the air. After looking it over, he pulled the cap off one end and held it out to me.

"You haven't peed yet, have you?" I narrowed my eyes at his amused smile but shook my head slowly. He knew I usually turned the shower on to heat up as soon as I woke up, then did my business before hopping in to wash the night away. "Good. Sit. Pee." He waved the stick toward the toilet.

How this man seemed to be so on top of every single thing in his life was a wonder I would probably never figure out. With a huff, I snatched the stick from him and stomped over to the toilet, but inside, I was a tangled mess of girlish delight. He didn't look bothered in the least that we could have made a baby after barely knowing each other. In fact, he looked rather smug.

I didn't even bother trying to tell him to leave. That had never worked yet, and with the way he was staring with intense eyes, I knew it would have been like telling a wall to move. As I held the stick, my breath caught. I wasn't sure what I wanted, though that wasn't true, was it? I wanted this man more than I wanted to breathe. He had become my everything, and now that the possibility was in front of us, I knew I wanted his child.

With a deep breath to center myself, I allowed myself to relax. Closing my eyes, I did what I needed to. Jack was there in a heartbeat, taking the stick from me, replacing the cap on the end, and setting it on the counter. He washed his hands as I cleaned myself up. He moved over so I could wash my own hands as my eyes stayed glued to the stick the whole time. I felt his fingers on my chin and broke the staredown with the test to meet his eyes.

"You're mine, you know that, right?" His black eyes were fierce as they looked into mine. I could read his emotions there, which he rarely showed, even to me. I lifted a hand to grasp his wrist.

"I'm yours."

"Good. No matter what, you will always be mine. You will never leave my side, Sally. You're here to stay."

Oh. Oh no. There was one thing I hadn't told him yet. Something that he wouldn't be happy about, and I wasn't sure how to tell him I had to leave in about three months. I started to open my mouth to tell him, dreading his reaction, when my phone rang from the other room. He let my face go, and his eyes softened.

"Go ahead." I nodded and started to step away but paused. I stepped up on my tiptoes and placed a kiss on his lips before dropping back to dart into the bedroom to grab my phone. There was only one person who would be calling me, and I hadn't heard from her in weeks.

"ADA Ramirez, how are you?" I kept my eyes on Jack, who had stepped into the room, following me with his eyes. His eyebrows drew together as he heard my greeting.

The urgent tone of her voice had my spine stiffening and cold dread, making the fine hairs on the back of my neck stand on end. "Sally, there's a problem. Listen, I don't know if he knows where you are, but you need to leave. Go somewhere else. Now, quickly."

I let out a sob and pressed my fist to my mouth. "What happened?" I asked, my voice barely above a whisper. The phone was snatched from my hand. Jack pressed the speaker button so we could both hear Ramirez's words as she said something that could only have come from my worst nightmares.

"The other girl that was a witness for Dr. Stein turned up dead three days ago. We had gotten an email from her saying she wanted to talk to us and that there was something we needed to know. Before we could meet with her, she disappeared. I didn't find out that she was dead until this morning." She paused and took a deep breath as if she were bracing herself. Just that sound made me want to run away. I grabbed Jack's hand and gripped it tightly.

"Sally, Dr. Stein has disappeared, too. I was just informed this morning that three days ago, he failed to report to his parole officer."

"Three days..." my voice was barely audible, but she must have heard them because she began to frantically demand that I leave my current location again.

"Please, Sally. You need to leave. He may already be wherever you are."

"How did he find her?" Jack's harsh, growled words had Ramirez fading into silence before asking me what was obviously a 'what the fuck' question.

"Sally?"

"It's okay, ADA Ramirez. You can speak freely. Jack is my... boyfriend," I finished lamely.

"I'm a lot more than her boyfriend. How did he find her?" He demanded again.

"I'm not sure that he has. Sally told no one where she was going, but her phone number was on file. It wouldn't take more than a two-bit hacker to trace her location. Look, Jack, if you care about Sally, you need to convince her to leave. And she needs to leave her phone behind. Sally, don't use any credit cards. Cash only. Don't use your ID for any reason that would have your information entering a computer system. Obviously, you won't need to be back here for the trial in three months. This stunt he's pulled has guaranteed him a spot in the penitentiary with or without your testimony."

"Do you know if he's the one that killed that other girl?" I dreaded the answer but needed to know. As far as I understood it, Dr. Stein was a monster, but he hadn't actually killed anyone.

She sighed, sounding much older than her thirty-something years. "Tests are still being run. The forensics system runs pretty fucking slowly and is always overtaxed. But, yes, it looks like he is likely the one that murdered her."

"I'll take care of everything," Jack said. Then, without waiting for anyone to say their goodbyes, he punched the disconnect button and tossed my phone onto the bed. He turned to me slowly, the look of a man ready to kill. I swallowed back any protests that I would have made about him being rude to Ramirez as I looked up at him. "There's more you needed to tell me." His voice was flat, hollow.

"I was going to tell you the rest of it today," I offered up lamely.

"It's too late for that."

I sighed and ran a hand through my hair, the fingers getting caught on the tangles I still hadn't brushed out. "You're right. I'm sorry."

I walked over to the dresser and opened the drawer that held my meager belongings that weren't hanging in the closet. I snatched my hand back when he stalked up behind me and slammed the drawer shut.

"You aren't going anywhere." His tone was final, and I looked up at him in disbelief.

"But, Dr. Stein—"

"Won't get anywhere near you. I won't let him."

Zero woofed from the end of the bed, where he was watching us with intelligent eyes. It seemed as if he agreed with his owner.

"Jack, I don't want to leave. But I don't want to put anyone else in danger. If I leave, he won't be able to find me. It's for the best." I sniffled, the tears filling my eyes, making my nose sting.

"You. Aren't. Leaving. Me." Jack growled. Then, I was tossed over his shoulder and carried into the bathroom, where the shower was still waiting.

TWENTY-FIVE

SALLY

It seemed as if both of our eyes zeroed in on the test at the same time, freezing us in our motions of washing away the shampoo and soap from our bodies. We hadn't spoken since he'd set me down on the tiled floor. We had just settled into a quiet rhythm of showering the night away. There had been a far-off expression on Jack's face whenever I chanced a glance at him, and I knew he was deep in thought about my situation. If I had to take a guess, I would say that he was planning how to keep me safe while also keeping me close. Honestly, if I could trust anyone in this world to do so, it would be him.

But now we seemed to both remember that there was something we had been in the middle of right before the phone call that seemed to blow my world up all over again. I tore my eyes away from the test, barely visible through the foggy, wet glass door, and up at Jack. He looked down at me. And I could see it there in his gaze, what I wanted from him more than anything. Hope. He wanted this, too.

"Jack?"

"Come on. We'll look at it together." I nodded and blinked rapidly, suddenly overcome by emotions. So many swamped me at once I wasn't sure how to deal with them other than to push them back down. If I didn't, I was afraid I would simply burst into uncontrollable tears.

He turned off the shower and grabbed a large fluffy towel, folding it around my body after patting me dry. His touch was always so gentle and caring, the complete opposite of what he showed to the outside world. How could I not have fallen so hard and so quickly for him? What woman wouldn't want someone like him to treat her like his queen while ready to slay her enemies for her without blinking an eye?

After a cursory swipe of the towel over his damp chest, he wrapped it around his waist, tucking the ends in, and took my hand. Together, we took the short steps to the counter and, as if in silent agreement, kept our eyes on each other until we were standing right in front of the test. He squeezed my trembling fingers. "Ready?"

I swallowed, then gave him a small, weak smile and nodded. "Okay."

As one, we turned our heads slowly and looked down. I stared, unsure at first what I should be looking for. I leaned closer, my dark red wet hair falling over my shoulder and landing with a splat on the counter next to the plastic stick.

"Is there supposed to be one and a half lines?" I squinted at the second line that was faint on one end and darker on the other. Did that mean it was positive or negative? Wasn't it supposed to be solid?

All of a sudden, my legs were swept up from underneath me, and I was being carried into the bedroom. Jack lay me on the bed and settled on top of me after yanking both of us free of our towels, leaving nothing between us. I was breathing heavily from the abruptness of the movements and blinked up at him, my mouth open, ready to ask him what was going on, my mind having been jolted from all thoughts of the test, when he swooped down and took my lips with a searing kiss that stole my breath and curled my toes.

I moaned in delight as he consumed my mouth with his lips,

tongue, and teeth. When he pulled away, nipping at my bottom lip, I let out a whimper, trying to chase his mouth, but he had already disappeared, lowering down my body and leaving small licks and nips along the way until he stopped at my lower abdomen. Then my whole body stilled. I stopped breathing and just stared as he spread his big, calloused hands over my soft skin. The black from the tattoo ink stood out starkly against the paleness of my flesh. He spread his fingers as he cupped my belly, his thumbs below my navel, brushing against my pelvic bone.

"Jack?" I let out a hoarse whisper.

He tried to speak, moving his lips, but all he did was choke on his words. Then he lowered his forehead, resting it against his hands. His shoulders began to shake. Seeing him like that, overcome with emotion, brought tears to my eyes, and I wrapped my hands around his shoulders, holding him tight, not saying a word. He needed time; I could see that. I stared up at the ceiling, blinking back my tears.

After several minutes of nothing but silence surrounding us in the bedroom, Jack finally brought his head up. At his movement, I looked down at him, seeing the red-rimmed eyes and the fierce promises held in their black depths.

"I will protect you with my dying breath," he vowed. "For the rest of my life, I will make sure you are safe. I will give you all the love I am capable of giving." He looked down at where his hands were still cupping my belly. "Both of you."

I let out a sob, my turn to be unable to say words. He was giving me more than I ever thought I would have. More than I had hoped for. I had just wanted love. He was giving me him. I tugged on his shoulders, pulling him back up to me, needing to kiss him, to show him how much I loved him. He let me, only after he placed a soft kiss below my navel.

Once he was face to face with me again, he thumbed away a tear, giving me another hot kiss. Then he flipped us, so I was on top of him.

"Ride me." His hands went to my breasts, thumbing my nipples and then pinching them harshly.

"Yes," I breathed out. With a shaky hand reaching between us, I gripped his swollen cock while steadying myself with my other hand on his broad chest. I ran the tip of him over my clit, bucking at the delicious feeling while the vibrations of his chest rumbled through the palm of my hand. I slid his cock just a bit further until it rested at my opening, then once it was in place, I lowered myself onto his thick shaft.

I felt every inch as he penetrated me, stretching me to the point where pleasure and pain became indistinguishable. As we became fully connected, I looked down into his half-lidded eyes, marveling at the emotion that shimmered there. This man said he didn't know what love was, but the way he was looking at me, the way he swore to protect me and our baby, he knew more than he realized.

"I love you, Jack."

The fingers holding tight to my hips flexed, digging in, and then he gripped firmly, lifting me back up, sliding me along the long length of him, holding all my weight in his strong arms. When he dropped me back down, he punched his hips up, impaling me so deeply I felt it in my very soul. I cried out, throwing my head back in a scream.

Over and over, it continued. Even though I was the one on top, he was the one in control. His hands directed every movement. His grunts and growls filled the room, mixing with my whimpers and cries. There was something new to our lovemaking, an added element that hadn't been there before. It had always been incredible, but all I could think through my lust-fogged mind was that we were now connected on a deeper level that went beyond a simple pairing of a woman and a man. He had let me in. More than that, he let himself believe that it was real.

"That's it. Squeeze my cock. Let me feel you drench it with your cunt." His dirty words and the bite he gave me on my breast sent me over the edge, and I came with a scream that echoed against the walls around us. With a final grunt, he pulled me down on him, grinding up into me as he spilled hotly inside my channel. I collapsed over his chest, breathing hard with my eyes squeezed shut. I would be feeling him for days on my skin, inside me, and I never wanted it to go away.

We lay there together, just taking each other in, enjoying the aftershocks, and letting our heartbeats return to normal. The shrill ringing of a cell phone broke into the moment, making Jack curse viciously. He held onto my back tightly as he reached over to grab his phone, then smoothed his hand over my back soothingly when he answered.

"Fuck off." He made to hang up the phone but paused before cursing again. "What?" he barked into the phone. "Where?" After listening for a few more minutes, he cursed loudly, then hung up, throwing the phone to the bed. I watched it bounce, then settle just before falling over the edge. "Goddammit!" he roared, making me flinch at the sheer volume.

He turned to me with a grimace, running his hand through his hair. "Sorry, baby." He let out a heavy sigh and climbed off the bed. I watched as he walked over to the dresser, pulled open a drawer, and took out a pair of boxer briefs. He yanked them up his legs, tucking himself away inside, then grabbed a pair of jeans off the floor.

"I'm really sorry. There's been a fucking accident. Fuck!" He stopped in the process of pulling his shirt on and shook his head. "I'm sorry, I have to go take care of some shit." He came over to the side of the bed where I was curled up with the blanket tucked under my chin as I watched him prowl around the room. He sat next to me and cupped my cheek. I blinked up at him, worry filling me. Jack generally didn't act concerned or agitated, not like this. Something awful must have happened for him to be so obviously distressed.

"I'm going to send someone over to stay with you so you aren't alone. I don't like leaving you like this." I nuzzled my cheek into his palm.

"Is everything alright?" It was a stupid question. Obviously, things weren't alright in the least, given the way Jack had been stomping around, looking like he was mere seconds from ripping someone's head off.

"No, little Queen. Things aren't alright. But they will be, just as soon as I put the Boogeymen into the ground." So it was the other motorcycle club that was the problem. Now, Jack's reaction made more sense. Very few things could seem to get him worked up, but The Boogeymen MC seemed to top the list. "I need you to listen to me very carefully, okay?" He waited until I nodded, my eyes wide and on his. "Do not leave this house. Don't open the door until one of my guys gets here. It will probably be Lock. Are you okay with him being here with you?"

"Yes, that's fine," I agreed. I didn't know Lock well, but I didn't have a problem with him. At least he hadn't given me any reason to have a problem.

"Good girl." He kissed my forehead, then glanced down at his phone and cursed again. "I have to go." He stood up and went to the closet. He disappeared inside for just a few seconds, then quickly reappeared with his heavy motorcycle boots in one hand and a pair of socks in the other. He took one more long look at me and opened his mouth as if he wanted to say something else before clamping his jaw shut tight. His eyes turned hard and practically frosted over with how cold they were, becoming the Jack that everyone else knew. And then he was gone, slipping out of the bedroom door. It was a couple more minutes before the front door opened and closed. I heard Jack give Zero a command to stay and guard the house right before the motorcycle started up.

I didn't move for a long time, even though I knew I needed to get up and get dressed since someone would be coming by sooner rather than later. But, I couldn't shake the feeling of dread that had covered me ever since Jack started getting ready to leave. I couldn't say for certain where the feeling stemmed from or what I was most worried about. It was just a deep, nearly overwhelming feeling of impending doom.

TWENTY-SIX

THE NIGHTMARE KING

Dust and gravel flew in my wake as my bike raced down the dirt road on the short drive to the clubhouse. Very little would have been able to take me away from my Queen's side at this time—my pregnant Queen–except the threat of war.

Three warehouses full of weapons were in flames, and one of my loyal club members was in the hospital with a bullet wound to the neck. It was nothing short of a declaration of war. Oogie was calling me out, and I was going to answer his call. He was going to regret stepping foot in Pumpkin Patch. This was my territory, and he could take it from my cold, dead claws.

I roared to a stop, not bothering to turn off the engine. Every single member of the Devil's Nightmares was ready and waiting for me outside the clubhouse. Before leaving my cabin, I had gone into my hidden safe and armed up. Every available inch of my body was covered in weapons, and it looked like each of my men were similarly armed.

I eyed Lock and waited for him to walk over to me. Before I could say a word, he nodded, his usual devilish grin gone from his face, replaced by a rarely seen seriousness. "I've got her, Prez."

I nodded once, understanding that he would protect her, but stared him down. "Lock," I knew my eyes offered nothing but death. "She's pregnant."

"Say no more, man. I was already going to protect her with my life. I swear it."

With nothing left to say, I turned to the gathered members of my club and looked them over one last time. They all wore the same looks on their faces, ones that said they were prepared to kill to protect our town and keep our territory out of the hands of our enemies. Without a word, I shot forward, leading the group as we rode toward The Four Corners. As neutral territory, no fighting was allowed to be conducted there other than during sanctioned fight nights. That didn't mean that we were going to ride into a meeting with our enemy unarmed.

The Boogeymen had burned three of our warehouses simultaneously to gain my attention and then shot one of my men, leaving him for dead when he got too close. They may say it was to get my attention, but it couldn't be considered anything other than a blatant call for war. Calling a meeting on neutral ground with the other clubs as witnesses was a play Oogie was making for a specific reason. I just didn't know why yet. And that pissed me the fuck off.

As we rolled up the long road to The Four Corners, the lot was already full of bikes from all the surrounding clubs. Some bikers were standing beside their bikes, smoking. Most looked to be pissed off to be called out on such short notice, their day interrupted by this bullshit. Nobody liked what the Boogeymen were attempting to do with Pumpkin Patch. If they managed to get my town, there would be no stopping the Boogeymen from taking each surrounding territory. Oogie might think that he had the strength and firepower behind him, but he would find out that the rest of the clubs weren't going to stand by with their thumbs up their asses.

As I pulled to a stop in an empty section of the lot reserved for my crew, each of my guys pulled in behind me. Shock and Barrel pulled in next to and just behind me, leaving me clearly in front as the President and leader of the Devil's Nightmares.

I swung my leg over the side of my motorcycle and stepped forward, my arms down at my sides, my hands open and ready to reach for a weapon. Rules of the neutral ground be damned if Oogie made one wrong move. The man himself stepped forward from where he was leaning against his big beast of a bike. It was painted red, a large pair of dice with grinning skulls on them on the gas tank. It was nice artwork that I wanted to see burned to ash along with its owner.

"Bones!" His hands were outstretched as if he were greeting an old friend he hadn't seen in a long time. "Good to have you join us today. I am sorry that it had to be under these circumstances. I heard your man in the hospital is hanging in there. Sorry to hear about him. What rotten luck that he happened to be around at the wrong time."

We both stepped no further than the front of our bikes and met each other's stares. Everyone around us had stopped all conversation, coming to attention to listen closely.

"You declared war today, Oogie." My words were gravel coming from my throat, the ice-cold tone held death and was clear to everyone, but the fucker just laughed.

"Aww, I was just getting your attention, Bones. You didn't even call me when I burned the last one. I had to step it up a little. No real harm done, right?"

Everyone on the lot shifted uncomfortably, knowing that it was bullshit. This was a dangerous game he was playing. You didn't burn down another club's territory as an alternative to picking up a goddamn phone.

"You got my attention, Boogeyman. What the fuck do you want?" It was the moment of truth. He either stated his intentions to take over, or he lied and revealed the coward that he was. Either way, he wouldn't get the backing he was likely hoping for.

"Where's my sister, Bones?"

His sister? He did this because of Daisy? After sending her to us the way he had, he'd proven he didn't give a fuck about her life. I suspected he just didn't like to lose in the game he had begun to play, and now his arrogance demanded he save face in front of his men.

"What sister?" I cocked my head at him, then turned to Barrel. "Did you know he had a sister, Barrel?"

Barrel scratched the side of his head, ruffling his green hair with his middle finger, and smirked. "Nope, can't say I did, Prez."

I looked back at Oogie to see his congenial smile had dropped, and the playfulness that he had started this meeting with had been replaced with rage. Ahh, his true colors at last.

"I want her back," he seethed, his dark eyes burning with hatred as he scanned my members as if he would find any trace of her among them.

"Well, now. That's too bad. You should keep your possessions on a tighter leash."

He took a step forward, his fist clenched at his sides. Every single man in the lot stiffened. Some reached inside their vests or behind their backs to palm their weapons.

"If you don't hand her over…"

It was my turn to step forward. All sense of civility dropped to show my burning rage. "You'll what, Boogeyman? Why would you think your sister would be with my club? Is it so she could spy on us? Give you intel?" I cocked my head. "To climb into my bed then slit my throat? That's what the plan was, right? To kill me to make it easier to take over Pumpkin Patch?" I lifted my arms and gestured wide. "What was next? Take the next town and the next? Are you so greedy to run your drugs through the whole fucking state that you were willing to sacrifice your own family to get what you wanted?"

There were murmurs around us as the other club members discussed what I said. For the majority of us, our women were to be protected. We didn't use them and throw them to the wolves. Sending in a woman as a spy was a dangerous game, a move that could have easily ended with her death. As it was, what I had done to her wasn't permanent, though the mental scars were something she would have to live with.

"Did you kill her?" he gritted out as he ground his jaw. He reached behind him, palmed a gun, and raised it to point at my chest. I smirked, crossed my arms, and stared him down.

"Unlike you, I don't send women to their deaths. She's safe. Far away from you. If she's smart, she will use the money I gave her to start over with a new life like I told her to. She knows that there is nothing here for her but a big brother that doesn't give a shit about her."

Oogie cocked his gun and the sound was followed by hundreds of others just like it. He glanced around to see that every other member of the surrounding clubs had their weapons trained on him. If his finger so much as twitched, he would be dead before his bullet left the chamber. He held up both hands and then slowly replaced his gun behind his back. With his angry gaze on me the whole time, he stepped back until he was next to his motorcycle.

"Are you a betting man, Bones?" he asked as he swung his leg over the side of the bike and sat down. I just stared back without answering as he replaced his scowl with the wide, friendly grin he had started the meeting with. "How's that little redhead of yours?"

Every muscle in my body stiffened at the mention of my Queen, but I showed no outward sign that I was letting him get to me. His grin grew wider.

"She's something special, right? You've never shown any interest in a woman until her. That night at fight night, mmhmmm, you couldn't take your eyes off of her. Do you think you can keep her safe, Bones? Want to place a bet on it?"

With his parting words, he started up his motorcycle, the sound a loud growl as the rest of his club started up their bikes all around him. He pulled out first as I watched him. He circled the parking lot once, making a show of it as the entire club of Boogeymen rode behind him. Then they pulled onto one of the long roads that led off into the distance, heading back toward his territory.

I didn't allow myself to move or speak, knowing that the remaining two clubs were still watching me. I trusted them as much as I could, believing that they wanted peace as much as I did, but I wasn't a man to give away any weakness. The president of the Midnight Demons broke away from where his club was gathered, followed shortly by the president of the Black Wolves.

I stood in place, unable to move, while every part of me wanted to destroy the Boogeymen for threatening my woman. Both men approached with grim expressions.

"Hey, man." Talon, the president of the Midnight Demons, held out his hand first, and I worked to unclench my fist so I could exchange his handshake. Blade was next, and I shook his hand, too, grateful for their greetings even if I were eager to return to the house, needing to have eyes on my pregnant woman.

"I'm just going to say it because it needs to be said," began Blade. "We need to work together on this. That man is unstable, and it's clear that he isn't going to stop until he has the whole state." He eyed me. "Not that I wouldn't help you if I weren't worried about my own territory. But it's going to take all of us to end that club."

Talon nodded his agreement. "I don't like having drugs show up on my streets, and I don't like having our women being threatened." He scratched at his long red beard and looked out at the cornfield in the distance. "I mean, it's not as if I don't run drugs, I ain't no saint, but our drugs are clean. And we don't deal to kids, ya know?" I nodded. People were going to buy drugs no matter what we did. But we could do our best to make sure the quality was good and wouldn't kill them when they tried to party.

"Did you really send his sister away with money?" Talon asked after we all agreed to have a meeting later to plan out how to end the Boogeymen for good.

I paused from where I had been about to climb back onto my motorcycle. "Yeah. Daisy's long gone from here with a new identity and enough cash to set her up in a new life." He nodded his head and turned to walk away.

"I knew you were a good man, Bones!" He called out over his shoulder. I just grunted as I started the engine and roared out of the parking lot, not giving a shit about what anyone else thought about me except my little Queen.

TWENTY-SEVEN

SALLY

I knew I had to get up and get dressed before one of the guys showed up at the door. I slid out of bed and made my way into the bathroom to clean up after our last round of sex. I wouldn't have time for another shower, so I used a washcloth to wipe the stickiness between my legs. The whole time I cleaned up and then brushed out my still damp hair, I couldn't shake the overwhelming sense that something terrible was going to happen. I wished I could call Jack and ask him to come back, but I knew I needed to be strong. As the woman of a ruthless motorcycle club president, eyes would be on me, and his club would start to resent it if I were seen as trying to control their leader.

I went back into the bedroom and got dressed in a pair of yoga pants and one of Jack's soft black T-shirts, needing the comfort it would bring me to have a piece of him against my skin. I suddenly remembered the test and returned to the bathroom to look at it.

I picked it up, still seeing the solid pink line and the second, half-solid, half-faint line. Noticing the box sitting there, I tilted it, letting the instructions slide out, and unfolded the paper. I was reading about the different types of positive results that could show up when I heard the knock on the door.

With a huge grin, I couldn't drop because, yeah, Jack had been right; I was pregnant. I wanted to go to a doctor to confirm for my own peace of mind, but the box boasted an over 99% accuracy rate. I disarmed the alarm and took the chain off the door after peeking through the peephole to see Lock standing there waiting to be let in. I turned the knob and pulled open the door.

"Hey, Lock—"

A loud bang and spray of blood cut off my greeting. I stared, horrified at the wet stain that was growing steadily on the front of Lock's red shirt. It was the same color as his shirt, but the wetness continued to expand as we both looked down at it. Lock looked up at me and opened his mouth to speak, but no words came out. Instead, a thick stream of blood rolled down his chin.

As I stood there frozen, I watched his wide eyes go blank as if the light went out in them. Then, as if in slow motion, his knees bent, collapsing, and he fell forward toward the open doorway. I jumped back before he could fall into me, still in shock by what I was seeing. Once he was face down on the ground, that was when I saw the hole in the center of his back. And the blood. So much blood. It began to run over the sides of the hole in his back and down until it started to pool on the entryway floor.

I finally opened my mouth to scream, but a voice I had never hoped to hear again trapped the sound in my throat, making it instead come out as a strangled gurgle.

"Ah, Sally, my little patchwork doll. Finally, I found you! You know you are mine, my dear. Why did you run from me?"

Without further thought, I spun on my heel and ran back down the hall toward the bedroom. I had no idea where to go or what to do. My only thought was to escape the monster that had kept me captive and destroyed my life. I let out a scream when my hair was yanked hard, and I was pulled back against the body of the man I hated and feared more than any other.

"Tsk tsk. I won't ever let you go again, Sally, love." He brought his nose to my neck and sniffed there, making me shiver. He hadn't done anything like that before. I had always been more like a doll to experiment on in the past. Having him press his face against me the way he was sent new waves of terror into my soul. "Things have changed, haven't they, sweet Sally? You need to be punished, and I have so many ways to do it."

He started to drag me back down the hall by my hair. I held onto his wrists to relieve the pain of my hair being ripped out by the roots as I screamed and begged him to let me go. He ignored my pleas, and when I told him that Jack would find me and kill him, he just laughed.

"No one is going to take you away from me again. Don't you see? You're all I have left. I have nothing else to live for. A man would do just about anything to keep his one last treasure. Let this Jack come. I'll be waiting."

"No! Please, Dr. Stein, please don't do this! I'm pregnant!" He paused as we reached the doorway and looked back at me. He seemed to stare at my belly for a long moment, then shrugged.

"It doesn't matter. Neither of us will live long enough for it to make a difference." Then he stepped over Lock's body, dragging me with him as I slid in the still warm blood. My bare feet left red footprints along the walkway, then over the rocky ground, until we reached the edge of the house before he pulled me around the corner. The rough gravel of the unfinished yard dug painfully into the soles of my feet, and my neck was beginning to hurt from the odd angle my head was being held by my hair.

I tried screaming at the top of my lungs, hoping that anyone would be able to hear me, knowing that the cabin was too far from the compound, that even if the entire club had been standing outside, no one would have been able to hear me from so far away. But still, I couldn't give up. I couldn't just let him take me without a fight. If I could get my hands on a weapon of some kind if I could hurt him...

A bright spot of white caught my attention through the tears that blurred my vision. I blinked rapidly, trying to clear away the tears enough to see what it was. When I realized what I was seeing, my heart gave a painful lurch in my chest. I cried out and pulled, trying to get to Zero. He was lying still in the dirt, not far from the house.

"Zero! No!" I sobbed, yanking, not caring that I was hurting myself in the process.

"Come on, girl."

"No! How could you!" I screamed desperately as I twisted painfully in his grip, wanting nothing more than to see if Zero was still alive. A sharp jab poked me hard in the side, making me freeze. I looked down to see the gun that had killed Lock was now pointed at my stomach.

"You're coming with me. Now!" He pressed the gun harder into my side, his threat clear.

With another sob, I gave one last long look at Zero and allowed the monster to lead me away from the dog that had saved my life. Inside, I was begging for forgiveness. I longed to go to Zero, to hold him and run my fingers through his soft fur. I wanted to thank him for being so brave and strong. For being my hero.

We turned the corner to the back of the house, which was covered by overgrown bushes. Jack had plans for the cabin; he just had yet to get around to them. Part of those plans he had told me about one night as we were lying in bed together was to put in a swimming pool and a bar-b-que grill. Eventually, there would be a lovely patio where he could hang out with his closest friends, but for now, it was a mess, and no one ever came out this way. Behind one of the large bushes was a small dark car.

The doctor opened the trunk and pushed me inside. Before I could even try to sit up or roll over, the trunk was slammed closed, and I was locked inside the dark. There was little room to move, but I did my best, feeling around in the darkness above my head for the latch that all vehicles come equipped with. I figured it was a long

shot, that he'd likely disabled it in some way or even removed it alto-
gether. All I found was warm metal.

The car began to move virtually silently. That's when I realized
that I was in an electric vehicle. No wonder we hadn't heard it
parking outside the small house. It might as well have been a ghost.
Jack was going to be infuriated when he realized all the simple
mistakes that were made today. If he even figured them all out since
it seemed the doctor had done a decent job outsmarting us all.
Apparently, Zero was the only one that caught on, and now he had
paid the price.

Before I allowed myself to get swallowed up by grief and fear
again, I continued my examination of the stuffy trunk, but it was
completely empty. There wasn't even the tiniest crack to allow the
smallest amount of light in, so I had to use my hands to feel where
the tail lights would be, hoping to break one, thinking maybe I could
stick my hand out and signal another car. That was impossible, too.
There was no easy access to the lights, hidden the way they were
behind a panel. I couldn't find a way to lift the floorboard, and there
wasn't a latch to gain access to the backseat. I was completely and
utterly fucked. I could only allow myself to be thankful that at least it
wasn't summer, so even though it was stuffy and uncomfortable, the
heat shouldn't become unbearable.

The car came to a stop much sooner than I had expected, and I
held my breath. I didn't know if we'd reached our destination or if he
was stopping for another reason after such a short drive, and I
wasn't certain what I wanted the answer to be. The man seemed to
have become even more unhinged since the last time I saw him. The
thought made a shiver run up my spine despite the warmth of the
unventilated trunk.

We hadn't been driving for long and couldn't be far from Jack's
home. I was afraid to allow myself to hope that being so close would
make it easier for him to find me. I lay in the darkness, hardly daring
to breathe while waiting to find out what was coming next.

I listened to footsteps outside the car and braced, but nothing could have prepared me for the blinding brightness of the sunlight after being in the dark for even such a short period. Dr. Stein didn't give me a chance to adjust, though. He grabbed the arm I had thrown up to shield my eyes and began to pull me roughly. I cried out in pain as I fell to my knees on the concrete.

"Come, girl. We don't have time for your dramatics." The doctor huffed at me impatiently as he pulled me quickly to my feet. I glanced to the left and right, wondering if I would have a chance to make a run for it, but the sight of where we were had me freezing long enough to have the gun pressed firmly into my side again. "Walk normally, sweetheart. We are just a man and a woman heading into their motel room." Another firm press had me nodding my head in agreement even as I wanted to turn to him with an incredulous look. Normal? He just pulled me from the trunk. What part of that would seem normal to anyone but a serial killer?

I allowed him to lead me to the row of rooms, limping beside him. He was no taller than I was, being a man of short stature, so his strides weren't very long, but my knees hurt from the fall. Not to mention, the soles of my feet were still sore from the walk on the rocky dirt back at the house. When we came up to the row of motel room doors, I nearly laughed out loud when I realized which one he was leading me to.

He opened the door and pulled me inside before shoving me toward the bed. He kept the gun trained on me as I fell facedown, immediately scrambling to sit up, hating to be in a vulnerable position around this man who haunted my dreams.

"Up on the bed, my dear. You'll find I already prepared for our stay." He waved the gun, gesturing for me to do as he instructed. I couldn't help but notice the same stains that had been on the cover when I stayed in the room more than a month ago were still there. Had they even cleaned the room at all? Since it was the least of my worries at the moment, I did what he said and warily crawled to the center of the bed. It wasn't until I was in the middle that I noticed the leather cuff lying by the pillow. Turning to look, I spotted the matching one on the other side.

"Go ahead, don't be shy. Slide your wrist into the cuff, dear. Once you have it attached, you can put the other one on."

With eyes burning with frustration, I picked up the first cuff and buckled my right wrist in. I only hesitated for a moment before reaching for the left one. I eyed him as I slid the leather through the loop. "Jack is going to come for me."

He scoffed while reaching into the pocket of his slacks to produce two small padlocks. "Sally, dear, even if that biker thug came looking for you, he won't get close enough to rescue you. I told you, I have nothing else to live for. I will finish what I started, and then..." He snatched my right arm and pulled it far away from my body, too far to be able to reach with my left hand to try to stop him as he slid the small padlock into place on the metal ring where the leather strap went through the cuff loop. "Once I'm done, I'll kill us both. So, you see? It doesn't matter who finds us. It will be too late."

TWENTY-EIGHT

THE NIGHTMARE KING

We were almost to the clubhouse, where I planned to leave the rest of the club behind to head to my cabin. I needed to see my woman. I needed to have my hands on her to reassure myself that she was okay. The urge had been beating at me since I had ridden away, nearly causing me to turn back a million times, but since leaving The Four Corners, I was almost desperate to reassure myself that she was safe.

I didn't even pause as I passed the large building; just waved a hand in the air to acknowledge that we were back on the clubhouse grounds. I would need to call church today, so I'd be back. There was a lot to discuss, and it couldn't wait, but this couldn't either.

I revved my engine, putting on speed and throwing up rocks on the long dirt road that led to the house. It was only a speck in the distance, surrounded on both sides by cornfields that were turning brown. The closer I got to the house, the more my need to get to her grew instead of lessening.

My breath froze in my lungs. The first thing I noticed as I pulled up was the open door. Lock's bike was sitting in the drive, so if the door was open, then that meant he hadn't been able to stop whoever had come for her. My heart rate was already beating out of control as I skidded to a halt, my tires squealing, then fishtailing. I dropped my motorcycle, jumping off, not caring to take the time to put the stand down. I had my gun in my hand before both feet hit the pavement, and I was already running for the door.

I saw the small bloody footprints before I saw the man lying on the ground. I stared in horrified shock at Lock lying with the upper half of his body in the house, keeping the door open. From the puddle of blood and the size of the hole in his back, I knew he was already gone. My heart squeezed painfully, stealing the breath from my lungs as I realized my long time friend and VP, the man I trusted above all others, was dead. I wanted to drop to my knees, but I couldn't take the time to check on him. He was already gone, but my girl might not be.

"Sally!" My desperation rang clearly through my choked yell as it echoed against the walls while I ran down the hall to our bedroom, darting my eyes in each open doorway I passed, but I could sense the house was already empty. When I reached the bathroom to see the white plastic test still sitting there from just a few hours before, I threw back my head and roared. My hand was through the wall, plaster raining down to the carpet before the sound died away. "Fuck!"

I stormed back the way I had come, remembering the footprints. I stepped over my fallen friend, anger and regret trying to make their way inside me, but I was too focused on finding my Queen to give Lock the proper attention he deserved.

I stared at the footsteps where she had slipped in the congealed blood that had still been fresh when she'd stepped in it. I eyed the trail and followed, jogging along where it had left the walkway and started over the rocky dirt that would one day become a grassy yard. I would need to work on that for our kid. Children needed soft grass to play on, not the rocks and dirt it was now. My mind tried to tell me that it was too late, that the future that had been in my grasp hours ago was already gone, but I clenched my teeth.

I forced the dark thoughts back, battling them with everything I had. Sally needed me to find her. There were only two possibilities that I knew of. Either the Boogeymen had killed Lock and taken my woman while we were distracted at the meeting, or she had been found by the man who had given her the scars that covered every inch of her beautiful body.

If the Boogeymen were responsible, nothing would stop me from reigning destruction on their club until every single one of them were dead, destroyed by my hands. If it was her captor, I would show him what it was like to be helpless as his body was being carved into. I would ensure he stayed alive while I sliced every single cut she had suffered by his hands into him. Once I was satisfied I hadn't missed a single scar, I would let him bleed out slowly. I would stand there and watch as the light died from his eyes.

The footprints faded until they disappeared, but there were still signs of her steps through the dirt. I followed them as they headed around the corner of the house and toward the back. There was a spot where it looked like there had been a slight struggle, as if she had tried to get away from whoever had led her. I looked up to see what might have caused her to start fighting at that spot, when I saw the white fur lying just a few feet away.

I quickly ran to my dog and slid to a stop, dropping to my knees beside him. I raised my hands, surprised to see them shaking, and hesitated before lying them over his side, fearing the worst. I nearly collapsed with relief when I felt a slow but steady rise and fall of his chest.

"Fuck, Zero. Goddamnit!"

I pulled the phone from my pocket. "Barrel! Get the van over to my house, now!" I tossed the phone to the ground beside me and squeezed my eyes shut. I clenched my fists in his fur and ground my jaw so hard it hurt. My mind was in a black haze of rage, and I needed to rain death and destruction on the fucker that had done this shit. Lock was dead. My woman was missing. My dog was hurt. I. Needed. To. Kill. Someone.

I blinked my eyes open and looked back over where the scuffle had taken place in the dirt. Sally had likely seen Zero and tried to go to him but had been forced to keep moving. Moving to where? I scanned the ground without leaving Zero's side, following the path left by my girl's bare feet. Fuck, she'd been walking over the rough ground full of small, jagged rocks. The fucker would pay for that, too.

As I followed the trail she'd made, I finally saw them. Tire marks. The fucker had been parked right behind my fucking house. It could have been parked there all night. Maybe he'd only been there a few minutes. Regardless, I didn't fucking know, and that was a stupid fucking mistake on my part. I had intended on putting security cameras around the place, but for so long, it had only been me living out here. I arrogantly thought that no one would ever be stupid enough to come onto my land. Now, too many others were paying the price for my foolishness.

The roar of several motorcycle engines signaled the arrival of more than just the van I had called for. Barrel's vicious cursing reminded me that Lock was still on my doorstep. Fuck. I grabbed my phone and shoved it into my pocket as I stood back up. I would have to answer to my men for the mistakes I made, too.

Carefully, I scooped Zero into my arms and tried not to think about how his head rolled to the side as if he were lifeless. I could feel his heartbeat under my hands. I had to hold on to that. I carried him over to the van, where a prospect stood next to the open side door with wide, round eyes. I gently lay Zero down on the floorboard, then backed away slowly, not taking my eyes off his chest, which was moving too shallowly for my liking.

"Take him to the vet. Don't leave his side. Ever." I stared the prospect down, letting him see just how serious I was with my command. "I don't care what the vet is doing right now. You make her stop and tend to Zero. Understand?"

He nodded, his Adam's apple bobbing with his nervous swallow. "Yes, Prez. I won't leave his side."

"Good." I nodded and turned to face Barrel, who was standing behind me, his face pale as he looked back at where our club brother lay dead on the ground. "Barrel, you're coming with me. Shock," I waited until my Sergeant at Arms tore his horrified gaze from the Vice President and met my cold stare. "Take care of Lock. Put the club on lockdown. All family members need to head straight for the clubhouse until we find the person who did this."

The van pulled away from the house quickly and back down the dirt road. I watched as it grew smaller in the distance before disappearing. I turned to my motorcycle, which was no longer on the ground. Someone had righted it, but I was too busy trying to keep a tight hold on my emotions to show my gratitude. I straddled the bike, started it up, and prepared to begin my search for my missing woman.

Barrel climbed onto his bike next to me and gave me a look. "How are we going to find her?"

"I don't fucking know," I growled, raking my hand through my hair in frustration. "But I do know it won't be by sitting here with my thumb up my ass." I glanced over at him and then revved the engine. "Let's head into town and ask questions. If I'm lucky, someone will have seen a strange car driving through."

It was all I had to go on. One thing was for sure. When I got my little Queen back, I was putting a tracking device on her ass.

TWENTY-NINE

SALLY

D r. Stein Was the picture of calm contentment as he moved around the room. I watched from the bed as he picked up a small black bag I hadn't noticed before, opened it, and began to rifle through the contents. My attempts to lick my lips to ease the dryness were stopped by the gag that was pulling painfully on the corners of my mouth.

I couldn't see what he was doing with his back to me, but I heard the sounds of metal instruments being placed carefully down on the wooden surface of the dresser. From past experience, I knew Dr. Stein was meticulous regarding his tools. Knowing what was coming, cold sweat began breaking out on my forehead, and tremors began to shake my arms.

The doctor turned around and looked at me with a giant smile on his face. "There's always been one thing I've always wanted to try. Unfortunately, I haven't had the opportunity until now. This is going to be fabulous."

With giddy excitement, Dr. Stein moved into the bathroom. I heard the water turn on, and I knew he was washing his hands.

Though he was preparing to undergo illegal surgery in a motel room, the doctor was still careful about following the protocols set for cleanliness, at least for himself. I didn't think he cared as much about my well-being.

He came out just a few minutes later and returned to the dresser. He pulled on a pair of gloves, snapping the fingertips into place one at a time. As I watched him prepare for a new surgery, the tears I cried began to soak into the sides of the gag. I had no idea what he had in store for me, but what I did know was that it was going to hurt. I also feared that Jack would not make it to me in time. I had no doubts that he was on his way. Jack would do anything to find me, but there was a real possibility that he'd be too late.

"So, you see, dear Sally, you already know that I've had to be the best as the finest and most respected plastic surgeon. I've never left a scar behind, never any evidence that someone had had work done. Isn't that such a strange thing? That people would spend so much money to look different only to want to ensure nobody knew?"

He slid on his white coat with his name embroidered on the breast. Then, he picked up a long, wicked, wicked-looking blade. It looked like it was made from surgical steel, just like the rest of the implements that he used, but this one was much larger and scary looking. It looked like something from a nightmare. I wasn't sure what he was planning to use it for, but it looked like it could do a lot of damage very quickly. He turned it back and forth, studying it under the dim lighting of the hotel room lamp. Even with such poor lighting, it still reflected brightly. It had a serrated edge, and I could guess what he was planning to use it for.

"Oh yes, this is going to be my greatest work yet. You see, Sally, the one thing that I've always wanted to do but have never been able to try is reattach a limb." He turned then and looked at me, and I stared back at him with wide-eyed fright. The implications of what he said terrified me to my core. Just imagining what he wanted to do was bad enough, but being in a filthy motel room that likely hadn't been cleaned properly in years, with no medication, no anesthesia, just a crazy doctor with wickedly sharp tools and my body at his mercy. There was no way I would make it out of this alive. And after he touched me with that blade, I wasn't sure I wanted to.

THE NIGHTMARE KING

Halfway into town, I spotted a black Town Car coming down the road heading in the direction of the club compound. There were very few reasons why anyone from town who didn't have a direct affiliation with the club would head out this way. When they flashed their lights, I gritted my teeth at the delay in getting on with the search in town. Only the hope that they would be coming out to give information to me had me slowing to a stop in the middle of the road.

The mayor rolled down his window with a forced smile. He was a weasel of a man, and he knew his position was mainly in name only. He did all the tedious work that went along with the position, but the real decisions regarding Pumpkin Patch were always passed through me first.

"Mr. Ellington. Nice day we are having."

I nodded curtly as I let the bike idle, ready to move on if this fucker was going to waste my time. "Mayor."

His smile dropped for a moment before he managed to force it back on his sweaty face. "I, uh, heard that you have a woman now. A redhead?"

I gave him a sharp look, needing him to get to the point. "Have you seen her?"

"Well, now. Uh," his eyes darted out the windshield, then back to me, his nervousness written in every movement. "It seems there was a car spotted in town yesterday. A stranger checked into the motel.

You know how the town notices these things during the off-season. We don't get many strangers in Pumpkin Patch, you know."

"What do you know, Mayor?" I demanded, needing him to get to the point. If this was the guy I was after, I needed information already. Sally didn't have any time to spare, and every second without her was killing me inside. The fucker could be hurting her while this asshole was taking his sweet fucking time chatting.

"Well, it seems that same car returned to the motel just a little bit ago. He, uh, pulled a woman from the trunk—a young woman with red hair. I was told she didn't look very happy. But they went into the motel room together without a fight, you know? I don't want to get involved if you and the little woman had a spat, but if she is in some kind of trouble, and, uh, you," he coughed into his hand as if he were afraid to say the words out loud, "cared about this woman, I thought you should know. So, here I am, coming out to tell you personally. Just in case. And, you know, if you are so inclined to be grateful, perhaps you could see to it that when the elections start up again in a few months, you might be interested in helping me retain my position as mayor of this fine town."

He looked hopeful, his eyebrows disappearing under the brim of the black hat he wore to cover his balding head. I revved the engine as Barrel cursed from his position next to me.

"Which room, Mayor?" I ground out between my teeth.

"Uh, I believe it was room 16 that they disappeared into together. You won't take it out on me if the little lady is stepping out on you, right?" He fidgeted with his tie and ran his fingers over the brim of his hat in his typical nervous gesture.

I gave a curt nod and prepared to take off, not caring to satisfy his curiosity about the situation.

"Oh, Mr. Ellington! About that election..."

I eyed him, letting him see my seriousness as he swallowed thickly, shrinking back a bit from where he had been leaning forward eagerly. "Mayor, I need you to send an ambulance to room 16 at the motel. If my girl is safe, I'll make sure you stay Mayor of Pumpkin Patch for the next decade."

As I peeled away with Barrel by my side, the mayor called out his window after me. "Thank you, Bones! Mr. Ellington! I'll make that call now!"

I didn't bother to acknowledge him. My only thought was to get to that motel room and save my Queen.

SALLY

My eyes stayed glued to the blade as the doctor approached the bedside, where I lay cuffed and unable to move. No matter how hard I pulled, the leather cuffs held me tight. I felt like I was going to suffocate while trying to breathe through my tears, the gag, and my fear.

The room felt stifling even though I knew from experience it was a steady 72 degrees. While my hair stuck to my sweaty forehead and my heart tried to beat out of my ribcage, the doctor remained calm and steady. He looked so content as he studied the weapon in his hand and then glanced over my body, looking for the perfect place to begin cutting.

I tried to scream. I tried to push the fabric from between my lips, hoping that if I could just get it to slide down to my chin I'd be able to scream the motel down. Then maybe somebody, anybody, would hear me. Instead, the gag held tight as it pulled hard on the flesh in the corners of my mouth. My throat felt raw from how hard I was screaming, but hardly any sound managed to escape.

I pulled on my legs, hoping in vain that maybe the ropes he had tied to my ankles would be loose enough to allow me to pull a foot free. Then, maybe I could at least kick out at him. If I could just kick that stupid saw from his hand, it would buy me a few seconds. Jack was coming for me; I knew he was. *Please, Jack. Please!*

He seemed to make a decision and nodded to himself. He came to the head of the bed and gripped me firmly at my forearm, stretching it out. On instinct, I jerked hard and almost sobbed with relief when I managed to jerk out of his hold. He turned to look at me, his eyes sinister with the anger he usually hid so well.

"Now, Sally. That's not being a good girl. I need you to hold still if we want this cut to be as clean as possible." He grabbed my arm again with a steely hold, his fingertips digging harshly into my flesh. He stretched it back out and pressed it down hard against the mattress. "I won't be able to reattach it properly if the cut is a jagged mess."

I moaned in despair as I watched the saw come closer to my skin.

THE NIGHTMARE KING

For the second time in my life, I let my motorcycle drop to the pavement as I rode directly up to the door of room 16. Suddenly, loud screams of agonized pain rent the air, making my heart pound so hard I was afraid it would break my fucking ribs to escape my chest. I didn't even wait for Barrel to join me as I raised my foot and kicked the handle as hard as I could with my gun drawn, ready to end the life of the man who stole my woman, who was *hurting* my woman.

The first kick splintered the wood. The second kick bent the lock. When Barrel joined me for the third kick, the door finally flew open. It only took a second to comprehend what I was seeing before red took over, and I flew forward.

I grabbed the doctor by the back of his neck and threw him to the floor, where he fell onto his back with a pained cry. I spared a glance at the bed to see that Sally was alive. She was strapped down, red and sweaty, tears soaking her pretty face, and her moans of pain filled the room, but she was alive. It was all I needed to see to allow me to focus back on the man I was about to kill.

I lifted my gun and pointed it at his face, my finger on the trigger. I was about to squeeze when a firm, steady voice stopped me.

"Bones."

I didn't move my eyes from where the doctor lay on the filthy floor. He was yelling something about interrupting his greatest achievement, so I kicked him in the mouth to shut him up.

"Bones. If you kill him in front of me, I will have no choice but to arrest you for murder." The sheriff's voice stayed reasonable, the only calm in the chaos. My mind was roiling with the need to end the man who had killed my friend, hurt my dog, and planned to hurt my woman. The same man that had hurt her and tortured her for months.

"He needs to pay," I seethed through my teeth, my finger flexing on the trigger again.

"And he will. But, unless you want to spend the rest of your life behind bars, I suggest you let me take him in."

I stared down at the man who was holding his bleeding mouth and sobbing hysterically. Regretfully, I removed my finger from the trigger and slid the gun back into my holster. Then, I lifted my heavy boot and brought it down with all my strength on his knee. Over and over, I stomped on both of his knees, feeling satisfaction at the grinding of bones under my foot. The man may live, but he would never walk again. The doctor would have to view the world from a wheelchair as he lived behind bars. He would never have a chance to hurt Sally again.

With a heavy sigh, the sheriff glanced down at the screaming man when I finally stepped back, chest heaving and fists clenched, but satisfied, even if I wished I would have been able to just put a bullet between his eyes. "Damn it, Bones." He stepped back and waved the paramedics inside the room. "Whatever," he mumbled. "I hate paperwork."

I gave him a look that told him that if he wanted to keep his job, he would do what I paid him to. Then, I turned to go to Sally. I rushed to the bed, reaching for the cuff to free her. And froze.

"Medic," I whispered brokenly. Then yelled to get their attention from where they were kneeling next to the doctor. "Medic!"

THIRTY

THE NIGHTMARE KING

I never left her side. Even when the veterinarian wanted to see me in person, they had to come to the hospital to talk to me. Zero had been sedated sometime early that morning. It was a heavy sedation, one that could have killed him, but luckily, he pulled through. The fucking doctor had used a medication commonly used for stress and motion sickness in canines, but with the overdose he was given, it had nearly stopped his heart. The vet reassured me that Zero would have a full recovery. As she patted my back and then left the room, I stared at Sally as she lay still in the hospital bed.

Her blood-red hair was fanned out around her, free from tangles after I brushed it. Her skin was paler than usual, making her scars even more prominent. And her arm was wrapped in a thick bandage where the doctors had to sew her mother fucking arm back together.

I cursed as I stood, needing to move as the never ending agitation ran through me. I dragged my hand through my hair, yanking as I strode over to the window and stared out over the small town that I ruled. Too many mistakes were made. I was too conceited, my ego thinking that no one would ever be stupid enough to make a direct threat against me or my woman.

I had to make changes to keep her safe. A security system for the house that included the outside instead of just the inside was already being installed. A gate with a wall was going to be built around the compound and all the surrounding properties that belonged to the club. No one was getting in without a code, and a guard would be posted at all times, day and night.

The town spread out below me, lights twinkling in the darkness. Beyond the streets filled with homes and businesses were fields of pumpkins and corn stalks. Halloween would be coming to Pumpkin Patch soon. With the holiday would come tourists. Strangers would flock to the Halloween town to take in the sights. Haunted houses would open for business. Corn mazes would soon be plowed with the sole purpose of confusing and scaring those who dared to enter.

It was what the town lived for.

I turned back to look at the hospital bed and saw the machines that beeped and the blinking lights that kept track of Sally's vitals. She was alive. She would have another scar to go with the many she already had, but she would live. I breathed out a heavy sigh. I hated seeing her lying in that bed, knowing it was my fault. In my tangled thoughts, there was one that repeated over and over, louder than the others.

Maybe she would have been better without me.

If I hadn't brought her into my life, she would have been safe. She would have done what the Assistant District Attorney told her to do and left town. She could have escaped somewhere new and stayed hidden until the doctor had been caught. It was my fault that she stayed.

Then I thought of our baby.

Somehow, she was still pregnant. Even through the stress and trauma of the day, the baby had survived. It was a fighter, just like its mother. Perhaps she would be better without me, but now she was stuck with me. I was never going to let her go. I would just do whatever it took to make sure that she was never in danger again.

I started to walk back over to the bed to take my seat at her side when the ringing of my phone stopped me. I fished it out of my leather vest and looked at the screen, expecting to see one of my men's names on the screen. I frowned down at the unknown number and then declined the call. I continued to the chair I had been sitting in all day and took Sally's small, cold hand in mine. I wasn't leaving until my Queen could leave with me.

My phone rang again, making me grunt in frustration. I withdrew it from the pocket to see the same unknown number flash across the screen. Again, I declined the call. I leaned over the bed, placing my forehead on Sally's cold hand, wishing she would wake up so I could see her beautiful blue eyes.

My phone beeped, indicating I had a voicemail. I considered ignoring it, but on the off chance that it was from the vet with news about Zero, I sat back up and hit the button to listen to the call. As soon as I heard the voice coming through, I froze, my blood heating and then turning to ice in my veins.

There was still one more threat against my woman that would need to be seen to—one that couldn't wait. The Boogeymen were calling, and they were promising death.

To be continued in The Queen of Nightmares...

THE QUEEN OF NIGHTMARES

THE QUEEN OF NIGHT MARES

USA TODAY BESTSELLING AUTHOR

R SULLINS

For my NBC girls, you know who you are! Long live the King!

CHAPTER

ONE

THE QUEEN OF NIGHTMARES

I rolled over, stretching out my arm, reaching for something that I instinctively knew wouldn't be there. Every day for the past two months has been the same. Ever since I left the hospital with the thick bandage on my forearm where the doctor had attempted to dismember it from my body, I have woken up alone. I knew Jack wasn't far away, and I also knew he slept beside me, the indentation in his pillow where his head lay the night before. I could also swear I could still feel the sensation of his arms holding me as I slept. Though, that was likely nothing more than wishful thinking on my part.

The moment I woke up in the hospital, confusion and pain over-whelmed me. I had searched the room with blurry vision, trying to blink back the mental fog as I searched the room, expecting to find Jack. Instead, I saw Kara sitting in a chair in the corner, typing away on her phone. I stared at her for several seconds, trying to come to terms with the fact that it was a casually dressed Kara wearing jeans and a T-shirt with me and not the man that I loved.

261

The door opened abruptly, and a nurse came into the room. Kara looked up from her phone for just a second, then returned to her screen before her head jerked back up.

"Oh my god, you're awake!" She quickly jumped out of her chair and rushed to my bedside. "Holy shit, girl. Everyone has been so worried about you!"

"Jack…" my voice was nothing but a harsh croak, making me realize how dry and raw my throat felt. I tried to lift my arm to rub at the soreness there when agonizing pain flooded through every part of me, starting at my arm.

The nurse tutted, then hit a button lying next to me on the bed.

"This is your morphine, sweetie. You press that whenever you feel you need to. It's a much lower dose than normal, considering the pregnancy, but it should help take the edge off. If you hit your limit and you're still in pain, you press that call button and let me know."

Immediately, a weightless feeling began to flood me, and I could feel my eyelids begin to droop. "Jack?"

"Sweetie, that man hasn't left your side since you were admitted here two days ago." The nurse smiled down at me with a dreamy look that told me what she thought of my luck at having Jack at my bedside. "He had to leave, but I'm sure he'll be back as soon as he can."

Kara rubbed my knee through the hospital blanket. "Sorry, I'm not who you want to see right now, but all the club members are at Lock's funeral. I'm sure Bones will be back later tonight if he can make it. Though, I heard they are having a huge party in Lock's honor instead of a wake. Bones will probably want to stay for that since Lock was his VP and all."

I stopped listening as memories of seeing Lock standing in front of me, his red shirt turning wet as blood seeped into it. I remembered seeing his lips move as if he were trying to speak. The memories morphed from watching Lock fall face forward toward me to the sight of Zero lying motionless in the dirt. I wanted to scream out at the agony that filled my chest, but all I could do was close my eyes and drift off to sleep again as a tear escaped from the corner of my eye.

That was two months ago, and though Kara was wrong and Jack had returned to my room as soon as the funeral was over instead of going to the party, his absence had remained just as vivid ever since. Despite his presence, I might as well have been alone.

Most of the time, even though Jack was near, he was distracted or on the phone speaking in a gruff, hushed tone. Pain medication made it difficult for me to understand what he was saying. Since we came home and I started getting better, he took his calls in another room. I understood that it was important club business. I couldn't imagine what he was going through. I just wished he would look at me for more than the few seconds he'd glance my way before his eyes turned hard as ice and his jaw clenched as he ground his molars. Whenever he'd jerk his gaze away from me again, my heart clenched a little bit harder. I didn't blame him, though. I hated me, too. Lock would still be alive if it weren't for me.

I gingerly sat up, hoping that it would be the morning I wouldn't have to run for the toilet, but the moment I was fully upright, sitting on the edge of the mattress, my stomach rebelled. I quickly scrambled around the end of the bed, nearly hitting my shin on the bedframe as I slid along the floor in my haste and made it to the toilet just in time to kneel carefully on the tile floor before losing the meager contents of my stomach.

When I was done, I flushed the toilet and waited patiently, breathing deeply through my nose while wiping my eyes and nose with toilet tissue. Sometimes, the nausea would linger, forcing me to drop right back down to the floor to heave a few more times. Fortunately, it seemed like it would be a good morning. As I let out a long exhale, the nausea seemed to stay at a manageable level.

I finally got up, rising just a little unsteadily to my feet. I crossed over to the sink, quickly brushing my teeth before heading back to the toilet to pee. I may have been squeezing my legs together there towards the end when I was spitting the toothpaste suds out into the sink, but getting the awful taste of vomit out of my mouth took priority over relieving my bladder.

I glanced at the shower, wanting to get cleaned up, but my energy levels were at rock bottom, and I just couldn't bring myself to care. I turned back to the bedroom, walking around the foot of the bed to my side much slower that time, as Zero sat there, thumping his tail on the floor as he stared up at me with his wide doggy eyes. I sat down on the mattress with a heavy sigh as I eyed the hot mint tea and ginger cookies on my nightstand. Jack may have been more like a ghost around the house since I came home from the hospital, but he was still taking care of me. I blinked back the tears that threatened and rubbed a finger under my suddenly stinging nose, refusing to cry. Zero jumped onto the bed beside me and shoved his wet nose against my leg with a low whine. I absently stroked his scruff as I stared down into the steam curling from the tea.

I hadn't allowed myself to cry since the first couple of weeks that we'd returned home after my release from the hospital. Jack's physical presence but mental and emotional separation from me hurt so keenly. It was as if I could literally feel my heart cracking into pieces in my chest with every beat. I used to lock myself in the bathroom and cry tears as silently as I could. But after I overheard Jack talking to someone on the phone about having difficulty replacing Lock as Vice President, I stopped letting the tears fall. I didn't deserve to let them. But I could do nothing about the ache in my chest.

I reached for the teacup with my left hand. As I wrapped my fingers around the handle, they were already beginning to tremble. I lifted the cup slowly, raising it two inches, then three off the wooden surface of the nightstand before the muscles in my arm started shaking so badly with the strain that a bit of the liquid sloshed over the side of the cup. I couldn't hold the weight any longer and had to use my right hand to support the steaming tea before I dropped it and made another mess like the one I had made a few days ago in the kitchen.

With the help of my right hand, I brought the cup to my lips, lightly blowing on it before taking a sip. Jack made it perfectly, exactly how I liked it, with just a bit of honey. I didn't know how a man who couldn't stand the sight of me still cared enough to ensure my needs were being met. I closed my eyes as a new wave of pain swept through me. Perhaps it wasn't me that he was caring for now. I was pregnant with his child. A part of me that got louder every day couldn't help but wonder if I would still be sitting here in his home if I had lost the baby.

I shook my head as my nose stung and my eyes filled with tears again. But I looked up at the ceiling and blinked them back before any could fall. I wouldn't allow myself to feel sorry for this situation I had found myself in. I thought of Lock and how he would smile as if he were always looking around the world and seeing how we were all fools. He was loyal and had a good heart. He had been the one responsible for Jack coming to my rescue the first night they had returned from the rally. If it wasn't for Lock, I might have ended up the victim of sexual assault.

With a shaky arm, I slowly lowered the teacup to the nightstand. As the hot liquid sloshed over onto my fingers, I hissed in pain. Before I knew what was happening, Jack was stomping through the bedroom and into the bathroom. I could hear the water turn on for a brief moment before turning off again, and then he was in front of me. His large tattooed fingers engulfed my hand as he pressed the cool washcloth to the slight burn.

With a quick glance at my face before putting all his concentration on the cloth in his hand, he rumbled out an admonishment that made me feel two inches tall. "You need to watch what you're doing."

I swallowed through the lump in my throat and nodded weakly as I stared at his fingers, holding the cloth in place. I couldn't speak. I knew he was right, but I could feel the irritation coming off of him in waves as he held my hand in his. In all the time we had been together, even at the beginning, I couldn't remember feeling this way with him, and it hurt so badly.

Through my lashes, I could see him glance back up at me with a frown. Without another word, he straightened to his full height from where he'd been leaning over me. I could no longer see any part of him other than the bottoms of his legs and feet. He was already wearing his heavy motorcycle boots, and I knew he was about to leave for the clubhouse. He never stayed around the house for long anymore, and he hadn't asked me to go with him to sit in his office while he worked since before the *incident*.

He paused for a long moment before turning and walking away. His footsteps stopped at the doorway, and I heard him tap his knuckles against the wooden door frame.

"I'll bring something back for dinner." A long pause. "Make sure you take your pill and stretch your arm." Then he was striding down the hall, his heavy footsteps fading away. There was a pause, and then the front door opened, and I could hear the double beep of the alarm followed by a series of beeps as he armed it.

I glanced at the pill bottle on my nightstand next to the ginger cookies, the prenatal vitamins staring at me. Jack wanted me to take them, reminded me daily, and those were often the only words he spoke to me. A part of me wanted to throw the bottle across the room. I sighed and reached for the vitamins with my left hand since I wouldn't have a strong enough grip to twist the lid off unless I used my right hand. I opened the bottle and then fished out one of the large pills. With a grimace, I placed it on my tongue and then picked up the fresh water bottle that was magically always there for me. I washed down the pill with several gulps of the cool water, then ate a cookie before my stomach could make too much of a fuss.

With a sigh, I settled back against my pillow and reclined on the bed, thinking about the long, boring day ahead. I didn't know if Kara would visit me today. She was the only one I ever saw aside from

Jack. The few short times I saw him each day should have made me happy. Instead, every time he left, it just widened the hole in my heart a little more. My chest was always aching these days. I had thought that nothing could hurt as badly as my arm when I first woke up in the hospital. I was wrong.

CHAPTER

TWO

I was washing the teacup and small plate in the kitchen sink when I heard the doorbell ringing from the front door. I quickly dried my hands with a kitchen towel and all but ran to let Kara in. I needed the company, or I was going to go out of my mind.

I peeked through the peephole to be safe, then grinned when I saw Kara holding up a bag that was clearly from the deli in town.

I swung the door open wide to let the gorgeous blonde enter. Immediately, the alarm started shrieking its ear-splitting scream. "Shit! Shit! Shit! I forgot to turn off the alarm! One second," I yelled as I frantically punched in the code to disarm the alarm, then let out a breath at the sudden silence. "Damn, Jack's going to be pissed," I whispered. I shut the door, punched the code back in to reset the alarm, and turned to see Kara watching me with shrewd eyes.

I pasted on a bright smile, trying to pretend that my chest wasn't heaving from the stressful moment. "Hey! I'm so glad you're here."

She returned my smile with one that looked almost as forced as

269

mine was. "Hey, girl. Are you okay? Is Bones going to do anything to you for setting the alarm off?"

I waved away her concern. No, I didn't think Jack would hurt me. I just hated seeing the disappointment or the frustration that he always seemed to look at me with these days. I longed to see him smile at me the way he used to, and setting off the alarm wasn't going to give him a reason to be happy. "No, of course not. I just know he will be concerned after what happened before, you know?"

I led her into the living room and gestured for her to take a seat on the leather sectional. "I'll go grab a couple of plates. Do you want a soda?"

Kara nodded as she sat down on one end of the couch, and I went into the kitchen. My phone was still on the counter where I left it, and I could see it was lighting up with a phone call from Jack already. The alarm company had likely called him the second the door opened. I let out a gust of breath, then picked it up, knowing I had probably already missed at least one call from him. If I didn't answer this time, I would bet every earthly possession I owned that he would send the entire club out here, guns blazing.

"Hey, Jack," I said quietly.

"Is everything okay? Do I need to come back to the house?" His voice was gravelly and rushed, the concern just barely discernable under the harsh tone.

"No, everything is alright. I forgot to turn the alarm off before I opened the door." I walked to the fridge and pulled on the door, having to give it a little extra effort with my left hand. "I'm sorry for worrying you."

There was a deep sigh from the phone as I grabbed two cans of soda from the fridge. "Damn it, Sally. You have to be more careful."

I swallowed back the retort that wanted to come to the surface. I wished I could say what I really wanted to. It was on the tip of my tongue to ask Jack if it was me he cared about or his baby, but I clamped my teeth shut. It wasn't until I heard nothing but silence that I blinked and pulled the cell phone away from my ear to look at the black screen. He hung up just like that, without a single word of goodbye.

I clenched my jaw and closed my eyes for a minute. *Damn it, Jack.* I couldn't keep doing this. Not for the next six months. Not for the next eighteen years. I loved that man more than life itself. But I couldn't, just couldn't keep going the way we were. I needed him to be my Jack again. I needed him to hold me and tell me everything was okay between us.

I picked up the plates and sodas when I heard Kara call out to me. When I walked back into the living room, she looked at me with concern. "Are you okay, Sally?"

I gave a small laugh that sounded as far from cheerful as I felt. I placed the plates down on the coffee table where the sandwiches had been set out. Kara had opened the wrappers on the subs and had two bags of chips sitting there waiting.

"Yeah, I'm okay. Jack was just worried, that's all."

She eyed me dubiously but picked up her sub sandwich, transferred it to her plate, and wadded up the paper it had been wrapped in. "You can talk to me, you know."

I sat down with a huff, then picked up the remote. I didn't want to talk about my issues with Jack. It felt like a betrayal to even have her asking. But I did appreciate that she worried about me.

"I know, Kara. I really appreciate it. But there isn't anything to worry about. I promise." I pushed the button to turn on the TV, ignoring her skeptical stare at the side of my face. "Which episode were we on?"

I flipped through the apps until I found the right one, quickly finding our show and starting it where we had left off before she could say anything else. She grunted from beside me and then took a huge bite of her food. I chose to ignore everything: the pain in my heart, the worry about the weakness in my still healing arm, and the baby that was my only tether to the man I would never stop loving. I picked up my sandwich and my plate, then settled back to get lost in the problems of the make-believe world on the TV.

"I THINK you should come to the party tonight."

Kara's words jarred me from the story playing out in front of me, and I turned to look at her, popping the last chip from the bag into my mouth. "What party?" I asked, covering my mouth as I chewed with one hand to ask her the question.

"You didn't know? There's a huge club party tonight. You've already missed the other ones. I think you should come out to the one tonight." She tipped back her head, finishing the last of her soda before leaning forward to set the empty can beside her plate. "People are starting to talk."

"Talk about what, exactly?" I turned to face her on the couch, the show forgotten.

She eyed me incredulously. "About what? Girl, no one has seen you since before the whole kidnap and murder thing. Bones is always at the club. People think you two aren't even together anymore."

Her words hurt, even if they were all true. "What does it matter if they see me?"

Her mouth dropped open for a long minute, then snapped shut. "Let me put it bluntly. Bones is a hot as fuck guy. He's powerful and important to the club and the town. There's not a single club girl that wouldn't give her right arm to have that man."

She winced as she seemed to realize what words just came out of her mouth. I looked down at my left arm. There was a long, bright pink line that was healed, but barely. The scar looked a million times better than the ones running next to it, but since it was so new, it looked awful. Dr. Stein had managed to cut pretty deep before he'd been stopped when Jack broke into the hotel room. He hadn't gotten a chance to begin sawing through my bone, but the damage he'd done to the muscle was making it hard for me to gain strength back.

"I'm really sorry, sweetie. That was insensitive of me. I wasn't thinking."

I waved away her concern, knowing she hadn't meant it. It was honestly a little funny when I thought about the stupid phrase. People didn't think about things when they said them. I knew I had said the same thing in the past when it came to ridiculous things that ultimately didn't even matter.

"Forget it. No big deal." I tilted my head and studied her. "There's not a single girl who doesn't want him, huh?"

"Girl, no! Anyone would want to be in your shoes. And since everyone now knows that he's actually into women, they all want him to choose them next."

"Even you?" I asked quietly.

She froze while reaching into her small bag of chips and looked at me with big blue eyes. Kara was gorgeous with her big breasts and perfect hourglass figure. She had big, plump lips and honey-blonde hair that she liked to play with, always running her fingers through it and adjusting the strands to curve around her breasts, accentuating them. She was also kind. She was the first nice person I had worked with at the bar, not treating me like I had a disease just because I was covered in scars. Jack could do worse. Any man would want Kara.

She choked out her words. "Me? What? No, I would never do that to you. I swear!" But I could see in her eyes the lie there. Jack was too much of a man to turn down. He was everything she had described and more. If he crooked his finger at her, she would go willingly, friendship be damned.

I gave her a small smile even as my gut twisted. "Okay, Kara. Tell me about this party."

She seemed to relax at the change of subject. "It's just the usual club party. There will be lots of music, lots of booze. Some girls will dance on the stage to the heavy rock music that always plays. It gets pretty wild. It usually doesn't take long for clothes to come off. People will start fucking on the pool tables while everyone watches or finds their own partner to fuck."

I cleared my throat and shifted uncomfortably in my seat. It wasn't something I was interested in seeing. That first night, when the whole club had shown up at the bar, and I had met Jack for the first time, was wild and crazy. I couldn't imagine sitting there watching something even more wild than that night had been.

"What does Jack usually do during these parties?" There was no way he participated. He hadn't touched a woman before me.

Kara scoffed. "That man just sits in the corner with a beer and watches. Nothing gets to him. He doesn't even allow the girls to try to get close." It was a relief to hear, even if I'd already known. Kara's tone was hesitant when she added, "But, girl, that's going to change now. You know that, right?"

I jerked my eyes back to her from where I was glancing at the TV, absently wondering what I had missed in the show. "What do you mean?"

"Once a man has had a pussy on his dick, do you *really* think that he's going to keep sitting back watching everyone else get off? Fuck no! He's going to want pussy, and there are plenty of girls just waiting for the first indication that he's ready."

I leaned back in my seat and stared at the TV, no longer seeing the show. Instead, all I could picture was a horny Jack seeing all the sex going on around him, deciding that he was bored and wanted a piece of the action. *Over my dead and dismembered body.*

CHAPTER

THREE

THE QUEEN OF NIGHTMARES

Kara helped me get ready after laughing at what I had walked into the living room wearing, telling me that I wasn't heading to church. Instead of dressing in the cute sundress with a cardigan to ward off the cold weather, I was sporting a pair of the short shorts Jack had bought me months ago. It paired nicely with a lacy tank top that showed a bit of the enhanced cleavage I'd gained thanks to my pregnancy. I had to struggle just a bit with the button on the shorts. My belly wasn't showing yet. I didn't even have the slightest bump, but my lower abdomen was firmer to the touch than it used to be. The baby was clearly growing, and I had no doubts that the bump I had been looking for in the last few days would be making its appearance soon.

I sat on the bathroom counter as Kara put the finishing touches on my makeup. I was afraid to look in the mirror. I didn't even own half of what she had applied to my face. She'd gone out to her car and returned with a makeup bag that was bulging on the sides with products. When she'd held up black eyeshadow and told me I'd look great with smokey eyes, I'd just sighed in defeat and let her do whatever she wanted.

Eventually, Kara stepped back, screwing closed the lid on the stain she'd just finished applying to my lips. "There! All done! The guys are going to be creaming in their pants when they get a look at you!" I cringed at the visual but hopped down carefully from my perch on the counter.

I turned slowly to face the mirror, not expecting to look like a clown but still worried about what I'd see. My face felt almost heavy with all the products that I was wearing. When I was trying to hide my scars, I used a pretty thick concealer and foundation, but since I started wearing makeup in high school, I have generally only worn some mascara and lipgloss.

My mouth dropped open in shock when I looked at my reflection. The scars on my face were barely discernible, but that wasn't what had surprised me. The dark eye makeup paired with the bright red lip stain made my blue eyes pop. The contouring she had done made my cheekbones look camera-ready. I almost looked like a model. I didn't know if I loved it or hated it. But there was no doubt I looked good, even if I barely resembled myself.

"Wow," I breathed as I turned my face from one side to the other, looking for the tell-tell signs of the scars that ran from the corners of my lip to nearly my ears, giving me the hideous smile I hated but had grown used to seeing whenever I looked in a mirror. She had done a fantastic job. "I might need some pointers for the future."

"I got you, girl. Any time, really." Kara quickly added some eyeshadow to her own lids as I watched and gave her eyes an exotic look with some liquid eyeliner that extended out past the corners of her eyes. I turned to look at the corners of my own eyes to see she had done the same to mine, though not quite as dramatically as she had with hers.

I heard her zip up her makeup bag and looked back to see she had already put on some lip stain. Her look was flawless, and I could imagine her easily making a killing as an influencer on social media.

She looked me up and down. "Ready to go wow the club?"

Nope. "Uh, yeah. I guess."

"That's the spirit!"

She giggled as she hooked her arm with mine and led me into the bedroom. I picked up the cardigan against her protests and shrugged it on. It was really freaking cold. No matter what she said, I wasn't going outside in just a tank top.

When we reached the door, I bit my lip before remembering the lip stain. Kara had promised it would last the whole night and that I would be able to eat and drink without having to stress about smudges or fading, but I couldn't help but be worried. I stared at the alarm panel a sucked in a huge breath. I hadn't been outside since the hospital except for brief trips to the doctor to have my stitches removed weeks ago and to check on my healing progress shortly after that. I was due for an appointment with my obstetrician in a couple of days, but this would be the first time I left without Jack by my side.

I let the breath out slowly, then punched in the code. There was a possibility that Jack would just think I was letting Kara out or she was retrieving something from the car like earlier. However, if he decided to look at the app on his phone, he would see that I set the alarm to AWAY instead of the STAY setting, indicating I was leaving. I shrugged one shoulder defiantly. Oh well. I wasn't his prisoner. I could leave any time I wanted to. Right. *Shit.*

My fingers trembled as I stepped out the door, followed by Kara, and fit the key into the lock. I wasn't so sure about this plan anymore. I didn't really mind staying inside the house where it was safe. I slipped the key into the back pocket of my shorts and lifted my chin defiantly. I couldn't live like a princess locked away in a tower. Maybe Jack would be mad; he would just have to get over it.

I followed Kara to her beat-up little car. It looked like it had been through a few battles and lost. I eyed it dubiously as she climbed inside the driver's seat. She leaned over and unlocked the passenger door for me. It gave a loud metallic groan as I pulled it open, and I gingerly sat down on the stained cloth seat. It was clean inside but obviously worn down with age.

The car started up with a little grumbling, like a kid who didn't want to wake up for school, but once she put it into drive, it rode smoothly. Kara ran her hand over the cracked dash and grinned at me. "My brother is a mechanic. Someone brought this little guy in but couldn't pay the bill. Since the garage keeps the cars from people who don't pay their bills, he fixed it up and gave it to me as a birthday gift a couple of years ago. It runs great, and he keeps up on the maintenance for free."

"Oh, that was nice of him. Who's your brother?"

She waved her hand as we approached the clubhouse. The heavy metal door was propped open, and light spilled into the parking lot that was filled with almost as many cars as there were bikes. "You don't know him. He doesn't live in Pumpkin Patch."

I was going to ask more questions, but the words died on my tongue as I got my first view of the new gate. It was a massive black wrought iron with wide brick posts on either side. There was a guy standing at the gate looking bored and wearing a leather vest. As he turned away, I could see his cut didn't have a patch on the back. I realized he was a prospect likely on gate duty for the night.

I turned and saw the wrought iron fencing stretched on as far as I could see, going toward Jack's place. Turning my head, I could see it stretching in the opposite direction as well. Jack had fenced in the Devil's Nightmares compound. My heart did a funny flip in my chest. I hadn't known he'd installed the fence. It hadn't been there the last time I came through, but that had been at least a few weeks ago. I never noticed a fence outside the house, but then I rarely looked outside. It also was possible the fence wasn't very close to the house, either. But one thing was certain: Jack wanted the compound safe from intruders like Dr. Stein.

I blew out a breath and looked over to Kara, who had walked to my side. "There's a fence."

She giggled and hooked her arm with mine, leading me toward the front door that was propped open, loud music blaring from inside. "Yeah. It has been all the town has been talking about for weeks." She bumped her hip into mine. "Ready to turn some heads?"

"Not even a little bit," I muttered under my breath as I took the first step inside the spacious room.

I had seen it before when I used to come with Jack to his office, but it had never looked the way it did now. The lights were on, but they were turned down low enough to give off the atmosphere of a club. An actual dance club, not a motorcycle club.

The small stage in the corner that had a pole on it was occupied by two girls writhing against each other, wearing next to nothing. A handful of bikers holding beer bottles shouted encouragement to the girls as they caressed each other while sliding around the pole. They weren't dancing or using the pole as intended. It was more like a prop as they got the men worked up into a frenzy.

The two pool tables in the middle of the room had several bikers surrounding them. A couple of the men were holding pool sticks, attempting to play an actual game, while the other guys were making out with or groping more scantily clad women. I watched as a biker picked up one girl by her butt and sat her heavily down on the table. He ripped her leather bikini top down over her breasts, laughing as they popped out, baring her pierced nipples.

I looked away quickly, only for my eyes to land on one of the leather couches. A girl was on her knees in front of Barrel, who had his legs spread wide, his thighs on either side of her chest as her head bobbed up and down furiously. His half-lidded eyes met mine, and I watched as his gaze slid lazily over my body. His lips turned up in a smile right before he froze, his eyes widening in shock.

I saw the second he recognized me and held back my cringe. I wanted to turn around and run back out the door before he could sound the alarm, but I squared back my shoulders. I wasn't going to run. I belonged here, didn't I? I was the President's woman. I may not have a tattoo on my wrist telling the world that I was Devil's Nightmare property, but I was owned just the same.

Barrel sat up straighter as his eyes narrowed on me while the head continued to bob quickly in his lap. I could feel his censure and knew he disapproved of me showing up here tonight. Well, fuck that. I started to turn away when I felt a heavy arm wrap around my waist and pull me into a hard, muscled body. It took me only a second to realize that the man holding me wasn't Jack.

"Hey, sweetheart. Haven't seen you around here before. Lucky me, I get to claim your hot little body before all my brothers get ahold of you. I do hate sloppy seconds." The voice was rough, slightly accented with a southern drawl, and definitely not what I wanted to hear. His hot breath fanned over my neck before I felt his wet tongue lick me there and slide up to my ear. "Oh yeah, I'm gonna have fun riding you tonight."

"Don't touch me. I belong to Jack." I tried to pull away, but he tightened his grip with a laugh.

"I don't know who Jack is, but baby, if you walk in here looking like that all alone, you're going to find out real quick that any *Jack* will do."

"I don't even know what that means!" I twisted to face the guy I had never seen before.

"It means you're fair game, baby." He grinned at me with straight white teeth. He was handsome, with dark hair and brown eyes. He had a thick beard that was nicely trimmed, but he was so, so wrong.

"The Nightmares don't take women against their will." I gritted out as I pushed against him again. "And Jack is..."

He cut me off before I could finish my sentence. "No, the Nightmares don't force girls. But then, you wouldn't come to a party here if you weren't looking for a biker to get between your thighs. So stop playing hard to get, sweetheart. If you want privacy, we can find a room to fuck in."

"Jack is Bones, you dimwitted fuckface. Now, let me *go.*" I yanked hard just as the man dropped me like I was on fire. The momentum had me falling backward with a yelp. He took a step forward as if to keep me from falling, but before he could reach me, I landed against a hard chest. Strong arms wrapped around me, much like the man's had just moments before. This time was different, though. This time, the arms belonged to the only man I craved.

I immediately settled into Jack's arms, my heart sighing at the feeling I had missed for the last couple of months. Now that they were wrapped around me again, I never wanted to leave them.

All too soon, Jack's hands left my body, and I opened my mouth to protest. His big hands gripped my waist and roughly moved me to the side. As I stumbled a few feet over, I watched as he stalked forward and wrapped one of those hands around the throat of the man who had thought he had a right to fuck me.

"Tell me one good reason I shouldn't gut you right here, Joker?" Jack's tone was low and deadly as I admired his back muscles flexing under his black T-shirt.

"I didn't know she was yours, Prez. She said she belonged to Jack. I don't know, man. I've been gone for almost a year. If you got an old lady, nobody mentioned it." His voice was raspy as he croaked out the words through the tight squeeze around his throat.

I stared at those tattooed fingers that were flexing as if trying to decide whether to squeeze or let go, and I brought my fingers up to my own neck. I ghosted my fingertips over the place where Jack used to hold me so possessively but no longer did. Tears blurred my vision as I turned away, pushing past the bodies that were surrounding us.

I stumbled away from the circle of onlookers and quickened my pace until I was running down the long hallway that led away from the common room where the party was being held. I ignored all the sounds coming from dark corners and passed a couple fucking up against the wall right in the hallway without a glance.

I stopped at the door to Jack's office, expecting it to be locked, surprised that it was ajar. I pushed it open to see the lamp on at the desk and a pile of papers covering the surface. Was he in here working while the party was going on down the hall?

I wiped at my eyes and looked down at my hand to see it covered in black mascara and eyeliner. Great. Now, I was going to look ridiculous. I sniffled as I stood in the center of the room and wrapped my arms around my middle. The voice from the doorway had me freezing in place while my heart immediately started pounding out of control.

JACK

"I'm going to let you live since you had no idea who she is to me. That's on me." I tightened my grip just enough that Joker couldn't mistake my intentions. "But if you even so much as breathe the same air as her with any purpose other than to protect her, I will strip the flesh from your bones and feed it to my dog." I shoved him away from me and quickly followed after my little Queen. I didn't give a fuck what anybody thought about their President chasing after his woman.

It was as if she were my beacon of light. I needed her. The only light in my darkness was my Queen. I had spent the last two months doing everything within my power to ensure her life was as safe as possible.

I pushed the door to my office open further to reveal my girl standing in the middle of the room. She was staring at my desk with a forlorn expression. I wanted to yell at her, to punish her for leaving the house unprotected. She'd entered my clubhouse without a guard and opened herself up to the lustful gazes of every biker present. I trusted them, but she was my woman. *Mine*. And nobody had the right to look at her but me. She looked beautiful with her sexy body and blood-red hair falling down to her waist. I wanted to cut the eyes out of every man who had seen her tonight, with her wearing those little shorts that showed off her toned legs.

"What are you doing here, little Queen?" I could hear the residual anger still seeping into my tone from seeing her wrapped in another man's arms. I didn't know what might have happened if Barrel hadn't come to get me. I know I would have had to kill Joker for touching more of her than he already had.

Her swift intake of breath was the only indication that she had heard me. I watched as her shoulders curled inward and her arms tightened around her middle. I took another step forward and swung the door shut before turning the lock with a loud snick.

I slowly stepped closer, afraid I would spook her. I was close enough to feel her body heat radiating off of her. I closed my eyes and dipped my head down until my nose was just a hairsbreadth away from skimming her neck. I took in a deep inhale, bringing her scent into my lungs. She smelled of sweet oranges and vanilla, and my stomach clenched at my desperate need for her.

For months, I had denied myself the feel and taste of her body. I couldn't allow myself the comfort, not when I had to make sure that what had happened could never happen again. *If I lost her...*

I clenched my fists at my sides to keep from reaching out. I had nearly lost my little Queen all because of my arrogance. Stupid mistakes had led to her being taken from me. Because of me, one of my best friends was dead. I was lucky that Zero had made a full recovery. But had Sally been killed, I wouldn't have survived the loss.

"You shouldn't have left the house. What were you thinking, coming here alone?"

"I wasn't alone."

I raised an eyebrow at her whispered words. She had been alone with my club brother in the crowded room. I thought of how she had spent her day as I watched from the cameras. She'd spent the time with the blonde friend she usually spent time with. The blonde was the only one to ever come and go. The blonde would have been the only way Sally would have even known about the party. Why did she bring my girl only to leave her on her own?

"If you wanted to come to the clubhouse, you should have asked me so I could keep an eye on you." I tried to soften my tone, but the anger still coursed through my veins. I stepped back as Sally suddenly whirled around, her long hair brushing against the bare skin of my arms, making me bite back a groan at the contact. She looked up at me with fire in her weary eyes.

She had smeared makeup on her cheek from where she had rubbed tears away, but she had never looked more beautiful than she did as she stood in front of me with her fists clenched and blue eyes flashing.

"And you would have brought me?" She scoffed, lifting her chin in such a haughty manner that it made her appear to be the queen I knew she was.

My fingers itched to swipe away the strands of red hair that stuck to her cheek. "Perhaps," I murmured.

She threw her arms out, then let them drop back to her side. "Perhaps? Perhaps you would have spent time with me? Perhaps you would have spoken more than two words to me?"

I furrowed my brows. It was true; I hadn't spent much time with Sally since the attack. I'd had a single-minded focus to fix all the security holes in my home and compound. She also needed time to heal. I glanced down at her arm to see the bright pink line where she had nearly lost her arm due to the almost nonexistent security two months ago.

"I've been busy."

"Busy doing what, Jack? Busy with who?" There was an accusation in her tone that I didn't like.

"I've been trying to make our world a safer place. You are going to have my child soon. I won't have it come into a world that is too dangerous for it to even play outside."

Her fight seemed to leave her almost as quickly as it had come. I watched as her shoulders slumped and her hands went to her abdomen. "The baby," she whispered brokenly. "Of course, you want the baby to be safe."

I tilted my head, confused by her sadness. "The baby means the world to me, Sally." Didn't she know that I would do anything, to give anything, to make sure that the piece of her currently safe in her belly would never know a moment of pain or be frightened by the world around us?

She looked back up at me, a small, sad smile on her face that didn't reach her eyes. Her eyes held nothing but bleak misery, and the sight of it made me want to howl at the moon in frustration. "I know that, Jack." She looked away from me to stare at the darkened window across the room. "I just wish..." Her words trailed off, fading away the way her light seemed to be right before my eyes. I finally gave in to my need to touch her.

I placed a finger under her chin and forced just enough pressure there to get her to turn her face back to me. I needed to see her eyes. My heart thumped wildly in my chest at the feel of her soft flesh against mine again. For so long, all I had allowed myself was to hold her at night. I have been so afraid I would hurt her. I suppose, in a way, I was also punishing myself for my mistakes that had led to her injury.

"You wish, what, little Queen?" I coaxed as I swept my thumb over her chin, close to her plump bottom lip. I couldn't see her scars under all the makeup. It made me want to demand that she wash it all off so I could see her, the real her. She always looked beautiful, but I loved her natural beauty the most.

She blinked up at me, and a tear escaped, sliding down her cheek and making a trail through the dark smears of her makeup. She let out a stuttering breath, and her voice was so soft I had to strain to hear her in the quiet room. "I wish you still loved me, too."

Her words nearly had me doubling over from the pain they caused. It felt as if someone had taken a red-hot blade and plunged it directly into my heart. My words sounded as broken and jagged as I felt.

"You don't think I love you?"

She gave me that small smile that was nothing but misery and what I suddenly recognized as heartbreak because I felt the same emotion now, too.

"I think that I wouldn't still be in your life if I weren't carrying your baby."

I closed my eyes as I felt her words hit me like serrated knives, slicing me to the bone. I thought back to every time I left her in the morning. I always ensured she had what she needed. The tea, I knew, helped with the sickness she woke up with. I didn't dare touch her while she felt so poorly. I hadn't wanted to cause her more discomfort, so I left her with the ginger cookies that the lady at the diner had assured me would help with the nausea. I would remind her to take her prenatal vitamin since the doctor had assured me it would be good for her health.

But all along, what she needed was *me.*

I opened my eyes, blinking back moisture, to see her head bowed in defeat again. I couldn't take it anymore. I had held back because she needed to heal. I had spent all my time away to ensure her safety. Most of my days were spent on the phone or in meetings with the other MC presidents, discussing plans to stop Oogie and the Boogeymen from their imminent invasion of my territory and the specific threats he had made against my woman. The only comfort I had been able to allow myself was the intimacy of holding her in her sleep. In doing what I had, I made the woman I love lose her hope.

I moved my hand, sliding it down from her chin until it rested on her neck. I could feel the soft fluttering of her heartbeat against my fingers and relished in the feel of the proof that she was alive and in front of me. I tightened my grasp until I could feel her heart beating steady and strong. She gasped and jerked her head up, her eyes meeting mine. A small spark of life flickered there as her gaze met mine.

"The baby is my world, little Queen. It exists because it's part of you. But you? You are my very existence. Without you, there is no me." Her lips trembled as she stared into my eyes, and I watched as that little flicker of life grew brighter. "I told you before that I didn't know what love is. But, Sally, the way I feel for you? It doesn't seem strong enough, but there is no other word that could describe the yearning, the obsession, the desire I feel for only you. I'm sorry I haven't shown you. But, I vow to you, not another day will go by in our very long lives that I won't show you with everything I am. I love you, little Queen."

I counted each tear that slid down her cheeks as I spoke the words from my heart until I lost count. Each tear was another misdeed I had made against her that I would strive to make up for.

"Jack." My name trembled on her lips.

"You're mine," I swore to her as I lowered my head to press my lips to hers, groaning at the contact I had been craving for months.

"I'm yours," she promised, her soft lips moving against mine. She wrapped her arms around my shoulders, diving a hand into the hair at the back of my head. "I love you, Jack. Make me yours again," she moaned against my mouth.

"You have never stopped being mine."

THE QUEEN OF NIGHTMARES

I t seemed as if mere seconds ticked by, and I was naked in front of a fully clothed Jack. I clawed frantically at his T-shirt, desperate to feel his skin against mine but too overwhelmed to think straight. He gently removed my fingers from the tight grasp I had on his shirt and shifted my hands to my sides. Then, he reached behind his head and pulled his shirt off the way that always had my heart beating faster and anticipation building in my core.

"You're so fucking beautiful," he breathed against my lips before reaching for my thighs. He gripped them firmly and lifted me while turning and taking a few long strides to the nearest wall. With his gaze trapping me in their bottomless black depths, he pressed my back against the wall, the cool surface making me hiss and arch my breasts into his smooth, muscled chest. "You will never doubt me again." He reached between us to pull at his belt and the button of his jeans. His growled words went straight to my clit, making me shudder, while at the same time, a small pang of regret twisted my heart.

"I'm sorry," I whispered, meaning it down to my soul. I should have trusted him. I should have known that the man I knew he was would never turn his back on me so easily. After giving me everything and knowing he had trouble expressing himself, I should have given him the benefit of the doubt. My stupid emotions had been all over the place after I had woken up in the hospital. Guilt, pain, sadness, it all tormented me into thinking I was unloveable, that I didn't deserve to be loved. So why wouldn't he turn away from me? It was nothing but lies and self-doubt.

"I'm sorry I didn't give you the reassurance you needed." His expression was so tortured that I raised my hands to cup his cheeks.

"We'll know to never do this to each other again," I whispered.

"Never," he agreed roughly.

With that vow, he shifted until his hard cock was at my entrance, then he slowly pressed forward, sliding into me inch by glorious inch. The burning stretch I felt as he filled me so completely made me gasp with the pleasure I had been missing. He took advantage of my open mouth, pressing his lips to mine and plunging his tongue inside. The kiss was so sweet as his lips caressed mine that my eyes teared up with an overflow of emotions.

Once he was at the point where he could sink no deeper, he paused, allowing me to adjust to being so full again. I watched in rapt fascination as he closed his eyes, the tendons on the side of his neck straining as he groaned with pleasure. Seeing this ruthless, hard man being so overwhelmed by the feel of me was such a beautiful sight. It made me wish I could take a picture to carry with me always.

"You feel so fucking good," he growled as he opened those intense eyes again to stare at me. He withdrew as slowly as he had entered me, his long length dragging against all the sensitive nerve endings in my channel. "My pussy." He slammed his cock back into me, making me cry out from the pleasure-pain. "My woman." He pulled back only to slam back in again just as hard. "My Queen," He growled as he began to piston his hips at a brutal pace that left me whimpering as I clawed at his shoulders.

I could feel everything inside me tightening as an orgasm so huge it almost terrified me began to build. My skin was so sensitive that goosebumps covered my arms and neck, and even my scalp tingled as my hair moved with his rapid thrusts.

I felt him shift and cracked open my eyes, not realizing I had closed them. He moved a hand from one of my thighs to slide it under my ass, then lifted the other hand to my throat. The gentle yet firm squeeze on my neck by his big tattooed hand was exactly what I needed to send me over the edge. I tilted my head back and screamed out my release, not caring at all that the entire club and all the guests at the party could hear me. Nothing mattered but Jack and what he was doing to my body.

As I came down from the most intense orgasm I'd ever had, aftershocks kept sweeping through me. Jack groaned in my ear as my pussy walls kept convulsing. He let go of my throat, sliding his hand around my back, and carried me away from the wall. All I could do was hang on, panting, as he strode over to his desk, each step making his cock move inside me deliciously.

When he reached his desk, he swept out his arm, sending everything flying to the floor. He laid me on the surface and then stared down as if he were memorizing the image of me naked and panting for him. With a groan, he pulled his thick cock from my pussy. I immediately reached for him, hating the loss, but my hands met nothing but air as he dropped to his knees on the floor in front of me.

With a jerk, he spread my thighs open wide. The look on his face, as he stared at me with ravenous hunger, had me whimpering as my need grew swiftly again, as if the orgasm that had nearly destroyed my sanity hadn't just ended.

"Fuck," he growled as he moved forward and took a long lick of my wet pussy. "I love the taste of your cunt." He licked me again, then speared his tongue into my entrance. "Never going to stay away from this cunt again. *Mine.*" Then there was no more talking, just grunts coming from him and moans of pleasure from me as he ate me as if he were making up for every day that he hadn't had a taste.

Just as I was about to come again, Jack pulled back, wiping his chin on my thigh. He stood to his feet, towering over me with his cock hard and pulsing with his heartbeat. It was still glistening from being inside me, the tip practically dripping from his precome.

I tilted my head back, an invitation as my neck stretched that he took full advantage of, sliding his hand there as he slid back inside me. I moaned, feeling complete once again. I lifted my hands to grip his wrist, holding onto him like an anchor. "Jack."

"Never again, Sally."

I opened my eyes to meet his half-lidded gaze as he slid out slowly, then thrust in hard and fast. "Never again," I agreed.

"Fuck! Too good. I'm going to come. *Fuck*." Jack reached for my breast and pinched my nipple, giving it a hard twist that had me arching my back and my walls clenching around him. "Come with me, little Queen. I want you to squeeze my cock as I fill you up."

I did exactly as he demanded, my whole body freezing and then convulsing as the orgasm took over. I could hear Jack grunt loudly as he pushed deep and then held still as his cock jerked inside me. He draped his body over mine, his face buried in my neck as he let the pleasure sweep through him.

Once we both came down from our orgasms, he withdrew from my body slowly. Then he gently swept me up in his arms. He walked over to the couch with me cradled against him and sat down. He held me against his chest with one arm. With the other, he swept my hair back from my face and then ran his hand over my body. His big, callused hand roamed over my back, arms, and legs, touching every part of me he could reach.

When I shivered from the chill of the room after the way my body had heated during our lovemaking, he reached over to grab the throw blanket he'd bought for me months ago. He tucked it around me, ensuring every part of me was covered. I reached up to stroke his cheek, and he leaned into my palm.

"You're going to make a good dad, Jack."

He stilled at my whispered words. "I'll need you to teach me."

I smiled at him. "You already know how. You take such good care of me. You treat Zero like he's your baby. You won't need me to teach you. But I'll be here to remind you when you need me to."

"Fuck." He pulled me against him, burying his face in my neck again. "I don't deserve you, Sally. I don't deserve any of this happiness you've given me." His words were muttered against my skin, hoarse and full of emotion.

"You deserve everything. Regardless of what you think, you are a good man, Jack. You take care of this town and its people. I've seen how everyone respects you because you treat *them* with respect. You may be gruff and appear mean, but inside, you have the heart of a true hero." I giggled as I teased him. "You're a marshmallow."

He pulled his head back as he narrowed his eyes, looking menacing and dangerous, sending shivers up my spine. I grinned.

"Take it back," he growled.

I shook my head and laughed. "Never."

"Take it back now, woman, or you'll regret it." His tone would have the bravest men trembling in their boots, and they'd be wise to fear Bones, the Devil's Nightmare President. The Nightmare King. But he was my Jack. I booped his nose.

"What will you do to me? Smoother me in kisses?"

I could see the corner of his mouth twitch and knew he was fighting back a grin. His eyes were still narrowed as he tried to glare at me, but there was a lightness there that he so rarely showed.

"Oh, no, little Queen. I'm going to do much worse than that."

Then, all I could do was squeal as I was suddenly lifted and turned, my back meeting the cold leather of the couch. My laughter rang out as his fingers went to my sides. I writhed on the leather as he tortured me with tickles. Not an inch of me was spared as he made sure I was sorry for calling him soft. Once he was satisfied he'd taught me a lesson, he proceeded to show me how much he appreciated my words with more orgasms.

We were too engrossed in each other's bodies and the love we were sharing to care that the bikers of The Devil's Nightmares all grinned at each other as they listened to the laughter and chuckles coming from their President's office. They shared knowing looks, relieved that their King and Queen were back. Then they returned to their party, doing what bikers did best.

JACK

I woke up with a crick in my neck and my bare ass sticking to the leather of the couch in my office. I wondered at first what had woken me until I realized my woman was reaching out, half asleep. Her arm reached into nothingness beyond where I held her tight to my chest. Her arm fell heavy to the base of the couch, startling her into full wakefulness.

She lifted her head, blinking her beautiful, confused blue eyes. "Jack?" The confusion cleared quickly as her eyes took in my face, bouncing from my eyes, my nose, down to my mouth before darting back up to my eyes. A radiant smile broke out over her face. "You're here," she breathed in wonder and relief.

My once dead heart gave an uncomfortable squeeze in my chest. I did that to her. I made her second guess my adoration for her. I tightened my hold across her back and nuzzled into her neck, breathing in the intoxicating fragrance of all that she was. Her scent was mixed with mine. The smell of us together, along with the feel of her sweet, soft body laying snugly against my hard muscles, had my already stiff cock turning hard as stone for her. You would think that I couldn't get hard again so soon after the marathon of sex we'd had the night before. Every surface and most of the walls had seen action last night, but I had learned from the beginning that just the thought of Sally could make me hard over and over again.

"I'm here, baby."

I held her tight and flipped us over in a swift move, grinning when she let out a small squeal of shock at the abrupt movement. I brushed the hair out of her eyes as she blinked up at me, then narrowed her eyes.

"You could warn a girl."

I grinned down at her, then spread my palm over her throat, reaching for her heartbeat. As I found that life force, proof that she was alive, I shifted my hips and slowly sank my cock inside her warm, wet heat carefully, knowing she was likely sore. I watched as her eyes clouded over with pleasure. The sound of her low moan made my heart squeeze for an entirely different reason.

With long, lazy strokes, I brought both of us to a satisfying climax as she ran her hands up and down my back. I could feel her fingers glide softly along the low ridges of the scars. They were nothing like her long, deep ones. The experience I'd had receiving mine was a different kind of torture than what she'd had to endure. We'd both had more traumatizing moments in our lives than most people could even begin to imagine, and it had shaped both of us. It had turned me into a monster that had only learned to feel again once this angel came into my life.

As I emptied myself into her gripping cunt, I buried my face into her neck. The overwhelming emotions threatened to bring tears to eyes that hadn't shed a tear since I held that first blade, feeling it slice through my personal monster's flesh. This woman had somehow brought humanity back to me. I still wasn't sure if I liked that or not. What I did know is that I would never trade her for anything. I would go through a thousand tortures if it led me to my Queen.

"Ummm," she purred as she stretched below me. Once her breathing steadied and her heart rate returned to normal, she whispered, "I love you, Jack."

Would I ever get used to hearing those words? I pressed a kiss to her neck and lifted my head to gaze directly into gorgeous blues. "I love you." My words were like gravel, pushing through a throat tight with emotion. "You are my everything."

Her smile was sweet and soft. She lifted a hand and smoothed it down my cheek, the raspy sound of my thick stubble sounding loud in the quiet office.

"What are we going to do today?"

I slowly withdrew my softened cock from her warmth, already missing the tight grasp of her cunt before I was even all the way out. As I fell out completely, I leaned up on my elbows to glance down her body at where I had been. One of her legs was pressed tightly to the back of the couch, and the other was over the side, spread as wide as she could be in the small space. I watched, fascinated as always, as my release slowly slid from her body.

With a grunt, I smoothed my fingers through the wetness and brought it up to her belly, where my child rested safely. I ran my fingers in slow circles and painted her with my essence. Then I took a finger and wrote four letters through the whole thing.

Once I was done, I looked back up to see her grinning at me. "I guess I'm going to have to wash you up." I looked back down where I had written MINE across her belly. "And because I want to keep those letters on you, I'll have to dirty you up again."

She let out a small laugh. "I think I might have to wait until tomorrow for that." She wiggled her hips and gave a slight wince. "I might be a little sore today."

I wish I could say I felt bad about that. But a part of me felt nothing but pride that I'd fucked my woman so well that she'd feel me even when I wasn't inside her. I got off the couch and held my tattooed hand out to her. "Come on then, little Queen. I'll wash you, then put some ice on your poor, abused cunt."

She blushed as red as her hair as she gripped my hand. "Jack!" Her laughing tone was admonishing, but there was no disguising her small whimper of need as I held her tight against me once we were both standing. I slid my hand down her back, past the lush curve of her ass, and slid further until my thumb was over the puckered hole of her ass, and my fingers were sliding through the wetness of her pussy lips.

I smirked down at her. "Are you sure you want to wait until tomorrow?" I sank a finger into her cunt and swirled my thumb over her asshole. I hadn't taken her there yet, but I would claim all of her one day. She was mine, and I needed to own every single part of her body.

Her little whimper turned into a moan, making my cock, which had finally been satisfied, twitch. Then, a knock sounded at the door, making Sally jump. Her sudden movement made my finger slide deeper. I was about to push back my plans for a shower when Barrel's muffled voice sounded through the door, the tone urgent.

"Sorry, Prez. I hate to interrupt. But, something important has come up that you are going to want to deal with yourself."

"Fuck," I grumbled, watching as Sally's expression went from pleasure to disappointment. With more reluctance than I would have imagined, I pulled my hand from between her legs, giving her one last sweep of my thumb. Her whole body shivered, but she smiled up at me with understanding, already forgiving me for leaving her before I'd even walked out the door. I let out a heavy sigh. "I'm sorry."

She cupped my face and raised up on her toes to press a soft kiss to my mouth. "Don't be, Mr. Biker President. Just be safe for me, okay?"

"Fuck, I don't deserve you." I pulled her tight, drawing her up my body until she wrapped those lithe little legs around my hips. I gripped her hair in my fist and angled her head to give her a proper kiss. It was fast, but it was everything I couldn't find the words to say. I pulled back. "But I'm never letting you go."

"Good," she sighed, letting her legs drop, then stepping back. She looked around the room for her clothes, walking over to where her shirt was peeking out from under my desk. I groaned as she bent over to pick it up, showing off her wet slit. I resisted stroking my cock before walking over to the door, cracking it open just far enough to see Barrel. The tired lines on his face and the tussled hair made it look like he'd enjoyed himself a little too much last night.

I glared at him as he leaned against the doorway. He yawned wide enough for me to see his tonsils, and I was ready to slam the door in his face until he shook his head as if he were shaking away the fatigue. I wondered if he'd even made it to a bed yet. His eyes opened, finally catching sight of my glare, but his gaze went down my body, the smirk that he had pasted on dropping as his mouth gaped open.

"Holy fuck, Prez! Everyone wondered, but no one really thought you'd have the balls to be tattooed literally everywhere."

I heard a snicker coming from behind me and turned my head to see that my girl had most of her clothes on and was pulling her top over her head. She gave me a saucy wink as she strolled over to me, ignoring the scowl I aimed at her for laughing. She walked up behind me and slid her arms around my waist from behind, laying her head on my back before placing a kiss there and poking her head around my arm.

"Hey, Barrel."

He started to give her the signature smirk that he sent all the ladies until I narrowed my eyes in warning. He cleared his throat instead and ran a hand through his messy hair. "Hey, Sally. Morning. Have a good night?"

She laughed softly. "Yeah, it was pretty good. Looks like you didn't get much sleep."

"Nope. There is too much of me to go around. Gotta please all the pretty things, ya know?"

"For fuck's sake. What's the emergency, Barrel?"

He looked back at me, then gestured with a wave of his hand.

"Maybe you, uh, should put that thing away before you give me an inferiority complex."

With a grunt, I turned away, striding over to where my jeans lay discarded on the floor. I tugged them on while Sally walked over to the couch and sat down, and Barrel leaned against the doorframe, yawning again.

"What's going on?" I asked while buttoning my jeans. I snagged my T-shirt off the desk chair and pulled it over my head. I needed a shower and hated putting yesterday's clothes back on, but that would have to wait.

He glanced over at where Sally was sitting, watching both of us with interest. "Do you think we should talk in the meeting room?"

I shook my head once. "No. Sally can hear anything you have to say." My tone was final, and there would be no arguments from anyone on the matter. Ever. If anyone disagreed with my Queen being privy to club business, they could get the fuck out. I almost lost her by keeping my distance. I wasn't making that mistake again. Sally was the strongest person I knew. She could handle anything, and I knew she would always stay by my side, no matter what she learned about the club.

Barrel shrugged, seeming to accept my command easily. "Whatever you say, Prez. One of the guys was on patrol and caught one of the Boogeymen in the act of setting one of the warehouses on fire. He's in the shed." He eyed Sally once more. "He may not last long. The fight to subdue him resulted in a few injuries. Had to call Doc in to patch up our member, too. He should be here soon."

Doc was on his way. Good. It was past time to have a talk with him. I needed men I could trust in my inner circle. Men who would have my back, and more importantly, men who would protect my Queen with their lives. I also had a Vice President position I needed to fill.

CHAPTER

SEVEN

THE QUEEN OF NIGHTMARES

The knock coming from the office door jerked me awake, and I had a feeling of déjàvu as I looked around the room.

"Sally? Are you in there?" Kara's voice called to me softly through the door, making me sit up. I had a brief moment of nausea as I rose from my lying position, but it passed fairly quickly after I called out to give me a minute.

I realized that I hadn't been sick at all earlier when Jack and I woke up. I had to laugh softly to myself at that. Jack was good for more than just the fantastic orgasms he could give me. He also seemed to help with the morning sickness, too. Now that I thought about it, maybe a lot of the illness had to do with how depressed I was. The mind is a strange thing, and stress can do a lot of damage to a body. At least, I hoped it was that easy, because morning sickness sucked.

After Jack kissed me goodbye, promising that he would be as quick as possible and making me swear not to leave the clubhouse, I went into the restroom and cleaned up as well as I could with the

311

soap and water there. It wasn't the best, and it definitely didn't come close to being shower-clean, but at least I felt fresher than I had when I woke up.

I walked barefoot over to the door and opened it to see Kara standing there with a smile. She looked a lot fresher than I did, obviously having had the shower I was craving. Her long blonde hair was pulled back in a ponytail, and she was wearing a pretty top with a pair of jeans and sneakers.

"Hey, Kara." I swung the door open wider in invitation, and she walked past me after giving me a one-armed hug. I noticed she was carrying a small package about the size of a shoebox.

"Hey, Sally." She sat down on the couch with the box resting on her lap. She looked me up and down critically as if searching for something. "Are you okay?"

I closed the door and sat down on the other end of the couch, turning sideways with one knee bent, my foot tucked under my other leg so I could face her. "Yes? I'm great. Why do you ask?"

"Well, first, I want to apologize. As soon as we walked in, my ex saw me and pulled me away." She bent her head down, looking embarrassed. "We, uh, stayed occupied for most of the night in one of the rooms." She looked me up and down again, her eyes stopping on a few of the fingerprint sized bruises left on my skin from Jack's hands on my upper thighs. "I heard that Bones was super pissed and dragged you back here to his office. I'm so sorry that I got you in trouble. I swear I didn't mean for that to happen."

I laughed at that. "I wasn't in trouble. It's fine. Jack just didn't like that one of the guys got too close to me. Honestly, coming here last night was the best thing I could have done."

Kara cocked her head, looking at me like I was crazy. "Sally, you have bruises. If he's hurting you..."

I waved my hand, cutting off her line of thinking before she could go further. "Jack would never hurt me. I'm a redhead. I bruise like a peach, Kara. Trust me, nothing he did was harmful in any way." I appreciated her concern. I wished that I'd had someone like her when I was growing up and needed someone to care more about my welfare.

I leaned forward and grabbed her hand, giving it a gentle squeeze. "Thank you for being worried about me. I really appreciate it." I let go and sat back against the arm of the couch again. "But, seriously, there is no need for concern about Jack. He loves me."

She let out a gust of air but still didn't look entirely convinced. "Sally, that's what a lot of abused women say. It's easy to make excuses when the person that is abusing you makes you think they are your whole world and that you need them."

My tone was a lot sharper when I replied. "I appreciate your concern. But, as I said, Jack is not abusing me. He treats me like a queen. In fact, he calls me his Queen. He loves me, and," I leaned forward, making sure to emphasize my words, "he does *not* harm me."

She stared at me for a long beat, her expression unreadable. "Okay, Sally," she finally said softly. She stood up after that. "Well, I just wanted to check on you and also to apologize for ghosting you last night." She gave me a smile that seemed a little forced, and I felt bad for being so harsh with her. "I'm really glad you're okay and that it looks like the two of you worked out whatever was going on between you."

"Thanks," I said softly. I stood up to follow her to the door.

As Kara opened the door and started to walk out, she stopped and spun around to face me, holding the box towards me. "Oh! I almost forgot. As I was coming through the gate, the postal guy showed up. I saw that he had this package addressed to you and offered to bring it in."

Surprised, I held out my hands to take the box. I couldn't think of a single reason I would have anything delivered to me, and definitely not at the clubhouse. "That's strange. I haven't ordered anything, and no one I know would send me mail." As I took the box, I was even more confused by how light it was. It almost felt empty.

"Well, maybe Bones ordered you something. Anyway, I've got to go. See you later!" She walked away with a wave.

"Yeah, see you later, Kara." I shut the door and stared at the box as I carried it over to the desk. The shipping label had my name and the address of the clubhouse on it, but I didn't see a sender. The return address was in Pumpkin Patch. "So strange," I murmured. I searched Jack's drawers for a pair of scissors with no luck but grinned when I found a small switchblade. "Typical."

I sliced through the tape and set the knife down, then opened the flaps of the cardboard box, only to see another box inside. The inner box was red and even lighter as I lifted it out. It felt like it was made out of a thin cardstock that could easily be crushed in my hands. There was a strange design on it, making the box look like it was one large die with black skulls instead of dots. I held it up to my ear and shook it gently.

At first, I didn't hear anything and thought that it truly was empty, but then I listened to the faint sound of several small objects bouncing around. I set the box back down with a frown. I didn't have a single solitary clue what it could be. I looked at where the flap was tucked in and reached to lift it. My hand froze for a second as a cold sensation went down my spine. I shook off the feeling of dread, telling myself that I was being ridiculous.

I slid my finger under the edge, sliding the lid out of where it was tucked in, and gripped the thin sides carefully. For a long second, I leaned over and stared into the interior, my mind unable to comprehend what I was seeing. My mind had stalled, maybe from the horror, maybe because what was inside was so unexpected. It wasn't until the insects began to crawl onto my fingers and up my hands that I reacted.

I screamed as my brain finally understood what was happening. In my panic, I brushed my hands against each other, trying desperately to swipe the bugs off me. As I shook my arms frantically, I knocked the box off the desk, the small thud as it hit the floor drowned out by my terrified screeches. I didn't notice more insects escaping the box until I felt them crawling up my legs.

The first bite took me by surprise. I slapped at my thigh, where the pain flared to life. Then I smacked my upper arm, where a second sting lit up my nerve endings. I was shaking, still screaming, and slapping at my body when I felt one on my scalp. I could feel it digging through my hair and immediately bent over to shake it out. I didn't know where to slap anymore. My hands were trembling, and my heart felt like it was going to explode out of my chest when the door flew open.

"What the fuck?" Doc stood stunned for a moment as he took in the scene. Bugs were all over me, crawling under my shirt, in my hair, and even on my face as I jumped around wildly. "Fuck, Sally!"

Doc ran over and immediately began to brush the insects off my arms. He began stomping his heavy shoes, doing a much better job than I had been at squashing anything that fell to the floor.

"Get them off! Get them off me!" I screeched with all the horrified panic I felt as I batted at my hair, shaking my head wildly. It took several long minutes for Doc to free me from most of the insects as I shook and cried.

"What the absolute fuck, Sally! Where did these bugs come from?" he demanded as he stomped on several more creepy crawlies as they tried to scatter once they hit the floor.

"I don't know!" I wailed, still rubbing vigorously at my skin, still feeling the ghostly sensation of a million tiny feet crawling all over me.

"How did they get in here?" His tone was incredulous as he smacked another bug off my shoulder and stomped on it.

I lifted a shaking finger and pointed to the red box that was lying on its side on the floor, now empty. "They were in there. I don't know!" I cried. "A package came addressed to me. When I opened it, they swarmed all over me." I let out a sob and held up my arm so I could look at it. I had red bite marks all over my arm. When I glanced at the rest of my body, I could see I was covered in insect bites. "Oh my god! Doc!"

"Shit. Are you allergic?"

I trembled. "I don't know. I don't even know what those bugs are!"

He pulled me into his body, wrapping a comforting arm around me. I rested my forehead against his chest as I sobbed. I needed Jack. Having Doc hold me was calming my racing heart, but I knew I wouldn't settle until I was in Jack's arms.

"We should get you to the hospital, just in case." He pulled back, peering down at me, "You're pregnant. This kind of trauma might not be good for you." He looked down at the floor to see all the mangled bodies of the bugs. "Fuck. I need one of them so we can identify what they are."

I backed away from the bodies, a shiver racking my body. I didn't want to see another bug as long as I lived. "I don't think anyone could identify any of those," I said with a shudder.

He sighed. "No, I don't think so either."

"Where's Jack?" I tried to keep the whimper out of my voice, but I didn't think I was very successful.

"I'll call him and tell him to meet us at the hospital. Okay?" He put his arm around my shoulders and started to lead me to the door. I spotted my shoes and bent over to slide them on my feet when I felt a tickle under my shirt. My high-pitched scream was loud, bouncing off the walls, as I started jumping around all over again, making it fall to the floor. Doc swiftly grabbed an empty water bottle out of the trash can and scooped the weird looking bug into it before it could escape.

"That'll do," he announced.

EIGHT

JACK

I strode into the shed to see a naked and shivering Boogeyman hanging from the hook in the center of the room. I had to admit, it was pretty cold in the processing room, considering how close it was to Christmas already. There was a furnace for disposing of deer carcasses that came in handy for disposing of other things as well, but it wouldn't be lit for this interaction. Not until later.

I wasn't so sure all the shivering was due to the cold as I stared at the enemy biker. He was scrawny and looked young. He couldn't have been far past twenty. I had no sympathy for his age, however. He made a choice to get in bed with the worst MC in the area. Now, he had to deal with the consequences.

"You don't look so good." I looked him over, taking in all of his injuries, including what looked like a knife wound in his ribs. Barrel was right; the guy wasn't going to last much longer. I needed to get what I could out of him before it was too late.

At the sound of my gravelly voice, his whole body jerked. He slowly lifted his head, revealing an eye swollen shut and a split in his lip, with a watery trail of blood going down past his chin. When he focused his one good eye on me, it widened before he put on a brave front and sneered. Instead of an answer, he spit a wad of blood onto the floor.

"Fuck you, Devil," he croaked out.

I stepped closer. "No thanks. Though, I could have been fucking my woman right now if I didn't have to deal with you. You'll pay for that, too."

"Fuck your whore. Oogie is going to ruin her pussy when he gets ahold of her." He tried to be brave with his foolish words, but the wobble at the end gave away how scared he really was. He was fucked, and he knew it.

Without responding to his taunt, I reared back and punched him in the ribs, right where the knife wound was. His body swayed wildly as his scream echoed around the room.

"Fuck, Prez. That was brutal." Shock winced and rubbed a hand over his own ribcage.

I grunted and walked over to the table already laid out with tools, selecting a long, thin blade typically used for filleting meat. "What do the Boogeymen have planned?" I gritted out as I strolled back over to the young man who had settled into whimpers. His wound was flowing freely with blood, a puddle forming underneath him and rolling into the drain. There was an interesting pattern of blood splatters over the floor where he had swung before one of my men stopped him.

I expected the man to be defiant and tell me to fuck myself again. Instead, he squeezed his eyes shut and whimpered.

"Prez plans to get your woman from behind your walls. He's pissed you built them and made it harder for us to get in." He let his head drop, and his voice was slurred as he continued spilling his secrets as his blood ran thickly from his side and down his leg. "He thinks if he gets the woman, he'll be able to control you. Once he has her, he'll have the town."

He wasn't fucking wrong. I would gladly give up everyone in the town to save my Queen. I ground my teeth so hard my jaw ached, and I could feel a throbbing pain behind my eye from the headache that was forming.

"How does he plan to get her?"

"D-don't know. I just fully patched in last—" he took a breath and then started coughing, blood spraying from his lips. "I'm new, so I don't know anything," he finished in a hoarse whisper.

The kid was almost gone. I wouldn't get anything further from him. I sighed, then swiped across his throat with the knife, making sure to cut deep enough that he would bleed out quickly. His body jerked once before going still. I turned away and dropped the knife on the table for one of the men to clean.

"I shouldn't have to say it, but I'm going to anyway," I said as I looked at each of my men in the eye. These were my closest men, the officers of the Devil's Nightmares, and my inner circle. I trusted them, but I still needed to make sure they understood the serious-ness of my words. "Sally is mine. She is to be protected at all costs. She never leaves the compound without me. There needs to be a guard on her location at all times. That means day and night, someone will be guarding my house." I glared at them, daring them to challenge me.

This was new territory for the club. A few members had old ladies, but none that had been under direct threat before. Sally was more than an old lady to me. She was my Queen, and that meant she was Queen of the fucking Nightmares, too.

"She is your Queen. You will protect her and show her the same respect you show me. Is that understood?" I jerked my head and narrowed my eyes to glare at Barrel as he stepped forward.

"Just saying, Prez, but that was a given. We get it." He looked around at the other guys, and they all nodded or grunted their agree-ment. Shock folded his arms over his chest with a grin on his face. "We're happy for you. We like Red, and we like seeing you happy."

My chest felt strangely warm at his words. As I glanced at each of my inner circle, they all had the same look of agreement and grins. I resisted the urge to rub at my chest. I grunted. "Good." I turned to walk to the door without looking back. I needed to get to my girl after hearing Oogie's plans for her. I would give him whatever he asked for to get her back, but I didn't want him to lay a finger on her. I knew if he did somehow get past me, he wouldn't leave much of her to retrieve. Just the thought alone had cold sweat trickling down my spine.

I punched in the code to the heavy door of the processing room and swung the door open to breathe in the fresh, cold air. Snow was coming soon. The clouds hung heavy and thick in the sky. My breath came in puffs of white as I strolled from the shed to the back of the clubhouse. Before I made it halfway to the main building, the back door flung open, and one of my men came running out. He stopped in his tracks when he saw me. I could clearly read the urgency on his face.

"What's wrong?" I demanded as I quickened my pace.

"It's Sally..."

Before he could finish speaking, I began to run, throwing the heavy back door open hard enough to bang against the wall, and ran down the hall to my office, where I'd left her to wait. The door was standing open, so I pushed inside.

"Sally!" I glanced around the room, not finding my woman. Instead, there was a cardboard box on my desk that hadn't been there before. Red caught my eye, and I looked down to see another box lying on the floor. I blinked at the disgusting mess of insect bodies squashed into the thin carpet.

Before I could turn around to search for my Queen, the same man who had run outside to tell me something about her came into the room, breathing heavily from running.

"Doc took her to the hospital. I don't know what happened. He just told me to find you and tell you to meet him there."

I knew what happened. I walked over to the red box and picked it up, looking inside. There was a bug about the size of a dime that tried to run out and down the side of the red box. I snatched it between my fingers and squeezed. I wiped my hand on the leg of my jeans and plucked the black card out of the bottom of the box.

I tried to do this the easy way, Bones.

I warned you two months ago.

You should have just done what I told you when I left you that message.

Give up the town, or your woman suffers.

This was only the beginning.

I flung the flimsy box to the ground, wishing it was made out of something fragile that would make a satisfying sound as it shattered. As it was, I simply turned away, my need to have Sally in my arms greater than my need to tear the box to pieces. I tucked the small card into my back pocket, then picked up the cardboard box to see a mailing label on it. I turned toward the door, ready to head to my bike. I strode past the man who had come to give me the message and paused just long enough to give him another job to do.

"Give this to Shock. Tell him I want to know who mailed it." I shoved the box at Horse and kept going as he fumbled it until he had a solid grip. "And have the carpet removed from my office. Have them put in a fucking wood floor."

"Got it, Prez. Good luck. Hope she's okay."

I ignored him. She was going to be okay. She fucking had to. But she was also outside the gates without me. If I had to guess, that was precisely the Boogeyman's plan all along. She'd be easy to grab at the hospital. I could only be glad as fuck that Doc was with her. If there was one person I could count on to protect her almost as well as I could, it was my brother.

Just because she belonged to me would have been enough for him to want to, but I knew that he had a soft spot for my girl. He had checked on her several times over the past few months. From the time she had first moved in with me after her attack in the alley and then after she'd nearly lost her arm, he always made sure to check on her to see how she was healing. After I was done ensuring my girl was going to be okay, I would be giving my brother a demand that he wouldn't be able to refuse this time.

I let the heavy steel door at the front of the clubhouse slam closed with a bang and strode to my bike. I heard steps from heavy boots running in my direction. Without pausing my long strides, I called out to Barrel.

"I'm heading to the hospital. Send out a message to every club member. I want all exits to Pumpkin Patch covered. If any Boogeymen are spotted, I want them captured for interrogation."

I heard the steps slow, then pick back up again as they headed in the opposite direction. I knew Barrel would likely be pissed that he wasn't coming with me, but I needed him to get the town protected and locked down more than I needed a shadow. Ever since Lock was murdered, Barrel had been determined to become my personal body-guard. His way of working through grief, I supposed, but he would understand my need for the order.

With a command for Zero to stay behind as he trotted up to me with a whine, I straddled my Harley, then took off with a deafening roar of the engine and a cloud of dust.

THE QUEEN OF NIGHTMARES

Doc was exasperating. From the time we'd left Jack's office, he had been fussing over me. He had already asked me how I felt no less than ten times in the fifteen-minute drive. And now he was trying to convince me to let him carry me into the hospital. I could see the worry written all over his face, though, so I could forgive him. But I still wasn't going to let him carry me.

"Doc, it's just some bug bites! What's the worst that could happen? I scratch until I bleed?" I turned and started following the signs that guided me toward the emergency entrance to the hospital. I felt a little silly for going to the ER for bug bites. If it weren't for my worry about the baby I was carrying, I probably would have just covered myself in Benadryl cream and taken some Tylenol.

"Anaphylaxis, necrosis, death."

His words spoken so matter of fact had me pausing. I swallowed hard before turning to look over my shoulder as he caught up with me.

"Isn't it past time to be worried about anaphylaxis?" I blinked up at him, picking out the features that he shared with Jack as a way to calm my sudden burst of nerves.

He sighed and put his arm around my shoulder, leading me over to a side entrance I hadn't noticed. "Yes. But there's still time to have a negative reaction. And necrosis could take a few days to start showing up." He pulled a card out of his wallet and scanned it before pulling the door open. He guided me inside the brightly lit hallway, straight to the busy desk in the center of the large room the hallway opened up into.

The nurse who sat behind the desk, typing away on a keyboard, asked in a tired, bored voice, "Can I help you?" before looking up. I had to bite down on both lips to stop myself from giggling at the double-take the pretty brunette did once she realized who was standing at her desk. Her entire demeanor changed from the harried, overworked nurse to a shy, blushing schoolgirl.

"Dr. Erickson." Her cheeks turned rosy, and I could see how hard she was clenching the arms of her chair. But what really caught my eye was the way Doc's eyes seemed to soften as he glanced down at her.

"Helen." His tone was unlike anything I'd ever heard come from him. His two default tones tended to be gruff and sarcastic. Hearing him speaking so softly and gently had my eyes widening in shock. Doc's hand that was still on my shoulder squeezed. "This is my sister-in-law, Sally. She got into some kind of bug nest and was bit quite a few times."

With a concentrated effort, Helen tore her eyes away from Doc's handsome face and looked me over. Seeing her own eyes widen at all the red, swollen bumps covering my scarred flesh had me ducking my head, ready to hide in a way I hadn't since Jack had come into my life and made me believe I was beautiful. To the nurse's credit, she didn't act like I was strange for wearing the stupid shorts and top in the freezing cold weather. I wished I had thought to ask to stop by the house for a quick change of clothes first.

"Usually, I would advise a patient to watch and wait with a dose of Benadryl. But Sally is pregnant." His jaw clenched as he got pissed off all over again at the memory of seeing me covered in crawling, biting insects. "My brother would be a little upset if anything happened to his girl." I grimaced. That was the understatement of the century. The last time someone had hurt me, Jack settled for destroying his ability to walk, only because he had witnesses and couldn't pull the trigger without ending up in prison. "So, I'm going to need full panels done as well as an ultrasound machine to check on the baby."

Helen stood up quickly. The brief flare of what I thought I recognized as jealousy was wiped clean and replaced by sympathy by the time Doc finished speaking. "Of course! I believe room seven is open. I'll go run and check. Just wait here."

I watched the pretty nurse speed walk down a hall, then turned to look up at Doc with a raised eyebrow. "Helen, huh?"

He turned his gaze from the direction she had disappeared and narrowed his dark eyes on me. Though more rich chocolate and less deep, bottomless abyss, Doc's eyes still reminded me of Jack. I wasn't exactly sure what it was about them. "Don't," he growled. I would have pushed him just for the fun of it, but Helen was already returning.

"Your room is ready for you, Sally. If you'll follow me, I can get you set up."

I looked back at Doc for a second, but his eyes were glued to a different woman, and I couldn't catch his eye. I didn't want to be left alone, even if I was in a hospital. It just seemed like a bad idea after what had happened today. Being here at all could be playing right into the person's hands. When I heard the footsteps coming, I let out a sigh of relief that he wasn't going to leave me alone.

"What kind of insects were they?"

The softly spoken question jarred me from my thoughts but brought me back to the feeling of all those creepy crawlies. I clenched my fist to keep from patting my hair for any strays. Again.

"Uh, I have no idea. Doc?" We both looked over our shoulders to see Doc jerk his eyes up from the general location of where our asses had been. I smirked as he cleared his throat.

"What?"

"Where's the bug you managed to save?"

"Shit. I left it in the truck. I'm going to need to run and get that. But it can wait until Bones gets here first."

I gave him a grateful smile and then turned to the nurse. "It was about an inch long, maybe less, and was brown. It had a lot of legs like a millipede, but it definitely wasn't as long, maybe more like a pill bug, only hairy instead of body armor. Oh," I winced as I gave in to the increasing urge to scratch one of the many bites."They bite or pinch or sting. I know that's not helpful. I'm sorry."

"Have you tried Googling the bug?" she asked, and I shook my head.

"It all happened so fast. I didn't even grab my phone before heading here."

Doc spoke up, already pulling his phone out of his pocket. "I'll start looking while you get dressed in the hospital gown. I'll be right outside the room, so don't worry." I nodded, my neck feeling stiff, and my smile was brittle as I followed Helen into the room.

She walked over to a cabinet and pulled a typical gown from a shelf before handing it to me. "Change into this. I'm assuming Dr. Erickson will be the one to run your tests, so I'll wait for him to give his instructions. I will get your ultrasound machine ordered, though." She smiled as she walked to the door and pulled the curtain toward the wall, blocking all view inside the room from the open door, before closing the door behind her.

I had the top and shorts I had been wearing off and folded neatly on the chair before struggling with the ties on the hospital gown. Suddenly, I was hot, sweaty, and finally feeling that nausea I hadn't missed waking up with this morning. It seemed that whatever charm Jack had for holding back the morning sickness had worn off.

I collapsed back on the bed and breathed deeply with my eyes closed. I wasn't sure if I was going to make it without having to sprint for the toilet. I heard the heavy knock on the door and swallowed thickly. "Come in," I croaked out before the wooden door swung inwards.

"You decent, Red?"

I grunted out my answer. I rolled up one hip to tug on the blanket I was lying on, barely having the energy.

"Hey, hey. What's going on? You were fine a minute ago?"

"I feel sick. And hot." I whined with a ridiculous pout as I felt sorry for myself.

"Come on. Get up so I can fix your sheets. Bones should be here in just a few minutes. Then you can get my brother to rub your back or whatever shit will make you feel better." I snorted as I lowered my feet back to the cold floor.

"Nice bedside manner you have there, *Dr. Erickson*," I swayed, and the room seemed to grow smaller as I watched through squinted eyes as Doc pulled the blanket and sheet back for me.

"Family and the club get the real me. The hospital gets the professional me. Don't you feel special?" He turned to look at me after I had stayed silent. I was patting my clammy cheek and taking in deep breaths through my nose.

"Oh, shit." Doc darted to the sink to grab a plastic bag attached to a bottomless cup from the small stack sitting there. With expert ease, he had the long blue bag stretched out and the cup shoved under my chin just in time.

I groaned once I was done. It probably wouldn't have been so bad if I had at least eaten something. But after Jack left, I had fallen back to sleep. Then Kara woke me up, and after that, the whole bug thing happened.

Heavy footsteps sounded outside in the corridor, seconds before my heavy room door was pushed open. I knew it was Jack before he even came around the curtain, but I was surprised to see Doc holding a gun and holding me back with his arm when I tried to get past him to get to Jack.

"Jack!" His name came out in a strangled sob. All of the emotions I had been trying to hold back, all the fear, pain, the sudden weakness from being sick. It all came out of me as Jack shoved past Doc when he didn't move back quickly enough. He scooped me up in his arms and held me cradled to his chest, giving a grateful nod of thanks to his brother before Doc slipped out the door. Without a word, he let me get it all out until I gave an exhausted hiccup.

Jack rested his cheek on the top of my head. "I'm so sorry I wasn't there for you."

I let out a shaky breath, then cringed. "You have nothing to feel bad about Jack." I covered my mouth with my hand. "But, if you love me, you will take me to the sink so I can rinse out my mouth. I kinda threw up right before you showed up."

He cursed as he stood up and carried me to the sink. He handed me a small paper cup and turned on the cold water. "I didn't get your ginger cookies and tea this morning."

I spat out the water and glared into Jack's beautiful dark eyes before turning back to the sink and rinsing again. When I spit it out, I reached for a paper towel, smacking Jack's hand away when he tried to do it for me.

"You can't control the world, no matter how big, bad, and tough you are. You just have to accept that some things you can't command and deal with the aftermath the way we mere mortals have had to do our entire lives."

"I don't like seeing you sick or injured," he growled as he walked me back over to the hospital bed. Then he sat down on the edge, swinging his legs up so he could rest comfortably against the raised head with me in his arms.

"I'm certain I wouldn't like seeing you hurt either, Jack. But if that were to happen, I would do everything I could to help you get better."

He raised a sexy eyebrow and ran his tattooed fingers over the red, swollen bites on my cheeks. While he inspected the bites, I ran a fingertip over his neck, lightly tracing the bones that were shaded so spectacularly. I couldn't help but admire the artistic talent. His T-shirt covered the base of his neck down, so I wasn't able to give into the enjoyment of tracing the rest of the bones down his chest.

"You wouldn't torture yourself with the thought that there might have been something you could have done to prevent it?"

I huffed. "I don't see why we have to play the semantics game."

Jack snorted, then kissed the tip of my nose. "Right. Semantics."

I tapped my fingertip on his stubbled chin and gave a decisive nod. "Thank you for seeing things my way, sir."

THE QUEEN OF NIGHTMARES

A knock on the door had Jack and I looking in that direction as if we held the ability to see through the fabric hanging in the way. The door cracked open just before the familiar voice of Helen called out. I covered Jack's hand with my own, giving a shake of my head so he'd slide the gun back under his vest before the sweet nurse that his brother had a crush on could see it and freak the fuck out.

"Hey, Sally. Dr. Erickson said his brother arrived." She was dragging something on wheels, and I saw her backside before the rest of her came into view.

I nudged Jack. "Go help her."

He didn't say a word; he just tightened his arms around me. Which I suppose was answer enough. Jack wasn't ready to let me go yet.

"Oh my." Helen's words trailed off once she caught sight of Jack holding me possessively in his arms. She looked away quickly as if she had caught us in a compromising position that wasn't as innocent as him holding me tightly with all our clothing on. Well, I mean, I was in just a thin gown with my ass completely exposed.

"I have the ultrasound machine here. I told the technician I would get it set up for them, but they should be here in just a few minutes," Her rambling was cute, but I didn't like the idea that I was making her uncomfortable. I nudge Jack again.

"Maybe you should let me up."

Again, he tightened his arms. "I can't, Sally. Don't ask me again."

"Oh, please don't get up if you're comfortable. It's okay." Helen gave a reassuring smile as she glanced over from where she had begun to sort wires and plugs for the big square machine.

"It's you I don't want to make uncomfortable. Jack can hold my hand from the chair." I stared pointedly at Jack as I said the words. He stared right back at me blankly.

Helen stopped prepping and turned to look us over again. "You don't make me uncomfortable. You make me wistful. I wish I had what you two so clearly do." She hit a button on the machine, and the screen came to life. "It might be a little jealousy, too." She laughed lightly, then walked back to the door. "I'll see you two soon. And don't worry, Dr. Erickson's brother, I'll inform the ultrasound tech that she needs to expect her patient to be held while she does her job." She gave a wink and a smile before pausing at the door. "She can work around you." With that, she was gone.

"What's going on with that nurse?" Jack jerked his chin in the direction of the now empty doorway.

"I think Doc has a crush on her. Or she has a crush on him? Maybe a mutual crush." I shrugged. "But it was clear they both liked each other. It's also clear that neither one of them has acted on it." I turned on Jack's lap to face him more. "Do you think—"

"No." His tone was flat. Final.

"But, Jack—"

"No."

I gave out a disgruntled huff and crossed my arms over my chest.

I wasn't going to agree not to meddle, no matter what Jack said. What could it hurt to give a little push?

"Little Queen," his tone was a warning, but I could hear the amusement he was failing to hide. I just gave a non-committal hum as I stared at the floral pattern on the curtain. Jack sighed and settled his chin on my shoulder. I absentmindedly scratched at the spots on my arms. The bites weren't too bad, but they were definitely itchy.

A large hand settled over mine, stopping my fingernails from doing any damage. "Baby, I don't want you to make yourself bleed. I'm barely holding it together here. If I see blood on your beautiful skin, I'm going to start tearing things apart."

I sighed and snuggled further into his warm body. I relaxed into him and allowed his comforting presence to soothe away the lingering terror. I let my eyes drift shut and let my mind wander back to last night and our conversation. Before the attack a couple of months ago, I had been the happiest I had ever been in my life. It was difficult just to erase all the pain and doubt that I had gone through in the recent weeks, but knowing that all of our problems stemmed from a lack of communication had gone a long way in making me get past it. We just needed to avoid anything like it in the future.

It wasn't long before another knock sounded on the door. It opened immediately, a feminine voice calling from behind the curtain.

"Sally? Are you ready for your sonogram?"

A small woman with a bright smile and a headful of long, shiny braids twisted back into a smooth updo stepped around the curtain at my answering, "Yes."

"Great!" She walked over to the machine that Helen had set up and started clicking on the multitude of buttons. "Helen warned me that we might have to do this with company." She grinned, eyeing Jack's arms that were still wrapped tight around me. "I don't blame you." She winked and held out a skinny white bottle. "But I'm going to need you as flat as possible."

With some maneuvering, I wiggled until I was flat on my back, my head in Jack's lap. My feet were hanging off the end of the bed, but the ultrasound technician didn't seem to mind the position I had to get into to keep Jack from losing his shit. When I lifted my gown up to tuck under my breasts, Jack made sure to keep my lower half covered while holding one arm over my breasts. His overprotectiveness had me wondering how he would react once it was time for me to deliver this baby. If he didn't want to see me in pain, he was going to be in for a rude awakening in a few more months.

"Okay, here we go. It's warm, so it shouldn't be too much of a shock." Shana, by the name on her badge, leaned over, squirted a large glob of the jelly substance over my lower belly, and then placed the doppler on my skin. It wasn't unpleasant, just a strange sensation that made me want to squirm.

All thoughts of weird jelly-like substances and exposed flesh flew from my mind as soon as the staticky sounds from the machine evened out into a steady beating. My breath caught at the sound, and Jack's arm tightened around me.

"There we are," Shana murmured quietly and used one hand to shift dials and press buttons while holding the wand steady. She shifted the wand a little and held still before shifting again. "It looks like your little bean is doing good. Heartbeat is nice and strong." She turned the screen so I wouldn't have to crane my neck. There, in a pool of black and white, was a small image of a heart beating wildly. "It isn't always easy to see the fetus this early in your pregnancy, but this is a great shot."

She spoke some more, but I couldn't focus on her words. All I could do was stare at the beautiful sight of the little heart fluttering. "Jack," I whispered in awe, reaching up and grabbing onto his hand.

"I see it, little Queen." His voice was gruff with the emotions he was holding in. "I love you." He whispered the words into my hair, and we both took in the moment we saw our baby and heard the heartbeat for the first time. I blinked back the tears that threatened to cloud my vision. I didn't want to miss a single second of this moment.

After several more minutes of tapping buttons and moving the wand around, Shana removed the doppler and smiled down at me. "I'll send the images to the doctor, but it looks like everything is right on track for your estimated date of conception." She handed me a towel and started cleaning up the doppler. "Congratulations!"

I gave her a watery smile as I swiped the towel over the gel on my abdomen. "Thank you."

"There's only one in there, right?" It was the first time I thought I'd ever heard Jack sound hesitant, but the girl laughed.

"Only one." She winked as she held out a strip of paper to Jack. He took it gingerly in his big, tattooed hand. I tilted my head back to see what he was holding but got stuck on the absolute awe on his face as he stared down at the images of our baby. Seeing Jack fall in love with our baby made my heart feel like it was swelling with more love than I could possibly contain.

Shana slipped out of the room quietly as we both stared at the grainy images. "I'm going to be the best father I can, Sally. I promise."

I turned in the bed and crawled back up to rest against his chest again. His arms wrapped around me, holding me close, his chin on my shoulder.

"I know you will, Jack. You're going to be an amazing father."

He tore his eyes from the pictures to gaze down at me as I tilted my head up to look at his handsome face. "Thank you."

I shrugged and gave him a lopsided smile. "It's the truth."

"No. I mean, thank you for giving me what I never thought I could have. Until you came into my life, I was barely living. I had my club, my bike, and my dog. Now, I have everything."

"Jack," I cupped his cheek and let out a breath heavy with emotion. "It's you that gave me hope for a better life. I was dead inside after what I had gone through. I was in constant fear, always wondering if I would ever be able to walk outside and not be afraid. I didn't know if I would ever be able to find a way to live again. You gave me back my life. You make me feel safe, loved, and cherished."

He closed his eyes and leaned into my touch before opening his dark eyes again. He looked deep into my soul. "We brought each other to life."

"Yes." His lips touched mine in a soft caress. His kiss was gentle, reverent.

"Marry me."

The words were whispered against my lips, and it took a long second for them to penetrate. I pulled back and stared up at him, eyes wide. My gaze took him in, seeing his fierce determination, the firm set to his jaw. I searched for any signs of regret that the words had come out of him. The longer I stared, the narrower his gaze became until he was glaring at me.

"You *will* marry me."

I let out a breathless laugh. "Are you sure?"

He let out a growl before grabbing me by the hips and turning me to face him on the hospital bed. His hands were tight, just shy of bruising, as he crushed me to him. His mouth took mine in the type of brutal kiss I was used to from him, making me melt against his hard chest. When he broke the kiss, he glared at me some more.

"I'm not asking. You are my woman, my Queen. You are going to marry me and make me the happiest fucking biker there has ever been, or I will put you over my knee and spank your ass until you do."

I burst into tears again for the hundredth time that day and threw my arms around his shoulders as I cried into his neck. He held me tight against him, rubbing my back as I let out the last bit of anxiety I'd been holding on to.

That was how Doc found us when he walked into the room a few minutes later. He stood there with a bemused look on his face, staring at the emotional mess I was, when Jack decided to announce loudly that Doc would be his best man and the club's Vice President —whether he liked it or not.

THE QUEEN OF NIGHTMARES

After Jack's declaration said in a tone full of stark finality coupled with a glare, daring Doc to argue, he and Doc stepped outside the room for a quiet discussion. Before leaving, Jack kissed me lightly on the lips and gave my still flat belly a gentle rub. He let me know that he was planning to run to the cafeteria for some terrible coffee, but there would be a prospect standing guard outside the room just in case the Boogeymen tried to make a move. At this point, it seemed unlikely, but the chance of an attack couldn't be eliminated completely, and I couldn't deny that having someone there made me feel better.

I lay in the bed, trying desperately not to scratch at the itchy spots, and waited for the Benadryl to kick in. Doc had assured both of us that it would be perfectly safe to take. Even so, Jack did a quick internet search to verify for himself while Doc stood by the door, glaring with his arms crossed over his chest. I had to smile, even as I rolled my eyes for Doc's benefit at Jack's overprotectiveness. The brothers were more alike than either of them realized.

I wanted to go home. I hated being in the hospital after what I had experienced at the hands of Dr. Stein. Just being in the building brought back horrible memories. More than once, the man had sent me to the hospital. But Doc wanted to ensure that everything looked good before we could go, so he refused to allow me to leave until the lab processed my bloodwork.

I was staring at the deep, red scar that ran across the upper part of my forearm when the door to the room opened again. There was no knock, so I had assumed it was Jack returning already, but whoever it was entering was quiet and definitely not my biker President.

A thin, young woman wearing blue scrubs edged around the curtain as I eyed her. She had her head down, her short, dark hair concealing her face as she slowly walked toward the machine to my left that was monitoring my heart rate. I watched warily, wondering why she was acting so strangely.

My phone began to vibrate on the bed next to me. Jack had placed it there when he first showed up. He'd wanted me to keep it close in case I needed to reach him, not happy that I had left it behind at the clubhouse. The ringing distracted me from the quiet nurse. When I glanced down at it, I saw an unknown number from California. With a frown, I declined the call, figuring it was a sales call or something equally unimportant from my time living there.

I glanced back up to see the nurse staring at me from the corner of her eye. It was obvious she wasn't there to take notes on my vitals. My hand moved to the call button on the side of the bed when she finally turned to look at me, a desperate look on her face.

"Please, don't."

I knew that voice. The woman looked different without the pink hair and the arrogant attitude, but there was no mistaking who it was.

"Daisy." I picked my phone up, already preparing to call Jack, when she reached over and snatched the phone from my hand.

"Sally, please listen to me!" she begged in a desperate whisper, eyeing the curtain that was concealing the door.

I glared up at Daisy. I could admit that I was shocked to see her standing in front of me, alive and well. A part of me had expected Jack to kill her. She had been a spy, after all. The last time I had seen her, she had taunted him to kill her as she spewed toxic venom at him. The threats she made about her brother and what he was planning on doing to me would have been enough to have Jack end her life. So, seeing her standing in my hospital room alive and apparently doing well had my head spinning.

"What are you doing here?" I demanded, eyeing the phone she now held in her hand. I glanced at the door, knowing all I needed to do was yell out to have the Nightmare prospect running inside.

Daisy glanced toward the door again and swallowed before slowly reaching out to hand my phone back to me. "I owe Bones my life. I need to repay him."

I opened my mouth to respond, but no words came out. I realized I should have asked questions back then, but I had thought at the time it was best I didn't think of Jack as a woman murderer. Even if I could understand his reasonings, it would have been difficult to reconcile the act with the man I had come to love. Now, it seemed there was a lot more to the man than I ever could have imagined.

Daisy gestured to the phone I was holding with a trembling hand. "I understand if you want to call him, but I hope you'll give me a few minutes to explain."

I eyed her, really taking her in. She looked the same, but there were subtle differences. The thick makeup was gone, allowing her natural beauty to shine. Her hair was dark in what I assumed was her natural shade, making her pretty eyes pop with color. She looked healthy, even if she seemed spooked.

"You have five minutes," I threatened, setting the phone in my lap and eyeing her with my best no-nonsense stare.

She gave me a small smile that wobbled just a little. "Thank you," she whispered. "Bones gave me enough money to disappear after I told him everything I knew about what my brother had planned for the Devil's Nightmares. I took the money and got on the first bus out of town. I made it to Tennessee, where I rented a small apartment and got a job at a bar." She shrugged a shoulder and gave a self-deprecating smile. "It's all I really know how to do."

She sighed, rubbing her forehead before continuing. "Anyway, I have a cousin back here that I was worried about, so I decided to call her, making her promise not to let Oogie know I was alive. I've been hiding with her while I tried to figure out a way to get a message to you." She paused and stared at me with a serious expression. "I found out that Oogie has someone else spying on the Nightmares."

I inhaled sharply at the news. With all the security Jack had been implementing and the plans they were making to take out the Boogeymen, it could mean disaster for everyone if there was another mole in the club. If they knew too much, it could mean death for everyone.

"Who is it?"

She was already shaking her head before I could get the words out. "I don't know. I wish I did, really. But Cherise didn't know either. She just overheard her old man talking about it with some of the guys who had come over for drinks one night. Cherise thought I was dead, too, and had been pissed at Oogie for putting me in the position in the first place, knowing what would happen if I were caught." She shook her head. "I should never have agreed to do it. I knew it was dangerous and that I probably wouldn't make it out alive, but Oogie has a way of forcing the issue.

"When I told Cherise about what Bones did for me, she insisted on telling me what she could, hoping to help. Sally," she looked at me with big eyes, "please know, not everyone is like my brother. Most of us don't agree with how he runs the club or the other horrible things he does." She shuddered and looked across the room to the window overlooking the town of Pumpkin Patch. The lights outside twinkled with the strange mix of Christmas and Halloween that the town seemed to thrive on. With Christmas just around the corner, the pumpkins decorating the town were more jovial than menacing, and much of the pumpkin artwork adorning the shop windows had Santa hats and other Christmas-themed items added.

"I can't stay," she said, glancing back at me. "Bones said if I ever returned, he wouldn't hesitate to kill me this time. I really can't blame him. But I needed to warn you. I couldn't find a way to get to you after the fences were put up around the compound."

"Are you the one that sent the box of insects to me?"

She looked shocked and took a step back, almost hitting the wall behind her. "No! I swear it wasn't me. It's something Oogie would do, though. He loves to terrorize." She got a faraway look in her eye and shuddered again as if remembering her own torment at her brother's hands. "I just heard that you were here. The town likes to talk, and gossip travels fast. I thought it would be my best chance to let you know." She stared at me, her look intense and serious. "Sally, he plans to take you. I didn't know how true my words were when I was threatening Bones that day, but my brother really does plan to take you. He thinks if he can get to you, he'll be able to control Bones and force him to give up the club and town. If Bones is no longer the President, he will be able to take down the entire club. You have to keep an eye out at all times. Someone close to you is working for him. You can't trust anyone."

Heavy footsteps could be heard outside the door, and both of our heads jerked in that direction. "Shit," she hissed and darted her eyes around frantically.

I made a split-second decision. "Quickly! Go into the bathroom!" I waved her in the direction of the open door. "I'll find a way to get you out of here, I promise."

She took a couple of steps toward the bathroom, stopped, and came back over to me with tears in her eyes. "Thank you, Sally. I really am sorry for everything. In case you ever need me." Then she turned and darted into the small room right before the door opened. I closed my hand over the small slip of paper she had placed in my lap.

I quickly thought of how I should handle the situation. I hated lying to Jack or keeping secrets from him, but even though I had little reason to, I believed Daisy. She was putting her life on the line to save mine, and that made me trust her. There was a good chance that Jack would react violently to having someone who used to be such a threat so close to me, especially after what happened today.

As Jack stepped around the curtain while holding a paper cup in both hands, I smiled. He really was a good man. Better than anyone knew. He could have killed Daisy; instead, he gave her a new life. It made my heart swell with love for him even more than I already had.

"Hey, little Queen. I got you some hot tea." He set the cup down on the table before leaning over to kiss the top of my head.

I closed my eyes, savoring the warmth of his breath on me as he lingered there. When I opened them, I glanced at the closed bathroom door. I needed to protect him as much as I did Daisy. I couldn't allow him to hurt her. And he would in a heartbeat if he thought I needed protecting, but if he did, his conscience would forever eat away at him.

"Jack?" I asked in a quiet voice.

"Hmmm?" He ran the backs of his tattooed fingers over my cheek, and I leaned into them.

"I'm a little hungry. Do you think that you can get me something small to eat? Maybe a sandwich? Or a muffin?" I looked up at him to see he was already straightening to his full height, ready to go get me whatever I asked for. It had my conscience pricking at me. I hesitated. "Maybe one of the guys could go get it for me?"

He shook his head. "I'll get you what you need, baby. Is turkey okay?"

I blinked back the tears that started stinging my eyes at his thoughtfulness. "Turkey would be perfect."

"Good. I'll be back before you know it. If you need me for any reason, call." He tapped the phone in my lap and bent down one last time to kiss me as I lifted my chin to meet his lips.

"Thank you," I whispered.

"Don't thank me for taking care of you, little Queen," he said before heading back out of the room.

After several long seconds, Daisy cracked the bathroom door open, peeking her head out. Without another word to each other, we both nodded and then she followed quietly behind Jack. I didn't know if I would ever see her again, but I wished her well and silently thanked her for risking everything just to bring me a warning.

CHAPTER

TWELVE

THE QUEEN OF NIGHTMARES

It was late before we finally made it back home. My bloodwork had come back clean, with no serious concerns for my health. Doc had insisted on a final ultrasound right before we left the hospital to check on the baby one last time. It was clear that he was going to be an overprotective uncle. I was already starting to tease him about it. He was still arguing with Jack about becoming the new Vice President, but I was certain that Jack would get his way.

Doc found an entomologist to send the bug to at a nearby university, though it didn't seem to matter at that point. The inflamed bites had lessened in swelling with the dose of Benadryl he had prescribed at the hospital. It seemed whatever they were, it wasn't venomous. The entomologist didn't seem concerned about the insect when he saw the picture but promised he would look at it closer once he received the body. It was a lesson I would never forget, though. I won't be taking any more chances on unknown packages in the future.

I collapsed on the couch, exhausted from the day, even though I

351

had spent the majority of it in a hospital bed. Jack dropped his keys on the table by the front door after waving off Doc, who had given me a ride back in his SUV. He locked the door and set the alarm before turning to look at me. Zero and I were huddled together with his fluffy white head in my lap as he stared up at Jack with baleful eyes. I had a feeling he could sense that something had happened. Either that, or he just didn't like how I had left him all alone all day after the last couple of months being available for cuddles any time he wanted.

Jack snorted, then shook his head as he shrugged off his leather cut. He folded it and laid it over the arm of the recliner adjacent to the couch. He sat down and then started removing his heavy motor-cycle boots. I couldn't tear my eyes away from the sight of his muscles bunching and moving under the black T-shirt he wore. It never failed to send a thrill through me when I watched him. He was so beautiful.

Once he tugged off his socks, laying them over the tops of his boots, he stood back up and disappeared in the direction of the kitchen. I closed my eyes as I listened to him moving around. It was so strange to think that this was my life now. I never could have imagined being here just a few short months ago. But as I dug my fingertips into Zero's thick fur, I relished every second.

Jack came back into the room with a bottle of beer and a water bottle. I gave him a smile when he handed me the water, then giggled at Zero's disgruntled huff when Jack shooed him off the couch, taking his place at my side. Jack's arm went around me, pulling me close, and we both sighed at the contact.

"Did you know you had voicemails?" He asked as he pulled my phone out of my pocket, about to toss it onto the coffee table.

"Hmmm?" I was sleepy, ready to end the night after such a long day. "Oh. I forgot. I was getting spam calls all day, I think." I frowned down at the phone he held toward me. "I didn't recognize the number, so I didn't pay attention to it."

He hesitated, then pushed the phone into my hand. "You should check, just in case," he suggested, "unless you want me to check for you."

I shrugged. "I doubt the Boogeymen are calling me from a California number." After unlocking the phone, I went to the voicemails, ready to delete them without looking, when the words of the first message caught my eye. My breath seized.

Jack tensed at my reaction, then slipped the phone from my suddenly trembling fingers. His vicious curse had me squeezing my eyes closed. He put the voicemail on speaker, and we listened to it together.

"Miss O'Hara? This is Marshall Douglas from the California State Penitentiary in Los Angeles County. I have been trying to reach you regarding a very serious matter that may be a cause for concern for your safety. As of 8:37 am this morning, the inmate by the name of Finkle Stein escaped the custody of his correctional officers during a routine doctor's visit. It is believed the prisoner exaggerated his inability to walk. At this time, we have no known location for his whereabouts. We feel you should be on high alert as we conduct our search for Finkle Stein. For any additional information, you can reach my office at 555-691-0102."

Once the voicemail ended, Jack played the second one that said much the same information. All I could do was sit there in stunned disbelief. How could it have happened? I was too out of it at the time, but it was my understanding that Jack had broken the doctor's knees so severely that he was never supposed to walk again. Dr. Stein was never supposed to be a threat to me or anyone else after going to prison.

Stunned, I stumbled up from the couch, refusing to listen to any more of the messages that were a warning to my safety. There was no doubt he was going to come for me. On stiff legs, I walked down the hallway, ignoring Jack's curses. By the time I made it to the bedroom, I was gasping for breath. My arm was throbbing painfully, the ache there vicious as the phantom feeling of the knife that had torn through my skin and muscle began its torturous slicing all over again.

I stumbled against the bathroom counter, my hand catching me before I could fall against the tile. My head was ringing with my own screams. *No. No. No.* He wasn't supposed to leave prison. I didn't have to testify against him because he was caught red-handed, literally, holding the knife. He had been sentenced to life. I was supposed to be free.

I rushed to the toilet, dropping to the floor. As I emptied my stomach, Jack gathered my hair. He knelt beside me, not saying a word. As I slumped over the toilet seat and blinked up at him through watery eyes, I could see what it was costing him to remain strong for me.

Jack was the kind of man that wanted to slay my demons. If he could, he would hunt down Dr. Stein and destroy him once and for all. I knew he had to be beating himself up inside, thinking that he had failed me.

"Jack," my voice was a croak as I reached out to him.

He took my fingers in his, shaking his head. He helped me to my feet and led me over to the counter, lifting me and then setting me on the cold tile. His jaw was locked tight, the muscles there bunched and straining under the pressure. I tried to reach for him again, but he stepped back from my grasp, instead turning to grab my toothbrush, readying it for me.

"Please," I hiccuped.

"I'm sorry," he ground out.

"It's not your fault, Jack." My voice was a plea. I desperately wanted Jack to hold me, to tell me everything would be okay. But I knew it wouldn't be that easy.

"I should have fucking killed him!" He finally shouted after I finished rinsing the toothpaste from my mouth.

"If you had, then you would be the one in prison." My gentle reminder did nothing to calm the rage burning in his eyes.

He finally looked at me and ran a fingertip over my lips as I fought my own internal battle between my fear and the need to keep Jack calm. "But, then, you would be safe, little Queen."

I shook my head. "From one monster, maybe. But what about the rest of them? I need you here, with me. I need you to be my hero."

He gave a derisive snort as he scooped me back into his arms and carried me to our bed. "I've never been anyone's hero, baby."

"You're mine," I whispered, thinking of all he had done for so many people. The way he protects the town. The way he refused to kill Daisy after everything she had done. "You are more a hero than you could possibly know, Jack."

Before he could deny it again, I leaned into him, kissing his stubbled jaw and moving to his lips. He accepted my kiss, but only for a brief moment before pulling away. I could tell he planned to leave me in our bed alone. He was putting me to bed like a child, but he was going to leave. My heart squeezed in my chest as he stood to his full height after pulling the blanket over me. I bit my lip to stop the trembling, but I couldn't keep the tears from filling my eyes.

"Jack, please don't do this," I whispered, fighting to hold back the sob that wanted to escape my chest. I needed him now more than any other time. After spending the last two months as little more than roommates that shared a bed, I couldn't take more distance from him. It felt too much like rejection all over again.

He hardly glanced my way as he seemed to firm his resolve, stepping away from the side of the bed and walking toward the door. I couldn't take it. My heart was breaking into pieces, and I wasn't sure if they'd ever be able to be put back together again.

I pushed back the covers that he had just tucked around me and got onto my knees. I would only plead with him once. If he walked away, I wouldn't forgive him. I wouldn't *trust him* anymore.

THIRTEEN

THE QUEEN OF NIGHTMARES

"Jack," I called out softly as he approached the door. He paused without turning around, his hands gripping both sides of the doorway until his knuckles turned white. I couldn't tell if he was trying to hold himself back from turning around or if he was that anxious to leave.

"I love you more than I ever could have imagined. But," I closed my eyes, knowing that my next words could destroy everything. He might never forgive me. I never wanted to see the look of hatred on his face in my direction, but I had to stand up for myself.

When I opened my eyes again, I could see he was glancing over his shoulder, his whole body tense as if readying himself for a blow. My voice was soft in the quiet room, and I could hear his ragged breathing. "If you walk out that door, I'll never forgive you. You'll be ripping my heart out. I know why you feel you need to leave, but we can't do this. We can't go back to how it's been these last couple of months." I took a deep breath as he turned around to face me, his nostrils flaring and his eyes narrowed, laser-focused on me as I begged on my knees.

"Are you threatening me, little Queen?" His tone was low, dangerous. He clenched his hands by his sides into fists as his chest heaved.

I shook my head slowly, bringing my hands together to rest in my lap, hoping to still the trembling in them. I looked down at them, seeing the scars there. "No, Jack. I'm not threatening you. I'm making myself a promise. I can't hold on to a man who doesn't want to be held onto. I am worth more." I looked up at him with a tear trailing down my cheek. "You're the one who taught me that."

Jack made a strangled sound in the back of his throat as he watched the tear slide across the scar by the corner of my lip before finally falling over. Suddenly, he pushed away from the door and rushed over to me. Both of his large hands gripped the sides of my face as he slammed his mouth on mine. Jack's kiss was fierce and rough, stealing my breath from my lungs. I tasted the beer he'd barely had a sip from and the saltiness of my tears as his lips moved over mine.

He swallowed my gasp with a growl as I clutched tightly to his shoulders. It felt like I was being swept away by a raging storm, and I never wanted to be drowned so much in my life. I dug my fingernails into his shoulders, hoping that somehow it would be enough to hold him to me forever.

He broke away as suddenly as he had started, and my heart sank to the floor. I didn't want to live without him. He had become my whole world in such a short amount of time. I didn't want to walk away. I didn't want to say goodbye. But I would. For my self-respect. For my self-worth. For my peace of mind. I would leave and never look back.

I tried in vain to hold back my tears, blinking furiously so I wouldn't lose a single second of seeing his beautiful face before he walked away.

"You won't leave me," he snarled, his face so close we shared each other's air. He was practically panting as his chest heaved with his heavy breaths. I could see how wide his pupils were, nearly drowning out what little color could be discerned in his dark eyes. It wasn't until that moment I realized he wasn't angry. He was terrified. "You're *mine*. You told me that you were mine. You promised me."

His tone was nothing but accusatory as he growled and snarled, snapping at me like an angry beast. But, just like when we'd first met, I could see the truth that he held inside. In his eyes, I could see the scared little boy he'd once been. The little boy who needed his mother and had been let down time and time again was still there. Only, this time, it was me he was afraid was going to hurt him. My heart ached.

I cupped his jaw with both hands and leaned in even closer, trying to make him see into my heart. "I never *want* to leave you, Jack. Please. Don't make me leave you to protect myself."

He closed his eyes and growled, resting his forehead on mine. His voice was hoarse as he spoke. "I need to stop the threats against you, Sally. There are too many—one after another. I'm so scared you're going to get hurt again or worse, goddamn it. I almost lost you." He opened his eyes to glare into mine. "And then you threatened to walk away."

"Because you were walking away," I sighed, my breath fanning over his lips. "I have to know you will be here when I need you. And tonight, I needed you, but you weren't listening. I know you have priorities. I understand that the club comes first. I understand that you have a lot of responsibilities, but I just want to know you will listen to me when it's important. You can't walk away and put me last." I sucked in a shocked gasp as my head was tugged back by a handful of my hair at the base of my neck.

"You listen to me," he snarled, his anger shocking me. I hadn't seen so much anger directed at me before, not from him. "You are the only thing that is important. The club is nothing," he spit out. "Next to you, it is meaningless. I told you before, you are my whole world.

Without you, there is no me. So, if you want to leave, you need to stab a dagger through my heart first because that is what it will feel like as I watch you walk away."

The fist in my hair wasn't painful, but he held me so tight I couldn't pull away if I tried. His body loomed over me as he eased his knees onto the bed beside mine. The hand in my hair tugged until my back arched, just on the verge of pain. He took my back to the mattress without letting go of his hold, and then his other hand moved to my throat in a tight grip. I could feel my pulse fluttering wildly under his thumb. Shame for my accelerated heart rate tried to surface, shame that instead of this large, violent man scaring me, I was growing wet from excitement. But he owned my body, and I had learned he would bring me nothing but pleasure when he touched me. I swallowed, then tilted my chin, giving him room to hold onto me more firmly.

He growled deep in his throat as he watched my reaction to his domination. He took my lips in a clashing of teeth and dueling tongues. My breath was taken from me as he carried me away on a tidal wave of lust and passion. I knew it would destroy both of us irreparably to be separated. I could only hold onto the deep hope that there was nothing we couldn't work out together. That there was no problem too big to overcome.

I knew it was harsh, giving him an ultimatum, but he was a stubborn man who didn't know the first thing about being in a relationship. But he'd quickly proven that he was the man I'd known he was. He was dedicated, loyal, and willing to do what it took to love me. The same as I was with him.

When black dots began to dance along the edges of my vision, Jack finally pulled back, allowing great, big, greedy gulps of air to fill my lungs. As I squirmed under him, Jack kissed along my chin, then down to my collarbone as his hand around my throat spasmed, even as the one in my hair released the tight hold.

I threw back my head as his hot mouth tightened around one of my sensitive nipples. I was hit with double the sensation as I felt the rough fingertips of his free hand skate along my neglected breast to settle over the nipple there. He pinched and pulled as I gasped at the pleasure mixed with pain.

With shock, I felt myself explode with an orgasm. Jack's rhythmic sucking on one nipple and the rolling, pinching of the other had sent an arrow of heat straight to my clit, until everything inside me tightened before expanding forcefully outward. My back bowed, and my screams echoed in the room, making my own ears ring.

I was lying, boneless, panting in a daze when Jack's smug tone had me cracking one eye open.

"We are going to be doing that again. Soon." He ran both of his palms over my breasts, the sensation soothing as much as it made me shiver with awareness of what had just happened.

I narrowed my eyes at him. I wasn't mad, but there was something about his overly self-satisfied expression that had me wanting to deny that he had anything to do with it. "I wonder if I can do it by myself." I immediately kicked myself mentally for taunting him. I knew better than to poke the beast, especially when he was still worked up from our argument.

The hand I adored collared my throat once again as he moved his face so close to mine our noses brushed against each other. "Mine."

Again, my breath was taken from me with another fierce kiss. His teeth nipped at my lips in between strokes of his tongue along mine. I melted back into the mattress, my whole body surrendering to anything and everything he was willing to do to me. By the time he was pulling back again, the self-satisfied smirk returned to his face. I was a melted puddle of bliss and willing to concede that he, indeed, was the only person alive capable of pleasuring me.

He tucked me into his still clothed body, his chest curving protectively over my back as his arms wrapped tightly around my waist. "Jack? Don't you want to…"

He shushed my sleepy murmur and kissed the back of my neck.

"You rest, little Queen. It's my punishment for making you doubt me again."

My eyelids were already fluttering closed for the last time, and I didn't have the energy to argue with him. Though, I was going to make a mental note to kick his ass for saying such a ridiculous thing.

FOURTEEN

JACK

I woke up the same way I had the last two months. The emotions that flooded me were all the same, with regret and shame filling me, quickly followed by determination. What was different were all the reasons. I had screwed up in so many fucking ways. I thought I had been protecting her by making her safe physically instead of staying by her side as she healed. I thought she needed space to recover instead of being the shoulder she needed to lean on. I had absolutely no experience in any kind of relationship, least of all with a woman, though that was no excuse.

I did have a fuckload of determination to make sure she understood how much I loved her and was never going to let her go. I may fuck up, but I learned from my mistakes. I didn't know if she realized that if she somehow did manage to leave me, I would have chased her down. It didn't matter how fast or how far. She wasn't getting away from me. I wouldn't survive it. How did someone live without their heart?

I pressed a kiss to her bare shoulder, inhaling deeply to take her scent into my lungs. Everything about her had quickly become vital to me. I needed her scent, her touch, the sight of her in my vision.

With a last brush of my nose against her soft skin, I slowly slid out of the bed. I was uncomfortable in my clothing all night, but just the thought of leaving her warmth was enough to have me sucking up any discomfort I felt.

Zero stretched in the corner where his bed was situated, his front paws extended with his rear high in the air, before giving a full body shake. He sat down and thumped his tail a few times. I jerked my head toward the door, letting him know he should go outside to do his thing before I expected him back in the room, keeping watch over our girl. He jumped to his feet, gave a quiet rumble, then turned tail to run out the door.

I did my own morning routine, making sure to keep quiet so Sally would be able to sleep in as long as she needed. After changing into fresh clothes, I had the electric tea kettle on, getting the water ready for when she finally woke. I wasn't sure if her morning sickness was getting better yet or not. Yesterday morning, she hadn't run straight to the toilet, but maybe that was just because I'd distracted her. Fuck if I knew how the shit worked. I eyed the drawer where I had last stashed the book I bought from the baby store in town nearly three months ago. It was informative, but every time I cracked the pages open, it felt like I was a voyeur into a world I didn't belong.

While I plated the ginger cookies that she seemed to love for more than their anti-nausea properties, I made a phone call to the one guy I knew could get his hand on any weapon in existence. I had an idea for a very specific handgun that I thought my little Queen would appreciate.

I watched as Zero trotted into the kitchen, going straight to his water bowl. He took a few licks of his water and ate a few bites of his dry kibble before heading back down the hall with his tail held high. His chin was up as he marched back to the woman he saw as his. I'd have to grab him a big meaty bone from the butcher later to show my appreciation for his dedication. Even when I hadn't been there for her, he had stayed by her side.

I set the empty cup next to the plate of cookies and placed a tea bag inside to wait for the moment I heard her stirring awake. I hoped she would sleep longer, but there was no telling when she'd wake up, and I wanted to be ready.

I felt my phone vibrate with a message and fished it out of my pocket. I wasn't surprised at the report of more fucking around with our warehouses. I had guys on watch every minute of the day and night, as well as patrols throughout town. I'd stepped up the patrols ever since the first attack. When the message from the Boogeyman President had come through with his threats, I'd tripled them. He wanted me to hand over the club and the town in order to save my girl from his clutches? Fuck that. The whole situation was killing me inside. I would gladly sacrifice anything for my girl, but I couldn't turn over an entire town to that motherfucker, not knowing that he would have it burned to ashes within twenty-four hours. There were too many innocent people that I had sworn to protect. No matter how much I needed Sally safe, I couldn't let those who'd done nothing but help me when I'd needed it the most suffer. Sally needed to be alive and with me, but I wouldn't be handing over control of my territory.

No. The answer wasn't to sacrifice the town. The only true way to end the threat was to cut the head off the one making it. Oogie needed to die. Now that I'd finally backed Doc into a corner to become my VP, it was time to gather the club together to make a solid plan. The Boogeymen couldn't hide away forever. I wasn't going to play little boy games the way they were. Oogie thought he would wear us down by systematically attacking our resources, but all it was doing was pissing me the fuck off.

We were going to need to take the fight to him. The only way to get it done swiftly was to prepare for an all-out assault on his compound. I didn't have the benefit of insider intel the way he did. I had a mole on the inside, but I could never get one into his inner circle. What I had would have to be good enough.

When I heard the bedcovers rustling from the bedroom down the hall, I sent off one last text calling for Church later that afternoon. Then, I poured the steaming hot water into the porcelain cup before turning off the kettle. Carefully, I walked the tea and cookies to my girl.

I heard the water running in the bathroom as I set the cup on the nightstand. Instead of slipping out of the door with the mistaken thought that she needed space from me and then heading to my home office to figure out what else I could do to provide security around the compound, I reclined on the bed and waited.

It didn't take long for the door to open and Sally to appear. She was wearing a pair of short sleep shorts and one of my T-shirts, looking fuckable with her long blood-red hair hanging to her waist in waves. But I noticed the way her head was down, staring at the floor as she shuffled back into the room. She looked miserable, and it made an ache form in my chest.

"Come here, little Queen."

Her head jerked up at the sound of my voice, her eyes immediately going to where I was sitting with my back against the headboard on her side of the bed. Her eyes widened as if she were surprised to see me, and I cursed myself for putting that doubt there.

I jerked my chin. "Now."

Her feet started moving then, and within seconds, she had her knees on the bed and was crawling toward me. I could see her heavy breasts hanging through the wide neck hole of my shirt. They had become larger and rounder in the last few weeks, a testament to the baby growing in her womb. My baby. The ache that had formed in my chest at the realization she still worried about me being here for her dissipated as pride surged through me. I had done that. I knocked up my woman. I marked her from the inside.

Mine.

I tugged her arm until she fell into my lap, her lithe legs straddling me, her weight settling onto my thighs. This was where we should have been every morning since the hospital. I was a fucking asshole.

I wrapped my hand around her long hair, relishing the softness as the strands wove through my fingers. With a light tug, I had her chin up and poised exactly the way I wanted her.

"Good morning, baby," I whispered gruffly before taking her mouth with mine the way I always needed to whenever she was near. By the time I had kissed her breathless, tasting the mint from the toothpaste on her tongue, she had melted into me. All of her weight was pressing into my chest, and my cock was rock solid beneath her.

She ground her hot little pussy against my thick cock, but as much as I always wanted her, needed to feel her under my hands and have her taste on my tongue, to have my scent on her skin, and my come dripping from her pussy, she was pregnant, and I needed to take care of her. Her needs came first. Always.

I gripped her hips firmly and gently pushed her back until there was space between us. She looked at me in confusion, immediately trying to lean forward for another kiss. I placed a hand on the center of her chest to hold her in place as I chuckled. Reaching over to the nightstand with my other hand, I carefully took the cup of tea and held it out to her. She took it with a pout but immediately inhaled the sweet scent.

"Drink first," I told her, my hands tightening on her hips as she blew gently across the surface of the tea. "Then we can play."

Her smile lit up my dark fucking world as she lifted the cup to her lips and drank.

CHAPTER

FIFTEEN

THE QUEEN OF NIGHTMARES

"I don't see why I have to learn this since I have you to protect me," I grumbled as Jack stood behind me. He held my arms in front of me, directing my stance until he was satisfied it was perfect. I felt him nuzzle the side of my neck, his scratchy day-old stubble rubbing along the sensitive skin there, sending goose-bumps and a wave of desire coursing through me.

"Because you're my Queen. Every queen needs to be able to defend herself. And," he rumbled as he placed his chin on my shoulder next to my ear, "you look like my every fucking wet dream standing here holding a gun like this." He nipped my ear with his teeth and growled. "Now focus."

I gave myself a mental shake to rid the lust from my brain. *Okay, focus.* Easier said than done with the sexy man plastered against my back, holding onto me like a second skin. I let out a nervous breath as I stared down the barrel of the gun toward the two-liter bottle of soda sitting on the fence several feet away. I wasn't scared of guns, but I also had never held one before. "Right. Focus," I repeated.

We'd been practicing shooting with Jack's big black handgun for a while already, and my arms were getting tired from the weight. My strength had been getting much better in my injured arm, but it still got tired quickly. I had to use my right hand to do almost everything, and holding the gun for so long was taking a toll.

Before he would even let me hold it, we'd spent at least an hour going over safety rules until I could recite them back to him.

Don't point a gun unless you're willing to pull the trigger.

Treat every gun as a loaded weapon.

Aim for the center of a body; it makes the biggest target, and you're less likely to miss.

I let out one more slightly steadier breath and then slowly squeezed the trigger, already squinting at the loud sound I knew was coming. Before my eyes, a fountain of soda sprayed through the air like a foamy geyser as the bullet met the target. I let out a squeal of delight and amazement as I realized I had actually hit the bottle.

I spun around to Jack with a giant smile on my face. "I did it!"

He chuckled as he slipped the gun from my hand and thumbed the safety back on. *Oops. That was another one of the rules.* "You did, baby. I'm so proud of you."

He set the big black handgun on the tree stump next to us and cupped my cheeks. I looked up into his black eyes and felt as if my insides were melting at the look he was giving me. I had been such an idiot for doubting him. When I'd woken up to an empty bed, I had immediately gone back to all those days before, thinking that he had reverted back to keeping his distance from me after hearing the voicemails. Seeing him now staring at me with so much love and pride in his eyes, I knew he would never hurt me again.

I lifted on my tiptoes to place a kiss on his lips, needing him to know how much I appreciated what he was doing for me. He made a low, rumbling sound in his throat as he wrapped an arm around my lower back to hold me against him. He didn't take over the kiss; he simply held me tight against his body and allowed me to lead.

A loud, ear-piercing whistle sounded from behind us, and we

broke away from each other to turn to see who it was. Jack's arms never left me as we watched Barrel strolling toward us with a huge grin on his face while carrying a small black case.

"Nice shot there, Red. Looks like I may have some competition for my title." Barrel gave me a wink, then Jack a chin lift. "Hey, Prez. Got that thing you requested." He rapped on the hard plastic case with his knuckles. His words had definitely piqued my curiosity, but luckily, I didn't have to wait long to find out what he meant.

Jack took the case with a nod of thanks as the men did a manly back pat. "You got it faster than I expected, even for you."

I tilted my head. "What does that mean?" I asked as I glanced between the two of them, confused as Barrel stood there grinning and Jack gave me a wink.

Jack set the case on the large tree stump next to his gun and popped the plastic tabs on the side. "Barrel can get his hands on just about any gun you could ask for. He's somewhat of a weapons expert, especially when it comes to guns, and can shoot better than anyone I've ever met. If he has you in his sights down the barrel of his gun, you're already dead."

"Barrel!" I gasped as the realization hit me. "That's how you got your name!" I grinned up at him and watched in fascination as his cheeks grew suspiciously pink. He reached up with one hand and ruffled his green hair in embarrassment. It seemed like the unapologetic cocky loverboy didn't take compliments well. "How did you get so good?"

He grunted. "I was a sniper in the military for a little while."

I could sense there was more to it than that, and my curiosity refused to allow the story to end there. "Only a little while?"

"Yeah. Uncle Sam and I thought it was best to end our relationship."

Jack snorted. "He punched his commanding officer in the nose when the guy found out Barrel fucked his daughter and tried to assign him to latrine duty as punishment."

I covered my mouth with my hand, not even trying to stop the giggles from erupting when Barrel turned a glare on Jack.

"Oh my god. Exactly how many times has your dick gotten you into trouble, Barrel?" I could barely get the words out through my laughter while Barrel switched his glare to me, crossed his arms over his chest, and refused to answer.

As I wiped at moisture from the corners of my eyes from all the laughing, Jack tugged me back to him, wrapping his hand loosely around my throat to growl in my ear. "No thinking about other men's cocks." I snorted, then turned so I could press a kiss to the underside of his chin, feeling the stubble there rasp against my lips.

"Trust me, the only cock I ever think about is yours." Then, a thought occurred to me. I started wondering about the others and how they got their names. "Doc's obvious, but what about Shock?"

Barrel finally laughed as Jack shook his head with a smirk. "Shock spent some time in a psychiatric hospital."

"That's awful," I said with a grimace. But it explained a lot when it came to that creepy smile. He was a nice guy and was the first to come to my rescue when I needed it the most by way of getting Jack to help me. But that smile made shivers run down my spine sometimes.

I hesitated to ask. "What about…" I was going to just forget about it, letting the question drop, but Jack answered anyway.

"There wasn't a padlock, safe, or door that Lock couldn't get into." We all got quiet after that as we remembered the man who'd been murdered. He'd been their friend for longer than I knew and was one of Jack's closest men. Hell, he'd been the Vice President of the club. I cleared my throat and poked him in the side, hoping to lighten the mood.

"We all know where *your* nickname came from." I traced a tattooed finger. "Maybe I should start calling you Bone Daddy," I snickered, though, secretly, I didn't hate the name.

Barrel laughed loudly while Jack just smirked and shook his head before sweeping me up into his arms. He held me so close to his chest that I barely had room to wiggle as he buried his head in my neck and bit me there just hard enough to make me gasp through my giggles.

"First of all, little Queen, it's a road name, not a nickname. Secondly, you can call me daddy all you want in bed while I'm giving you my bone."

I groaned in mock disgust as I playfully slapped his chest. "Oh, that was lame. Starting with the dad jokes already?" I squirmed as he nipped at my skin again in retaliation. I glanced over where Barrel was still laughing hard enough to double over, grabbing his sides.

"Holy shit, that was fucking funny." Barrel wiped at his eyes once his laughter had died down to the occasional chuckle. He pointed his finger at Jack. "His road name has nothing to do with being tatted up like a walking Halloween sideshow. Naw, his name actually comes from the fact that he enjoys filleting a man open to the bone. It's his favorite form of torture. He didn't start getting the ink done until after his uncle gave him the road name."

I stood there, slack-jawed, as the words tumbled around in my brain. I wasn't sure what to think about what it said about Jack that he could do that to someone. I knew he was cold and ruthless. I even knew that he could kill someone without losing sleep, but to slowly torture someone? I slowly turned until I could see Jack's face, his expression carefully blank. I decided right then that there was no way I would judge him.

I cleared my throat. "And here, all I got was the nickname Red. I feel cheated."

A look of relief swiftly crossed his features before he wiped it away. A small smirk toyed with the corner of Jack's mouth as he stared down at me. "Did you forget? You're much more than just Red. You're my little Queen, and the queen is the most powerful piece on the board. The king needs his queen. Without her, he is destined to fall."

CHAPTER
SIXTEEN

I watched Sally as she lovingly wiped a microfiber cloth over the short barrel of her new Sig Sauer P238. It was a tiny little weapon that barely fit into the palm of my hand, but it was fucking powerful. All I cared about was that it did the job it was intended for. The fact that my little Queen had nearly lost her mind when she saw it for the first time was just a sweet bonus.

"Alright, baby, I think your new gun is clean," I chuckled as she glared up at me before smiling back down at the shiny purple Sig.

"But it's so pretty," she practically fucking cooed at it. I snorted.

"Alright, I'm glad you like it. But we need to head to the club-house. I called everyone to Church in about fifteen minutes. I don't think it's a good idea for the President to be late to his own meeting."

She gave a long, put-out sigh. I thought she was going to kiss the fucking gun for a second but seemed to refrain at the last second. Instead, she looked up at me with hopeful eyes. "Can I bring it with me?"

"I want you to take the fuckin' thing everywhere with you. But you don't have anything to carry it in yet. I'll get you a shoulder holster so you can keep it by your side. Your little sweater things will cover it."

She looked puzzled for a second before she let out a cute as fuck giggle. "Oh! You mean cardigan."

I rolled my eyes, took the small purple Sig from her hand, checked the safety out of habit, and set it on the counter. "Whatever. Let's go."

I tugged her into my body, giving her a swift kiss, then walked her to the door where her jacket was waiting. It had started snowing again since our morning shooting practice, so I held her boots out. "Sit."

"I'm not a dog. No offense, Zero," she grumbled but sat on the bench, letting me slide her boots over her tiny feet. Zero sat next to us, his tail thumping the floor.

Once I had her bundled up, I set the alarm and led her to the garage, Zero following on our heels.

"We aren't taking the bike?"

I shook my head. "Not in this weather. We won't be able to ride again for the next three months or so. Now that winter has started to really set in, it will be icy more often than not. Too dangerous for a motorcycle. Not to mention, the cold wind fucking hurts, and I don't want frostbite to take my nose off. Even wearing a balaclava can't keep the icy wind out at these temps."

As soon as we stepped into the garage, my girl's jaw dropped. Yeah, my truck was pretty fucking massive. It was all black with shiny chrome that I had the prospects keep polished whether I was going to be driving it or not. But it probably wasn't the large truck that she would need a boost to get into that had her in awe. I took in the intricately painted emblem of the Devil's Nightmare on the hood. Even I had to admire the detailed paint job.

"Wow," she breathed as she took a step forward to get a better look. "That's amazing artwork."

I grunted my agreement, then took her arm to lead her to the passenger side. "One of the town's people has a business doing custom art. They did all the brother's work on their bikes, too."

She side-eyed me. "Let me guess—you bankrolled them to get them started."

I just shrugged, not denying it. It wasn't something I talked about or advertised. I may have helped a lot of people get their businesses up and running, but it was their hard work that kept it solid. Those people were successful because of what they did and how well they did it. My only hand in it was giving them the start-up capital.

I jumped into the cab behind the wheel, double-checking to make sure Sally was buckled before starting the truck and pulling out of the garage, hitting the button to close it as soon as I was clear. Zero had already run back into the house through his dog door to get back into the warmth of the house. I glanced at the dash, noting the time. I should make the meeting. Others would arrive before I got there, but I wouldn't be late.

From the corner of my eye, I could see Sally running her hand over her belly with a thoughtful look. I reached over and took her free hand in mine, lacing our fingers together and resting our joined hands on the seat between us. I frowned at the distance, making a mental note to seat her next to me on the bench seat from now on. I didn't like that she would no longer be pressed up against me the way she was on the back of my bike. Then I thought of her growing our child in her womb. I supposed there wouldn't be any more riding for her even after winter was over. Her belly would be too large to ride, and the thought that it wouldn't be safe for the two of them and what kind of injuries it could cause if we were to get into an accident was enough to have me gripping the steering wheel so hard it creaked.

"What's wrong, little Queen? Is it the baby?" I tried to keep the anxiousness out of my tone, but I was sure it had slipped through by the way she shook her head, giving me a reassuring smile.

"Nothing's wrong. It's just... I could swear my belly feels rounder.

Like, I didn't notice it earlier today. But now, sitting here, I think it might have grown."

My heart rate picked up at the thought of visible proof that she was carrying my baby. I untangled our fingers to reach over. She moved her own hand aside to allow me to run my hand over her belly. It did seem to be a little more rounded than I remember. I swallowed hard and had to clear my throat before speaking.

"I think you're right, baby."

She grinned over at me, placing her hand on top of mine. "It's starting to seem so real."

I growled. "It *is* real. That's my baby in there. I have pictures to prove it." I thought of the strip of grainy black and white photos tucked safely away in my cut pocket under the leather jacket I was wearing.

"I know that," she laughed. "It's just that actually feeling it makes it undeniable. I don't know," she shrugged a shoulder while caressing my hand that I didn't want to move yet. "I just like feeling it instead of just knowing it. Pretty soon, we'll be able to feel it move." She sounded excited at the thought. I could picture it in my mind now that she said it. I didn't know what it would feel like since I had never felt a woman's pregnant belly before, but I couldn't wait to find out. I would never admit it out loud to anyone, but it terrified as much as it excited me.

I pulled into the clubhouse parking lot, parking in the designated spot for the President along with the rows of other vehicles that bikers liked to refer to as cages. My men were going to be a bit grumpy now that it had grown far too cold to ride our bikes. It was always that way for the first few days. Once spring hit and everyone pulled their bikes out of storage, it would be the exact opposite. They would all act like little boys who'd gotten their birthday wish.

After parking, I got out and went around to the passenger side to lift Sally down. I waited, with my hands gripping her arms firmly, to make sure she had her footing on the icy gravel. "Watch your step." I eyed the rocks, wondering if I should have the lot paved. In the meantime, one of the prospects needed to salt the fucking ground. I wouldn't have my girl slipping and hurting herself.

We walked to the front door together as I eyed the ground warily. I gripped the heavy door, glad we would finally get out of the cold. "Do you want to wait in here or in my office?"

Sally looked around and smiled, spotting a few of the club girls. "I'll wait here." She lifted on her toes to kiss under my chin. Every time she did that, I got that tight feeling in my chest. Once she dropped back to her feet, I wrapped my fingers around her slender neck, feeling her steady heartbeat.

"Don't leave. I won't be long." The kiss I pressed to her lips was hard and fast before I let her go, striding away. If I didn't leave quickly, I'd be tempted to stay. I hated not having her by my side, especially with all the danger that seemed to surround her right now.

I stomped into the meeting room, my mood souring with every step I took away from my little Queen. Almost everyone was already around the table, only the spot at the head and two others empty. I eyed Doc, who was sitting back in his chair, arms crossed and glaring holes into me. I smirked.

"Hello, brother."

He flipped me off. "Fuck you, Bones."

Everyone around the table laughed at his display of irritation. We all knew that if he didn't want to be sitting in that seat, he wouldn't be. We also knew that it was long overdue. There was no better choice for the VP position than Doc. And there was no one I trusted more than him to have my back. As VP, if anything happened to me, he would be next in line to take over. He may not have been a patched member of the club all these years, but he'd been a part of it just as long as I had. The one and only thing that had held him back from making it official was the hours he had to spend at the hospital at the beginning of his career. He was still a busy doctor, but he was at the point where he wasn't captive to his job any longer. I knew he would put the club first as much as he was able.

I shrugged off my leather jacket, draping it over the back of my chair, and sat down just as the remaining brothers walked in and took their seats with a nod to the rest of the gathered club members.

"Alright, let's get this meeting started." I looked around the table with the gavel next to my fingers. "Let's talk about how we are going to annihilate the mother fucking Boogeymen once and for all."

SEVENTEEN

THE QUEEN OF NIGHTMARES

"Hey, Kara!" I walked over, excited to see my friend. She looked me over from head to toe as she examined me closely.

"Hey, girl. I heard some shit happened yesterday after I left."

I nodded to the other girls with a small smile in greeting. We weren't close and had barely spoken more than polite words to each other, but they hadn't been mean. I wished I could make friends easier, but I had a hard time putting myself out there, especially with these girls. They were so beautiful, and I could never forget my scars. Even if Jack made me feel so good about myself that I often forgot about them while we were together, the self-consciousness always came roaring back as soon as I was around other people.

I shuddered at the memory of those thousands of little feet crawling over me. "Yeah, that package you dropped off had a nasty surprise in it. I ended up spending most of the day in the hospital with dozens of bug bites. Luckily, they weren't venomous. I just had to take some Benedryl for the itching."

I lifted my sleeve, where several bites were still red. Though they were smaller in size than they had been the day before, they were still slightly raised.

One of the other girls gasped in genuine shock at the sight. "I'd heard you had some kind of attack, but no one knew what it was. Are you okay?"

If I thought about them too much, I would start scratching at them again, so I quickly pulled my sleeve back down. "I am. It was pretty boring in the hospital, to be honest. Though, Jack and I did get to see the baby."

There was a chorus of exclamations. Apparently, it wasn't common knowledge that I was even pregnant. That honestly didn't surprise me. I hadn't been around long after we first found out, and then I had spent months in the house pretty much alone, with Zero and Kara for occasional visits.

"Oh my gosh! I didn't know the Prez had a baby on the way!" One of the girls gushed. "I bet the baby grows up to be just as handsome as he is." Her voice was dreamy as she got a faraway look, either imagining Jack or my baby. Either way, I felt a spark of jealousy. Both were mine.

I forced a laugh. "Yeah, I bet."

Kara eyed me knowingly. She was the one who had convinced me that other girls would want Jack even more now that he'd proven he was interested in women. She gestured with her eyes at the other women, who seemed to be looking at me with jealousy. Or maybe it was that they were sizing me up? Maybe they thought they could win Jack away from me. They had the skills, I was sure. But Jack was devoted to me, and I could tell in the truck how much he was already in love with our baby, too. No one could take that away from me.

I lifted my chin a little higher, trying to be the Queen he always called me. I was the one he'd chosen, not these women. Even though he'd been surrounded by their beauty night and day for years, it wasn't until *me* that he'd changed. It sucked for them, but for me, it was glorious being his girl.

I looked back over at Kara, giving her a smile and showing her that it didn't matter who wanted him. She was frowning but gave me a reassuring smile once she noticed me looking her way.

"You want something to drink, Sal? I can get them to pour you some ginger ale?" Kara asked as she slid off the stool she was perched on. I stepped back to allow her room to move around me, already heading to the other end of the bar where a prospect was drying glasses with a bar towel.

"Umm, sure. That would be great, thanks," I called as I stood there awkwardly. I wasn't sure if I should take a stool near one of the other girls or move over toward the couches. I remembered what I had seen a couple of nights ago and shuddered. No, thank you. I wrapped an arm around my middle. Perhaps I should just go to Jack's office. I'd be comfortable there, and I wouldn't feel like I was on display for the club girls as they carried on a conversation between themselves about how cute babies were and how they bet the Prez's baby was going to be the cutest they'd ever seen.

"Sally?"

I jerked my head in the direction of the voice to notice one of the girls smiling at me.

"I asked if you got a sonogram picture printed yesterday?" I couldn't remember her name since I hadn't worked with her much. It was Mindy or Mandy. Maybe Cindy?

"Oh, yeah, sorry. Jack kept most of them, but I did manage to keep one for myself." I reached into my small crossbody bag and pulled out my wallet. I slipped the little square picture from inside and held it to me protectively while everyone giggled, talking about how adorable it was for big, bad men to go crazy over their babies. I smiled in agreement, but inside, I was thinking, *you can't take him from me. I need him!*

"You're so lucky, Sally. You have what we all want." All the girls nodded in agreement as one of them spoke.

"Yeah. These bikers are just so much, you know!" Another gushed. "When they claim someone, they go all out. A bit caveman, I guess, but who wouldn't want to be claimed by a man who would do anything to protect you?"

I laughed awkwardly. "Yeah, Jack is pretty caveman, I suppose. But he makes sure I know that I'm all his." I reluctantly held out the piece of paper with my baby on it and watched as they all got as close as they could. They oohed and awed over the little dot in the middle that resembled a peanut. I couldn't help but smile a real smile as I watched them fawn over my son or daughter.

"I can't wait to hold him!"

"I bet it's a girl!"

"No way. There's no way a man like Bones would make anything other than a boy."

Kara walked back over to the group, holding a bubbling glass of ginger ale and a beer bottle. "Just as long as you bitches know that I get aunt privileges."

"I don't care, just as long as I can get baby snuggles," Mindy or Cindy sighed. "I should get one of these bikers to settle down so I can have a baby." She looked back up at me as I pulled the picture back, carefully tucking it away in my wallet again. "How'd you do it?"

I jerked my head up at the question, zipping up my purse and picking up my glass of ginger ale with a frown. "What did I do?"

"You got one of the Devil's Nightmares to fall in love with you."

A short blonde nodded with a sassy grin. "Not just any Nightmare, *the* Nightmare. He was so unattainable. None of us ever stood a chance. We're just curious what you did."

I took a small step back as I glanced at all their eager faces one by one. As I looked closer, I didn't see malice. Maybe a hint of jealousy, but it didn't seem to be directed at me personally. They all looked genuinely... happy for me. Maybe Kara was wrong. I didn't think these girls were trying to steal Jack from me at all.

"Uh, I didn't really do anything. I mean, the first time I saw him, I felt like, a spark. Then, I didn't really see him very much, but when he was around, he always seemed to be watching me. It wasn't until a month had passed before he even spoke to me." I laughed as I thought back. When I thought about the Jack I knew then, to the Jack I know now, I realized that he was just as confused as I was. I sort of loved that he didn't know what he was doing.

"That's super sweet. Though, I wouldn't mind having one of them just stomp up to me and throw me over his shoulder. None of that staring for a month bullshit. No offense, Sally."

I giggled. "None taken."

"I like how you think, Sherry," the little blonde nudged one of the others. "Carry me off to his cave and lay his claim as he lay his pipe."

I choked on my ginger ale, sputtering as everyone laughed at her words.

"Agreed. Anyone that claims me better have a big ass pipe, too. I've had it with tiny little pencil dicks."

"Pencil dicks aren't the problem, it's what they do with it. Some guys think just because they're hot, they don't have to work it. A hot guy can have an anaconda in his pants. If he can't make that thing do the mamba, then he's worthless. Throw him back and find an average fucker that really knows how to work those hips."

All the girls agreed with a cheer and took a big swig of their drinks, all giggling and talking excitedly about guys and their experiences. I was surprised that I found myself enjoying their company. I glanced over at Kara to see her sitting back, sipping her beer and watching everyone with a small smile. I nudged her with my elbow with a grin, glad she had been wrong. It was nice having girlfriends for once.

EIGHTEEN

JACK

"I will send out the drones later tonight around three a.m. Less chance any patched member will be out, and prospects likely won't know what they are looking at. That's if I'm even noticed." Tech's tone was smug, but then, he'd earned the right to be. He could probably send out a drone at high noon during a barbeque and still go unnoticed.

I jerked my chin, giving him all the permission necessary to start getting his plan in order. The meeting had been productive. We had a working plan to take out the Boogeymen once and for all. As much as I would love to ride up guns blazing or, better yet, shoot off a few dozen rocket-propelled grenades to wipe them out, we needed to be smart and stealthy. And the first step was surveillance. But we had already lined up steps two through ten as well.

"I'll check our stash for C4 and all the fixings for bombing the buildings. Once we know what we are looking at," Rash jerked his chin in Tech's direction, "Once we have the layout, I'll draw up the compound diagram and figure out the best places for them."

I sat back, running my hand over my scruffy chin. I needed to shave so I didn't hurt my girl with it. I didn't like the thought that I could damage her delicate skin. "Sounds like we have a working plan. We'll need to call our inside guy back. Shock, get ahold of him, and tell him to make himself scarce. I don't care what excuse he comes up with. If he's not out of there by the end of the week, then it's his ass."

Shock nodded with a grim smile. "On it, Prez."

"There's one more thing we need to discuss." I glared down the table. "I just got word this morning that the doctor fucker that hurt Sally escaped prison. According to the voicemails, He escaped yesterday morning from his own doctor's appointment. The mother fucker walked out of there after killing his guards and the doctor."

Barell sighed and shook his head. "I saw what you did to his knees. There's no way he's able to walk long or far. He's going to need a cane, at the very least. I will put the information out around town to be on the lookout for a stranger with a cane, wheelchair, or crutches. Fuck!" He shook his head again. "How is Red taking the news?"

I thought about her panic attack last night. I knew the only reason she managed to get control of her emotions was because she had to deal with mine. "She's handling it. But she shouldn't need to. I don't want this fucker to get within one hundred yards of this town. Do I make myself clear?" I eyed everyone around the table.

All heads nodded their agreement, but it didn't satisfy me. Nothing would until the threat was eradicated once and for all. "He won't be going back to prison." I didn't have to clarify. He would be dead. We had an incinerator that needed feeding. "It's going to be all hands on deck for the next several days around here. If you have families, I suggest you move them onto the compound. Or send them away to stay with extended family. Hell, put them on a plane to fucking Jamaica for vacation. Somewhere warm out of this damn cold. Whatever you choose to do, make sure they are safe."

After everyone agreed and any questions they had were

answered, I called an end to Church. I stood up quickly, nodding to my men and slapping Doc on the back as thanks. I appreciated that he'd finally stepped into his role, even if it was reluctantly.

"One sec, Prez," Horse called out before I could leave. I paused and stared, waiting for whatever he had to say. "That package that arrived yesterday? The one you wanted information on?"

I nodded, anger rising as the memory of what had happened to my girl all over again. I clenched my fists, ready to rip apart whoever had sent it. I didn't care who it was. "Who sent it?" I demanded, getting impatient.

He scratched his head as he looked at me. "That's the thing, Prez. It wasn't mailed. The shipping label was fake. Whoever sent it didn't mail it. It was delivered, but not by the post office."

I thought about that, my anger rising. We wouldn't have an address to trace it back to. It just got a fuck of a lot harder to find the person responsible. Even though I knew Oogie was behind it, I wanted my hands around the throat of whoever handed it over.

"Check the camera at the front gate. See who it was that delivered it. My girl said that a postal worker dropped it off. I want his face, then find the mother fucker." I didn't have to say what I wanted done with him. He would be in the processing room as soon as he was identified.

"You got it, Prez. I'll go talk to Tech now." With a chin lift, he was out the door.

I strolled down the hall, heading for the main room where I'd left my girl, needing to see her. Sounds of laughter and music greeted my ears before I'd even made it through the doorway. I stopped for a second to just take in the sight. Sally was sitting on a stool in the middle of a group of club girls. They were obviously drunk while she held a glass, sipping what I assumed was soda. It didn't stop her from enjoying herself and giggling at whatever one of the girls said, though.

I walked straight to her, interrupting their conversation and not giving a single fuck. Once I reached her, she looked up at me, her eyes sparkling with joy. I hadn't thought much about what her place in the club would be as my old lady when it came to the club girls, but it looked like she would be fine. I was proud as fuck to see she was genuinely enjoying herself and not acting like she had to hide or hold herself back.

"Little Queen."

She sighed happily, leaning into me. "Jack."

I couldn't resist taking her mouth right there in front of everyone. If they saw the President falling over his ass for a woman, then so be it. It would ensure they knew who she belonged to, so they would know to never fuck with her. "Did you enjoy your visit?" I asked against her lips when I reluctantly broke off the kiss.

She grinned up at me, then looked over my shoulder at the others. "I did. I made friends with Brittany, Cindy, Sherry, and Carla. We had a lot of fun talking about men."

I rolled my eyes. "Of course you did." I smacked her ass to get her moving. "Let's get home before the snow comes down any more than it already has."

She laughed as she slid off the stool. "It's like a mile down the road, Jack."

"I don't give a fuck. I don't want you out in the snow. Say goodbye."

She waved at the women and then hugged the blonde, who was a regular visitor to our home. Before we walked away, the girl, Kara, spoke up.

"Oh! I wanted to ask you if you wanted to go to the maze with me tomorrow. It will be a lot of fun, and the weather is supposed to be nice."

Sally perked up. "Maze?"

I was already shaking my head before Kara began to explain, but she ignored me, continuing to speak, making me turn my glare on her. The girl had balls because she pretended she didn't see me. "Yeah. You missed it when they had it running for Halloween because of your..." She trailed off and waved toward Sally's arm.

"Well, they switch it up after Halloween, turning it into a haunted Christmas theme. It's a lot of fun. They serve hot chocolate and hot apple cider. The decorations are Christmassy but spooky. We should go."

I wanted to say fuck no. There was no way I would let my girl out in public with the kinds of threats after her. But I took one look at her pleading expression, making the words die on my lips. I narrowed my eyes at her.

"Please, Jack? The only time I've even been off the compound was to go to the hospital. I didn't get to have any Halloween fun, and now it's nearly Christmas. If you're with me, I know I'll be safe. Maybe some of the others can come, too?"

She looked behind me to where I knew Barrel and Doc were standing with beers in their hands, watching my girl tuck my nutsack into her purse. "Fuck," I growled. I turned to look at my men over my shoulder. "Get the fucking prospects to check the safety of the maze. I want them standing on guard while we are there." I pointed at a grinning Shock. "You fuckers are all coming with."

Sally clapped her hands. "Yay!"

I gripped the back of her neck. "You're going to pay for this, little Queen."

I felt her shiver as she swallowed and watched as her pupils dilated with lust. Fuck. A punishment wasn't meant to be a turn-on. My cock twitched at the ways I could punish her without letting her come. My favorite option was her on her knees.

"Let's go, troublemaker."

She huffed but came willingly, waving at the room.

"I'll text you the time!" Kara called out as we made it to the door. A blast of cold air swept into the room as I pulled the heavy door open. A quick glance showed the snow hadn't accumulated much since we'd been inside, and only small flurries swirled through the air. I grunted. If there wasn't much snow or ice on the ground, I wouldn't have an excuse to call off the trip tomorrow.

I helped Sally across the gravel lot and over to my truck,

watching to make sure there weren't any patches of ice for her to slip on. I noted the salt dotting the lot with satisfaction. The current prospects we had seemed to be good at following orders. It was a good sign. With any luck, they'd be able to complete their probation period without any fuck ups.

I helped Sally up into the driver's side of my truck. When she started to slide all the way over, I gripped her thigh and tugged her back into the middle. "This is where you sit from now on."

She huffed but put on her seatbelt without complaint. "The girls are right. You bikers really are a bunch of cavemen."

"I'll show you caveman when I toss you over my shoulder and carry you to our room."

She grinned. "That doesn't sound too bad."

I raised an eyebrow, looking at her after I pulled out of the parking space. "No? What about when I pull your hair and stuff my fat cock down your throat, making you choke on it in apology."

She gasped, but I didn't miss the way she squirmed in her seat. "Apology for what?"

"For making me agree to this stupid fucking idea of going out in public while you're in danger."

She sighed and leaned into me. "You're right. I just thought it sounded fun. We don't have to go if you think it's too dangerous."

"It *is* fucking dangerous. But I will do everything I can to make it as safe as possible. I don't want you to feel like a prisoner in your own home."

"Thank you, Jack." She brushed a kiss on the underside of my jaw.

"You're still going to be punished," I warned, my tone low and full of threat.

Her voice was breathy when she replied. "Oh, I figured."

NINETEEN

THE QUEEN OF NIGHTMARES

I was so excited I was practically vibrating as we headed into town. The signs indicating the maze were easy to follow. I looked out of the rear window to see Doc's SUV following close behind. He seemed to be just as reserved about the whole outing as Jack was and swore he wouldn't be leaving our sides.

Jack had mentioned the prospects had already checked the whole area for any possible threats without signs of trouble. Even so, they would be standing guard around the property just in case. I felt bad about that because, even though the sky was clear today, it was still really freaking cold.

There hadn't been any sign of Dr. Stein in or around town yet. When I called the number from the voicemail, I was told they had no further information. No one had any idea where Dr. Stein had disappeared to. It was strange to think that a man who could barely walk managed to get away in the first place. To think he was also able to evade the authorities was just unbelievable. Maybe Jack was right, and this whole thing was a really bad idea. I was about to call the whole thing off when Jack slowed down to turn into the maze parking lot.

It was almost like a carnival had come to town. There was a huge tent set up in the middle with rows of tables where people could sit and drink their hot beverages. Right next to the seating area was a long, enclosed building with a small line of people waiting to order.

As we climbed out of the truck, I could hear the music playing over loudspeakers. It was Christmas music but played on what sounded like an old pipe organ, giving it a decidedly spooky vibe. This town was nuts but in such a fun way. It was no wonder people came from miles around to enjoy what they had to offer.

We stood and waited near the truck as the others parked before making their way over to us. Jack fussed with my scarf, ensuring it was wrapped securely around my neck and sufficiently covered my ears while checking that my stocking cap was in place.

"I'm fine, Jack," I huffed as he tugged the zipper of my heavy coat up even though it was already as high as it could go. "Is this how you're going to be with your son or daughter?" I cocked an eyebrow, amused. He paused for a second before adjusting my scarf again.

"Probably. Why would I not make sure those that I love most are completely taken care of?"

My heart melted at his words. Okay, there was no arguing with that. When he put it that way, I would let him fuss over me as much as he wanted.

"Hey, Sally!" Kara called, and I turned to see her walking out from between two cars. "Glad the Prez let you out of the house finally."

I cleared my throat, uncomfortable at her words and the way her tone implied that he'd been purposely keeping me locked away. "It's too bad my injury kept me away for so long. But I'm here now!" I smiled, squeezing Jack's hand in apology, even though it wasn't my fault that Kara seemed to be in a weird mood.

"Yeah, you're here." She almost sounded unimpressed. I wanted to ask her what was up with her attitude, wondering if she was having issues with her boyfriend or something. "So let's go have some fun." She hooked her arm in mine and began leading me toward the large red tent. "Hot cocoa first, then we can go explore."

I looked over my shoulder to see Jack scowling but close on our heels, with Doc and the others following right behind him. We went straight to the first open window and ordered our drinks. I chose hot apple cider while Jack and the other bikers in our entourage ordered coffee. Kara sucked the whipped cream off her hot cocoa before blowing on it.

We stood near a tall patio heater that gave off more radiant heat than I expected it to. While glancing around, I realized there were several throughout the tent area, making it a pretty comfortable place to relax and warm up.

"This place is amazing!" I said as I took a tiny sip of my cider. It was delicious.

"You should see the place when it's set up for Halloween. Which, honestly, is all the time except for Christmas. That's the only time they switch it up a bit. But Halloween is something else. It's one of the biggest attractions for the town." Kara looked around at the grounds beyond the tent and pointed.

"The maze entrance is right there. It's about a half-mile long and a quarter-mile wide. It usually takes about an hour to make your way through it. Every year, they change the design so the locals don't memorize it."

"That's huge! I can't wait to try it out." I couldn't contain my bubbling excitement.

"That's what she said," Barrel snickered, letting out an oof when Doc elbowed him in the ribs. "Hey, man. Watch the goods. I've got a date later with a hot brunette," he said as he massaged the area.

"Yeah?" Shock asked with a grin. "Is her name Palm-ela?"

We all laughed as Barrel smirked. "Yeah, yeah. Whatever. No need for self-love when the ladies crave all this." He gestured down his body before making a crude gesture at his crotch. I groaned as he laughed uproariously.

"What are you? Twelve?"

He winked at me with a smirk. "I haven't measured, but I have it on good authority that…"

"Shut the fuck up, Barrel. My woman doesn't need to know how tiny your cock is," Jack growled, cutting off Barrel before he could go into any kind of detail.

"Anyway," Kara spoke up, putting an end to the jokes. "Over there is where they have pumpkin carving during fall. It's obviously too cold for that, so they have cookie decorating instead." She pointed to a smaller tent, which had a few children laughing as they used giant bags of colorful frosting to draw on some rather large cookies. I couldn't tell the shapes from where we were standing, but it was a fair assumption that they were probably pumpkins.

"That building is where all the locals can sell homemade goods like pies or preserves. One of the farms even has honey for sale."

"Wow. I don't think I've ever had honey that wasn't in a little plastic bear." I was impressed and excited to explore. I could also see a small play area for the kids and couldn't wait to bring my own child once they were old enough to enjoy it.

Jack draped his arm over my shoulders as I sipped at my rapidly cooling cider. "We'll get some honey before we go home."

I beamed up at him. "Yay!" My stomach did a twist when he smirked down at me and gave me a wink. God, he was just so handsome.

Kara chucked her empty cup in the closest trash can and then rubbed her gloved hands together. "Okay, there obviously isn't nearly as much to do since it's now winter and absolutely fucking cold, but I'm sure we'll be ready to call it a day by the time we make it through the maze. I can't wait for you to see all the spooky Christmas decorations inside. It's great! There will be bloody toys and Santa with an axe." She turned to me. "Are you ready?"

I gulped down the last of my apple cider, letting Jack take the paper cup from me before I could throw it away for myself. "Yep! I'm ready. Let's go."

"We go together." Jack's deep, gravelly tone was firm. "You stay with me at all times."

"Of course I will." I agreed quickly. I had made a promise, and I trusted his judgment. I already felt terrible that I had pushed to be here when he didn't think it was a good idea. Just the thought of why had me looking around nervously. Dr. Stein could be anywhere between here and California. He already knew where the town was. His only issues were traveling while trying to stay off the radar of law enforcement and his mobility. I hoped his knees were giving him hell.

Kara's expression hardened at Jack's words, and I grimaced. I really didn't want her to think that all he did was make demands of me. I knew that's what she had mostly seen of our relationship, and it made it hard to convince her he wasn't overbearing. Or an abuser. I left his side to take her arm with mine this time. I leaned closer so I could whisper low enough that only she could hear.

"He's really worried about my safety right now, that's all."

She tugged me forward and started walking toward the entrance to the maze. I glanced behind me to see Jack scowling at where Kara and I were connected. I gave him a quick smile, but it didn't seem to pacify him any. I knew he'd prefer it if I were next to him instead, but he could compromise just a little. He could protect just as well from five feet away as he could two.

We passed empty stands on our way to the maze, and I wondered what was usually there. I was excited to come back next year when everything was set up. I could imagine face painting for the kids, or vendor stalls, selling Halloween or pumpkin themed items. I only hoped all the threats were gone by then. I ran my fingers over the slight swell of my belly and smiled. Next Halloween, Jack and I would have a baby to bring.

THE QUEEN OF NIGHTMARES

We stepped up to the entrance to the maze and waited while Jack paid for everyone to enter. I held out my hand for a bright orange pumpkin shaped stamp. I was going to wait for the guys to get their stamps, too, but Kara immediately started pulling me through the first row of corn stalks. I looked back to make sure Jack stayed in sight.

"Relax. Geez, we are only a fucking foot away." Kara's annoyed tone took me aback. I hadn't expected her to still be so irritated with Jack after I told her how worried he was.

"Kara, I told you. Jack's worried about my safety. There's a lot going on right now that you don't know about. He just doesn't want anything to happen to me. Especially after what happened a couple of months ago."

She blew out a heavy breath, then turned her head to glance at me quickly with a forced smile before looking back at the path in front of us. "I get it. But don't you think he goes too far? I mean, look how controlling he is."

I was already shaking my head before she finished speaking. "No. He doesn't control me, Kara. I swear he doesn't. He just... I don't know. It's a scary time right now. I think he feels like everything is out of his control. He can't stop the threats and is worried that I could be attacked at any time."

Kara stiffened, her whole body turning rigid at my words. I hurried to reassure her. "You aren't in danger by being around me, I promise. Besides, Jack made sure the whole place was as secure as possible before he let me come."

Alright, my last words probably played right into her concerns, but I didn't care. I trusted Jack. That was all that mattered. I looked back again and realized I could barely see the top of Jack's head. He was going to start getting pissed if I didn't slow down to let him catch up. Right on cue, I heard him call out, telling me to stop.

I turned to Kara to let her know we needed to slow down, but the words froze, my throat constricting until there was nothing but a strangled sound. Kara's free hand that wasn't looped through my arm had a gun pointed right at my side. Her now gloveless hand had a firm hold on the trigger. Flashbacks of the last time I was threatened with a gun had my vision going spotty, and I swayed on my feet at the sudden lightheadedness.

"Call out to him. Tell him you're fine, or I'll shoot him." This wasn't the Kara I knew and had come to care about. Her eyes were cold as they focused on me, and I knew then that she wasn't bluffing.

I swallowed back the nausea churning, threatening to come up. "I'm fine, Jack!" I called out, unable to control the shakiness. "Kara and I are just around the corner."

I could hear him curse and Doc reassuring him that the place was secure. I wished that was true, but I couldn't take my eyes off the barrel of the gun. I stumbled over a root, making Kara jerk me upright. She turned a corner and sped up her steps, dragging me along as I bit my lip to hold back a whimper.

"Please don't do this," I begged.

She didn't answer my plea, just firmed her jaw as she dragged me around another corner.

"Why?" It was all I could think. Why had she pretended to be my friend? Why had she taken so much time to get to know me? Was everything a lie? "Where are you taking me?" I guess there was another question I needed answers to.

"You wouldn't understand," she muttered, ignoring my second question completely.

"I thought you were my friend."

My whispered words made her scoff.

"I *was* your friend, Sally. I tried to convince you to leave Bones. But you just can't see how he controls you. He bruises you, for god's sake."

I shook my head. "I told you, he doesn't. I know it may look like it, but he loves me. He would never hurt me. Is that what this is all about? If we stop, we can discuss this. I can prove that Jack isn't hurting me." If she was doing this to protect me, I could forgive her, even though the method was a little extreme.

"No," she snapped, "That's not what this is about. I was trying to protect you. If you would have just left him, there wouldn't be a reason to use you as leverage against him. But you just wouldn't listen. Now, I have no choice."

I blinked back tears as her words settled on me. She pulled me further and further away, traversing the maze as if she had it memorized. I didn't know where she was leading me, but I knew it was somewhere I really didn't want to go.

"Please tell me why you are betraying me this way," I pleaded. My eyes were bouncing from the gun still pointed at my side to the trail in front of us, hoping that she wouldn't trip and accidentally shoot me in the stomach. I knew my baby would never survive that.

"Things aren't always about you," she snapped, turning to glare at me. She huffed out a breath. "I have no choice. My brother is the Boogeyman VP. He called me home from college two years ago.

Once I do this last thing for them, I can go back to my own life. I never wanted to be here. I grew up in Texas with my mom, while my brother lived in the next town over with his dad. I hate this place. But as soon as I hand you over, I'm out of this frozen hell hole."

"And my life will be over," I muttered, the sense of betrayal making my heart ache.

"Don't be so dramatic," she scoffed.

"Dramatic? You think that me being offered to the Boogeyman MC on a silver platter to be violated is being dramatic?" My voice rose with my words as I stared at her, incredulous.

"Lower your voice." She hissed as she thumbed off the safety. I held out my free hand, begging her again.

"Please. Put the safety back on. I will do what you say, but please, put it back on." More visions of her tripping and me ending up dead danced in my frantic mind.

We turned another corner to see a Christmas display in an alcove decorated with tinsel and toys around the base. But someone had painted them to look like a bloody massacre had happened in the scene. I shuddered as we passed it.

"You know, Sally, I don't think I will. I don't trust you not to grow a backbone and try to fight me for it."

My heart dropped. She wasn't wrong. I had been contemplating that very thing. I knew if she managed to get me to our destination, it would be all over for me. Would it be better to fight her now and risk being shot? I wasn't sure Jack would be able to save me this time. I chanced a glance over my shoulder, but there was no sign of him. As I tried to listen, the only footsteps I could hear were Kara's and mine, along with our heavy breathing.

Our steps crunched over the frozen roots that were lying across the path periodically. For the most part, the path was clear. It was obvious it had been worn down with so many people having gone through the maze before us. There were also patches of ice and snow. Seeing the snow there in little drifts along the bases of the stalks reminded me of how cold it was outside. I was trembling from fear but also from the frostiness in the air.

After walking quite a distance, passing different twisted Christmas displays, I heard Jack faintly as he called out to me. I opened my mouth to respond, but Kara jabbed me in the side with the gun. "Don't even think about opening your mouth." I held my breath in terror.

"Please," I whispered, almost too quiet to hear. "Please be careful with that gun."

"Then shut up and do as I say," she snapped.

A tear slid down my cheek, and I wiped it away furiously with my gloved hand. "You were like a sister to me," I muttered as my heart ached. "You were the first real friend I had."

She let out a heavy sigh, and for the first time, she sounded truly sorry. "I never wanted to do this. You're a nice person. When I started talking to you, you were just another girl who worked at the bar. I liked you, Sally. But then Bones moved you into his house." She shook her head. "That's when everything changed."

I sniffled at her words. "And there's no way you will just let me go?" She scoffed. "What about Daisy?" A thought crossed my mind. "Were you in on it together?"

"I never knew her. As I said, I grew up in Texas. It doesn't surprise me, though. Oogie likes to cover as many bases as he can. He was pretty fucking pissed, though, when he found out your man killed his sister. Not that he cared about her or anything. He just hates to lose."

She pulled me to a stop at the edge of the maze. I could clearly see an empty field on the other side of the last row of stalks as she pulled her arm from mine. I wrapped both of my arms around my middle, as much for protection as comfort. She took her stocking cap off her head and stuffed it into her pocket, then straightened her blonde hair with a sigh, never taking her gun or eyes off of me.

"It's too late for that, Sally. If I didn't have to do this, I wouldn't. You have no idea how many opportunities I've had to incapacitate you and hand you over to Oogie. I could have drugged you so many times but didn't. Now, time has run out for both of us."

"I'm glad you said that, little Kara." A deep, masculine voice had both of us turning as a tall man slipped through a row of corn stalks. He was almost as tall as Jack, but he was brawnier, with a beer belly starting to form over his belt. His cut was showing through his open leather jacket, letting me know that this was the infamous Boogeyman President.

Kara straightened, one hand going to her hair to smooth it down over her breasts like I've seen her do so many times. "Oogie." Her tone was breathless as she stared up at the man who had been threatening the club for months. I glanced between the two of them as I watched him smirk and Kara smile shyly. So she was in love with the monster. So much made a little more sense now. She was hoping to impress him. What a freaking joke. It made me want to slap her until she came to her senses.

"It's good to know you disobeyed my direct orders, little girl. I could have had my hands on Bone's woman months ago and had the town in my clutches. But you kept that from happening."

She shook her head as her smile dropped, and her eyes widened in alarm. "No, it wasn't like that—"

The gunshot rang out, cutting off her words, and I jumped as the blood spray spattered across my cheek. Kara dropped to the cold, frozen ground in the next instant. As I stared at the growing puddle of blood that turned her blonde hair dark crimson, a large hand grabbed my upper arm in a hold hard enough to bruise through the heavy jacket and layers of clothes I was wearing.

I didn't even cry out as he pulled me roughly through the cornstalks to the field outside. It wasn't until the sound of Jack's bellow from somewhere in the maze jarred me from the shock of seeing yet another person murdered in front of me.

TWENTY-ONE

THE QUEEN OF NIGHTMARES

With a hard pull that I knew I only got away with due to surprise, I slid away from Oogie. I didn't even make it two feet before I was snatched roughly by my hair. That time, I did cry out as my neck jerked back, wrenching with pain.

Oogie laughed, not even attempting to hide his amusement at my weak attempt at running away. "Oh, no, love. You aren't going anywhere." He brought me closer with his tight grip to put his nose behind my ear and inhale deeply. "I'm going to have fun with you. Maybe I'll keep you for a while, hmmm?"

"Please, don't," I whimpered as I brought my hands up, grabbing his wrists to relieve some of the pressure on my scalp.

He shook me roughly, pulling several strands out with a snarl before shoving me to the ground. I landed on my hip, bracing myself from the fall with one hand, my wrist screaming with the hard impact of the icy ground.

"Grab her, throw her into the van." Oogie turned dismissively and walked away. It was then I noticed a dark van parked several feet away at the edge of the corn maze. I wondered where Jack's men were. They had said the place was secure.

A tall, skinny man with pockmarks on his face grinned down at me with stained teeth as he stood there wearing a dirty bomber jacket that had seen better days. He turned and spit, a long stream of saliva mixed with chewing tobacco hitting the ground a foot from my leg. I shuddered with disgust and tried to scoot away from the mess.

"I hope the Prez lets the rest of us have a turn with you, too. You look like fun."

"Fuck you, asshole," I hissed out the words, batting at his hands as he reached down for me. I swung my fist and managed to get him in the nose. He snarled, then spit more brown saliva on my chest, ruining the beautiful white jacket Jack had gifted me with. I gagged viciously, turning my head away from the sight. As he managed to get a hold of my arm and yanked me to my feet, I knew the nausea I had been battling since Kara had taken me was going to win.

As I swayed on my feet, I could feel the vomit rising. Before I could turn to the side, it erupted from me. All the apple cider I had just drunk, as well as my breakfast of French toast, came rushing out in a torrent all over the front of the greasy biker.

"What the fuck!" He cried out, letting me go to hold his arms wide at his sides. I fell back to the ground, heaving with tears running down my cheeks.

"What's going on over there?" Oogie demanded from the side of the van as he drew on a cigarette. Jack had stopped smoking months ago when he realized the smell made my morning sickness flare. I didn't care if he smoked; he was an adult who could do what he wanted, but Jack respected me enough to quit when he saw how uncomfortable it made me. As Oogie walked over with his lit cigarette in his hand, the smoke wafted toward me, and my stomach immediately rebelled again.

As I turned to my side to heave into the packed dirt ground next to me, the pale, sweaty-faced biker I had thrown up on started gagging.

"Oh, man," he whined as he bent over. "I don't do puke, Prez." I may have been lying there on the frozen ground, covered in blood, spit, and likely splatters of my own vomit, but I couldn't stop the grin at seeing what I had reduced this man to. As soon as he emptied his stomach on the ground with a moan, I had to quickly turn my head to avoid seeing it and heaving with my own nausea again.

"Fuck. We're gonna be here all day with this shit." Oogie stood over me, glaring daggers at my face. "Are you done?" I thought about lying, but in the end, I simply nodded my head weakly. "Good. Get your scrawny ass up and let's get going."

He reached down and once again dragged me to my feet, then over toward the van. As I got nearer to the open doors of the van, I could see a body inside. That's when I realized what had happened to Jack's men. I recognized the shaggy hair of the one lying motionless in the van, but that was all I could see through the blood covering him. I didn't know his name, but he had always been smiling.

Before Oogie could pull me close enough to toss me inside the van next to the dead prospect, heavy footsteps thundered on the other side of the corn stalks, coming closer by the second. Everyone turned in the direction of the maze. Oogie had his gun up and pointed just as Jack came storming through the stalks with rage in his eyes and a gun in his hand. Barrel and Doc followed right behind him.

Just as Oogie pulled the trigger, I shoved his arm up, making the shot go wide. With my ears ringing, I saw Jack snarl viciously and come storming toward us. I would have described him as a deadly avenging angel, but that would have been wrong. He resembled a demon more than he ever would an angel, with his black eyes and the tattoos climbing up his neck and covering his gloveless hands.

"Jack!" I cried out, so glad to see him. I took a step toward him, but once again, I was yanked back, falling into the hard body behind me. Oogie wrapped one hand around my throat, squeezing hard enough to cut off my air supply. His other hand jammed the barrel of the gun into the side of my head. My hat lay somewhere in the dirt after our first scuffle, so it hurt as the metal dug roughly into my scalp.

I whimpered with pain and terror, looking at Jack as he stood only a few feet away. He appeared ready to rip off Oogie's head with his bare hands as he eyed the gun the man had pressed against me. The greasy biker must have finally finished his vomiting because he grinned as he walked over to where we were standing by the van's open doors.

"Stupid fucker. We win!" His laugh cut off abruptly with a loud bang. Jack shifted his gun back to aim at Oogie, not even bothering to watch as the other guy fell to the ground with a thud.

Oogie sighed and shook his head. "That was my VP you just shot." His tone said he was more bothered by the inconvenience than losing his second in command.

I stared at the dead man in disbelief. "That was Kara's brother?" I mumbled.

Everyone ignored me.

"Let her go, Oogie," Jack growled, his tone low and deadly.

I could feel Oogie's chest move against my back as he chuckled. "Never gonna happen. I warned you, didn't I? I told you what was going to happen. Then I discovered that you are planning to destroy my compound. Did you really think I wouldn't find out that you sent a drone to map my territory? I have spies everywhere, *Jack*. You pushed my hand. This is really all your fault."

"I won't let you take her," Jack ground out between clenched teeth. His fingers shifted on the gun he was holding, adjusting his grip, and I knew he was itching to pull the trigger. "You're outmanned, Oogie. You can't walk away from this. But if you let her go, I'll let you leave."

The Boogeyman President threw back his head and gave a short bark of laughter, immediately bringing his eyes back to Jack. "Oh, how wrong you are." His tone went from amused to deadly serious with his words. He gave a loud, piercing whistle, making me wince. While my ears rang, I watched as Jack's expression didn't change, but his eyes went from deadly intent to dread. They darted from the left, where the maze was, then back to my face. I knew whatever he'd seen wasn't good. I had never seen Jack afraid before, but what was there scared the shit out of him. I sucked in my breath and held it, knowing that what happened next was going to be bad.

Movement from the corner of my eye had me shifting enough to try to get a look. That was when I realized Oogie hadn't come unprepared. Several members of his club had entered the scene, emerging from the maze where they had likely been waiting for the signal from Oogie.

I closed my eyes, inhaling through my nose as it stung with the sudden stark terror that swept over me. When I reopened them, I blinked rapidly to clear my vision, wanting one last look at Jack before my entire world was ripped away from me. As I tried to tell him how much I loved him with eyes, Jack's expression became filled with so much impotent rage that my heart ached for him.

"As you can see, gentlemen, you lost before you even played your first hand. The game is over. I win." He laughed again, then gestured to one of his men. "We're done here." He looked back at Jack. He pulled me backward with him as we awkwardly climbed into the back of the van. "If you ever want to see her again, you know what to do."

The body of the prospect was kicked unceremoniously out of the back of the van onto the cold, hard ground. Barrel and Doc had moved to stand next to Jack, both of them with a hand on an arm, attempting to hold Jack back. He shoved them off with a snarl and stepped forward.

"Stop!" He shouted. "Don't take her. You can't take her." His deep voice became gravelly, cracking at the end. "Take me instead."

"Prez—" Barrel spoke low next to Jack, sending me an apologetic look. I understood. Without Jack, it was almost certain that the club, as well as the town, would fall under Boogeyman rule. I was just a woman. Jack was going to need his men to remind him of that. I gave Barrel a small smile.

Jack growled. "No!" He strode forward, dropping his gun to the ground, leaving it lying there as he came forward. "You fucking take me. Not her, goddamnit."

"Jack, no!" I didn't want to be taken, and I didn't want what I knew would most assuredly happen to me. But I loved Jack more than I loved myself. It would destroy me if Oogie got a hold of him. I knew it was what Jack was thinking, too, though. Both of us were willing to sacrifice ourselves for each other. A sob broke through when I realized there was no winning this. Not for me and Jack.

"Done." Oogie shoved me forward as his men immediately swarmed Jack, taking him by the arms as one of them slammed a meaty fist into his gut. I fell to the edge of the van, barely stopping myself from tumbling over the side before one of the Boogeymen grabbed me roughly. He pulled me through the cold, congealed blood of the dead prospect and dropped me with a bone-jarring thud back onto the ground several feet from where they were punching Jack. He never fought back as he watched Doc and Barrel rush forward to grab me and pull me a safe distance away. I cried out as a particularly vicious punch knocked his head back, and blood sprayed from his mouth.

Watching them beat on Jack was one of the hardest things I had ever done, but I didn't want to lose a single minute of seeing his beautiful face. Doc tugged me into his arms, attempting to offer me comfort, but my body and mind were going numb as I watched them finally pull Jack into the back of the van as they heaved out heavy breaths. Jack was bent over, wheezing. He spit a mouthful of blood on the ground and raised his head to look at me. One of his eyes was already nearly completely swollen, and the other had blood dripping into it from a cut above his eyebrow.

As I sobbed in Doc's arms, Oogie paused at the doors he was closing. "I'll be seeing you soon, little girl," and then he winked at me. Jack roared from inside the van and rushed forward, heading for Oogie as the doors slammed closed. Muffled sounds of fighting could be heard through the walls of the van as the whole vehicle rocked back and forth. I held my breath, terrified of what was happening. Jack was outnumbered, with at least four Boogeymen in there with him. The sound of a gunshot made me jump and shriek. All sounds of the fighting ended abruptly. When the van started up and began rolling away a second later, I cried out, screaming Jack's name.

TWENTY-TWO

THE QUEEN OF NIGHTMARES

Doc carried me through the crowd of gawkers back to the parking lot as I sobbed uncontrollably. I ignored all of it, even when we stopped for a brief moment to speak quietly with a man who looked vaguely familiar. I didn't care about anything except for Jack. That gunshot played over and over in my mind on a horrible loop.

Once we got to the SUV, Doc shoved me up into the seat, quickly belting me in. Through my tears, I could see other Devil's Nightmares climbing into their own vehicles but turned away. When Doc slid behind the wheel, an unexpected torrent of rage came bursting out of me.

I slapped and punched as much as I could, trapped behind the restricting belt, too far gone to even think about undoing and making my assault on my would-be brother-in-law easier. I screamed and sobbed at Doc while he just held up his arms to protect his grim face. "You should have stopped him! You should have let them take me! I hate you! I hate you! Get him back!" My door opened behind me, and I felt large arms wrap around me, holding me still as I struggled to free myself as my chest heaved. "It should have been me!" I screamed, ending with a sob.

"No, Red." I recognized the voice as Barrel, and that just spurred me on. He had been there, too. He should have stopped Jack from sacrificing himself for me. That shot reverberated in my mind like a broken record, making my shoulders shake from how hard I was crying.

"I'm sorry, Sally," Doc muttered.

I felt a prick in my upper arm and glanced down through blurry eyes to see Doc pulling a syringe back. I moaned in defeat. "Jack."

"I know, Red," Barrel whispered into my hair as his grip loosened. "I know."

I slumped back into my seat. My whole body trembled even as my sobs quieted to whimpering while the tears continued to stream down my cheeks to drip off my chin. I rolled my head against the headrest. "Not Jack. Not Jack." I whispered. "It should have been me."

I felt the door close, and the vehicle start up. "Red, the town would be in ashes anyway if they had taken you. Bones would have burned down the whole fucking town in a rage." I heard Doc's words, but I didn't care. I didn't care about anything but Jack. Let the whole fucking world burn.

My eyes must have closed as we drove through the town. Once we pulled back into the compound and parked in the lot in front of the clubhouse, my door opened again. Barrel clicked my seatbelt, and I felt it loosen from around me. He lifted my arm to allow it to slide from around my body. I blinked at him, my eyelids feeling heavy.

Doc moved to his side, and Barrel stepped back, a sad expression on his face as he looked down at me. I glanced over at Doc as he reached for me. I allowed him to slide his arms under and lift me. As I stared at his profile I could see the same features that both he and

Jack shared. I squeezed my eyes closed to shut out the image as a fresh wave of tears began to fall.

"I hate you," I whispered.

Doc heaved out a heavy sigh. "Not as much as I hate myself, little Red."

A few minutes later, I felt myself being lowered. I felt the familiar leather of the couch in Jack's office under me. I almost begged for him to take me anywhere else, but when he placed the throw over me, I got a whiff of Jack's scent on it and pulled it closer. Quiet sobs took over, not allowing me to say anything else.

A hand rested on my shoulder. Doc's deep voice was soft as he told me to sleep. "We're going to be in Church, Red. I swear, we are going to do everything we can to get my brother back." Without waiting for a response, he turned and strode out of the room, the door closing behind him with a soft snick.

I hiccuped as my heart ached so much it felt like my chest was literally being ripped apart. I had to rub there just to make sure I wasn't bleeding out all over the leather.

DOC

We sat around the conference table. Every patched member of the Devil's Nightmares filled the room. Every seat was taken, and a few were leaning against the walls. Several men were chain-smoking, making the air in the room hazy as we discussed the situation. Each of the men were filled with rage. We all pretended to ignore the empty chair at the head of the table.

"We have the aerial footage of the compound. I say we ride over there with every single weapon we have and blow the whole fucking compound to hell."

There were several agreements to the biker's suggestion. Fuck, I wanted to agree, too. But we had to be smart.

"We can't just ram into them like two virgins on prom night," Shock spoke quietly, a grim look on his face replacing his usual smile. He played with a knife as he kept his eyes on the table in front of him. I knew he was feeling a fuck-ton of guilt for not having stayed with us when we all went into the maze. At the time, he thought it would have been better to stay outside to keep an eye on anyone entering. Jack had agreed, no one knowing the threat lay on the opposite side.

We had been discussing this shit for what felt like fucking hours and had gotten nowhere. I was tired, emotionally and physically. Barrel sighed and pulled at his green hair. "The Boogeymen know what we were planning. We have to do something else. We have to be smart about this."

Tech had already scanned the room for bugs and found two. That fucking bitch who had played Red had likely planted them at some time. She'd been around the club for two fucking years, so there was no telling what kind of damage she had done or how much The Boogeymen knew about our club. It was no wonder they had been able to cause so much mayhem over the last few months. They knew every move we were making before we even made it. It was also clear now that she had been the one behind the delivery of the insects all along. I wished she were alive and standing in front of me right now so I could put my own bullet in her forehead.

Still, though, I looked around the table. It was a real possibility that one of the men in this room was another mole. "Does anyone have any other suggestions?" I asked, heaving out a sigh as I sat back and crossed my arms. "The longer we leave him there, the worse his chances are of survival. What about the other clubs? Didn't Bones have an agreement with them?"

"What if..." one of the guys leaning against the wall spoke up as he stared pointedly at the empty chair.

"Don't fucking say it," I growled, slamming my fist on the table in front of me.

He held up his hands as several club members turned to glare at him. "I'm just saying. We have to be realistic. There is a possibility that he's already dead. Sending the rest of us in there to retrieve a dead body will just end up killing off the rest of the club."

"He's not dead."

The quiet voice coming from the doorway had everyone turning to look at her. Sally looked gaunt with dark circles under her puffy eyes. Seeing her had me trying to swallow past the lump in my throat. My little brother was in love with this woman when he hadn't let a single other soul past his walls. A part of him was with her. I glanced down at her belly, the slightest curve to her lower abdomen visible through the T-shirt she was wearing.

The biker who had spoken before she came in scoffed in derision at her words. I took a close look at him, trying to remember anything about him, but came up blank. He was average height, maybe five foot ten, with a bit of a beer belly. He was likely in his mid-thirties. But I had no idea how long he'd been a part of the club.

"I get that you want your man back, sweetheart, but get your head out of the fucking clouds. No way is the Boogeyman President going to keep Bones alive."

Sally's expression hardened as she stepped forward. "Don't call me sweetheart." She walked right up to the man, and my whole body stiffened as I watched him clench his fists. "He's. Not. Dead."

"You can have your fucking delusional dreams all you want, but I'm not dying for anyone." His words had everyone in the room bristling with anger. A club only worked when every member cared more about the club than they did themselves. It was part of the reason I hadn't joined years ago. I knew I didn't have the time to make such a commitment.

I was about to jump to my feet when I watched in what felt like slow motion as Sally brought her hand up, the glint of steel shining under the bright light in the room. She held the blade to the man's throat as he snarled down at her. I stood slowly, along with several others, as we watched and waited. This was something Sally needed to do, but if he made a single wrong move toward her, I was going to slice his throat myself.

I watched as she lowered the blade a few inches, then sucked in a breath as she slid the knife under the name patch on his chest and began sawing.

"What the fuck are you doing, bitch?" He made to move into her, but before I could round the table to get to them, the bikers on both sides of him grabbed him by his arms. With them holding him steady, Sally continued to cut until his name patch that read Bear was hanging by a thread. She pulled back the knife, and while staring into his eyes, she used her free hand to grip the patch and pull, breaking the last of the thread and tugging it off the leather. Everyone ignored his curses as he ranted the whole time she was slicing.

"I may not be a member of this club, but even I know what it's supposed to mean to be in a brotherhood. You don't care about your President? Then you're not a part of this club either."

The man looked ready to commit murder. He looked up, glancing around at the faces looking back at him with disgust. "You all are going to let this bitch come into Church and do this shit?" His gaze settled on me.

I sat back in my chair with a grin. "Yep."

TWENTY-THREE

THE QUEEN OF NIGHTMARES

It took a couple of the men to drag Bear out of the door. It was easy to hear him yelling as he was dragged down the hall. There wasn't a single ounce of regret in me as I walked to the head of the table. I stared down at the empty chair for several seconds until someone cleared their throat, jarring me from the thoughts of Jack that swirled through my head.

I tossed the patch down on the table, watching as it skittered to a stop in the middle of the polished wood. Without a word, I pulled the chair out and took a seat, daring anyone to tell me I wasn't allowed to be in the room, let alone sit in the President's spot. I knew I had already crossed several lines and broken a dozen rules, but Jack had made me his Queen, and in my eyes, that gave me every right.

I looked around the room, meeting each man's gaze individually. "Does anyone else have an objection to saving Jack from the Boogeymen?" When there were no grumbles or words of dissent, I clasped my hands and placed them in front of me on the table. "Good. Now, tell me what the plan is."

I expected there to be pushback. I had no business being in this room, after all, but the men just glanced at each other as if asking, *are we really letting her do this?* Doc was the first to speak up.

"The plan is to take as many weapons as we can to the compound later tonight. One of our guys," he nodded to a tall, skinny guy with shaggy brown hair and glasses. He was wearing a patch reading Tech on his vest. "Sent out a drone the other night, mapping out all the buildings." He leaned forward and gave me a grave look. "We know where buildings are, but this won't be easy. The Boogeymen will be expecting us. We can set C4 with charges to blow up buildings. We can take a shit-ton of ammunition, but we don't know where they are keeping Bones, and we know they will be waiting for us. There will likely be a massive gunfight, and several of us could end up dead."

Doc sat back and sighed, running his hands over his face. Looking haggard, he dropped his hands and stared at me. All the pain and hopelessness he felt was easy to read. "Even if we do all that, we still may not find Bones alive."

I bit my lip to stop it from trembling. Everything he said was true. As I looked around the room, I saw looks of determination. There was a heavy dose of fear, but I could see each of these men were willing to take the chance, knowing that they could very well lose their own life by saving Jack's.

I nodded. "I understand. You can't go in guns blazing. It won't work, and Jack wouldn't want the rest of you to lose your lives to save him. Perhaps what we need to do is the unexpected."

"What do you suggest?" Shock asked, watching me with an intense expression. I could feel him trying to read me as if he could dig into my brain and find all my secrets.

"I think we need someone who is familiar with the compound. Someone who will know where Jack is being held. Someone that no one will expect."

Barrel snorted. "That includes... absolutely no one. It sounds like a great plan, but unless you know something the rest of us don't, then we are back at square one." He looked around the table. "Maybe one of us can sneak in to take a look around. If we are careful, we should be able to find where he is. We can take out whatever guards there might be quietly. Once we have him back, then we can return to Plan A and wipe the fuckers off the planet."

There were a lot of agreements around the table. Most of the guys started discussing who would be best for the job, with several volunteers ready to take the risk. As I sat there and watched, I could feel eyes on me. I looked up to see both Doc and Shock staring at me intently. I chose to ignore their probing eyes. There were questions I couldn't answer at the moment.

I stood up from Jack's chair and nodded at the two men while the rest of them continued to discuss the plan. Someone had opened a notebook and was making notes. A small bit of warmth filled me at the sight of so many of Jack's men ready to charge into danger for him. It was too small to override the aching coldness that had taken over from the moment those van doors closed, though.

I walked out of the conference room as the two bikers who had dragged Bear out were coming back in.

"Hey, Sally, watch out for that guy, okay? We gave him a warning, but assholes like that can react kinda stupid, you know?" I nodded my head, grateful for the warning.

"I understand. I will keep an eye out for trouble."

As I walked away, my shoulders sagged under the heavy weight of emotions I was battling. I had slept for a while after Doc had dosed me with whatever the sedative was in that injection, but I was still groggy, and depression threatened to pull me under. The only thing I could fight it with was determination. I wasn't going to stop until Jack was in front of me.

I entered the office then closed and locked the door behind me. I glanced around the room, taking in the simple decor. The desk was to the left, and the leather couch to the right. Behind the desk by the window was a filing cabinet with a small fake Christmas tree on top. I didn't know how long it had been there and wondered if it was

Jack's doing or someone else's. I saw a small box on the floor under the window and walked over to peer inside. I had no desire for any more nasty surprises, so I pulled the knife back out of my pocket. Using the tip, I lifted the flap of the box. I relaxed, my muscles loosening and shoulders dropping once I saw it was filled with Christmas ornaments.

I set the knife on top of the filing cabinet next to the tree and reached in for the first ornament. It was a ceramic gingerbread man, made to look as if it had been decorated with frosting. It was adorable and so well made it almost looked like a real cookie. With a small smile, I hung the gingerbread man up on one of the branches before reaching back into the box for another.

It didn't take long to cover the tree since it was only about three feet tall, but it was festive and colorful, the majority of the ornaments being gingerbread men with slightly different colors. There were no lights or garland in the box, so it was a fairly basic decorated tree. But I liked it in its simplicity.

I backed up to take in the full effect of the Christmas tree until my hip hit the side of the desk, taking my attention. When I turned to look down at it, I noticed stacks of paperwork sitting there. Out of curiosity, and a feeble attempt to take my mind off things, I shuffled through the papers and realized I was looking at reports from the various businesses Jack owned in town. There was also a stack of invoices as well as written requests for all kinds of things like changing inventory and updating logos and signage. It seemed Jack did a lot more than financially back the town's people the way he'd like me to believe. Maybe he was embarrassed, or maybe he truly believed he had no hand in what the businesses did. But from what I was discovering by looking through the papers, he actively aided them in business decisions and was still paying bills for a few of them. My guess was that the money was recorded as a loan to the ones who were still getting steady on their feet. From another financial ledger, it was clear that the repayment plans on his business loans were very generous.

My pride in Jack, the man, grew as I took in what I suspected was only the tip of the iceberg when it came to the town. I picked up the pen lying next to the paperwork and started reading through the requests again from the beginning, paying closer attention. I pulled a notebook closer to me and began making notes.

As I worked in silence, my mind kept drifting to what I had said in the conference room. I knew what had to be done, and like the men of the club, I hesitated. I wanted Jack freed more than anything, but I would be putting a woman in grave danger. Did I ask her to risk her life? Did Jack have a choice? I had no doubts that the club's plan to send in a man would fail. Jack needed someone who knew exactly where he was being kept and could get him out undetected.

With a heavy dose of trepidation fueled by hope, I reached for my phone. With trembling fingers, I withdrew the piece of paper from my pocket. I didn't know why I had suddenly needed to keep it close. After getting home from the hospital, I placed it in my shirt drawer underneath a blouse I never wore. When I was getting dressed this morning, I saw it sitting there, staring at me like a bold neon sign, so I picked it up and slipped it into my pocket. Now, as I sat at Jack's desk, I typed the number into my phone.

It rang three times, and I was about to hang up when the person answered.

"Sally?"

"Hey, Daisy. Remember when you gave me your number, you said if I ever needed anything, I could call you?" I took a deep breath. "There's something I need your help with."

CHAPTER
TWENTY-FOUR

JACK

Everything hurt. Even my fucking eyelashes hurt as they brushed against the skin of my bruised and swollen eye socket. I kept my eyes closed as I listened to the shouts outside that had started up just a few minutes ago. The sudden commotion had drawn them outside and ended the latest fun the Boogeymen were having at my expense, so I was grateful for the distraction.

If I had to guess, one of my men, or all of them, had come in an attempt to rescue me. I cursed silently. I didn't have time to relay any orders when I had been taken, but Doc should have known that his priority should be on keeping my woman and child safe. I could die happy knowing that they would live. If the club angered Oogie, there was no doubt he would take it out on my little Queen. He'd already threatened her several times, but his final words to her had been what made me see red.

When I heard him say those words, I'd lost my shit. It wasn't until the bullet slammed through my shoulder that I slowed down, but it was the strike to my skull from behind that had put my struggles to an end. I'd woken already strung up like a fucking deer, which was pretty fucking ironic since that was the same method of torture the Devil's Nightmares employed.

Instead of hanging me by my arms, though, I was hanging by my fucking feet. My one arm was useless. I couldn't move it at all, thanks to the bullet I had taken to my shoulder. My other arm could move, but I chose to wait until I had a chance to act. If they did anything to that arm, I wouldn't have a snowball's chance in hell of getting free. My only option was to bide my time and play the good little captive until the perfect moment came. Hopefully, it will come sooner than later.

When the yelling died down, I cracked open my bloodshot eyes. After hanging for so long, I was having trouble seeing straight. Of course, that may also have something to do with the blow I'd taken to my head or one of the numerous punches they'd landed. I was hanging like a fucking piñata for them, and they were taking full advantage. I knew I had at least a couple of broken ribs, making it difficult to breathe.

There was another concern I was facing. I wasn't sure how long I'd been hanging here by my feet, but a body could only take about ten hours before it shut down. The best case scenario would be that I died from a brain hemorrhage. The worst case would be that my internal organs slowly crush my lungs until I could no longer breathe.

I blinked to clear my vision, giving my head a small shake. The first thing I saw was the puddle of blood under me. Blood was still dripping from my fingertips at a fairly steady rate. It was likely another reason I felt so goddamn woozy. The sound of the door opening caused my body to tense involuntarily, and I had to stifle my groan of pain. I wasn't going to let these mother fuckers see they had made me weak.

"Get him down and throw him in the cage." There was no mistaking the voice of Oogie. Even through the constant woosh of my heartbeat pounding through my head, I could still hear his fucking voice. I was going to make sure I killed him real fucking slow. As soon as I could move.

Rough hands grabbed and lifted me until the chain wrapped around my legs and feet was clear of the hook in the ceiling. My body landed hard on the cold cement ground, stealing what little oxygen I had. The cement might as well have been the icy ground outside; it was so fucking cold. The place was what I would have expected from a torture room. The temperature was cold enough to make me involuntarily shiver while the heat was kept so low it barely kept the room above freezing.

I coughed and groaned, but thankful as fuck that I was no longer hanging even as I worked to stop myself from writhing on the floor with the pain. My entire body was adjusting to the sudden change of position. My ribs felt like they were being pried out of my chest with a pair of pliers, while my skin felt electrified as feeling rushed back into my fingers and toes.

Hands grabbed my chained feet and began to drag me across the room. I was pulled inside a large metal cage that looked like it was meant for a dog. If I had to guess, it was six by six by six. It would be large enough to sit comfortably, but if I were to stand, I'd have to hunch over. I also wouldn't be able to lay out straight.

The cage was welcome, though. It meant that I would be left alone. If I could rest, I could escape. I would do anything to get back to Sally. But only if I were able to kill Oogie before I left. I couldn't leave him alive, or he would just keep showing up like a fucking cockroach.

Heavy boots walked closer as the cage door was slammed, and a padlock clicked into place. "I should really just kill you and be done with it." Oogie stared down at me with triumph. It was the same look he'd been wearing ever since I'd woken up chained and bleeding. "But you have caused me so much trouble that I just can't help but want to play with you for a little while. The boys have bets going on about how long you'll last. A few of them think it could be weeks."

He tilted his head as he grinned at me. "But I think you'll only make it a few more days."

He turned around and barked an order at one of the men standing by the door. "Bring him in." He turned back to me, crossing his arms over his broad chest. "Just so you know, every man that comes to my compound in an attempt to rescue you will die swiftly. Or slowly. It depends on my mood at the time." He shrugged.

The door opened, and a body was dragged inside. They pulled him over, stopping just outside the cage before dropping his arm. Oogie kicked his side, and by his lack of response, it was apparent he was already dead.

"This one came waving a white flag. Can you believe that shit?" He laughed. "Waving a white fucking flag like this was the Civil War or some such bullshit. He tried to say that your woman kicked him out of the club, and he wanted to join me." I narrowed my eyes and looked closer. The man was wearing a cut, but his name patch was missing. His face was a mess, but after blinking to clear my vision a little more, I finally recognized him as Bear. I huffed, ignoring the pain it caused. My woman had good fucking instincts. That fucker had been pushing back too much lately, and the club leaders had already voted to put him on his last fucking warning.

"I'll be watching closely for any other tactics your men try to use. You won't be able to make a dupe out of me, Jack Ellington. You will die here. The only thing that will change is whether you're still alive when I bring your old lady in. Will you still be alive when you watch me fuck her? Have you opened her ass yet? I think a sweet peach like that would have a nice tight asshole. I can't wait to make her bleed."

He turned to walk away as I seethed through my teeth. I had to grip my ribs tight with my good arm as my breathing sped up from the picture he'd painted. I wanted to rip him apart with my bare hands and my teeth in his throat. I closed my eyes, trying to get the image he'd painted out of my head as I panted shallow breaths. Before he left the small concrete building that was hardly bigger than a shed, he paused again, his hand on the metal door.

"Oh, there is one more thing," he said in a cheerful tone. I just knew that whatever he was about to say next was going to put me over the edge of sanity. And I was right.

"I know about the baby, Bones. Imagine if I let her have your spawn and raised it as my own. Your son will grow up to be just... like... me." As the door shut behind him, his laughter echoed around the room before fading away.

TWENTY-FIVE

THE QUEEN OF NIGHTMARES

Aloud commotion woke me from my fitful sleep. I was startled, sitting up with a jerk as I listened intently. It took me a minute to shake away the disorientation and realize I was on the couch in Jack's office. Late last night, Doc had brought Zero to the clubhouse along with a duffle bag holding clothes and necessities for an extended stay. The men had decided that I wouldn't be safe at the house. As much as I longed to be in the space that Jack and I had shared, one that held his touch and smell, I had to agree. I wouldn't have felt safe there, even with a guard.

I slowly stood up, glad I was wearing sweats and a long-sleeved shirt, and patted Zero's head as he whined next to my feet. "I know, boy, let's go see what's going on out there." He huffed out his agreement, and together, we walked out of the office and down the hall to the main room to see Barrel pacing back and forth with a grim expression.

He was dressed in all black, wearing what I could only assume was tactical gear. He walked over to one of the tables and began taking off a heavy looking sack from his back and setting it down.

"I couldn't get through to look around the fucking compound." He sounded pissed. More than just a failed assignment should have caused. "That fucking weasel should have been put down instead of kicked out," he seethed.

"Who?" I asked, making every head turn my way.

"Fucking Bear was there." He started pacing again, yanking at his green hair in agitation. "As I was sneaking up to the compound, ready to get to work on the plan, the fucker showed up waving a white flag and bringing every fucking member of the club outside. There were so many men and so much shouting I couldn't sneak past. I had to stay hidden where I was until the uproar had calmed down. Luckily, no one believed him when he tried to say he wanted to jump ship." Barrel sighed in defeat. "As soon as they killed him, Oogie put every single club member on guard. They surrounded the whole fucking compound."

"Bear showed up?" Doc demanded in angry shock.

Barrel snorted. "Yeah. He started shouting about Sally kicking him out of the club. He demanded to see their President so he could join them in taking us down. Instead of listening, they killed him. That fucker thought he was going to spill our secrets, but Oogie assumed he was just a mole. Killed him without hearing him out." A few of the guys chuckled.

"Good," I said, turning around to head back to the office. I was bone weary and needed to sleep. I'd been a mess of emotions since the maze, and I knew it wasn't good for the baby. Now, more than ever, I wanted to make sure my baby was safe and healthy.

As I passed through the doorway with Zero on my heels, a phone rang from behind the bar along the wall. Everyone turned to look with surprise and wariness. It was the first time I'd ever heard the phone ring. I hadn't even known the clubhouse had a landline.

Tech was the one who walked over and picked the receiver up from the cradle on the wall. "Hello?"

His back went ramrod straight as he listened to whoever was on the other end of the line. My stomach twisted when his head turned to look straight at me with a troubled expression. We all waited as he listened without saying a word. Thankfully, the call was brief, and Tech snarled out, "We'll be there."

He turned to the room and looked at Doc. "The Boogeymen are calling another meeting at The Warehouse. He wants every club to be there for an important announcement." He glanced my way briefly, darting his eyes to my face, then looking away quickly. "He wants Red to be there, too."

"Fuck no!" Doc shouted as several of the other men cursed. I stood there frozen in shock as what he was saying penetrated.

I stepped further into the room again. "Maybe he will trade Jack for me." My words were quiet, but the bikers all heard by the way their curses got louder.

Doc stormed over to me and grabbed my shoulders, giving me a short shake as I stared up at his angry expression. He glared down into my face, his mouth tight in anger. "Never going to happen, Red."

"But—"

He cut me off with another small shake. "No fucking buts. You aren't going to be a fucking sacrificial lamb to these assholes. We will get Bones back, but you aren't going to be handed over to the fucking Boogeymen. So get that thought out of your stubborn head. You got me?" His chest was heaving as he shouted at me, but he lowered his voice, speaking in a softer tone. "You have a baby to protect now. Jack would want both of you safe."

I closed my eyes to hold back my tears. I thought about my baby and nodded. "Okay, Doc." I wrapped my arms protectively around my stomach and whispered again. "Okay."

"Good."

I nodded and turned, walking away from the angry men who still ranted to each other in low, angry tones. I swiped the moisture on my cheeks away with the back of my hand and sniffled. I had to protect the life inside me. That meant I couldn't save Jack, not by offering myself in trade the way he had. I needed another way. I thought of what I'd asked Daisy to do. She was my only hope. She had to come through for me. For Jack.

I pushed the door open to the office and waited until Zero followed me in to close and lock the door. I felt safe at the clubhouse, but I couldn't stop myself from adding that extra barrier, flimsy as it was.

I lay back down on the couch and pulled the throw over me even though Doc had brought in a comforter earlier that evening. The comforter was thick and warm, but it didn't have Jack's scent on it.

I reached down to pet Zero, running my fingers through his scruff. He let out a small whine as he lay his head between his paws. "I know. You miss him as much as I do," I whispered.

I could still hear angry voices out in the common room. Sometimes, there was shouting. Most of the time, it was just a noise in the background, like the hum of angry bees. It eventually lulled me back to sleep.

As I GOT DRESSED for the meeting that would be taking place in an hour, I carefully chose my outfit. There weren't a lot of options, considering Doc had only grabbed essentials, but I kept in mind what would be happening.

Doc had informed me that everyone would be riding in on their motorcycles. Though it was bitterly cold, there was no ice on the roads, and it hadn't snowed in the last few days. Apparently, going to an official meeting at The Warehouse necessitated a show of club force. The lack of ice meant it would be safe, even if the men would have to bundle up to protect themselves from frostbite.

I decided layers were the only way to go. I put a T-shirt on first, then a sweater over that, and would wear a borrowed jacket when we left. My pants were loose denim jeans, but I wore my tightest pair of yoga pants underneath for added warmth. My pants had deep pockets and were perfect for what I had in mind.

I had never stopped thinking that if I'd only had my gun on me while in the damn maze, Kara wouldn't have been able to force me to go with her. I could have been an ally instead of a hindrance to the men when we were confronted by Oogie. Jack may not have been taken. When I saw my little purple gun in the duffle along with my clothes, I knew I would never leave the compound without it ever again.

I picked up the gun and ran my fingers over the smooth, shiny metal. The purple shone in the light, and I smiled for the first time in what seemed like years. My heart never stopped hurting, but seeing that present from Jack was a small bit of sunshine to what had turned into a drab and dreary world.

I turned the gun over to check that the safety was on before popping out the magazine. I checked the bullets the way Jack had shown me, and then I pushed it back in with the heel of my hand. I lifted the gun and looked down the barrel as I aimed. I narrowed my gaze on the gingerbread tree, focusing on only one of the cute ornaments, before lowering the gun.

With one last swipe of my fingers over the gleaming metal, I slid it into my pocket. I wasn't going to face Oogie unprepared. I may have an entire club of bikers at my back, but I was going to have the means to protect myself. I was going to make Jack proud of me.

TWENTY-SIX

THE QUEEN OF NIGHTMARES

The ride was worse than I had expected. By the time we pulled into the dirt parking lot, I was frozen to the bone and wondered if I'd ever be able to feel my nose or cheeks again. Or my legs. I slowly slid off the back of Jack's bike, holding on to the seat as I waited for my legs to start working again.

Doc had borrowed Jack's motorcycle for the drive out to the meeting. Apparently, he had his own bike, but it was at his home. He felt it was easier to take Jack's since it was sitting there, unused, instead of taking his out of storage. As much as I wanted to yell at him, to tell him to keep his hands off Jack's things, what he'd said made sense. Besides, when I thought about it, I knew Jack wouldn't deny his brother the use of his motorcycle. Others, perhaps, but not Doc.

I started unwrapping myself from the protective layers Doc had insisted on. I pulled the balaclava off, glad I had braided my long hair so it wouldn't be a tangled mess. The balaclava probably helped keep my nose from getting frostbite, but at the moment, it didn't feel as if it had done anything to help. Once I stuffed it into my pocket, I pulled my stocking cap down over my head and ears. Everything else could stay on. I pulled my scarf up over my chin and hunched into it. Fuck it was cold.

The lot was already full with so many motorcycles, it was awe inspiring. I knew that there were clubs in the surrounding area, and had even witnessed it from the one time I had spent at The Warehouse months ago. The lot had been full, and the inside of the building had been packed with bikers of all shapes, sizes, and ages. That night, mostly, everyone got along pretty well and seemed more like allies instead of competitors or rivals.

Looking around now, though, I couldn't help but stare. As many as I thought there had been that night, there hadn't been nearly as many as what I was seeing now. Several of the men from the other clubs were leaning on their bikes, smoking cigarettes or joints. They were talking quietly among themselves. The atmosphere seemed subdued as they huddled into their jackets, breathing warm air into their cupped hands to warm them up and stomping their feet. It was different from how I usually saw bikers act when they were together as a group. I didn't think it was all due to the frigid weather.

A couple of the men broke away from their groups and headed over. Both of them were eyeing me closely as they approached. I didn't sense any negative vibes coming from either of them. The looks they had were more curious than anything. Perhaps there was a bit of pity, too. One of them, a tall man with a thick black beard and kind blue eyes, reached out his hand to me. He was wearing a President patch, and I blinked at it in surprise before sliding my gloved hand into his bare one. I didn't know how his fingers hadn't turned blue.

"I'm really sorry about your man. Bones is a good President. I wanted to let you know, we will do anything we can to help get him back. Like him and his club, we respect our women and protect them."

"Thank you, Talon," I murmured, glancing at the stitched name below his President patch.

He winked. "Midnight Demons at your service."

The other President, just as tall but with auburn hair and a shaved face, stepped forward, shoving Talon out of the way with a beefy arm. He also held out his hand for a shake. "The Black Wolves will also be of any help." He looked over to Doc beside me and shifted, extending his hand to my would-be brother-in-law. "I hear you're the new VP. It's nice to meet you. You have big shoes to fill. Lock was one of the good ones."

I looked at the ground at his words. My guilt over his death would likely never fade.

"He was, and I do," Doc agreed.

After dropping their hands back to their sides, everyone glanced around at the gathered bikers.

"Does anyone know what this meeting is about?" Blade, the Black Wolves President asked.

Doc shook his head. "No, but I'm sure we all have our guesses."

They all nodded grimly but didn't speak the words I knew were on everyone's minds. I clenched my hands into fists and shoved them into my jacket pockets. Jack wasn't dead. I would scream it to the sky if I had to.

The sound of dozens of engines broke into the murmuring of the bikers already gathered. I watched as every man who had been relaxed, leaning against their bikes, came to attention, tossing down their cigarettes. Their hands went to the clearly displayed weapons resting on their hips. The entire assembled group fairly vibrated with tension as the Boogeymen circled the lot and then came to a stop in the empty space in front of us.

I tugged off my gloves and tucked them into my pockets as they climbed off their bikes, laughing and joking with each other as if they didn't have a care in the world. As if they weren't holding my whole world captive somewhere, doing things to him, I didn't even want to try to imagine.

I seethed with an almost overwhelming rage as I watched Oogie swing his leg over his motorcycle with a huge grin on his face. Oogie glanced around at the grim faces of everyone standing opposite him and chuckled before landing his dark, piercing gaze on me.

"Well, well, well, what do we have here, boys? The little woman herself actually came." He looked around at the Devil's Nightmares assembled around me. "I honestly didn't think you all had the balls to bring her." He looked back at me with a nasty smirk on his face. "You caused me a lot of trouble, little girl," he tsked as if chiding a small child.

He turned around with his arms outstretched, taking in the combined groups of motorcycle clubs who had come to witness whatever it was he had called this meeting for. My entire body was trembling in fear and hatred. This man had tried to take me, but Jack had stepped in, willing to fight for me, ready to die for me. And this piece of shit monster had taken him instead. I wanted Jack back.

"It's over, fellas," he bellowed. "Or," he faced the Devil's Nightmares again, "should I say, it's just beginning?" He looked over his shoulder, and all the Boogeymen raised their fists and yelled a victory yell so loud it shook the ground and made me want to cover my ears. "This town and the entire area is now Boogeyman territory." He declared his words loud and clear as soon as the cheers died down. "With this territory in my control, nothing will stop me from using the highway from here clear to Canada. My product will be on a fast track to every town, city, school, and club for thousands of miles."

Every single biker that wasn't a Boogeyman shifted nervously on his feet and eyed one another warily. Doc stepped forward with his fists clenched.

"What the fuck are you talking about?" he demanded, his jaw tight and menace lacing his tone, hatred lacing every word. "Where the fuck is our President?"

Oogie let out a guffaw so obnoxious I wanted to punch him in the face to wipe the mirth right off it. "Your President? Oh, that's funny." He wiped at his eyes, still chuckling. "Old Bones gave himself up for his old lady here. Did you really think I was going to let him walk away? That I wasn't going to put him in the ground for the disrespect he's shown me over the years?"

My body froze, my breath refusing to release from my lungs. A loud ringing began to fill my head as his words played over and over in my brain. It wasn't until Oogie pointed at me, smiled wickedly, and began chanting "Yes, yes, yes" obnoxiously that I realized that I had been repeating "No" over and over out loud.

Someone handed Oogie a bloody vest that he took in his big, meaty fists and held up for everyone to see. It clearly had patches that read *Bones* and *President* on the front. It was covered in blood and what could only be a bullet hole just over the name.

"The King is dead." He dropped his hands and then tossed the leather cut in the dirt. It skittered across the rocks, dirt, and ice until it stopped just inches away from my shoes. I stared down at the vest, seeing that hole and all the blood. My stomach rolled, and I had to swallow hard several times to keep the vomit back. I shook my head slowly. I didn't want to believe what I was seeing. Not Jack. Not my Jack. The Nightmare King couldn't be gone. *No.* That was impossible.

As I stared at the vest, I could vaguely hear the words that the Boogeyman President was saying in his booming voice. Through a haze, I heard him demanding that the Nightmares clear out of his territory. Anyone that was still in town or anywhere around it by dark would be dead by morning. Including me.

But all I could focus on was that vest.

I felt the weight of that little purple gun that Jack had bought me sitting in my pocket. For hours, Jack had patiently taught me the way to use it. I learned how to load it, clean it, and how to aim for a man. He taught me never to aim a gun at a person unless I planned to kill. With that thought running through my mind, I slipped the little gun out of my pocket and lifted it while using my thumb to slide the safety off. With my left hand holding it steady, I let out a breath and placed my finger on the trigger. While everyone was arguing and cursing what Oogie was saying to the crowd, no one paid any attention to me. I gently squeezed the trigger, aiming right at the center of the chest of the man who had destroyed my life so much worse than Dr. Stein ever had.

The sound was deafening, and everyone in the big dirt lot went deadly still as I stood there and stared at the blood. I let my hands drop back down to my sides. It was amazing how something so small, almost insignificant in weight, could cause so much destruction. Jack had been right; the caliber that went in this tiny weapon was enough to kill a man with one well-placed shot.

TWENTY-SEVEN

THE QUEEN OF NIGHTMARES

Oogie looked down at his chest. He even lifted his hand and placed it over the hole that was allowing his blood to pump from his body in a steady rhythm with his heartbeat. As thick blood flowed from between his fingers, he looked back up at me and snarled. Before I could react to the promise of my death in his eyes, he fell to the ground with a heavy thud.

I leaned over and gingerly picked up Jack's vest, knowing he would want it back.

Angry shouts suddenly exploded from the Boogeymen as what had just happened finally penetrated. Someone threw themselves at me from behind, knocking me to the ground with a jarring impact. Even as I was rolled under the body, I held Jack's cut close to my chest. I lay on the cold ground, not feeling anything but the stitching of those letters that spelled out his name.

I heard a pained grunt, jarring me from my haze, and the body over me jerked. I knew immediately from the sound of the grunt that it was Doc who was covering me. I gasped as I realized he had taken a bullet meant for me, the same way Jack had protected me. I started crying then, hating myself for everything I had put these men through. Lock had lost his life for me. Jack had given himself for me. Now Doc was hurt because of me. He couldn't die, too. It was all too much. Too much pain, too much loss.

I lay there and sobbed for everything I had lost, for everything I had found. I only wanted to find a place to hide. I wanted a place to belong. In coming to Pumpkin Patch, Utah on a whim, I had found love in the Devil's Nightmares. But, I had also torn them apart.

Once the gunfire stopped and everything went blessedly quiet again, hands shifted Doc from his position over me. He was rolled over onto the frozen ground next to me, but I couldn't bring myself to look. A distant part of me was aware that I was firmly in denial, that I had locked myself away in my brain. Maybe I was suffering some kind of delusional episode, and my mind trying to protect me from the horrors of the last couple of days.

Hands lifted me from the ground as more shouts could be heard around us. As if in a tunnel, I could hear someone saying that we needed an ambulance. That was good, right? If Doc were alive, he would need a hospital, and they couldn't get him there on a motorcycle.

Hands were brushing over me, checking for injuries, I thought. Then I was gripped firmly by the shoulders and shaken roughly, a man yelling in my face. I just blinked up at him, not really recognizing who was shouting at me but knowing it was someone I trusted. Suddenly, the arms went around me and crushed me to his chest. I let out a small sob, my lips trembling as I squeezed my eyes closed until I saw stars behind my eyelids.

"Is he going to be okay?" I asked in a broken whimper.

"Doc's fine. He will be okay, Red, I promise," Barrel said with a sigh.

I nodded weakly and tucked the leather vest closer to me,

holding onto it like a lifeline. "Jack's going to be okay, too," I whispered.

He shook his head at my words but didn't answer me. "Come on, Red. Let's get you home."

As Barrel led me to his motorcycle, I glanced around numbly at the carnage. There were bodies and blood everywhere. From what I could tell, they mostly seemed to be those of the Boogeymen. It appeared that once all three rival clubs targeted them at the same time, they had no hope of winning.

Home.

Barrel was taking me to an empty house. It was home, but it wouldn't be the same until Jack was back.

I HELD Doc's hand in mine as the machines beeped rhythmically. It was almost strange being the one comforting instead of the one in the bed.

The door opened, and quiet footsteps walked in. I didn't glance up from the grip I had on Doc's hand, but I knew who it was without needing to look. When Helen placed a hand on my shoulder, I blinked to clear my vision before looking up at her.

"Hey, Sally. Do you want anything to eat or drink?" Without saying a word, I shook my head and dropped my gaze down to my lap to stare at Jack's road name. I knew I was being rude, but I just couldn't find it in me to care.

"I'm good, Helen. Thanks." She gave my shoulder a squeeze before moving over to Doc's other side, where she looked over the many IV bags closely, even though she had done that same thing just a short time ago.

"He still hasn't woken up?" Helen turned to me with a hopeful look on her face. She looked as tired as I felt. I knew she hadn't left the hospital for long in the two days since Doc had been admitted. I shook my head and watched as her shoulders slumped. "It's okay. The body needs to heal, and sometimes, it will put itself in a kind of stasis to protect itself. He'll wake up soon. The doctor who operated on him said the damage was minimal."

I nodded, knowing all that because she'd already told it to me. But I figured it was more of a way to convince herself at that point. I appreciated the effort, anyway.

"Still no word about his brother?" she asked softly.

I squeezed my eyes closed and shook my head again. "No," I whispered brokenly.

It had been two days since the Boogeymen were all wiped out. The few that were left behind that day to guard the compound were rounded up quickly and systematically tortured for information about Jack. But not one of them said a word as they died. I didn't know what they thought they were achieving by being loyal to that monster. I had a hard time believing that Oogie was that great of a leader.

Barrel and Shock made sure I knew that they were doing everything they could to locate him, but I could tell they'd given up hope. After every inch of the compound had been searched, the club was at a loss for what to do. The only sign that Jack had been there at all was a bloody cage and chains. With their newest Vice President in the hospital fighting for his life and their President missing, Shock and Barrel were sharing the responsibility of being in charge.

I had been spending my days at Doc's bedside, not knowing what else I should do with myself. I had been calling Daisy's phone non-stop until it stopped ringing and began to go straight to voicemail. Text messages had gone unread, but I refused to think the worst. If Daisy was dead, then that meant...*no*. I bit my lip hard enough to bleed. I wasn't even going to entertain the idea.

"Okay, Sally. I'll be back again in a little bit. Don't hesitate to push the call button if there are any changes, okay?" Helen said quietly. I nodded my agreement, and she turned to leave but paused with her hand on the door handle. "Sally? Maybe you could go down to the cafeteria and get something to eat. Maybe just a hot cup of tea to soothe your nerves?"

I thought of the tea that Jack used to make me every morning, and my heart gave a painful twist in my chest. "No," I said a little too loudly, then lowered my tone. "No, thank you. I'm good for now, Helen. I appreciate your concern, though."

Helen smiled sadly and then pulled open the door to step out. The prospect at the door glanced into the room when it opened. When he saw my eyes on him, he quickly looked away, his head turning to look forward again. The last thing I saw was him pulling his phone out of his pocket to text who I knew would be Barrel with an update.

After another hour of listening to the monitors, I finally decided I had to get up. My bladder had been screaming at me for the last thirty minutes. As I headed into the ensuite bathroom, my stomach rumbled in protest of being empty for too long. I wasn't even sure what time it was, but I figured it had to be close to dinner time.

After I washed my hands, I stepped back into the room while stretching out my aching back. I held a faint glimmer of hope that Doc would have woken up in the few minutes I had been away from his side. That glimmer died a quick death once I saw absolutely nothing had changed.

I walked over to the bedside and slid a finger over Jack's President patch before whispering to Doc. "I'm going to go down to the cafeteria for a sandwich. I'll be right back, though. Okay?" I sighed when there was no response, just the continuous steady beeping of the machines he was hooked up to. I tucked Jack's cut close to Doc's side.

Opening the door had the prospect quickly straightening up in his seat and tucking his phone away.

"There's no change," I muttered, walking past him. "I'm heading to the cafeteria for a quick bite to eat." I paused. "Do you want me to grab you anything while I'm there?"

"A coffee would be great. Black, thanks." He pulled out his wallet and held out a few bills. I tried to wave him off, but he shoved the money into my hand. "I insist. And use that money to pay for your food, too."

I didn't have the energy to argue with him, so I just nodded and mumbled my thanks. I continued on to the bank of elevators and waited for one of them to arrive. Once the doors closed behind me, I leaned against the back wall of the empty elevator and watched the numbers slowly tick down.

When the doors slid back open with a ding, I moved forward, having to dodge a nurse who was in an obvious hurry. On my way to the cafeteria, I noticed the sign for the gift shop and decided to take a small detour. I hoped it could take my mind off everything horrible in my life for just a few minutes.

The shop was typical of what I had come to expect from the town of Pumpkin Patch. Grinning jack o'lanterns filled the small store. Everything from T-shirts to glass figurines was pumpkin or Halloween themed. I shook my head as I walked around another display and stopped.

Baby items filled the corner shelves. I had found the section of the shop meant for newborn baby gifts. I reached out and stroked the soft fur of a stuffed blue rabbit. Next to the rabbit was a lamb holding a pink satin heart with the word "girl" written across it. My hands itched to pick up the stuffed animals and cradle them to my chest. Instead, I backed away from the display.

"Is there anything I can do to help you, miss?"

I jerked my head to the side to see an older woman with gray hair piled up in a bun on top of her head and reading glasses hanging from a chain around her neck. She was wearing a smock with another pumpkin on the front. I could have sworn I had seen the same one hanging by one of the shelves.

I shook my head. "No. Thank you, though. I was just looking."

The woman gave me a sympathetic look, and I turned my head away so I couldn't see it. For the first time since I left Kentucky, I suddenly missed my mom. I walked to the entrance but paused before leaving. "Have a merry Christmas," I said softly.

I heard her say just as softly, "You, too, dear."

As I headed to the cafeteria, I pulled out my phone. My finger hovered over the name on the display before I took a deep breath and touched the screen to dial.

TWENTY-EIGHT

THE QUEEN OF NIGHTMARES

I sat at the desk staring at the paperwork I knew Jack would need done. Jack's cut was sitting to the side, within easy reach. Running my fingertips over the bloodied lettering had become a habit I didn't want to break. It was comforting in a strange, perhaps even morbid way I couldn't explain.

Zero sat near my feet on the blanket from the couch. Jack's lingering scent was there, but it was beginning to fade. I knew Zero missed Jack as much as I did, so I passed the throw blanket to him, hoping it would help. I wasn't sure it did, though, by the way he would often let out a random whine.

It had been three days since Doc had been shot, and he still hadn't woken up. When I had gotten up on the couch that morning and walked to the front door of the clubhouse, expecting to be given a ride to the hospital, Barrel had stood there with his arms crossed over his chest and a determined expression on his stubborn face.

"You're not going to spend all day at the hospital today. I'll take you later for a couple of hours, but today, you're going to do literally anything else, Red."

I stared him down for several long seconds in silence, neither one of us blinking, before finally turning around to head back down the hallway. "Your roots are showing," I mumbled as I returned to the office. I ignored the gasp of outrage as I thought of the paperwork I had neglected the last couple of days. I knew exactly how to spend my day.

I walked straight to the desk. Before I sat down, I took the gun out of my pocket and placed it next to Jack's vest. Then, I rolled the chair closer and got to work.

THE DOOR OPENED QUIETLY, and someone slipped inside, shutting the door behind them with a click. I internally groaned that I had forgotten to lock it behind me when I'd returned to the office after breakfast with the guys out front. I had a lot of work to do to keep Jack caught up on his businesses, and it was proving to be a great distraction. I didn't need to be disturbed by one of the well-meaning club brothers wanting to check if I was alright for the hundredth time.

It wasn't until I heard the voice that my blood ran icy cold, and dread slithered up my spine.

"Ah, finally, my patchwork doll. I have come for you, my dear. Aren't you going to greet your father?"

I jerked my head up in disbelief. "How did you get in here?" I asked in utter disbelief.

After everything that had happened recently, I had completely forgotten about Dr. Stein and the threat he had posed. Seeing him standing there now after the hell the Boogeymen had put me through was almost anticlimactic. As if he were a weak man playing at being a villain. His overly theatrical announcement made in his nasal tone almost had me rolling my eyes.

Dr. Stein smiled while leaning heavily on a cane. "You seem to forget how long I can wait in silence, my dear. My hours of standing over a body doing surgery have well prepared me for waiting for the precise moment to make my move."

"What is that supposed to mean?" I snapped, tired of his weirdly formal way of speaking and the way he always acted as if he were the most intelligent person in the room. After the long months I spent listening to his monologues about how wonderful he was, I had been ready to poke my eardrums, just so I wouldn't have to hear it anymore.

He shook his head as if he were disappointed in a particularly dense child. "I was hiding in a shed until late last night. Once everything was quiet, I snuck into the building and hid in a storage closet." He grinned, proud of himself.

I stared in disbelief. "Where did you go to the bathroom?"

"One does what one must to accomplish their goals," he said without really answering the question. I wrinkled my nose. Did that mean he went in his pants, or did he go on the floor?

Dr. Stein reached into his pocket and pulled out a black gun, pointing it at my chest. I froze and could do nothing but stare at the barrel, the small black hole taunting me. I had seen firsthand what a bullet could do to a person's chest.

"Get up, Sally," he demanded, finally deciding to do what he'd apparently been waiting hours for. In the dark. In his own shit. *Eww.* "And shut that dog up before I put a bullet in it. I won't leave him alive this time."

I glanced down at Zero, finally noticing his vicious snarls. His wickedly sharp canines were bared, and he had drool dripping from his muzzle. Zero stood by my side, his hackles raised along his back. It was an impressive show of doggy rage.

"Zero," I whispered, "sit, boy. Quiet." He immediately sat at my command, his growls easing, but his displeasure was still projected through his snarls. He likely recognized this man from what had been done to him months ago. I figured he could also sense the threat coming from Dr. Stein and wasn't going to ignore it, no matter what I said.

"Good boy," I murmured. As much as I knew Zero could handle the doctor, the man was holding a gun. I didn't want anything to happen to Jack's dog. I loved Zero with all my heart, but I also didn't want Jack to return to me only to find out his beloved pet had been killed while trying to protect me.

I was jarred out of the wayward thoughts of Jack by the hand that reached out to grip my chin. I'd been doing that a lot lately, getting lost in my thoughts and letting the world fade away around me. This time, it had gotten me in trouble. Dr. Stein had limped around the desk and was right in front of me. He brought my face up to meet his gaze, jerking it roughly. Zero gave another warning growl that would have had me cowering in fright had it been directed at me. The Doctor was more stupid than I thought.

"It's time to end this, girl."

"Yes. It is," I said with a finality that I felt deep inside. I was sick and fucking tired of others getting killed or seriously injured from trying to protect me. And I was seriously god damned tired of having a gun pointed at me. I was done with being a victim or allowing others to take the hit that was meant for me. *I was done.* With my hand curled around one of the knives that was always in Jack's desk, I lifted it swiftly and plunged it directly into Dr. Stein's shoulder, effectively making him let me go. He dropped his cane, letting it clatter to the floor as he stumbled back several steps. He held his shoulder with one hand with a pained grunt. He continued to stumble backward until he was near the window, leaning against the wall next to the filing cabinet that held the small Christmas tree.

"You fucking bitch! You're going to pay for that! I am your father! I created you! I made you what you are. It is my right to take your life away."

I shook my head as I stared at him, at the gun that was once again raised and trained on me. The man was unhinged; I already knew that. Looking at him now, though, I could see he was at the end of his tether. The very fragile, broken fibers that were barely keeping him sane were snapping at a rapid pace.

"You didn't create me, Finkle Stein. You destroyed me. A beautiful man put me back together. He made me whole again. You are nothing but a monster. You aren't my father, and I'm not your patchwork doll. I am the Queen of Nightmares."

I reached over to Jack's leather cut and withdrew the shiny purple gun, the same gun I had recently used to end the life of the man who had taken my King from me. With a steady hand, I lifted it, flipped the safety off, and aimed. Without a single moment of hesitation, I pulled the trigger.

The impact of the bullet knocked Dr. Stein back against the wall. The only indication the man gave that he knew his life was over was the brief flare of shock in his eyes before they drooped. There was a strange, macabre image of a rose that bloomed from the center of his forehead before it began to run in thick rivulets down his eyes, nose, and chin.

"That was for Lock, you piece of shit," I whispered.

His body slumped against the wall and slid to the ground as his legs crumpled underneath him. As it came to rest on the floor, I stared at the Christmas tree that was now covered in dripping red, the gingerbread ornaments splattered in crimson, somehow making them almost more festive than before.

Heavy boots thundered down the hall, and the door was flung open with so much force it bounced off the wall, making a deep dent in the plaster where it hit. I frowned at the hole, thinking how Jack wasn't going to be happy with the damage.

Several men stormed into the room, weapons raised as they took in the scene. Zero was still growling and barking, still unsettled by the entire event. I set my pretty purple gun down on the desk before placing my hand on his head to calm him. His whole body shook with pent-up rage. I knew he would have wanted to be the one to end the threat, but I just couldn't take the chance that he'd be hurt.

"What the fuck, Red? He could have killed you!" Barrel yelled as the entire contingent of Devil's Nightmares holstered their weapons and stared in disbelief at the small man who lay dead against the office wall.

"His safety was on," I mumbled. "It was about as harmless as a paperweight."

I heard someone mutter from the group, and others rumbled their agreement while giving me the side eye. "That was a good shot," one of them said.

I shrugged. "I was aiming for his chest."

Shock stepped forward with a grin on his face. "Jack would have been proud of you, Red. You did good."

I looked up at him with a blank stare. "Will be."

His usual devil-may-care grin dropped, and that familiar look of sadness that everyone seemed to be wearing lately crossed his features. "Sally..."

I turned away, not wanting to hear it again. No one believed in him, and that pissed me off. If anyone could survive the Boogeymen, it was my Jack.

TWENTY-NINE

THE QUEEN OF NIGHTMARES

"Can someone get the body out of the President's office? Jack's not going to want him there when he returns."

I could see the men eyeing each other warily before a couple of them stepped toward the body.

"Wait!" I called out. "Get a trash bag to cover his head and tape it closed. I don't want his blood to get all over the clubhouse." I sat back down in Jack's chair and picked up the pen I had been holding before Dr. Stein snuck into the office. I stared down at the columns of numbers, not seeing them but needing to do *something* as I waited. With my left hand, I absently ran my fingers over my slightly swelling baby bump, mentally apologizing for all of the violence our little boy had been subjected to recently.

"We searched the entire compound. Every building. He was gone." Barrel muttered at the floor as his heavy boots shifted where he stood. I ignored him. I knew they had searched for Jack after I killed Oogie. But just because they didn't find his body didn't mean he was dead. Quite the opposite.

I looked back up when I heard footsteps returning to see the office had cleared out of bikers except for Barrel and Shock. Two walked back in carrying a plastic bag and a roll of tape and quickly got to work while Jack's right-hand men sat gingerly on the couch, staring at me as if I were a bomb that might explode at any moment. I ignored them and the two guys who made quick work of securing the body and carrying it out between them. I had no idea what they would do with it, but I had no doubts that there would be no evidence that he had ever been here. I knew I would never be blamed for his death. Frankly, I couldn't care less that I had killed two men. They had both been evil and had done so many terrible things to innocent people. They deserved far worse than a bullet.

Zero suddenly jumped to his feet and started barking like mad. For the first time since Oogie had tossed Jack's bloody leather vest in the dirt at my feet, my heart began to race. Adrenaline spiked through my system, and I flew out of the chair and raced over to the window, ignoring the way the sticky wetness oozed between my toes.

I couldn't see anything through the window but the long stretch of road leading to mine and Jack's house. I spun around, nearly slipping in the blood as Zero turned and raced out the open doorway. Barrel and Shock jumped up to follow me as I raced after Zero.

"Red, wait!" I could hear Barrel calling after me, but there was no way I was stopping.

Zero was far ahead of me but was stopped by the closed main door. He was jumping against it, trying to push his way through the heavy door. I pulled it open, hard, and he flew through it like a shot, heading straight for the gate. A car was idling just outside the gate as the Nightmare manning it held a gun at the driver.

"Open the gate!" I screamed as I ran forward, ignoring the stares of the gathering crowd and the rocks that bit into the bare soles of my feet. "Open the fucking gate, *now!*" I screamed again, my throat feeling raw at the intensity of my cries.

The man looked startled, staring at me in disbelief, but ultimately, he turned and did what I said without question. Barrel and Shock caught up with me, and someone, I wasn't sure which, put a hand on my shoulder to hold me back. I turned without looking and punched whoever it was right in the jaw, making him stumble back as the car rolled forward, coming to a stop a few feet away from me.

Zero ran to the back door of the car and barked furiously. His barks intermingled with whines as he jumped and pawed at the door. Daisy jumped out of the driver's side and looked at me with tears flowing down her battered face.

"He saved me, Sal. He saved me again. I couldn't leave him there. Even if you hadn't sent me for him, I wouldn't have left him."

"Daisy," I breathed as I looked her over. Her clothes were dirty and torn. She looked as if she'd been through hell and back. I didn't want to imagine what had been done to her on her brother's compound with him knowing she had betrayed him.

"It's okay, Sally. I'm okay." She stepped back and then reached for the door behind her. I held my breath as Zero stepped back, allowing her to open the back door of the small sedan. As soon as the door was open, he charged forward, making Daisy stumble back. His barks turned to nothing but high-pitched whines as he jumped inside the car.

It wasn't until I heard a low groan coming from the back seat that my breathing sped up. Suddenly, I was breathing so fast, too fast, and the world began to spin around me. Shock ran forward to the car, looking inside. I could barely see what was happening. Tears were clouding my vision, which was already turning dark around the edges as I fought to take in enough oxygen.

"He's here! He's alive!" Shock's shouts brought everyone back to life. Every man that had been brought out to the yard because of my screaming and Zero's barking ran forward as I stood there in shock, my knees trembling until they started to collapse underneath. As I fell to my knees on the cold ground, Shock shoved the door closed again with Zero still inside.

The last thing I saw before everything around me faded was the sight of the car that Jack was in being backed through the gate and out of the compound.

JACK

"I don't understand, Prez. We searched that whole fucking compound for you for two days! You're telling me you were there the whole time?" Barrel was pacing the hospital room from end to end, relentlessly, making the headache from hell throb even worse until I finally snapped.

"Sit the fuck down," I roared, immediately regretting it as the sharp pain at the back of my skull felt like an ice pick was drilling for brain matter. I was fucking pissed that I was in this god-forsaken hospital room instead of at home. And if I had a gun handy, every single one of my men would have been nothing but puddles of blood on the floor.

They'd left my woman behind at the compound. Someone was going to pay for that. Depending on what kind of condition she was in once I caught sight of her, it might be with a bullet through the skull instead of just through the leg. Or arm. Or both.

As Barrel collapsed into the chair, he immediately began drumming his fingers. I wanted to yell at him again, but if I did, my brain could possibly start leaking from my ears.

"The shed they use for their prisoners has a pit underneath. When I managed to break out of the cage they had me in, Daisy came in," I snorted as I remembered the shock of seeing her cracking open the door I had been working on unlocking. We'd both stared in disbelief at one another. I had been angry enough at the sight of her to start reaching for her neck, ready to squeeze, until she whispered those little words that had me freezing in place.

"Sally sent me."

Disbelief had nearly overwhelmed me, but it had certainly made me stop reaching for her. She'd told me about the car she had waiting and that the entire club would leave soon for a meeting at The Warehouse. She was right; it would have been the perfect time to escape, except someone came in, immediately raising the alarm. With one loud shout, several of the Boogeymen had converged on the both of us. Oogie, himself, was the one that had beaten the shit out of Daisy. He hadn't taken it well that his own sister was trying to save me.

I had done my best to protect her from them all, knowing that if they got their hands on her, she would never survive. It had earned me a couple new bruised ribs and a few more cuts that would prob- ably scar, but in the end, we both survived. As it was, only the fact that they had run out of time and needed to leave for the meeting saved both of us from more serious injury. I had no doubt that if Oogie had returned from that meeting alive, Daisy would have wished she were dead before he finally killed her.

"Since he was running out of time to make the meeting, Oogie decided to throw Daisy and me in the pit together until they got back." I sighed, laying my head back on the flat pillow. "They never came back though."

It was Barrel's turn to snort. Then he started laughing so hard he nearly choked. I did my best to ignore him as I wondered what the fuck was taking so long to get my little Queen here.

"You can thank Red for that shit," he finally rasped out.

I frowned, picking my head back up to look at him with a glare. "What the fuck is that supposed to mean?"

"She shot and killed Oogie right there in the middle of the meeting in front of his whole crew." He shook his head and snorted again as I stared in disbelief at the side of his face. "He tossed your cut in the dirt and said you were dead. She just fucking lost it. Cold as ice, she pulled that tiny purple gun you got her out of her pocket and shot him dead center in the chest. It was awesome, to be honest, but she started a fucking gunfight, man. We were lucky that all three clubs were there. We managed to take out every single Boogeyman in minutes. Only a few of our guys took a bullet. In the chaos, one of the Black Wolves tripped and fell over his own bike and broke his leg. Pretty sure that was the worst injury on our side of the fight."

"Sally. Killed. Oogie." I couldn't believe what I was hearing. My sweet girl killed one of the most ruthless, murdering bastards in the state.

Barrel's smile faded as I watched, his expression turning serious. "She's been a little messed up since you were taken. Fuck, you don't know yet." He sighed and shook his head before standing to his feet again and walking over to the window. "Doc took a bullet for her, Prez. He's in an ICU room. Hasn't woken up yet that I'm aware of," he looked back at me with an apologetic shrug. "Today has been a fucked up day, and no one has had a chance to check on him yet. Between that fucking doctor showing up and then you—"

"What the fucking fuck!" I roared, not even giving a shit about my aching ribs or my pounding head. I started yanking the shit off my arms, ready to get out of this fucking hospital to get to my little Queen. I couldn't go another second without seeing for myself that she was okay. "Where the fuck is Sally?" I demanded as I swung my legs over the side of the bed. "Is she alive? Why the fuck isn't she here? What are you keeping from me?"

Barrel rushed over and pressed down on my shoulders to push me back in the bed, immediately making pain explode like a mother fucking supernova from the gunshot wound in my shoulder. I clenched my jaw and panted through my teeth as I waited for the wave of dizziness and nausea to subside.

"Fuck, Prez, I'm sorry! All right? I'm sorry. She's really okay, I promise. I'm not trying to hide anything from you. You'll see for yourself as soon as Shock gets back with her. Just sit back, and I'll tell you the rest, alright?"

A nurse entered the room, ready to turn off all the screaming alarms. She scowled as soon as she saw I had pulled all that shit off me and grabbed several gauze pads from the nearby cabinet to stop the bleeding from where I'd yanked the IV out.

"Mr. Ellington—"

"Just shut off the alarms," I growled, my head swimming with pain and nausea, making me swallow. I'd be fucking pissed as hell if I threw up. There was nothing I hated more than throwing up. And with the way my ribs were aching, I'd probably want to die. "I won't get up again. Just make it stop."

I groaned and leaned back in the bed. I was done for the moment of trying to be tough. I needed a fucking break. And I needed Sally. I eyed Barrel as he backed up to the chair and huffed out a breath.

"Goddamn, between you and that woman, I've never seen a more obsessed couple in my whole fucking life."

I grunted and closed my eyes, waiting for the nurse to do her thing before we could talk freely again. She kept glaring as she got the blood pressure cuff back into place and started a new IV.

"If this happens again, I will have no choice but to restrain you to the bed, Mr. Ellington."

"It won't." I met her glare for glare until she finally huffed, turned on her ugly, sensible hospital shoes, and walked out the door. I turned back to Barrel and waited impatiently.

"Well?"

He sighed dramatically before resting his elbows on his knees and holding his head in his hands. "She's been walking around like a zombie. We've all been encouraging her to eat, but I'm not sure how much she's actually put in her mouth. She's been insisting for days that you were alive, no matter what anyone said. Then, when Oogie said you were dead, it was like the light went out, but her determination became even stronger all at the same time. She has been worrying the fuck out of us. She spent the last couple of days here at the hospital, refusing to leave Doc's side." He sat back in the chair and looked up at the ceiling. "Until today. We insisted she stay at the compound and get some rest instead of sitting in that chair all day, you know? But then, I guess the doctor snuck onto the property somehow."

I narrowed my eyes at him, the heart rate monitor attached to my finger picking up the increased speed as my anger started to boil over again. "How the *fuck* did a stranger sneak onto the compound and make it into the motherfucking clubhouse, Barrel?" My tone was deadly.

Barrel rubbed the back of his neck. "Tech is looking into it, Prez. But right now, the answer is we just don't know."

"So what happened when the asshole broke in?"

"Red happened. Shot the fucker right between his eyes. There's, uh, actually a bit of a mess in your office. She was working on your invoices or some shit since you've been gone."

I closed my eyes and rested my head back against the pillow. I'd heard enough. I needed to see my brother, and I would get someone to take me to him soon. But I had to lay eyes on my woman before I could even think about anything else. Somehow, my sweet, pregnant woman had saved the fucking club, town, herself, and me all in a matter of days. But at what cost to herself?

THIRTY-ONE

THE QUEEN OF NIGHTMARES

A rhythmic beeping was the first thing I heard as I was pulled slowly from sleep. I tried to rub my nose, but a small, sharp pain had me hissing. I cracked open my eyes to look at my hand, seeing the tube taped there. I followed the tube until my gaze landed on the IV hanging from a metal pole. I glanced around, realizing with groggy resignation that I was in yet another hospital room. Only, there was something different this time.

I glanced down at my waist, where I could feel a hand resting on my bare belly underneath the hospital-issued cotton gown. My whole body froze as I took stock of what else I was feeling.

A large body was tucked in close to my back, spooning me from behind. Warm breath tickled the fine hairs at the nape of my neck. And a long, hairy leg was tangled in mine.

"Jack," I breathed, not daring to believe it was true. Tears immediately filled my eyes and began to fall, soaking the pillow under my face as my shoulders shook. I tried to hold the sobs back, but so many overwhelming feelings flooded in too quickly. It was impossible to stop.

"Shhh..." The hand over my belly lightly caressed me there. "I'm here, little Queen. Everything is going to be alright now." He continued to caress me as he brushed soft kisses against the back of my neck, just holding me as my body and mind purged the pain, anguish, terror, worry, and anger in great, big, wracking sobs. He spoke softly next to my ear, his deep, gravelly voice soothing my raw nerves.

"You did so good while I was gone, little Queen. You saved me. You saved the town. You were so strong, but you can relax now." He clenched me tighter to him as he paused before placing a tender kiss below my ear. "You are more than I could have ever dreamed of in a woman. You are more than just my equal. You are better than I could ever be. I love you, Sally. With my entire being, I love you."

As he spoke quietly, pieces of the jagged edges inside me smoothed out. Some of the pieces fit back together perfectly. Some of the pieces would always remain broken. But at least they weren't sharp anymore. Too much had happened in the last year for me to ever be the same as I was.

I had been held captive and tortured.

I had fallen in love.

I had watched the father of my child taken by his enemy without knowing if I'd ever see him alive again.

I had been told the love of my life was dead.

I had killed not one, but *two* men.

No, I would never be the same. In some ways, I was better. I had found the woman I was meant to be. I had found strength I didn't know I could possess. Maybe I was crying, but that's okay. Crying didn't mean weakness. Crying just meant that my emotions were so big, they needed a little release. Besides, wasn't it okay to be weak every once in a while?

My heart was twisting in my chest for the first time in days, not in fear or pain, but in happiness. Jack was here, he was alive, he was *holding me.* I shifted, turning to my back slowly, needing to see his face.

I had to swallow past the sudden lump in my throat as I blinked away a fresh round of tears. I would not cry. He was alive, and he was here. That was a cause for joy. So he looked a bit worse for wear, but that was okay. He would heal.

I raised my hand, heedless of the tube attached to it, and gently touched his battered face. Both of his eyes were swollen and bloodshot. It was so swollen I could tell he could barely see from one of them, if at all. Multiple areas had been either taped or sewn on his eyebrows, cheeks bone, the bridge of his nose, and upper lip.

He pressed harder into my hand. Instinct told me to pull away so I wouldn't cause him pain, but I held still, allowing him to choose how much touch he could handle.

"Jack." His name was hardly more than a whisper, I wasn't even sure if it made it past my lips, but he knew I said it.

Jack leaned down and softly pressed his lips to mine in a sweet caress. I could feel the intensity of his gaze as he leaned back to peer at me through his one good eye. "You are the most beautiful thing I've ever seen, little Queen."

He tried to lift his hand to touch me the way I was touching him, but our IV lines got caught together. I choked out a watery laugh as we pulled apart.

"You should rest more, baby. The doctor said you were suffering from exhaustion and dehydration." I only sighed and carefully returned to the position I had woken up in. I had no idea how long I'd been asleep in his arms, but now that he was with me, I felt as if I could sleep for days, finally able to truly relax and rest.

I yawned as I settled in. "How are they letting us stay in the same bed?" I murmured, not caring. I loved it, but I knew it went against policy.

"It was either this," he grumbled as he tightened his arm around me, "or I walked out of here without treatment."

I hummed. I knew there was more to the story, but I doubted he would elaborate. "Will you tell me what happened while you were there?" I asked sleepily.

"Not now," he said, kissing the top of my head. "Maybe if you get some rest, and after the doctor says you're back to full strength." I pouted with my eyes closed. I'd say I could handle it, but I knew there would be no arguing with him. "And, little Queen?"

I tensed at his suddenly serious tone. "Yes?" My eyes popped open to stare at the window across the room.

"Once we are both back home, I'm going to punish you for not taking care of yourself better." I swallowed hard, not liking what that would mean, but also, Jack was alive and capable of punishing me. So, as I drifted off to sleep, it was with a smile on my face.

A DOOR BANGING open startled me awake, nearly making me bolt upright in the unfamiliar bed I was lying in. Only the heavy arm wrapped across my middle kept me in place.

"Shit, Prez, I'm sorry." The sound of Barrel's gruff voice coming from the other side of the room had me settling again, my heart rate slowing back to its normal rhythm. "But I thought you'd like to know that Doc just woke up."

I gasped, trying to sit up again, but Jack gently pushed me right back down. His tone was calm, though I could hear the urgency he was trying to hide. "Good. Let the nurse know that we want to go see him as soon as they are done looking him over." Barrel jerked his chin and immediately left to do what Jack had ordered.

Once the door closed, much softer than it had been opened, I turned over the way I had the last time I had woken. Jack was already looking down at me. I could see that I didn't have to tell him, but the words slipped out anyway through my tight throat.

"He took a bullet for me, Jack. I'm so sorry. He covered me with his body. It's all my fault."

"He did what any man in the club would do, little Queen."

I shook my head. "No. It's my fault that they were even shooting. I started it by shooting Oogie and killing him." I closed my eyes, remembering the scene. The way the blood had poured from his chest as everyone stood in stunned disbelief. "I just didn't think about what I was doing. He tossed your cut in the dirt, and suddenly, my gun was in my hand. I just...pulled the trigger, and then he was on the ground."

"You thought I was dead." He said softly in the deep, gravelly voice I loved. I shook my head.

"No. I knew you weren't dead. I tried to tell everyone, but no one believed me. They were walking around, sad and angry. I just wanted you back." I blinked up at him. "They said they searched the whole compound, but the only sign of you alive was an empty cage. Where were you? How did Daisy find you?"

He huffed out a breath. "That's something else we are going to need to talk about." He kissed the tip of my nose. "Later. But to appease your curiosity, there was a pit under the room where the cage was. There was a trap door hidden in the floor. Daisy and I were thrown in there before they left for the meeting."

I gasped in horror. "You were in a hole in the floor for two days? How did you escape?" Then I thought of something else. "Did you have any food or water?"

He grimaced. "Unfortunately, they left us with nothing before heading out to the meeting with the other clubs. I don't know if they would have given us food or water once they returned, but," he lifted his arm, indicating the IV fluids. "This is the first drink I've had since that shitty coffee at the maze."

I scowled. "That's not funny, Jack. How did you get out?"

He sighed and ran his hand over my hair carefully so as to not pull either one of our IV lines. "Daisy was unconscious for an entire day with a bit of a head injury." He didn't elaborate, but I could just imagine what had happened to her after seeing her appearance at the compound. "Once she came to, I had to lift her up to push the hatch open. We're just really fucking lucky it wasn't bolted shut. I guess they hadn't thought anyone could escape."

"You lifted her?" I asked as I looked him over, noticing the way his arm was bandaged and the stiff way he held his torso.

"I had to get back to you."

THIRTY-TWO

THE QUEEN OF NIGHTMARES

The nurse wasn't happy when she came into the room. She scowled the entire time she separated our lines. I was incredibly grateful when Helen came in a few minutes later with a huge smile on her face and an announcement that my IV could come out.

Once I was freed, I put my own clothes back on, then sat back in a chair to watch as Jack was fussed over. He growled when he was informed that he would have to ride in a wheelchair or he wasn't leaving the bed at all. He only gave in when I promised I would ride in his lap. That earned both of us another glare, but neither one of us cared.

Once he was situated, I carefully climbed up onto his lap. I attempted to keep most of my weight on his thighs and off his chest, but with a heavy hand to my middle, he pulled me snugly against him, all while ignoring the shrill protests of the nurse. She finally huffed out an angry retort and stomped out of the room. As she passed Helen, she told her she didn't want to have anything to do with us and that she could take over. Everyone breathed a little easier after that.

Helen was all smiles as we passed the patched member who had been standing guard at the door. As she wheeled us down the corridor and to the elevator, I glanced back to see the biker following us closely with a clearly relieved expression.

After a short elevator ride to the next floor, we got off, Helen easily pushing the wheelchair with our combined weight in it. I knew she had to be as excited that Doc was awake as we were. If Doc didn't pull his head out of his ass and ask Helen out on a date soon, I was going to kick his ass.

I didn't have to guess which room Doc was in since there was another patched member standing at the door with his arms crossed. When he saw us, he dropped his arms and stared at Jack as if he thought he'd never see him again. There was disbelief, relief, and regret written all over his features. He stepped forward to meet us.

"She swore you were alive, Prez." He shook his head. "We should have known. A bastard like you wouldn't die that easy." He held out his hand, and Jack took it in a firm hold. "Glad to have you back, Prez."

I smiled but pretended not to see the glassy sheen to the biker's eyes as Jack grunted a response. He stepped back and reached for Doc's door, holding it open for Helen to push us through.

I heard the beeping machines right away, but Doc's pale, tired face was the first thing I saw. When he turned his head and saw Jack sitting there, alive, for the first time, a smile curved his lips, and his eyes lit up. I slowly slid from Jack's lap, careful not to jostle him, ignoring his reaching hand.

"Get back here."

I ignored his growl and stepped back, keeping my head down.

"Red." Doc's soft voice had me reluctantly leaving my examination of the tiled floor. I hesitantly glanced up at Doc. "Get over here." Jack sighed but didn't argue.

With a stifled sob, I stepped toward Doc's outstretched arms and carefully wrapped my arms around him. "I'm so sorry."

"Don't ever be sorry, Red. You're my sister. I would die for you." Doc's words were soft as he spoke into my hair. I breathed out a ragged breath, so grateful that he was alive.

Jack was wheeled forward until he was right up against the side of the bed so he could reach out his good hand to his brother as I straightened back up. "Thank you," he said as they grasped hands firmly.

He and Doc stared at each other for a long minute, communicating something between them that wasn't for anyone else. My heart ached with warmth and gratitude that my little family was whole again. Everyone had made it through this nightmare. We were all a mess, some of us more than others, but we were alive.

I stepped back so the brothers could have a quiet moment to talk without an audience. I moved over to Helen's side and did something Jack had forbidden me to do.

"Don't give up on him, Helen. If you care about him, make him see it. He needs a good woman by his side."

She blinked at me with a hopeful smile. "You think I can be that woman for him?"

"I think you're the only one who can." I wrapped an arm around her waist and gave her a small, one-armed hug. "What do you think about dogs?"

Her giggle had both men turning to look at us. Jack had a narrowed-eyed look as he took in our close positions, but a smile teased the corner of his mouth. Doc's expression turned soft and warm when he looked over the nurse. Yeah, they would be just fine. A little bit of pushing never hurt anyone.

We stayed in Doc's room, talking and laughing quietly until it was obvious that Doc was getting tired. We said goodbye, promising to see him again the next day. I was sad as we left the room, anxious for everyone to be well enough to leave. Doc's bullet wound had missed his spine but had hit a rib, bouncing over into his spleen before nicking something else. He'd be one organ short by the time he healed, but otherwise, he would fully recover.

When we rolled back into Jack's room, we came to an abrupt stop when we realized someone was in there. Daisy was standing with her back to the room as she stared out the window at the twinkling lights of Pumpkin Patch. I could see her whole body stiffen with our arrival.

I climbed off Jack's lap again, surprised when he didn't fight me that time. I walked over to Daisy and stepped beside her, seeing the town lit up below.

"Thank you, Daisy," I said softly. "What you did can never be repaid."

She inhaled sharply, then let it out in a whoosh. "I wish I could have done more. If I'd known who the other mole was…"

"Kara played her part well. Too well. I was certainly fooled." I shook my head in disgust at who I thought was my friend but who instead walked me right over to the devil with a smile on her face. "All that matters is that we all made it out alive. I'm sorry for killing your brother."

Daisy shrugged. "He was a shitty brother."

I tried to stifle a laugh, but Daisy started giggling, making me lose control until I was doubled over, clutching my side with tears leaking from the corners of my eyes. By the time we were done and brushing away the remnants of our laughter, Daisy was facing me with a smile.

"I'm really glad it's over."

I sighed as I looked over toward the bed where Jack was lying hooked back up to the machines and looking grumpy about it. "So am I. I just want to get back home and pretend none of this ever happened." I looked back at Daisy to see her swipe at her face. "You know you're welcome to stay."

She shook her head. "No. There's nothing here for me. I don't have any more family, and I burned too many bridges to stay. Besides, I found a nice place to land, and there is this guy I kinda like.

I think I want to explore things with him and see if we have something special. Something like what you and Bones have."

I wrapped my arms around her shoulders and pulled her in for a big hug. Even after all the shit she had pulled and the hell she had put me through when we'd worked together, I knew, deep down, that she was a good person. Someone I would have liked to know.

"You'll stay in touch?" I asked as I stepped back.

She smiled, her lips trembling just a bit. "I'd like that."

I nodded. "Good."

She gestured toward the bed. "Do you mind if I say goodbye?"

I grinned at her. "I'd be pissed if you didn't."

I stayed by the window as Daisy slowly, but without hesitance, stepped over to Jack while he watched her approach. "Bones, I just wanted to let you know I'm leaving. I also wanted to say thank you for everything you have done for me. I wouldn't have survived if it wasn't for you. I didn't deserve your help, not before, and not at my brother's compound." She swiped at her eyes. "You're a good man, Bones."

She stepped back and gave me a small wave as she headed for the door, but paused when Jack called out to her.

"Stay safe. If you ever need anything, you let me know."

Daisy looked like she might cry but straightened her shoulders and firmed her lips as she acknowledged his words with a quick nod. Then she was leaving through the door, letting it close softly behind her.

After kicking off my shoes, I climbed into the bed with Jack and let him tuck me into his side. Neither of us said a word as we lay there quietly. We were both eager to get home. The doctor had promised that he might be able to leave tomorrow as long as Jack took care of himself. That was a promise I intended to make sure happened.

THIRTY-THREE

JACK

I lay back on the bed, listening as Sally moved around the house. I fucking hated being restricted. What I hated even more was not being able to help out with the daily things that needed to be done around the house and club. With Doc and I both laid up while healing from our injuries, it had been up to Barrel, Shock, and Tech to run the club, while Sally insisted on taking care of the majority of my business work. I finally insisted that I would have no issues dealing with paperwork while sitting on my ass. She fought me at first, but once I convinced her that I would lose my fucking mind if I didn't have something to occupy it, she gave in, bringing the stack of papers from my desk at the club.

Zero jumped on the bed where I was reclining against the head-board, and I ruffled his fur while Sally walked through the bedroom after turning off all the lights in the rest of the house. She smiled sweetly as she walked through the room, pausing at my side to drop a kiss on my cheek before heading to the bathroom. I heard the shower turn on, and I'd had enough.

"Bed, Zero." He gave a low woof, but after licking my hand, he jumped from the bed. I watched as he circled three times and pawed at his pillow before laying down with a huff. I thought of Sally as she climbed under the spray, pictured her naked body, and groaned. This invalid shit was more than I could take.

I climbed off the bed and held back a wince as my ribs groaned in protest. I pulled the sweatpants down my legs and kicked them into the corner. It was still too hard to bend down to pick things off the floor. I would have to make it up to my little Queen later. Once I was fully healed, I would treat her like the queen she was, making sure she didn't have to lift a finger. I was damn lucky she looked after me and took care of all the things I couldn't while I was laid up.

I gingerly climbed back onto the bed and thought about what I was going to do tonight. What I was going to have *her* do. I may not be able to give her the dicking I wanted and what I knew she really craved from me, but I would make tonight enjoyable. It would only be a couple more weeks before I would be able to give her all of me. But there was no way I could wait that long.

I heard the shower turn off and closed my eyes as I pictured her wet body. The way the water would drip off her perky nipples that had grown darker with her pregnancy. I licked my lips as I thought about the way they felt in my mouth. I would have that tonight. I fisted my cock as I waited. It wouldn't be long before she was finished in the bathroom.

When she walked into the room wearing a small pair of sleep shorts that showed off her toned legs and the smallest, thinnest fucking tank top known to man, I growled with my hand squeezing my cock.

"Get over here."

She startled with her hand on the light switch.

"Go ahead and turn it off." The bedside lamp was on. It would give me plenty of light to see what I had missed in the last two weeks. With a blush that rose from the tops of her breasts to spread up her neck and onto her beautiful face, she hit the lights. The lamp cast a warm glow over the bed, guiding her straight to me.

"Take off your clothes and climb on my face."

She brought a hand to the front of her neck and rubbed absently as her thighs pressed together. "Jack, I don't think—"

"Little Queen, if you don't climb on my face right now, I am going to get out of this bed and bend you over it. Would you rather do all the work or take the chance I could hurt myself more?"

"That's coercion, Jack." Her tone may have been admonishing, but her sweet giggle told me she wasn't opposed.

"I don't give a fuck. It's been almost three weeks since I had your taste in my mouth. I'm dying without it. Seeing you walk around this house with your sexy tits swaying and your hot as fuck body teasing me has my cock ready to explode." I took my hand off my length so she could see how swollen I was for her. "See what you do to me, little Queen?" I rubbed my thumb over the precome that was leaking from the tip and almost groaned at the sensation. I couldn't resist another pump of my tight fist before letting go and reaching down to grip my balls. "I need you. Now."

She swallowed hard as she watched my hand move. She looked like she wanted to argue, but I could see the moment her resolve broke, and her hands went to her top. With one swift movement, she had it torn over her head and dropped to the floor. I groaned as my hand involuntarily squeezed.

Her shorts were next. I licked my lips as I saw her wet cunt exposed to me. I needed her in my mouth. No more waiting. I shifted on the bed until my back was flat. "Climb up here. I want your pussy in my mouth. I need you to ride my face, baby."

She walked over, her nipples hard points on her breasts, and goosebumps spread over her arms. She hesitated at the side of the bed. "You'll tell me if you hurt?" I grunted, wanting to grab her and yank her to me, but I knew it would make her stop, and my plans would be ruined.

"I swear I won't move. You can do all the work, and I will stay perfectly still. But, little Queen, if you don't get on my face right now, the punishment you have coming to you when I am better will be so much worse." My words were barely understandable even to my own ears as I growled.

"Okay, Jack." She put one knee on the bed and hesitated until I gripped her hips in frustration and pulled. She grabbed onto the headboard with both hands. It was her turn to glare as she stared down at me. Her pussy was so close, I could smell it, but she held herself back. "I know you're used to being in control, but if you move a single muscle other than your tongue, I will stop."

I grinned up at her. "You're cute when you're mad. It's like a spitting kitten."

She narrowed her eyes. "I'm not messing around, Jack. No moving, or we're done. Got it?"

"Yes, ma'am. Now, give me my pussy."

She sighed in exasperation but shifted up my body. I could feel the heat of her wet cunt as it moved up my abdomen and chest. My cock was so hard I was worried I would come the second her taste hit my tongue. That was alright; I knew I had more than enough to give her. I'd be hard again before I was done eating her.

She hovered over my face, and I could see how wet she was, the moisture glistening on her folds and inner thighs.

"Sit!" I commanded. I had to grip the sheets at my sides to stop myself from grabbing her again. I knew my fierce little kitten would carry out her threat of stopping. She had grown so much since I had first seen her. She'd evolved from a scared little girl hiding behind her hair to the warrior queen who stared down two different evil men and won. I loved her so much more with every day that passed. I never knew it was possible to care about someone the way I did her. For so many years, I had just moved through life with a cold, dead heart. She brought me to life with one look of her beautiful blue eyes.

Gingerly, she lowered her pussy until it hovered just above my mouth. "Oh my god, this is so awkward," she mumbled. I stuck my tongue out and swiped through her wetness, my eyes nearly rolling in the back of my head.

"Don't think, just feel."

When my tongue glanced over her clit, she quivered, her knees lowering her a little more. When I slid my tongue through her wetness to swirl around her entrance, she trembled, gripping the headboard tight. When I sucked on her clit, she lost her battle with the grip on the bed and sank the rest of the way, nearly suffocating me. I groaned. I would die a happy man.

She gasped and rubbed frantically as I chuckled. Suddenly, her shyness and reservations were gone, and I was just the tool to be used to get her off. I had to grip my hard cock firmly at the base, hard, to stop myself from coming all over my stomach and her ass.

Within minutes, she was throwing her head back and screaming her pleasure to the ceiling. I wanted nothing more than to grab her, turn her onto her back, and pound my hard cock into her until I released every bit of my hot come into her depths. Instead, all I could do was pant as if I'd run a fucking marathon and hope that she would take pity on my aching balls.

She scooted back until her wet pussy rested on my abs, my hard cock trapped and throbbing as she rested her face in my neck. Her hot breath coated my skin as I squeezed my eyes shut and gritted my teeth. She had given me what I asked for. I wouldn't beg her to drop her cunt down on my cock and ride me into oblivion.

I kept my eyes closed and continued to pant when she lifted her head and shifted. I felt her pussy lips slide over my cock head and had to bite my tongue to keep in my groan. It was when she angled her hips to glide up and then back down to notch the head of my dick at her entrance that I finally opened my eyes.

Her voice was husky when she whispered down to me. "You're going to be a good boy and stay perfectly still."

I growled at her words, every part of me wanting to retake control, but I didn't dare move a muscle. I nearly whimpered when she glided down until I bottomed out inside of her.

"Fuck. Fuck, yes!" I finally broke, throwing back my head and shouting. It was a fight to stop from coming as her hot walls gripped me as tight as a fist. Soon, she was raising and lowering herself as she leaned back, balancing her hands on my thighs as her hair tickled my balls. I made the mistake of looking at where we were joined. Seeing my length glisten with her wetness in the lamplight as she slid up and down was more than I could take. With a primal grunt I felt deep in my chest, I was unloading every drop of come I had into her.

When my mind finally started working again, it was to see Sally leaning over me, her hands resting on the bed next to my head. She had a wicked grin on her face, and seeing her like that, I fell in love with her all over again. I would never stop falling for her.

"You were such a good boy," she cooed.

As I growled and snapped my teeth at her throat, she giggled before moving off my softening cock and curled up against my side. I moved my good arm around her shoulders, pulling her closer to me.

"I love you, little Queen."

"I love you, too, Jack Ellington."

EPILOGUE - FOUR MONTHS LATER

SALLY

Even though it's spring, and it still gets pretty freaking cold at night in April, the world around us had finally thawed out. To celebrate, bikers did it in the only way they knew how - with booze and fighting. And fucking, too, I was sure. Though I doubted they ever let a little ice and snow stop them from having a woman.

Jack helped me down from his big black truck, his hands sliding around to rest on my belly for a few extra long seconds as he felt his son kick against his hands with a grin. Jack rarely hid his smiles anymore. He was still the deadly cold President of the Devil's Night-mares, but he no longer felt the need to suppress his emotions. At least when it came to his little family.

The truck was the only vehicle in The Warehouse parking lot that wasn't on two wheels, but I thought it was pretty sweet of all the clubs to leave a spot just for us at the front of the building. I wasn't *that* big, though Jack's giant baby did leave me feeling like a beached whale most of the time. And to think I still had two more months to go. The obstetrician had already informed us that I would have to have a C-section due to the size of the baby. Jack had been pretty upset, but I just told him it was only one more scar. It was one that I would wear with pride.

Jack took my hand and led me over the dirt and gravel, carefully watching my every step to make sure I wouldn't slip, trip, or fall. It had been the same way for the last few months, and as much as I loved his overprotectiveness most of the time, sometimes I just wanted to pretend that I wasn't pregnant so he'd be rough with me again.

The doors were propped open just like they had been the last time I'd been here. It seemed like a lifetime ago when I entered this massive building for the first time. Back then, I'd been a scared little mouse, afraid of the noise and all the men that filled the place. I had wanted to hide myself from everyone, even if it had been impossible in those skimpy clothes the servers have to wear. There would be no shorts riding up my ass and tight crop tops showing far too much cleavage for me tonight. Instead, I was wearing what I hoped was a cute dress with a cardigan. I knew I was going to look ridiculous walking into a biker venue wearing a sundress, but there were only so many things I could wear these days that didn't include giant sweatpants and one of Jack's T-shirts.

As we walked inside, we were greeted by so many people I couldn't keep track. I did know that the President of the Black Wolves tried to touch my belly but backed off with a grin when Jack withdrew his knife from his belt. Luckily, he hadn't pulled the same move with all the club girls who cooed over my baby bump.

It took a while to reach Jack's designated table, which was already occupied by Doc. Shock and Barrel wandered over a few minutes later to shake hands as well as give Jack a hard time about driving a cage to fight night. Jack took their teasing good naturedly, though, flipping them off with a grin.

I snuggled into his side as the first round of drinks was brought to our table by one of the girls. I thanked Mindy and slipped her a nice tip for her trouble as she winked then walked away. We all turned when the announcer started speaking from the center of the huge ring in the middle of the concrete floor.

"Who's ready for fight night?"

Cheers went up through the building at the commencement of the first fight night of the year. The announcer looked extremely disappointed as he shook his head, playing it up for all the bikers.

"I *said*, who's ready for mother fucking FIGHT NIGHT?"

The yells, stomping, and banging on the tables were so loud I had to cover my ears while I laughed. The excitement was infectious, and my heart started pounding with anticipation.

The first couple of guys were called into the ring. They were young and were obviously new. I figured they were likely newly patched members trying to prove something to their clubs. I gasped when the first fight ended with the two on the ground. The one on top was pounding the one trapped on the mat so hard that blood flew, adding to the many stains that already covered the surface. As disturbing as it was, I couldn't look away.

The fights continued the same way. Most of the fighters seemed to be evenly matched, but sometimes, someone would go in and get knocked out in the first few seconds. The poor guy was heckled so badly I felt bad for him. But when his club brothers would retrieve the loser, it was always with good natured pats on the back and a little bit of ribbing thrown in. They never left too upset, though.

Then the moment came I had been anticipating with equal parts excitement and dread. Jack's name was called, and just like months ago, the whole room went wild. A flash of fear filled me for a moment when I thought of his broken ribs and bullet wound, but I forced myself to relax. The doctor had cleared him months ago. Since then, Jack has been lifting weights and running in an effort to get his strength and stamina back. I had been thrilled to see him able to work out again because he was the biggest fucking baby on the planet while injured.

Jack stood up from his seat and turned to look at me, a small smirk playing on the corner of his lips. I licked my lips as he began to take his leather cut off. He had never replaced it. There was still a bullet hole above his name and title, which made it look pretty badass if I were being honest. But the blood stains made me shiver every time I looked at them. He folded it carefully and handed it to me, which I took and immediately hugged to my chest.

The other guy he was set to fight was already in the ring, doing his best to get the crowd to back him. I wasn't certain it was working the way he'd hoped, though. Jack pulled off his shirt from over his head, making me squeeze my thighs together at the sight. I would never get over how handsome he was. The stark black of his tattooed body just added a wild, untouchable effect to the whole package that was him. Well, untouchable to everyone but me. He welcomed my touch anytime I wanted to run my hands over him. Which I seriously was tempted to do right at that moment while his arms flexed as he handed me his shirt.

He leaned down, placing his hand on my throat with gentle pressure. "I'll be right back, little Queen.

"Okay, Jack," I whispered against his lips right before he placed a hot kiss on my mouth. As he straightened up and began to walk away, I licked his taste that still lingered on my lips.

"Jesus, don't you two ever take a break?""

I flipped Barrel off without taking my eyes off Jack and listened to him roar in laughter. Jack gripped the side of the ring and vaulted himself up onto the edge with a nimble jump. He turned back to me with a wink before turning back around to step over the top rope.

His opponent stuck his finger out, pointing at Jack, and said something, probably taunting and stupid, but Jack just twisted his neck side to side, loosening up. As soon as the bell rang, the other biker ran full force at Jack. I shook my head in disgust. Didn't they ever learn? Jack took a step to the side just as the man reached him with his fist out, ready to swing. As he flew past, Jack kicked out his foot and shoved the guy in the ass, making him stumble forward into the ropes.

As everyone erupted in laughter, the guy turned around, his face beet red from embarrassment. Jack said something to him and then gestured in a come hither motion with two fingers at the biker. I cringed while unable to hold in my laughter.

From there, the fight continued, with Jack evading punches while getting hits in every time. The other guy was covered in blood from his leaking nose, and the last punch he'd received had him holding his back. Even from where I was sitting, I could see his face twisted in pain.

"That guy's gonna be pissing blood for a few days," Doc mumbled, then took a swig of his beer. It made me glad that Jack was as good as he was. I would have hated to see him hurt again.

Finally, it seemed like Jack was done playing cat and mouse and descended on the other biker. With a few swift punches to the gut and then one hard uppercut to the chin, the fight was over. The guy was lying on his back, breathing heavily, when Jack strolled over to him and bent down. I didn't know what he said to him, but the other man laughed and held out his hand. Jack gripped it tightly and then hauled the man to his feet. With a final shake of hands, Jack turned back to me.

Like last time, he ignored the crowd as he jumped down from the ring. He didn't even acknowledge anyone as they tried to congratulate him. Instead, his eyes were on me as he strode forward with long strides.

The look on his face was like a hungry panther. I swallowed hard as I stood up from the bench and waited. By the time he reached me, I was already panting, my panties damp, and my heart racing. I was eager for what I saw in his gaze.

His hand went straight to my neck as I raised my chin in offering.

Without a word, he led me to the same back door we had had our first encounter. The hand that had slid from my throat to the back of my neck was tight with tension as we stepped outside. Nothing had changed from that first night. The tables were still arranged in the dirt, and there was still one single yellow bulb that barely lit up the yard.

There was no one outside this time as Jack kicked the door closed with one foot. He led me over to our table, and I started to sit.

"Not this time, little Queen," he rumbled in his deep, gravelly voice.

"Where do you want me, Bones?" I asked, hiding my grin.

He growled at me and then took my mouth in a rough kiss that I moaned into immediately. My Jack could be tender sometimes, but there was nothing I loved more than when he lost control and showed me his wild side. With firm hands, he gripped my hips and effortlessly lifted me to sit on top of the table.

With quick movements, he had the skirt of my dress flipped up, and my panties ripped down and off my legs. He bent over and licked up the center of my pussy. I leaned back on my elbows and moaned to the sky. I opened my eyes to stare at the stars filling the sky as he shoved my thighs wider to taste every part of me. When he wrapped his lips around my clit, the stars were behind my eyelids, flashing with brilliant lights as I screamed my release.

Before I could come back from nirvana, Jack had already undone his belt and had his pants open and shoved down his hips. He gripped my thighs hard enough to leave fingerprints as he pulled me to the edge of the table, careful not to make me collapse with his roughness, always mindful even through his raging lust. With one swift thrust, he was buried to the hilt inside me. Just like that, I was whole again.

I laid back fully on the table, needing to grip the wood above my head as he began to pound into me wildly. Every thrust sent a wave of euphoria through my entire being. Every glide of his hard cock hit just the right nerve ending to have me climbing higher and higher until I reached that pinnacle all over again.

Jack cursed and grunted above me as his cock grew impossibly thicker inside my channel. When his thrusts lost their rhythm, I was ready. Together, we broke apart, finding the bliss we had only ever found in each other. It would only be each other for us. There was no one else in the universe who could give us what each other could.

EPILOGUE - TWO YEARS LATER

THE NIGHTMARE KING

I rolled over and nuzzled into the back of my wife's neck. It was early morning; everything was quiet inside the house and in the world outside. No one was calling me, texting, or asking me questions. It was just me and my wife's sexy as fuck body cuddled against mine under our warm blankets.

"Ummm, Jack," she murmured sleepily without opening her eyes.

"Merry Christmas, baby. Go back to sleep," I said softly as my hand drifted up to cup her soft breast. Pregnancy and breastfeeding had given them more weight and size, and I was just enough of a horny man to admit they turned me the fuck on. I could hardly keep my hands, eyes, or dick off her gorgeous tits. When I titty fucked her several months ago while her milk rolled down to coat my cock, I thought I would lose my goddamn mind. I needed to get her pregnant again soon so I could experience that again.

I lifted her leg and placed it over my hip, widening her for my cock. I placed the tip of my cock at her entrance while she moaned into her pillow.

"Hurry up, Jack. Your son is going to be awake and ready to burn the world down soon." Her muffled words had me chuckling as I angled my hips and pressed forward as far as I could in our current positions.

Slow and steady, I rocked back and forth, giving my woman just enough of me to make her moan for more as she woke up fully. Once her moans changed to pleas for more, I rolled us until she was under me. I slid my arm under her hips and lifted, titling until she was at the perfect angle. Then I gripped her long braid, wrapping it around my fist.

With hard thrusts that would have put the headboard through the wall if I hadn't anchored it down more than a year ago, I gave Sally the Christmas morning wakeup call I had given her for the last two years and would continue to give until I was dead in the ground.

When she started to scream as her cunt began to spasm around my cock, I used my hold on her hair to muffle her cries with the pillow.

"Fuck. Fuck. Fuck. Always so fucking good, baby," I panted, doing my best to hold off my orgasm but knowing that it was a futile effort. Her heat, wetness, and tight stranglehold on my cock all worked against me, forcing me to come in several powerful spurts as I held my hips pressed as tight against her ass as I could get.

I rolled her back over onto her side, refusing to pull out of her, as we both panted for air. "You're going to kill me," she groaned as I felt an aftershock run through her body.

"Never," I growled back, nipping her chin with my teeth.

She giggled, slapping my face away weakly when the sound of our son suddenly drifted to us. Zero jumped to his feet and ran to the door. He sat there and cocked his head one way then the other as he listened to the increasingly loud demand came from down the hall.

"Da da da da da da da!"

"It's times like this that I'm glad he hasn't said mama yet."

I swatted Sally's ass before sliding out of her, wishing I had time to enjoy the sight of my come leaking from her body.

"Get your ass up and go pee," I demanded, even more determined than when we'd first started our relationship, that my little Queen take good care of herself. Sometimes, she grumbled about my insistence that she pee to prevent a UTI after sex, but she still did it, knowing that it was out of concern for her wellbeing and not a need to control her.

I slid out of bed and quickly pulled a pair of sweatpants on. As soon as I opened the door, Zero took off, running to the next door down the hall, pawing at it impatiently. I was pretty sure he loved my son more than me at this point. When I opened Timmy's door, Zero ran straight to the side of the crib and immediately began to bark and whine while Timothy giggled uproariously.

"Come on, little monster." I scooped my son up and held him close to my chest, taking in the feel of him against me and hating that he seemed to be growing faster than I could keep up. It seemed just a week ago he'd been so small I was afraid I would crush him if my hand spasmed. Sally swore that he had always been a giant baby, but holding him now, all I remembered was how tiny he was. It's too bad I couldn't turn back time and start it over again from the moment he was placed in my arms.

I scrunched up my nose as soon as the smell hit me. I looked over my shoulder to our bedroom, then down at Zero, who gave me a chastising "woof."

"Fine, I'll do it myself."

After cleaning up the mess of breakfast that somehow ended up on the ceiling, Sally and I began the long process of getting ready to take our eighteen-month-old out of the house. While Sally triple-checked the diaper bag, I pulled the truck up to the front of the house to get it warm and to keep the trip in the icy weather as short as possible for both my wife and son.

I closed the door behind me and rubbed my hands together to warm them up. "Looks like you're getting the white Christmas you hoped for."

Sally gasped and ran to the front door, jerking it open to stare in wonder at the white wonderland outside. "It's so pretty," she breathed. I chuckled softly and wrapped my arm around her waist. No matter how often she saw the world covered in snow, she always reacted the same.

Zero gave a warning bark, and I bent down to scoop up my little monster before he could get past our legs and run out into the snow. The last time he had done that, he landed face-first in the cold wetness and cried for fifteen minutes straight.

"Come on, we have Christmas to celebrate." I nibbled on his neck, making his whines turn to giggles. I waited until Sally set the alarm and locked the front door as I held Timothy. Together, we walked to the idling truck as I scanned the ground for rocks or ice. I had the prospects keep all the walkways clear, but I still checked for myself every night, so it should be clear of hazards, but it was always best to be sure.

THE RIDE to the clubhouse was short, as usual. As we drove slowly past the house that Doc built this last summer, I watched him and Helen step out onto their front porch. Sally waved frantically as if we hadn't just had dinner with them last night. Doc scowled at the ground and wrapped his arm around his wife's waist as he practically carried her to his SUV. He lifted her inside while she kept one hand on her huge belly and waved back as we passed.

As soon as I parked in my designated spot, the front door of the clubhouse flew open, and three children with various shades of red hair came running out.

"Sally! Sally! Come inside, quick! Santa came!"

"Mama said we had to wait for you to get here before we can open our presents," the youngest grumbled with their arms folded over their chest.

"Well, then, I guess we better get inside!" Sally told her siblings as they turned around and ran back the way they came.

Sally's parents only came around once a year, and while they were around, they mostly sat alone on the couch. They seemed happy to let their children run around while my brothers or club girls attempted to corral them. I always waved off Sally's apologies. I knew she felt bad about her family's behavior, but I was just glad they were communicating. It had been a rocky start when Sally made the first phone call to her parents. But after a few rough minutes, everyone calmed down, and her parents listened carefully to every word as Sally described what she had been through. Sally was happy to have them back in her life, even if it was mostly long distance. I was just glad I didn't have to murder my woman's parents.

I LOOKED around the mess in the room, seeing piles of ripped paper and ribbons. There were torn boxes from where the kids had hastily removed toys from their packaging before quickly discarding them for the next present.

It was complete mayhem.

But as I glanced down at my wife tucked snugly under my arm and our son asleep against my chest with his new stuffed dinosaur held loosely in his arms, I realized I didn't care.

I had everything I could ever want in my arms.

Everyone I cared about was within these walls.

My woman looked up at me, sensing my stare. I leaned down and pressed a kiss to her lips. It had been a hard beginning. My mother-in-law once said that we were lucky our lives together ended the way they did. She thought we might not have made it through, that any little thing could have changed the outcome. The possibilities were endless. I could have died if Daisy hadn't grown a conscience. Sally may not have even come to Pumpkin Patch if her finger had landed an inch over. I could have been sitting in prison if I hadn't stopped myself from killing Dr. Stein in the hotel room.

But I refused to believe that. Sometimes, fate refused to be messed with, and the outcome would always end the same, regardless of the journey. That's what I believed as I looked into the gorgeous blue eyes of my wife as she mouthed the words that I had hoped to hear today. I squeezed her closer to my side as I grinned down at her and slid my hand over her belly, which was softer than it had been a couple of years ago before giving me our first child. Soon, our little family would grow larger. I hadn't known I was capable of loving someone the way I loved my little Queen, but it was written in the stars.

We were simply meant to be.

THE END

Acknowledgments

Thank you so much for reading! This was a fun story to write since it combined my love of NBC, creativity, and romance! I already know that it is impossible to do Jack and Sally justice, I just hope that I was able to somehow create an entertaining story that you could enjoy.

Nicole, I couldn't do this without you. Those aren't just words, they come from the depths of my heart.

As always, I welcome feedback. If there is something you find that needs correcting, I'd love to hear about. Please feel free to contact me at rsullinsauthor@gmail.com.
Please join my Facebook group for giveaways, and sneak peeks into what I might currently be working on.

RSullins Book Group

If you enjoyed the story, please consider leaving a review! It truly is the best way to show an author that you care.

ABOUT THE AUTHOR

R. Sullins is a USA Today bestselling author, an International Bestseller, and a KDP All Star.

Family is number one in her life, followed by her menagerie of pets. Be patient with her, she's not very good at peopling.

She is a lover of fairies, tattoos, and coffee cups, has a vast collection of them all, and receives a glare from her teenager every time she brings home a new cup to squeeze into the cabinet.

When she's not writing, you will probably be able to find her reading a book. But, no matter what genre you find her immersed in, there is always one thing that her favorite stories have in common... you will never, ever find her reading any book with cheating. So rest assured! She will never write one, either.

A bit of drama, a dash of spice, a little bit of innocence, and a large dab of alpha is what makes up the recipe for her stories. Find more of her here: www.rsullins.com

Also by R Sullins

<u>Crimson Fate</u>

A standalone in The Hunter series